SELECTED STORIES
of Philip K. Dick

NOVELS BY PHILIP K. DICK

Clans of the Alphane Moon

Confessions of a Crap Artist

The Cosmic Puppets

Counter-Clock World

The Crack in Space

Deus Irae (*with Roger Zelazny*)

The Divine Invasion

Do Androids Dream of Electric Sheep?

Dr. Bloodmoney

Dr. Futurity

Eye in the Sky

Flow My Tears, the Policeman Said

Galactic Pot-Healer

The Game-Players of Titan

The Man in the High Castle

The Man Who Japed

Martian Time-Slip

A Maze of Death

Now Wait for Last Year

Our Friends from Frolix-8

The Penultimate Truth

Radio Free Albemuth

A Scanner Darkly

Simulacra

Solar Lottery

The Three Stigmata of Palmer Eldritch

Time Out of Joint

The Transmigration of Timothy Archer

Ubik

The Unteleported Man

VALIS

Vulcan's Hammer

We Can Build You

The World Jones Made

The Zap Gun

SELECTED STORIES
of Philip K. Dick

Introduction by

Jonathan Lethem

Pantheon Books, New York

Pantheon Books and colophon are registered trademarks
of Random House, Inc.

Library of Congress Cataloging-in-Publication Data

Dick, Philip K.
[Short stories. Selections]
Selected stories of Philip K. Dick.
p.   cm.
ISBN 0-375-42151-3
1. Science fiction, American.   I. Title.

PS3554.I3 A6 2002   813'.54—DC21   2002025798

www.pantheonbooks.com

Book design by Johanna S. Roebas

Printed in the United States of America

First Edition

4   6   8   9   7   5

CONTENTS

INTRODUCTION

Jonathan Lethem

Philip K. Dick is a necessary writer, in the someone-would-have-had-to-invent-him sense. He's American literature's Lenny Bruce. Like Bruce, he can seem a pure product of the 1950s (and, as William Carlos Williams warned, *pure products of America go crazy*), one whose iconoclastic mal-adaptation to the conformity of that era seems to shout ahead to our contemporary understanding. And, as with Bruce, the urge to claim him for any cultural role—Hippie, Postmodern Theorist, Political Dissident, Metaphysical Guru—is defeated by the contradictions generated by a singular and irascible persona. Still, no matter what problems he presents, Dick wielded a sardonic yet heartbroken acuity about the plight of being alive in the twentieth century, one that makes him a lonely hero to the readers who cherish him.

Dick's great accomplishment, on view in the twenty-one stories collected here, was to turn the materials of American pulp-style science fiction into a vocabulary for a remarkably personal vision of paranoia and dislocation. It's a vision as yearning and anxious as Kafka's, if considerably more homely. It's also as funny. Dick is a kitchen-sink surrealist, gaining energy and invention from a mad piling of pulp SF tropes—and clichés—into his fiction: time travel, extrasensory powers, tentacled aliens, ray guns, androids and robots. He loves fakes and simulacra as much as he fears them: illusory worlds, bogus religions, placebo drugs, impersonated police, cyborgs. Tyrannical world governments and ruined dystopian cities are default settings here. Not only have Orwell and Huxley been taken as givens in Dick's worlds, so have Old Masters of genre SF like Clifford

Simak, Robert Heinlein, and A. E. Van Vogt. American SF by the mid-1950s was a kind of jazz, stories built by riffing on stories. The conversation they formed might be forbiddingly hermetic, if it hadn't quickly been incorporated by Rod Serling and Marvel Comics and Steven Spielberg (among many others) to become one of the prime vocabularies of our age.

Dick is one of the first writers to use these materials with self-conscious absurdity—a "look at what I found!" glee which prefigures that of writers like Kurt Vonnegut, George Saunders, and Mark Leyner. Yet having set his characters loose inside his Rube Goldbergian inventions, Dick detailed their emotional abreactions with meticulous sympathy. His people eke out their days precariously, never knowing whether disaster is about to come at the level of the psychological, the ontological, or the pharmacological. Even his tyrannical world dictators glance neurotically over their shoulders, wondering if some higher authority is about to cause their reality to crumble or in some other way be exposed as fake. Alternately, they could always simply be arrested. Dick earned his collar as High Priest of the Paranoids the old-fashioned way: in his fiction, everyone is *always* about to be arrested.

The second set of motifs Dick employed was more prosaic: a perfectly typical 1950s obsession with the images of the suburbs, the consumer, the bureaucrat, and with the plight of small men struggling under the imperatives of capitalism. If Dick, as a bearded, drug-taking Californian, might have seemed a candidate for Beatdom (and in fact did hang out with the San Francisco poets), his persistent engagement with the main materials of his culture kept him from floating off into reveries of escape. It links him instead to writers like Richard Yates, John Cheever, and Arthur Miller (the British satirist John Sladek's bull's-eye Dick parody was titled "Solar Shoe Salesman"). Dick's treatment of his "realist" material can seem oddly cursory, as though the pressing agenda of his paranoiac fantasizing, which would require him to rip the facade off, drop the atomic bomb onto, or otherwise renovate ordinary reality, made that reality's actual *depiction* unimportant. But no matter how many times Dick unmasks or destroys the Black Iron Prison of American suburban life, he always returns to it. Unlike the characters in William S. Burroughs, Richard Brautigan, or Thomas Pynchon, Dick's characters, in novels and stories written well into the 1970s, go on working for grumbling bosses, carrying briefcases, sending interoffice memos, tinkering with cars in driveways, sweating alimony payments, and dreaming of getting away from it all—even when they've already emigrated to Mars.

Though Dick's primary importance is as a novelist, no single volume better encompasses his accomplishment than this collection, which doubles as a kind of writer's autobiography, a growth chart. From Twilight Zone–ish social satires ("Roog," "Foster, You're Dead") to grapplings with a pulp-adventure chase-scene mode that was already weary before Dick picked it up ("Paycheck," "Imposter"), the earliest pieces nevertheless declare obsessions and locate methods that would serve for thirty-odd years. In "Adjustment Team" and "Autofac" we begin to meet the Dick of the great sixties novels, his characters defined by how they endure more than by any triumph over circumstance. "Upon the Dull Earth" presents an eerie path-not-taken into Gothic fantasy, one that reads like a Shirley Jackson outtake. Then there is the Martian-farmer-émigré mode, which always showed Dick at his best: "Precious Artifact" and "A Game of Unchance." Later, in "Faith of Our Fathers," we encounter the Dick of his late masterpiece *A Scanner Darkly,* working with the *I Ching* at one elbow and the *Physicians' Desk Reference* at the other. "Faith of Our Fathers," together with "The Electric Ant" and "A Little Something for Us Tempunauts," offers among the most distilled and perfect statements of Dick's career: black-humor politics melting away to Gnostic theology, theology to dire solipsism, solipsism to despair, then love. And back again.

If Dick thrived on the materials of SF, he was less than thrilled with the fate of being *only* an SF writer. Whether or not he was ready for the world, or the world ready for him, he longed for a respectable recognition, and sought it variously and unsuccessfully throughout his life. In fact, he wrote eight novels in a somber realist mode during the 1950s and early 1960s, a shadow career known mainly to the agents who failed to place the books with various New York publishers. It's stirring to wonder what Dick might have done with a wider professional opportunity, but there's little doubt that his SF grew more interesting for being fed by the frustrated energies of his "mainstream" ambition. Possibly, too, a restless streak in Dick's personality better suited him for the outsider-artist status he tasted during his lifetime. Dick was obsessed with stigma, with mutation and exile, and with the recurrent image of a spark of life or love arising from unlikely or ruined places: robot pets, discarded appliances, autistic children. SF was Dick's ruined site. Keenly engaged with his own outcast identity, he worked brilliantly from the margins (in this regard, it may be possible to consider the story "The King of the Elves" as an allegory of Dick's career). "Sci-Fi Writer" became a kind of *identity politics* for Dick, as did "Drug Burnout" and "Religious Mystic"—these during the period when identity politics weren't otherwise the province of white American males. Here, from an introduction written for *Golden Man,* a collection of stories assembled in 1980, Dick reminisces:

> In reading the stories in this volume you should bear in mind that most were written when SF was so looked down upon that it virtually was not there, in the eyes of all America. This was not funny, the derision felt toward SF writers. It made our lives wretched. Even in Berkeley—or especially in Berkeley—people would say, "But are you writing anything serious?" To select SF writing as a career was an act of self-destruction; in fact, most *writers,* let alone most other people, could not even conceive of someone considering it. The only non-SF writer who ever treated me with courtesy was Herbert Gold, who I met at a literary party in San Francisco. He autographed a file card to me this way: "To a colleague, Philip K. Dick." I kept the card until the ink faded and was gone, and I still feel grateful to him for this charity. . . . So in my head I have to collate the experience in 1977 of the mayor of Metz shaking hands with me at an official city function [Dick had just received an arts medal in France], and the ordeal of the Fifties when Kleo and I lived on ninety dollars a month, when we could not even pay the fine on an overdue library book, and when we were literally living on dog food. But I think you should know this—specifically, in case you are, say, in your twenties and rather poor and perhaps becoming filled with despair, whether you are an SF writer or not, whatever you want to make of your life. There can be a lot of fear, and often it is a justified fear. People do starve in America. I have seen uneducated street girls survive horrors that beggar description. I have seen the faces of men whose brains have been burned-out by drugs, men who could still think enough to be able to

realize what had happened to them; I watched their clumsy attempt to weather that which cannot be weathered. . . . Kabir, the sixteenth-century Sufi poet, wrote, "If you have not lived through something, it is not true." So live through it; I mean, go all the way to the end. Only then can it be understood, not along the way.

The conflations in this passage are so perfectly typical—SF writer and uneducated street girl, Dick's suffering and yours. His self-mocking humility at Herbert Gold's "charity" is balanced against that treasured, ink-fading file card: a certainty that value resides in the smallest gestures, in scraps of empathy. Dick was a writer doomed to be himself, and the themes of his most searching and personal writing of the 1970s and early 1980s surface helplessly in even the earliest stories: the fragility of connection, the allure and risk of illusion, the poignancy of artifacts, and the necessity of carrying on in the face of the demoralizing brokenness of the world. Dick famously posed two questions—"What is human?" and "What is real?"—and then sought to answer them in any framework he thought might suffice. By the time of his death he'd tried and discarded many dozen such frameworks. The questions remained. It is the absurd beauty of their asking that lasts.

On a personal note, I'm proud to make this introduction. Dick's is a voice that matters to me, a voice I love. He's one of my life's companions. As Bob Dylan sang of Lenny Bruce, *he's gone, but his spirit lingers on and on.* In that spirit, let Phil have the final word here. Again, from the *Golden Man* essay:

What helps for me—if help comes at all—is to find the mustard seed of the funny at the core of the horrible and futile. I've been researching ponderous and solemn theological matters for five years now, for my novel-in-progress, and much of the Wisdom of the World has passed from the printed page and into my brain, there to be processed and secreted out in the form of more words: words in, words out, and a brain in the middle wearily trying to determine the meaning of it all. Anyhow, the other night I started on the article on Indian Philosophy in the *Encyclopedia of Philosophy* . . . the time was 4 A.M.; I was exhausted . . . and there, at the heart of this solemn article, was this: "The Buddhist idealists used various arguments to show that perception does not yield knowledge of external objects distinct from the percipient. . . . The external world supposedly consists of a number of different objects, but they can be known as different only because there are different sorts of experiences 'of' them. Yet if the experiences are thus distinguishable, there is no need to hold the superfluous hypothesis of external objects. . . ."

That night I went to bed laughing. I laughed for an hour. I am still laughing. Push philosophy and theology to their ultimate and what do you wind up with? Nothing. Nothing exists. As I said earlier, there is only one way out: seeing it all as ultimately funny. Kabir, who I quoted, saw dancing and joy and love as ways out, too; and he wrote about the sound of "the anklets on the feet of an insect as it walks." I would like to hear that sound; perhaps if I could my anger and fear, and my high blood pressure, would go away.

*   *   *   *

Thanks to Pamela Jackson, whose 1999 dissertation "The World Philip K. Dick Made" helped clarify my thinking in writing this introduction.

SELECTED STORIES
of Philip K. Dick

BEYOND LIES THE WUB

They had almost finished with the loading. Outside stood the Optus, his arms folded, his face sunk in gloom. Captain Franco walked leisurely down the gangplank, grinning.

"What's the matter?" he said. "You're getting paid for all this."

The Optus said nothing. He turned away, collecting his robes. The Captain put his boot on the hem of the robe.

"Just a minute. Don't go off. I'm not finished."

"Oh?" The Optus turned with dignity. "I am going back to the village." He looked toward the animals and birds being driven up the gangplank into the spaceship. "I must organize new hunts."

Franco lit a cigarette. "Why not? You people can go out into the veldt and track it all down again. But when we run halfway between Mars and Earth—"

The Optus went off, wordless. Franco joined the first mate at the bottom of the gangplank.

"How's it coming?" he asked. He looked at his watch. "We got a good bargain here."

The mate glanced at him sourly. "How do you explain that?"

"What's the matter with you? We need it more than they do."

"I'll see you later, Captain." The mate threaded his way up the plank, between the long-legged Martian go-birds, into the ship. Franco watched him disappear. He was just starting up after him, up the plank toward the port, when he saw *it*.

"My God!" He stood staring, his hands on his hips. Peterson was walking along the path, his face red, leading *it* by a string.

"I'm sorry, Captain," he said, tugging at the string. Franco walked toward him.

"What is it?"

The wub stood sagging, its great body settling slowly. It was sitting down, its eyes half shut. A few flies buzzed about its flank, and it switched its tail.

It sat. There was silence.

"It's a wub," Peterson said. "I got it from a native for fifty cents. He said it was a very unusual animal. Very respected."

"This?" Franco poked the great sloping side of the wub. "It's a pig! A huge dirty pig!"

"Yes sir, it's a pig. The natives call it a wub."

"A huge pig. It must weigh four hundred pounds." Franco grabbed a tuft of the rough hair. The wub gasped. Its eyes opened, small and moist. Then its great mouth twitched.

A tear rolled down the wub's cheek and splashed on the floor.

"Maybe it's good to eat," Peterson said nervously.

"We'll soon find out," Franco said.

The wub survived the takeoff, sound asleep in the hold of the ship. When they were out in space and everything was running smoothly, Captain Franco bade his men fetch the wub upstairs so that he might perceive what manner of beast it was.

The wub grunted and wheezed, squeezing up the passageway.

"Come on," Jones grated, pulling at the rope. The wub twisted, rubbing its skin off on the smooth chrome walls. It burst into the anteroom, tumbling down in a heap. The men leaped up.

"Good Lord," French said. "What is it?"

"Peterson says it's a wub," Jones said. "It belongs to him." He kicked at the wub. The wub stood up unsteadily, panting.

"What's the matter with it?" French came over. "Is it going to be sick?"

They watched. The wub rolled its eyes mournfully. It gazed around at the men.

"I think it's thirsty," Peterson said. He went to get some water. French shook his head.

"No wonder we had so much trouble taking off. I had to reset all my ballast calculations."

Peterson came back with the water. The wub began to lap gratefully, splashing the men.

Captain Franco appeared at the door.

"Let's have a look at it." He advanced, squinting critically. "You got this for fifty cents?"

"Yes, sir," Peterson said. "It eats almost anything. I fed it on grain and it liked that. And then potatoes, and mash, and scraps from the table, and milk. It seems to enjoy eating. After it eats it lies down and goes to sleep."

"I see," Captain Franco said. "Now, as to its taste. That's the real question. I doubt if there's much point in fattening it up any more. It seems fat enough to me already. Where's the cook? I want him here. I want to find out—"

The wub stopped lapping and looked up at the Captain.

"Really, Captain," the wub said. "I suggest we talk of other matters."

The room was silent.

"What was that?" Franco said. "Just now."

"The wub, sir," Peterson said. "It spoke."

They all looked at the wub.

"What did it say? What did it say?"

"It suggested we talk about other things."

Franco walked toward the wub. He went all around it, examining it from every side. Then he came back over and stood with the men.

"I wonder if there's a native inside it," he said thoughtfully. "Maybe we should open it up and have a look."

"Oh, goodness!" the wub cried. "Is that all you people can think of, killing and cutting?"

Franco clenched his fists. "Come out of there! Whoever you are, come out!"

Nothing stirred. The men stood together, their faces blank, staring at the wub. The wub swished its tail. It belched suddenly.

"I beg your pardon," the wub said.

"I don't think there's anyone in there," Jones said in a low voice. They all looked at each other.

The cook came in.

"You wanted me, Captain?" he said. "What's this thing?"

"This is a wub," Franco said. "It's to be eaten. Will you measure it and figure out—"

"I think we should have a talk," the wub said. "I'd like to discuss this with you, Captain, if I might. I can see that you and I do not agree on some basic issues."

The Captain took a long time to answer. The wub waited good-naturedly, licking the water from its jowls.

"Come into my office," the Captain said at last. He turned and walked out of the room. The wub rose and padded after him. The men watched it go out. They heard it climbing the stairs.

"I wonder what the outcome will be," the cook said. "Well, I'll be in the kitchen. Let me know as soon as you hear."

"Sure," Jones said. "Sure."

The wub eased itself down in the corner with a sigh. "You must forgive me," it said. "I'm afraid I'm addicted to various forms of relaxation. When one is as large as I—"

The Captain nodded impatiently. He sat down at his desk and folded his hands.

"All right," he said. "Let's get started. You're a wub? Is that correct?"

The wub shrugged. "I suppose so. That's what they call us, the natives, I mean. We have our own term."

"And you speak English? You've been in contact with Earthmen before?"

"No."

"Then how do you do it?"

"Speak English? Am I speaking English? I'm not conscious of speaking anything in particular. I examined your mind—"

"My mind?"

"I studied the contents, especially the semantic warehouse, as I refer to it—"

"I see," the Captain said. "Telepathy. Of course."

"We are a very old race," the wub said. "Very old and very ponderous. It is difficult for us to move around. You can appreciate anything so slow and heavy would be at the mercy of more agile forms of life. There was no use in our relying on physical defenses. How could we win? Too heavy to run, too soft to fight, too good-natured to hunt for game—"

"How do you live?"

"Plants. Vegetables. We can eat almost anything. We're very catholic. Tolerant, eclectic, catholic. We live and let live. That's how we've gotten along."

The wub eyed the Captain.

"And that's why I so violently objected to this business about having me boiled. I could see the image in your mind—most of me in the frozen food locker, some of me in the kettle, a bit for your pet cat—"

"So you read minds?" the Captain said. "How interesting. Anything else? I mean, what else can you do along those lines?"

"A few odds and ends," the wub said absently, staring around the room. "A nice apartment you have here, Captain. You keep it quite neat. I respect life-forms that are tidy. Some Martian birds are quite tidy. They throw things out of their nests and sweep them—"

"Indeed." The Captain nodded. "But to get back to the problem—"

"Quite so. You spoke of dining on me. The taste, I am told, is good. A little fatty, but tender. But how can any lasting contact be established between your people and mine if you resort to such barbaric attitudes? Eat me? Rather you should discuss questions with me, philosophy, the arts—"

The Captain stood up. "Philosophy. It might interest you to know that we will be hard put to find something to eat for the next month. An unfortunate spoilage—"

"I know." The wub nodded. "But wouldn't it be more in accord with your principles of democracy if we all drew straws, or something along that line? After all, democracy is to protect the minority from just such infringements. Now, if each of us casts one vote—"

The Captain walked to the door.

"Nuts to you," he said. He opened the door. He opened his mouth.

He stood frozen, his mouth wide, his eyes staring, his fingers still on the knob.

The wub watched him. Presently it padded out of the room, edging past the Captain. It went down the hall, deep in meditation.

The room was quiet.

"So you see," the wub said, "we have a common myth. Your mind contains many familiar myth symbols. Ishtar, Odysseus—"

Peterson sat silently, staring at the floor. He shifted in his chair.

"Go on," he said. "Please go on."

"I find in your Odysseus a figure common to the mythology of most self-conscious races. As I interpret it, Odysseus wanders as an individual aware of himself as such. This is the idea of separation, of separation from family and country. The process of individuation."

"But Odysseus returns to his home." Peterson looked out the port window, at the stars, endless stars, burning intently in the empty universe. "Finally he goes home."

"As must all creatures. The moment of separation is a temporary period, a brief journey of the soul. It begins, it ends. The wanderer returns to land and race. . . ."

The door opened. The wub stopped, turning its great head.

Captain Franco came into the room, the men behind him. They hesitated at the door.

"Are you all right?" French said.

"Do you mean me?" Peterson said, surprised. "Why me?"

Franco lowered his gun. "Come over here," he said to Peterson. "Get up and come here."

There was silence.

"Go ahead," the wub said. "It doesn't matter."

Peterson stood up. "What for?"

"It's an order."

Peterson walked to the door. French caught his arm.

"What's going on?" Peterson wrenched loose. "What's the matter with you?"

Captain Franco moved toward the wub. The wub looked up from where it lay in the corner, pressed against the wall.

"It is interesting," the wub said, "that you are obsessed with the idea of eating me. I wonder why."

"Get up," Franco said.

"If you wish." The wub rose, grunting. "Be patient. It is difficult for me." It stood, gasping, its tongue lolling foolishly.

"Shoot it now," French said.

"For God's sake!" Peterson exclaimed. Jones turned to him quickly, his eyes gray with fear.

"You didn't see him—like a statue, standing there, his mouth open. If we hadn't come down, he'd still be there."

"Who? The Captain?" Peterson stared around. "But he's all right now."

They looked at the wub, standing in the middle of the room, its great chest rising and falling.

"Come on," Franco said. "Out of the way."

The men pulled aside toward the door.

"You are quite afraid, aren't you?" the wub said. "Have I done anything to you? I am against the idea of hurting. All I have done is try to protect myself. Can you expect me to rush eagerly to my death? I am a sensible being like yourselves. I was curious to see your ship, learn about you. I suggested to the native—"

The gun jerked.

"See," Franco said. "I thought so."

The wub settled down, panting. It put its paws out, pulling its tail around it.

"It is very warm," the wub said. "I understand that we are close to the jets. Atomic power. You have done many wonderful things with it—technically. Apparently your scientific hierarchy is not equipped to solve moral, ethical—"

Franco turned to the men, crowding behind him, wide-eyed, silent.

"I'll do it. You can watch."

French nodded. "Try to hit the brain. It's no good for eating. Don't hit the chest. If the rib cage shatters, we'll have to pick bones out."

"Listen," Peterson said, licking his lips. "Has it done anything? What harm has it done? I'm asking you. And anyhow, it's still mine. You have no right to shoot it. It doesn't belong to you."

Franco raised his gun.

"I'm going out," Jones said, his face white and sick. "I don't want to see it."

"Me, too," French said. The men straggled out, murmuring. Peterson lingered at the door.

"It was talking to me about myths," he said. "It wouldn't hurt anyone."

He went outside.

Franco walked toward the wub. The wub looked up slowly. It swallowed.

"A very foolish thing," it said. "I am sorry that you want to do it. There was a parable that your Saviour related—"

It stopped, staring at the gun.

"Can you look me in the eye and do it?" the wub said. "Can you do that?"

The Captain gazed down. "I can look you in the eye," he said. "Back on the farm we had hogs, dirty razorback hogs. I can do it."

Staring down at the wub, into the gleaming, moist eyes, he pressed the trigger.

The taste was excellent.

They sat glumly around the table, some of them hardly eating at all. The only one who seemed to be enjoying himself was Captain Franco.

"More?" he said, looking around. "More? And some wine, perhaps."

"Not me," French said. "I think I'll go back to the chart room."

"Me, too." Jones stood up, pushing his chair back. "I'll see you later."

The Captain watched them go. Some of the others excused themselves.

"What do you suppose the matter is?" the Captain said. He turned to Peterson. Peterson sat staring down at his plate, at the potatoes, the green peas, and at the thick slab of tender, warm meat.

He opened his mouth. No sound came.

The Captain put his hand on Peterson's shoulder.

"It is only organic matter, now," he said. "The life essence is gone." He ate, spooning up the gravy with some bread. "I, myself, love to eat. It is one of the greatest things that a living creature can enjoy. Eating, resting, meditation, discussing things."

Peterson nodded. Two more men got up and went out. The Captain drank some water and sighed.

"Well," he said. "I must say that this was a very enjoyable meal. All the reports I had heard were quite true—the taste of wub. Very fine. But I was prevented from enjoying this in times past."

He dabbed at his lips with his napkin and leaned back in his chair. Peterson stared dejectedly at the table.

The Captain watched him intently. He leaned over.

"Come, come," he said. "Cheer up! Let's discuss things."

He smiled.

"As I was saying before I was interrupted, the role of Odysseus in the myths—"

Peterson jerked up, staring.

"To go on," the Captain said. "Odysseus, as I understand him—"

ROOG

"Roog!" the dog said. He rested his paws on the top of the fence and looked around him.

The Roog came running into the yard.

It was early morning, and the sun had not really come up yet. The air was cold and gray, and the walls of the house were damp with moisture. The dog opened his jaws a little as he watched, his big black paws clutching the wood of the fence.

The Roog stood by the open gate, looking into the yard. He was a small Roog, thin and white, on wobbly legs. The Roog blinked at the dog, and the dog showed his teeth.

"Roog!" he said again. The sound echoed into the silent half darkness. Nothing moved nor stirred. The dog dropped down and walked back across the yard to the porch steps. He sat down on the bottom step and watched the Roog. The Roog glanced at him. Then he stretched his neck up to the window of the house, just above him. He sniffed at the window.

The dog came flashing across the yard. He hit the fence, and the gate shuddered and groaned. The Roog was walking quickly up the path, hurrying with funny little steps, mincing along. The dog lay down against the slats of the gate, breathing heavily, his red tongue hanging. He watched the Roog disappear.

The dog lay silently, his eyes bright and black. The day was beginning to come. The sky turned a little whiter, and from all around the sounds of people echoed through the morning air. Lights popped on behind shades. In the chilly dawn a window was opened.

The dog did not move. He watched the path.

In the kitchen Mrs. Cardossi poured water into the coffee pot. Steam rose from the water, blinding her. She set the pot down on the edge of the stove and went into the pantry. When she came back Alf was standing at the door of the kitchen. He put his glasses on.

"You bring the paper?" he said.

"It's outside."

Alf Cardossi walked across the kitchen. He threw the bolt on the back door and stepped out onto the porch. He looked into the gray, damp morning. At the fence Boris lay, black and furry, his tongue out.

"Put the tongue in," Alf said. The dog looked quickly up. His tail beat against the ground. "The tongue," Alf said. "Put the tongue in."

The dog and the man looked at one another. The dog whined. His eyes were bright and feverish.

"Roog!" he said softly.

"What?" Alf looked around. "Someone coming? The paperboy come?"

The dog stared at him, his mouth open.

"You certainly upset these days," Alf said. "You better take it easy. We both getting too old for excitement."

He went inside the house.

The sun came up. The street became bright and alive with color. The postman went along the sidewalk with his letters and magazines. Some children hurried by, laughing and talking.

About 11:00, Mrs. Cardossi swept the front porch. She sniffed the air, pausing for a moment.

"It smells good today," she said. "That means it's going to be warm."

In the heat of the noonday sun the black dog lay stretched out full length, under the porch. His chest rose and fell. In the cherry tree the birds were playing, squawking and chattering to each other. Once in a while Boris raised his head and looked at them. Presently he got to his feet and trotted down under the tree.

He was standing under the tree when he saw the two Roogs sitting on the fence, watching him.

"He's big," the first Roog said. "Most Guardians aren't as big as this."

The other Roog nodded, his head wobbling on his neck. Boris watched them without moving, his body stiff and hard. The Roogs were silent now, looking at the big dog with his shaggy ruff of white around his neck.

"How is the offering urn?" the first Roog said. "Is it almost full?"

"Yes." The other nodded. "Almost ready."

"You, there!" the first Roog said, raising his voice. "Do you hear me? We've decided to accept the offering, this time. So you remember to let us in. No nonsense, now."

"Don't forget," the other added. "It won't be long."

Boris said nothing.

The two Roogs leaped off the fence and went over together just beyond the walk. One of them brought out a map and they studied it.

"This area really is none too good for a first trial," the first Roog said. "Too many Guardians . . . Now, the northside area—"

"*They* decided," the other Roog said. "There are so many factors—"

"Of course." They glanced at Boris and moved back farther from the fence. He could not hear the rest of what they were saying.

Presently the Roogs put their map away and went off down the path.

Boris walked over to the fence and sniffed at the boards. He smelled the sickly, rotten odor of Roogs and the hair stood up on his back.

That night when Alf Cardossi came home the dog was standing at the gate, looking up the walk. Alf opened the gate and went into the yard.

"How are you?" he said, thumping the dog's side. "You stopped worrying? Seems like you been nervous of late. You didn't used to be that way."

Boris whined, looking intently up into the man's face.

"You a good dog, Boris," Alf said. "You pretty big, too, for a dog. You don't remember long ago how you used to be only a little bit of a puppy."

Boris leaned against the man's leg.

"You a good dog," Alf murmured. "I sure wish I knew what is on your mind."

He went inside the house. Mrs. Cardossi was setting the table for dinner. Alf went into the living room and took his coat and hat off. He set his lunch pail down on the sideboard and came back into the kitchen.

"What's the matter?" Mrs. Cardossi said.

"That dog got to stop making all that noise, barking. The neighbors going to complain to the police again."

"I hope we don't have to give him to your brother," Mrs. Cardossi said, folding her arms. "But he sure goes crazy, especially on Friday morning, when the garbage men come."

"Maybe he'll calm down," Alf said. He lit his pipe and smoked solemnly. "He didn't used to be that way. Maybe he'll get better, like he was."

"We'll see," Mrs. Cardossi said.

The sun rose up, cold and ominous. Mist hung over all the trees and in the low places.

It was Friday morning.

The black dog lay under the porch, listening, his eyes wide and staring. His coat was stiff with hoarfrost and the breath from his nostrils made clouds of steam in the thin air. Suddenly he turned his head and leaped up.

From far off, a long way away, a faint sound came, a kind of crashing sound.

"Roog!" Boris cried, looking around. He hurried to the gate and stood up, his paws on top of the fence.

In the distance the sound came again, louder now, not as far away as before. It was a crashing, clanging sound, as if something were being rolled back, as if a great door were being opened.

"Roog!" Boris cried. He stared up anxiously at the darkened windows above him. Nothing stirred, nothing.

And along the street the Roogs came. The Roogs and their truck moved along, bouncing against the rough stones, crashing and whirring.

"Roog!" Boris cried, and he leaped, his eyes blazing. Then he became more calm. He settled himself down on the ground and waited, listening.

Out in front the Roogs stopped their truck. He could hear them opening the doors, stepping down onto the sidewalk. Boris ran around in a little circle. He whined, and his muzzle turned once again toward the house.

Inside the warm, dark bedroom, Mr. Cardossi sat up a little in bed and squinted at the clock.

"That damn dog," he muttered. "That damn dog." He turned his face toward the pillow and closed his eyes.

The Roogs were coming down the path now. The first Roog pushed against the gate and the gate opened. The Roogs came into the yard. The dog backed away from them.

"Roog! Roog!" he cried. The horrid, bitter smell of Roogs came to his nose, and he turned away.

"The offering urn," the first Roog said. "It is full, I think." He smiled at the rigid, angry dog. "How very good of you," he said.

The Roogs came toward the metal can, and one of them took the lid from it.

"Roog! Roog!" Boris cried, huddled against the bottom of the porch steps. His body shook with horror. The Roogs were lifting up the big metal can, turning it on its side. The contents poured out onto the ground, and the Roogs scooped the sacks of bulging, splitting paper together, catching at the orange peels and fragments, the bits of toast and egg shells.

One of the Roogs popped an egg shell into his mouth. His teeth crunched the egg shell.

"Roog!" Boris cried hopelessly, almost to himself. The Roogs were almost finished with their work of gathering up the offering. They stopped for a moment, looking at Boris.

Then, slowly, silently, the Roogs looked up, up the side of the house, along the stucco, to the window, with its brown shade pulled tightly down.

"ROOG!" Boris screamed, and he came toward them, dancing with fury and dismay. Reluctantly, the Roogs turned away from the window. They went out through the gate, closing it behind them.

"Look at him," the last Roog said with contempt, pulling his corner of the blanket up on his shoulder. Boris strained against the fence, his mouth open, snapping wildly. The biggest Roog began to wave his arms furiously and Boris retreated. He settled down at the bottom of the porch steps, his mouth still open, and from the depths of him an unhappy, terrible moan issued forth, a wail of misery and despair.

"Come on," the other Roog said to the lingering Roog at the fence.

They walked up the path.

"Well, except for these little places around the Guardians, this area is well cleared," the biggest Roog said. "I'll be glad when this particular Guardian is done. He certainly causes us a lot of trouble."

"Don't be impatient," one of the Roogs said. He grinned. "Our truck is full enough as it is. Let's leave something for next week."

All the Roogs laughed.

They went on up the path, carrying the offering in the dirty, sagging blanket.

PAYCHECK

All at once he was in motion. Around him smooth jets hummed. He was on a small private rocket cruiser, moving leisurely across the afternoon sky, between cities.

"Ugh!" he said, sitting up in his seat and rubbing his head. Beside him Earl Rethrick was staring keenly at him, his eyes bright.

"Coming around?"

"Where are we?" Jennings shook his head, trying to clear the dull ache. "Or maybe I should ask that a different way." Already, he could see that it was not late fall. It was spring. Below the cruiser the fields were green. The last thing he remembered was stepping into an elevator with Rethrick. And it was late fall. And in New York.

"Yes," Rethrick said. "It's almost two years later. You'll find a lot of things have changed. The Government fell a few months ago. The new Government is even stronger. The SP, Security Police, have almost unlimited power. They're teaching the schoolchildren to inform, now. But we all saw that coming. Let's see, what else? New York is larger. I understand they've finished filling in San Francisco Bay."

"What I want to know is what the hell I've been doing the last two years!" Jennings lit a cigarette nervously, pressing the strike end. "Will you tell me that?"

"No. Of course I won't tell you that."

"Where are we going?"

"Back to the New York Office. Where you first met me. Remember? You probably remember it better than I. After all, it was just a day or so ago for you."

Jennings nodded. Two years! Two years out of his life, gone forever. It didn't seem possible. He had still been considering, debating, when he stepped into the elevator. Should he change his mind? Even if he were getting that much money—and it was a lot, even for him—it didn't really seem worth it. He would always wonder what work he had been doing. Was it legal? Was it—But that was past speculation, now. Even while he was trying to make up his mind the curtain had fallen. He looked ruefully out the window at the afternoon sky. Below, the earth was moist and alive. Spring, spring two years later. And what did he have to show for the two years?

"Have I been paid?" he asked. He slipped his wallet out and glanced into it. "Apparently not."

"No. You'll be paid at the Office. Kelly will pay you."

"The whole works at once?"

"Fifty thousand credits."

Jennings smiled. He felt a little better, now that the sum had been spoken aloud. Maybe it wasn't so bad, after all. Almost like being paid to sleep. But he was two years older; he had just that much less to live. It was like selling part of himself, part of his life. And life was worth plenty, these days. He shrugged. Anyhow, it was in the past.

"We're almost there," the older man said. The robot pilot dropped the cruiser down, sinking toward the ground. The edge of New York City became visible below them. "Well, Jennings, I may never see you again." He held out his hand. "It's been a pleasure working with you. We did work together, you know. Side by side. You're one of the best mechanics I've ever seen. We were right in hiring you, even at that salary. You paid us back many times—although you don't realize it."

"I'm glad you got your money's worth."

"You sound angry."

"No. I'm just trying to get used to the idea of being two years older."

Rethrick laughed. "You're still a very young man. And you'll feel better when she gives you your pay."

They stepped out onto the tiny rooftop field of the New York office building. Rethrick led him over to an elevator. As the doors slid shut Jennings got a mental shock. This was the last thing he remembered, this elevator. After that he had blacked out.

"Kelly will be glad to see you," Rethrick said, as they came out into a lighted hall. "She asks about you, once in a while."

"Why?"

"She says you're good-looking." Rethrick pushed a code key against a door. The door responded, swinging wide. They entered the luxurious office of Rethrick Construction. Behind a long mahogany desk a young woman was sitting, studying a report.

"Kelly," Rethrick said, "look whose time finally expired."

The girl looked up, smiling. "Hello, Mr. Jennings. How does it feel to be back in the world?"

"Fine." Jennings walked over to her. "Rethrick says you're the paymaster."

Rethrick clapped Jennings on the back. "So long, my friend. I'll go back to the plant. If you ever need a lot of money in a hurry come around and we'll work out another contract with you."

Jennings nodded. As Rethrick went back out he sat down beside the desk, crossing his legs. Kelly slid a drawer open, moving her chair back. "All right. Your time is up, so Rethrick Construction is ready to pay. Do you have your copy of the contract?"

Jennings took an envelope from his pocket and tossed it on the desk. "There it is."

Kelly removed a small cloth sack and some sheets of handwritten paper from the desk drawer. For a time she read over the sheets, her small face intent.

"What is it?"

"I think you're going to be surprised." Kelly handed him his contract back. "Read that over again."

"Why?" Jennings unfastened the envelope.

"There's an alternate clause. 'If the party of the second part so desires, at any time during his time of contract to the aforesaid Rethrick Construction Company—'"

"'If he so desires, instead of the monetary sum specified, he may choose instead, according to his own wish, articles or products which, in his own opinion, are of sufficient value to stand in lieu of the sum—'"

Jennings snatched up the cloth sack, pulling it open. He poured the contents into his palm. Kelly watched.

"Where's Rethrick?" Jennings stood up. "If he has an idea that this—"

"Rethrick has nothing to do with it. It was your own request. Here, look at this." Kelly passed him the sheets of paper. "In your own hand. Read them. It was your idea, not ours. Honest." She smiled up at him. "This happens every once in a while with people we take on contract. During their time they decide to take something else instead of money. Why, I don't know. But they come out with their minds clean, having agreed—"

Jennings scanned the pages. It was his own writing. There was no doubt of it. His hands shook. "I can't believe it. Even if it is my own writing." He folded up the paper, his jaw set. "Something was done to me while I was back there. I never would have agreed to this."

"You must have had a reason. I admit it doesn't make sense. But you don't know what factors might have persuaded you, before your mind was cleaned. You aren't the first. There have been several others before you."

Jennings stared down at what he held in his palm. From the cloth sack he had spilled a little assortment of items. A code key. A ticket stub. A parcel receipt. A length of fine wire. Half a poker chip, broken across. A green strip of cloth. A bus token.

"This, instead of fifty thousand credits," he murmured. "Two years . . ."

He went out of the building, onto the busy afternoon street. He was still dazed, dazed and confused. Had he been swindled? He felt in his pocket for the little trinkets, the wire, the ticket stub, all the rest. *That,* for two years of work! But he had seen his own handwriting, the statement of waiver, the request for the substitution. Like Jack and the Beanstalk. Why? What for? What had made him do it?

He turned, starting down the sidewalk. At the corner he stopped for a surface cruiser that was turning.

"All right, Jennings. Get in."

His head jerked up. The door of the cruiser was open. A man was kneeling, pointing a heat-rifle straight at his face. A man in blue-green. The Security Police.

Jennings got in. The door closed, magnetic locks slipping into place behind him. Like a vault. The cruiser glided off down the street. Jennings sank back against the seat. Beside him the SP man lowered his gun. On the other side a second officer ran his hands expertly over him, searching for weapons. He brought out Jennings's wallet and the handful of trinkets. The envelope and contract.

"What does he have?" the driver said.

"Wallet, money. Contract with Rethrick Construction. No weapons." He gave Jennings back his things.

"What's this all about?" Jennings said.

"We want to ask you a few questions. That's all. You've been working for Rethrick?"

"Yes."

"Two years?"

"Almost two years."

"At the Plant?"

Jennings nodded. "I suppose so."

The officer leaned toward him. "Where is that Plant, Mr. Jennings? Where is it located?"

"I don't know."

The two officers looked at each other. The first one moistened his lips, his face sharp and alert. "You don't know? The next question. The last. In those two years, what kind of work did you do? What was your job?"

"Mechanic. I repaired electronic machinery."

"What *kind* of electronic machinery?"

"I don't know." Jennings looked up at him. He could not help smiling, his lips twisting ironically. "I'm sorry, but I don't know. It's the truth."

There was silence.

"What do you mean, you don't know? You mean you worked on machinery for two years without knowing what it was? Without even knowing where you were?"

Jennings roused himself. "What is all this? What did you pick me up for? I haven't done anything. I've been—"

"We know. We're not arresting you. We only want to get information for our records. About Rethrick Construction. You've been working for them, in their Plant. In an important capacity. You're an electronic mechanic?"

"Yes."

"You repair high-quality computers and allied equipment?" The officer consulted his notebook. "You're considered one of the best in the country, according to this."

Jennings said nothing.

"Tell us the two things we want to know, and you'll be released at once. Where is Rethrick's Plant? What kind of work are they doing? You serviced their machines for them, didn't you? Isn't that right? For two years."

"I don't know. I suppose so. I don't have any idea what I did during the two years. You can believe me or not." Jennings stared wearily down at the floor.

"What'll we do?" the driver said finally. "We have no instructions past this."

"Take him to the station. We can't do any more questioning here." Beyond the cruiser, men and women hurried along the sidewalk. The streets were choked with cruisers, workers going to their homes in the country.

"Jennings, why don't you answer us? What's the matter with you? There's no reason why you can't tell us a couple of simple things like that. Don't you want to cooperate with your Government? Why should you conceal information from us?"

"I'd tell you if I knew."

The officer grunted. No one spoke. Presently the cruiser drew up before a great stone building. The driver turned the motor off, removing the control cap and putting it in his pocket. He touched the door with a code key, releasing the magnetic lock.

"What shall we do, take him in? Actually, we don't—"

"Wait." The driver stepped out. The other two went with him, closing and locking the doors behind them. They stood on the pavement before the Security Station, talking.

Jennings sat silently, staring down at the floor. The SP wanted to know about Rethrick Construction. Well, there was nothing he could tell them. They had come to the wrong person, but how could he prove that? The whole thing was impossible. Two years wiped clean from his mind. Who would believe him? It seemed unbelievable to him, too.

His mind wandered, back to when he had first read the ad. It had hit home, hit him direct. *Mechanic wanted,* and a general outline of the work, vague, indirect, but enough to tell him that it was right up his line. And the pay! Interviews at the Office. Tests, forms. And then the gradual realization that Rethrick Construction was finding all about him while he knew nothing about them. What kind of work did they do? Construction, but what kind? What sort of machines did they have? Fifty thousand credits for two years . . .

And he had come out with his mind washed clean. Two years, and he remembered nothing. It took him a long time to agree to that part of the contract. But he *had* agreed.

Jennings looked out the window. The three officers were still talking on the sidewalk, trying to decide what to do with him. He was in a tough spot. They wanted information he couldn't give, information he didn't know. But how could he prove it? How could he prove that he had worked two years and come out knowing no more than when he had gone in! The SP would work him over. It would be a long time before they'd believe him, and by that time—

He glanced quickly around. Was there any escape? In a second they would be back. He touched the door. Locked, the triple-ring magnetic locks. He had worked on magnetic locks many times. He had even designed part of a trigger core. There was no way to open the doors without the right code key. No way, unless by some chance he could short out the lock. But with what?

He felt in his pockets. What could he use? If he could short the locks, blow them out, there was a faint chance. Outside, men and women were swarming by, on their way home from work. It was past five; the great office buildings were shutting down, the streets were alive with traffic. If he once got out they wouldn't dare fire. —If he could get out.

The three officers separated. One went up the steps into the Station building. In a second the others would reenter the cruiser. Jennings dug into his pocket, bringing out the code key, the ticket stub, the wire. The wire! Thin wire, thin as human hair. Was it insulated? He unwound it quickly. No.

He knelt down, running his fingers expertly across the surface of the door. At the edge of the lock was a thin line, a groove between the lock and the door. He brought the end of the wire up to it, delicately maneuvering the wire into the almost invisible space. The wire disappeared an inch or so. Sweat rolled down Jennings' forehead. He moved the wire a fraction of an inch, twisting it. He held his breath. The relay should be—

A flash.

Half blinded, he threw his weight against the door. The door fell open, the lock fused and smoking. Jennings tumbled into the street and leaped to his feet. Cruisers were all around him, honking and sweeping past. He ducked behind a lumbering truck, entering the middle lane of traffic. On the sidewalk he caught a momentary glimpse of the SP men starting after him.

A bus came along, swaying from side to side, loaded with shoppers and workers. Jennings caught hold of the back rail, pulling himself up onto the platform. Astonished faces loomed up, pale moons thrust suddenly at him. The robot conductor was coming toward him, whirring angrily.

"Sir—" the conductor began. The bus was slowing down. "Sir, it is not allowed—"

"It's all right," Jennings said. He was filled, all at once, with a strange elation. A moment ago he had been trapped, with no way to escape. Two years of his life had been lost for nothing. The Security Police had arrested him, demanding information he couldn't give. A hopeless situation! But now things were beginning to click in his mind.

He reached into his pocket and brought out the bus token. He put it calmly into the conductor's coin slot.

"Okay?" he said. Under his feet the bus wavered, the driver hesitating. Then the bus resumed pace, going on. The conductor turned away, its whirrs subsiding. Everything was all right. Jennings smiled. He eased past the standing people, looking for a seat, some place to sit down. Where he could think.

He had plenty to think about. His mind was racing.

The bus moved on, flowing with the restless stream of urban traffic. Jennings only half saw the people sitting around him. There was no doubt of it: he had not been swindled. It was on the level. The decision had actually been his. Amazingly, after two years of work he had preferred a handful of trinkets instead of fifty thousand credits. But more amazingly, the handful of trinkets was turning out to be worth more than the money.

With a piece of wire and a bus token he had escaped from the Security Police. That was worth plenty. Money would have been useless to him once he disappeared inside the great stone Station. Even fifty thousand credits wouldn't have helped him. And there were five trinkets left. He felt around in his pocket. Five more things. He had used two. The others—what were they for? Something as important?

But the big puzzle: how had *he*—his earlier self—known that a piece of wire and a bus token would save his life? *He* had known, all right. Known in advance. But how? And the other five. Probably they were just as precious, or would be.

The *he* of those two years had known things that he did not know now, things that had been washed away when the company cleaned his mind. Like an adding machine which had been cleared. Everything was slate-clean. What *he* had known was gone, now. Gone, except for seven trinkets, five of which were still in his pocket.

But the real problem right now was not a problem of speculation. It was very concrete. The Security Police were looking for him. They had his name and description. There was no use thinking of going to his apart-ment—if he even still had an apartment. But where, then? Hotels? The SP combed them daily. Friends? That would mean putting them in jeopardy, along with him. It was only a question of time before the SP found him, walking along the street, eating in a restaurant, in a show, sleeping in some rooming house. The SP were everywhere.

Everywhere? Not quite. When an individual person was defenseless, a business was not. The big economic forces had managed to remain free, although virtually everything else had been absorbed by the Government. Laws that had been eased away from the private person still protected property and industry. The SP could pick up any given person, but they could not enter and seize a company, a business. That had been clearly established in the middle of the twentieth century.

Business, industry, corporations were safe from the Security Police. Due process was required. Rethrick Construction was a target of SP inter-est, but they could do nothing until some statute was violated. If he could get back to the Company, get inside its doors, he would be safe. Jennings smiled grimly. The modern church, sanctuary. It was the Government against the corporation, rather than the State against the Church. The new Notre Dame of the world. Where the law could not follow.

Would Rethrick take him back? Yes, on the old basis. He had already said so. Another two years sliced from him, and then back onto the streets.

Would that help him? He felt suddenly in his pocket. And there were the remaining trinkets. Surely *he* had intended them to be used! No, he could not go back to Rethrick and work another contract time. Something else was indicated. Something more permanent. Jennings pondered. Rethrick Construction. What did it construct? What had *he* known, found out, during those two years? And why were the SP so interested?

He brought out the five objects and studied them. The green strip of cloth. The code key. The ticket stub. The parcel receipt. The half poker chip. Strange, that little things like that could be important.

And Rethrick Construction was involved.

There was no doubt. The answer, all the answers, lay at Rethrick. But where *was* Rethrick? He had no idea where the plant was, no idea at all. He knew where the Office was, the big, luxurious room with the young woman and her desk. But that was not Rethrick Construction. Did anyone know, beside Rethrick? Kelly didn't know. Did the SP know?

It was out of town. That was certain. He had gone there by rocket. It was probably in the United States, maybe in the farmlands, the country, between cities. What a hell of a situation! Any moment the SP might pick him up. The next time he might not get away. His only chance, his own real chance for safety, lay in reaching Rethrick. And his only chance to find out the things he had to know. The plant—a place where he had been, but which he could not recall. He looked down at the five trinkets. Would any of them help?

A burst of despair swept through him. Maybe it was just coincidence, the wire and the token. Maybe—

He examined the parcel receipt, turning it over and holding it up to the light. Suddenly his stomach muscles knotted. His pulse changed. He had been right. No, it was not a coincidence, the wire and the token. The parcel receipt was dated two days hence. The parcel, whatever it might be, had not even been deposited yet. Not for forty-eight more hours.

He looked at the other things. The ticket stub. What good was a ticket stub? It was creased and bent, folded over, again and again. He couldn't go anyplace with that. A stub didn't take you anywhere. It only told you where you had been.

Where you had been!

He bent down, peering at it, smoothing the creases. The printing had been torn through the middle. Only part of each word could be made out.

PORTOLA T
STUARTSVI
IOW

He smiled. That was it. Where he had been. He could fill in the missing letters. It was enough. There was no doubt: *he* had foreseen this, too. Three of the seven trinkets used. Four left. Stuartsville, Iowa. Was there such a place? He looked out the window of the bus. The Intercity rocket station was only a block or so away. He could be there in a second. A quick sprint from the bus, hoping the Police wouldn't be there to stop him—

But somehow he knew they wouldn't. Not with the other four things in his pocket. And once he was on the rocket he would be safe. Intercity was big, big enough to keep free of the SP. Jennings put the remaining trinkets back into his pocket and stood up, pulling the bellcord.

A moment later he stepped gingerly out onto the sidewalk.

The rocket let him off at the edge of town, at a tiny brown field. A few disinterested porters moved about, stacking luggage, resting from the heat of the sun.

Jennings crossed the field to the waiting room, studying the people around him. Ordinary people, workmen, businessmen, housewives. Stuartsville was a small Middle Western town. Truck drivers. High school kids.

He went through the waiting room, out onto the street. So this was where Rethrick's Plant was located—perhaps. If he had used the stub correctly. Anyhow, *something* was here, or *he* wouldn't have included the stub with the other trinkets.

Stuartsville, Iowa. A faint plan was beginning to form in the back of his mind, still vague and nebulous. He began to walk, his hands in his pockets, looking around him. A newspaper office, lunch counters, hotels, poolrooms, a barber shop, a television repair shop. A rocket sales store with huge showrooms of gleaming rockets. Family size. And at the end of the block the Portola Theater.

The town thinned out. Farms, fields. Miles of green country. In the sky above a few transport rockets lumbered, carrying farm supplies and equipment back and forth. A small, unimportant town. Just right for Rethrick Construction. The Plant would be lost here, away from the city, away from the SP.

Jennings walked back. He entered a lunchroom, BOB'S PLACE. A young man with glasses came over as he sat down at the counter, wiping his hands on his white apron.

"Coffee," Jennings said.

"Coffee." The man brought the cup. There were only a few people in the lunchroom. A couple of flies buzzed, against the window.

Outside in the street shoppers and farmers moved leisurely by.

"Say," Jennings said, stirring his coffee. "Where can a man get work around here? Do you know?"

"What kind of work?" The young man came back, leaning against the counter.

"Electrical wiring. I'm an electrician. Television, rockets, computers. That sort of stuff."

"Why don't you try the big industrial areas? Detroit. Chicago. New York."

Jennings shook his head. "Can't stand the big cities. I never liked cities."

The young man laughed. "A lot of people here would be glad to work in Detroit. You're an electrician?"

"Are there any plants around here? Any repair shops or plants?"

"None that I know of." The young man went off to wait on some men who had come in. Jennings sipped his coffee. Had he made a mistake? Maybe he should go back and forget about Stuartsville, Iowa. Maybe he had made the wrong inference from the ticket stub. But the ticket meant something, unless he was completely wrong about everything. It was a little late to decide that, though.

The young man came back. "Is there *any* kind of work I can get here?" Jennings said. "Just to tide me over."

"There's always farm work."

"How about the retail repair shops? Garages. TV."

"There's a TV repair shop down the street. Maybe you might get something there. You could try. Farm work pays good. They can't get many men, anymore. Most men in the military. You want to pitch hay?"

Jennings laughed. He paid for his coffee. "Not very much. Thanks."

"Once in a while some of the men go up the road and work. There's some sort of Government station."

Jennings nodded. He pushed the screen door open, stepping outside onto the hot sidewalk. He walked aimlessly for a time, deep in thought, turning his nebulous plan over and over. It was a good plan; it would solve everything, all his problems at once. But right now it hinged on one thing: finding Rethrick Construction. And he had only one clue, if it really was a clue. The ticket stub, folded and creased, in his pocket. And a faith that *he* had known what he was doing.

A Government station. Jennings paused, looking around him. Across the street was a taxi stand, a couple of cabbies sitting in their cabs, smoking and reading the newspaper. It was worth a try, at least. There wasn't much else to do. Rethrick would be something else, on the surface. If it posed as a Government project no one would ask any questions. They were all too accustomed to Government projects working without explanation, in secrecy.

He went over to the first cab. "Mister," he said, "can you tell me something?"

The cabbie looked up. "What do you want?"

"They tell me there's work to be had, out at the Government station. Is that right?"

The cabbie studied him. He nodded.

"What kind of work is it?"

"I don't know."

"Where do they do the hiring?"

"I don't know." The cabbie lifted his paper.

"Thanks." Jennings turned away.

"They don't do any hiring. Maybe once in a long while. They don't take many on. You better go someplace else if you're looking for work."

"All right."

The other cabbie leaned out of his cab. "They use only a few day laborers, buddy. That's all. And they're very choosy. They don't hardly let anybody in. Some kind of war work."

Jennings pricked up his ears. "Secret?"

"They come into town and pick up a load of construction workers. Maybe a truck full. That's all. They're real careful who they pick."

Jennings walked back toward the cabbie. "That right?"

"It's a big place. Steel wall. Charged. Guards. Work going on day and night. But nobody gets in. Set up on top of a hill, out the old Henderson Road. About two miles and a half." The cabbie poked at his shoulder. "You can't get in unless you're identified. They identify their laborers, after they pick them out. You know."

Jennings stared at him. The cabbie was tracing a line on his shoulder. Suddenly Jennings understood. A flood of relief rushed over him.

"Sure," he said. "I understand what you mean. At least, I think so." He reached into his pocket, bringing out the four trinkets. Carefully, he unfolded the strip of green cloth, holding it up. "Like this?"

The cabbies stared at the cloth. "That's right," one of them said slowly, staring at the cloth. "Where did you get it?"

Jennings laughed. "A friend." He put the cloth back in his pocket. "A friend gave it to me."

He went off, toward the Intercity field. He had plenty to do, now that the first step was over. Rethrick was here, all right. And apparently the trinkets were going to see him through. One for every crisis. A pocketful of miracles, from someone who knew the future!

But the next step couldn't be done alone. He needed help. Somebody else was needed for this part. But who? He pondered, entering the Intercity waiting room. There was only one person he could possibly go to. It was a long chance, but he had to take it. He couldn't work alone, here on out. If the Rethrick plant was here then Kelly would be too . . .

The street was dark. At the corner a lamppost cast a fitful beam. A few cruisers moved by.

From the apartment building entrance a slim shape came, a young woman in a coat, a purse in her hand. Jennings watched as she passed under the streetlamp. Kelly McVane was going someplace, probably to a party. Smartly dressed, high heels tap-tapping on the pavement, a little coat and hat.

He stepped out behind her. "Kelly."

She turned quickly, her mouth open. "Oh!"

Jennings took her arm. "Don't worry. It's just me. Where are you going, all dressed up?"

"No place." She blinked. "My golly, you scared me. What is it? What's going on?"

"Nothing. Can you spare a few minutes? I want to talk to you."

Kelly nodded. "I guess so." She looked around. "Where'll we go?"

"Where's a place we can talk? I don't want anyone to overhear us."

"Can't we just walk along?"

"No. The Police."

"The Police?"

"They're looking for me."

"For you? But why?"

"Let's not stand here," Jennings said grimly. "Where can we go?"

Kelly hesitated. "We can go up to my apartment. No one's there."

They went up in the elevator. Kelly unlocked the door, pressing the code key against it. The door swung open and they went inside, the heater and lights coming on automatically at her step. She closed the door and took off her coat.

"I won't stay long," Jennings said.

"That's all right. I'll fix you a drink." She went into the kitchen. Jennings sat down on the couch, looking around at the neat little apartment. Presently the girl came back. She sat down beside him and Jennings took his drink. Scotch and water, cold.

"Thanks."

Kelly smiled. "Not at all." The two of them sat silently for a time. "Well?" she said at last. "What's this all about? Why are the Police looking for you?"

"They want to find out about Rethrick Construction. I'm only a pawn in this. They think I know something because I worked two years at Rethrick's Plant."

"But you don't!"

"I can't prove that."

Kelly reached out, touching Jennings's head, just above the ear. "Feel there. That spot."

Jennings reached up. Above his ear, under the hair, was a tiny hard spot. "What is it?"

"They burned through the skull there. Cut a tiny wedge from the brain. All your memories of the two years. They located them and burned them out. The SP couldn't possibly make you remember. It's gone. You don't have it."

"By the time they realize that there won't be much left of me."

Kelly said nothing.

"You can see the spot I'm in. It would be better for me if I did remember. Then I could tell them and they'd—"

"And destroy Rethrick!"

Jennings shrugged. "Why not? Rethrick means nothing to me. I don't even know what they're doing. And why are the Police so interested? From the very start, all the secrecy, cleaning my mind—"

"There's reason. Good reason."

"Do you know why?"

"No." Kelly shook her head. "But I'm sure there's a reason. If the SP are interested, there's reason." She set down her drink, turning toward him. "I hate the Police. We all do, every one of us. They're after us all the time. I don't know anything about Rethrick. If I did my life wouldn't be safe. There's not much standing between Rethrick and them. A few laws, a handful of laws. Nothing more."

"I have the feeling Rethrick is a great deal more than just another construction company the SP wants to control."

"I suppose it is. I really don't know. I'm just a receptionist. I've never been to the Plant. I don't even know where it is."

"But you wouldn't want anything to happen to it."

"Of course not! They're fighting the Police. Anyone that's fighting the Police is on our side."

"Really? I've heard that kind of logic before. Anyone fighting communism was automatically good, a few decades ago. Well, time will tell. As far as I'm concerned I'm an individual caught between two ruthless forces. Government and business. The Government has men and wealth. Rethrick Construction has its technocracy. What they've done with it, I don't know. I did, a few weeks ago. All I have now is a faint glimmer, a few references. A theory."

Kelly glanced at him. "A theory?"

"And my pocketful of trinkets. Seven. Three or four now. I've used some. They're the basis of my theory. If Rethrick is doing what I think it's doing, I can understand the SP's interest. As a matter of fact, I'm beginning to share their interest."

"What is Rethrick doing?"

"It's developed a time scoop."

"What?"

"A time scoop. It's been theoretically possible for several years. But it's illegal to experiment with time scoops and mirrors. It's a felony, and if you're caught, all your equipment and data becomes the property of the Government." Jennings smiled crookedly. "No wonder the Government's interested. If they can catch Rethrick with the goods—"

"A time scoop. It's hard to believe."

"Don't you think I'm right?"

"I don't know. Perhaps. Your trinkets. You're not the first to come out with a little cloth sack of odds and ends. You've used some? How?"

"First, the wire and the bus token. Getting away from the Police. It seems funny, but if I hadn't had them, I'd be there yet. A piece of wire and a ten-cent token. But I don't usually carry such things. That's the point."

"Time travel."

"No. Not time travel. Berkowsky demonstrated that time travel is impossible. This is a time scoop, a mirror to see and a scoop to pick up things. These trinkets. At least one of them is from the future. Scooped up. Brought back."

"How do you know?"

"It's dated. The others, perhaps not. Things like tokens and wire belong to classes of things. Any one token is as good as another. There, *he* must have used a mirror."

"*He?*"

"When I was working with Rethrick. I must have used the mirror. I looked into my own future. If I was repairing their equipment I could hardly keep from it! I must have looked ahead, seen what was coming. The SP picking me up. I must have seen that, and seen what a piece of thin wire and a bus token would do—if I had them with me at the exact moment."

Kelly considered. "Well? What do you want me for?"

"I'm not sure, now. Do you really look on Rethrick as a benevolent institution, waging war against the Police? A sort of Roland at Roncesvalles—"

"What does it matter how I feel about the Company?"

"It matters a lot." Jennings finished his drink, pushing the glass aside. "It matters a lot, because I want you to help me. I'm going to blackmail Rethrick Construction."

Kelly stared at him.

"It's my one chance to stay alive. I've got to get a hold over Rethrick, a big hold. Enough of a hold so they'll let me in, on my own terms. There's no other place I can go. Sooner or later the Police are going to pick me up. If I'm not inside the Plant, and soon—"

"Help you blackmail the Company? Destroy Rethrick?"

"No. Not destroy. I don't want to destroy it—my life depends on the Company. My life depends on Rethrick being strong enough to defy the SP. But if I'm on the *outside* it doesn't much matter how strong Rethrick is. Do you see? I want to get in. I want to get inside before it's too late. And I want in on my own terms, not as a two-year worker who gets pushed out again afterward."

"For the Police to pick up."

Jennings nodded. "Exactly."

"How are you going to blackmail the Company?"

"I'm going to enter the Plant and carry out enough material to prove Rethrick is operating a time scoop."

Kelly laughed. "Enter the Plant? Let's see you *find* the Plant. The SP have been looking for it for years."

"I've already found it." Jennings leaned back, lighting a cigarette. "I've located it with my trinkets. And I have four left, enough to get me inside, I think. And to get me what I want. I'll be able to carry out enough papers and photographs to hang Rethrick. But I don't want to hang Rethrick. I only want to bargain. That's where you come in."

"I?"

"You can be trusted not to go to the Police. I need someone I can turn the material over to. I don't dare keep it myself. As soon as I have it I must turn it over to someone else, someone who'll hide it where I won't be able to find it."

"Why?"

"Because," Jennings said calmly, "any minute the SP may pick me up. I have no love for Rethrick, but I don't want to scuttle it. That's why you've got to help me. I'm going to turn the information over to you, to hold, while I bargain with Rethrick. Otherwise I'll have to hold it myself. And if I have it on me—"

He glanced at her. Kelly was staring at the floor, her face tense. Set.

"Well? What do you say? Will you help me, or shall I take the chance the SP won't pick me up with the material? Data enough to destroy Rethrick. Well? Which will it be? Do you want to see Rethrick destroyed? What's your answer?"

The two of them crouched, looking across the fields at the hill beyond. The hill rose up, naked and brown, burned clean of vegetation. Nothing grew on its sides. Halfway up a long steel fence twisted, topped with charged barbed wire. On the other side a guard walked slowly, a tiny figure patrolling with a rifle and helmet.

At the top of the hill lay an enormous concrete block, a towering structure without windows or doors. Mounted guns caught the early morning sunlight, glinting in a row along the roof of the building.

"So that's the Plant," Kelly said softly.

"That's it. It would take an army to get up there, up that hill and over the fence. Unless they were allowed in." Jennings got to his feet, helping Kelly up. They walked back along the path, through the trees, to where Kelly had parked the cruiser.

"Do you really think your green cloth band will get you in?" Kelly said, sliding behind the wheel.

"According to the people in the town, a truckload of laborers will be brought in to the Plant sometime this morning. The truck is unloaded at the entrance and the men examined. If everything's in order they're let inside the grounds, past the fence. For construction work, manual labor. At the end of the day they're let out again and driven back to town."

"Will that get you close enough?"

"I'll be on the other side of the fence, at least."

"How will you get to the time scoop? That must be inside the building, someplace."

Jennings brought out a small code key. "This will get me in. I hope. I assume it will."

Kelly took the key, examining it. "So that's one of your trinkets. We should have taken a better look inside your little cloth bag."

"We?"

"The Company. I saw several little bags of trinkets pass out, through my hands. Rethrick never said anything."

"Probably the Company assumed no one would ever want to get back inside again." Jennings took the code key from her. "Now, do you know what you're supposed to do?"

"I'm supposed to stay here with the cruiser until you get back. You're to give me the material. Then I'm to carry it back to New York and wait for you to contact me."

"That's right." Jennings studied the distant road, leading through the trees to the Plant gate. "I better get down there. The truck may be along any time."

"What if they decide to count the number of workers?"

"I'll have to take the chance. But I'm not worried. I'm sure *he* foresaw everything."

Kelly smiled. "You and your friend, your helpful friend. I hope *he* left you enough things to get you out again, after you have the photographs."

"Do you?"

"Why not?" Kelly said easily. "I always liked you. You know that. You knew when you came to me."

Jennings stepped out of the cruiser. He had on overalls and workshoes, and a gray sweatshirt. "I'll see you later. If everything goes all right. I think it will." He patted his pocket. "With my charms here, my good-luck charms."

He went off through the trees, walking swiftly.

The trees led to the very edge of the road. He stayed with them, not coming out into the open. The Plant guards were certainly scanning the hillside. They had burned it clean, so that anyone trying to creep up to the fence would be spotted at once. And he had seen infrared searchlights.

Jennings crouched low, resting against his heels, watching the road. A few yards up the road was a roadblock, just ahead of the gate. He examined his watch. Ten-thirty. He might have a wait, a long wait. He tried to relax.

It was after eleven when the great truck came down the road, rumbling and wheezing.

Jennings came to life. He took out the strip of green cloth and fastened it around his arm. The truck came closer. He could see its load now. The back was full of workmen, men in jeans and workshirts, bounced and jolted as the truck moved along. Sure enough, each had an arm band like his own, a swathe of green around his upper arm. So far so good.

The truck came slowly to a halt, stopping at the roadblock. The men got down slowly onto the road, sending up a cloud of dust into the hot midday sun. They slapped the dust from their jeans, some of them lighting cigarettes. Two guards came leisurely from behind the roadblock. Jennings tensed. In a moment it would be time. The guards moved among the men, examining them, their arm bands, their faces, looking at the identification tabs of a few.

The roadblock slid back. The gate opened. The guards returned to their positions.

Jennings slid forward, slithering through the brush, toward the road. The men were stamping out their cigarettes, climbing back up into the truck. The truck was gunning its motor, the driver releasing the brakes. Jennings dropped onto the road, behind the truck. A rattle of leaves and dirt showered after him. Where he had landed, the view of the guards was cut off by the truck. Jennings held his breath. He ran toward the back of the truck.

The men stared at him curiously as he pulled himself up among them, his chest rising and falling. Their faces were weathered, gray and lined. Men of the soil. Jennings took his place between two burly farmers as the truck started up. They did not seem to notice him. He had rubbed dirt into his skin and let his beard grow for a day. At a quick glance he didn't look much different from the others. But if anyone made a count—

The truck passed through the gate, into the grounds. The gate slid shut behind. Now they were going up, up the steep side of the hill, the truck rattling and swaying from side to side. The vast concrete structure loomed nearer. Were they going to enter it? Jennings watched, fascinated. A thin high door was sliding back, revealing a dark interior. A row of artificial lights gleamed.

The truck stopped. The workmen began to get down again. Some mechanics came around them.

"What's this crew for?" one of them asked.

"Digging. Inside." Another jerked a thumb. "They're digging again. Send them inside."

Jennings's heart thudded. He was going inside! He felt at his neck. There, inside the gray sweater, a flatplate camera hung like a bib around his neck. He could scarcely feel it, even knowing it was there. Maybe this would be less difficult than he had thought.

The workmen pushed through the door on foot, Jennings with them. They were in an immense workroom, long benches with half-completed machinery, booms and cranes, and the constant roar of work. The door closed after them, cutting them off from outside. He was in the Plant. But where was the time scoop, and the mirror?

"This way," a foreman said. The workmen plodded over to the right. A freight lift rose to meet them from the bowels of the building. "You're going down below. How many of you have experience with drills?"

A few hands went up.

"You can show the others. We are moving earth with drills and eaters. Any of you work eaters?"

No hands. Jennings glanced at the worktables. Had he worked here, not so long ago? A sudden chill went through him. Suppose he were recognized? Maybe he had worked with these very mechanics.

"Come on," the foreman said impatiently. "Hurry up."

Jennings got into the freight lift with the others. A moment later they began to descend, down the black tube. Down, down, into the lower levels of the Plant. Rethrick Construction was *big*, a lot bigger than it looked above ground. A lot bigger than he had imagined. Floors, underground levels, flashing past one after the other.

The elevator stopped. The doors opened. He was looking down a long corridor. The floor was thick with stone dust. The air was moist. Around him, the workmen began to crowd out. Suddenly Jennings stiffened, pulling back.

At the end of the corridor before a steel door, was Earl Rethrick. Talking to a group of technicians.

"All out," the foreman said. "Let's go."

Jennings left the elevator, keeping behind the others. Rethrick! His heart beat dully. If Rethrick saw him he was finished. He felt in his pockets. He had a miniature Boris gun, but it wouldn't be much use if he was discovered. Once Rethrick saw him it would be all over.

"Down this way." The foreman led them toward what seemed to be an underground railway, to one side of the corridor. The men were getting into metal cars along a track. Jennings watched Rethrick. He saw him gesture angrily, his voice coming faintly down the hall. Suddenly Rethrick turned. He held up his hand and the great steel door behind him opened.

Jennings's heart almost stopped beating.

There, beyond the steel door, was the time scoop. He recognized it at once. The mirror. The long metal rods, ending in claws. Like Berkowsky's theoretical model—only this was real.

Rethrick went into the room, the technicians following behind him. Men were working at the scoop, standing all around it. Part of the shield was off. They were digging into the works. Jennings stared, hanging back.

"Say you—" the foreman said, coming toward him. The steel door shut. The view was cut off. Rethrick, the scoop, the technicians, were gone.

"Sorry," Jennings murmured.

"You know you're not supposed to be curious around here." The foreman was studying him intently. "I don't remember you. Let me see your tab."

"My tab?"

"Your identification tab." The foreman turned away. "Bill, bring me the board." He looked Jennings up and down. "I'm going to check you from the board, mister. I've never seen you in the crew before. Stay here." A man was coming from a side door with a check board in his hands.

It was now or never.

Jennings sprinted, down the corridor, toward the great steel door. Behind there was a startled shout, the foreman and his helper. Jennings whipped out the code key, praying fervently as he ran. He came up to the door, holding out the key. With the other hand he brought out the Boris gun. Beyond the door was the time scoop. A few photographs, some schematics snatched up, and then, if he could get out—

The door did not move. Sweat leaped out on his face. He knocked the key against the door. Why didn't it open? Surely— He began to shake, panic rising up in him. Down the corridor people were coming, racing after him. Open—

But the door did not open. The key he held in his hand was the wrong key.

He was defeated. The door and the key did not match. Either *he* had been wrong, or the key was to be used someplace else. But where? Jennings looked frantically around. Where? Where could he go?

To one side a door was half open, a regular bolt-lock door. He crossed the corridor, pushing it open. He was in a storeroom of some sort. He slammed the door, throwing the bolt. He could hear them outside, confused, calling for guards. Soon armed guards would be along. Jennings held the Boris gun tightly, gazing around. Was he trapped? Was there a second way out?

He ran through the room, pushing among bales and boxes, towering stacks of silent cartons, end on end. At the rear was an emergency hatch. He opened it immediately. An impulse came to throw the code key away. What good had it been? But surely *he* had known what he was doing. *He* had already seen all this. Like God, it had already happened for *him*. Predetermined. *He* could not err. Or could he?

A chill went through him. Maybe the future was variable. Maybe this had been the right key, once. But not anymore!

There were sounds behind him. They were melting the storeroom door. Jennings scrambled through the emergency hatch, into a low concrete passage, damp and ill lit. He ran quickly along it, turning corners. It was like a sewer. Other passages ran into it, from all sides.

He stopped. Which way? Where could he hide? The mouth of a major vent pipe gaped above his head. He caught hold and pulled himself up. Grimly, he eased his body onto it. They'd ignore a pipe, go on past. He crawled cautiously down the pipe. Warm air blew into his face. Why such a big vent? It implied an unusual chamber at the other end. He came to a metal grill and stopped.

And gasped.

He was looking into the great room, the room he had glimpsed beyond the steel door. Only now he was at the other end. There was the time scoop.

And far down, beyond the scoop, was Rethrick, conferring at an active vidscreen. An alarm was sounding, whining shrilly, echoing everywhere. Technicians were running in all directions. Guards in uniform poured in and out of doors.

The scoop. Jennings examined the grill. It was slotted in place. He moved it laterally and it fell into his hands. No one was watching. He slid cautiously out, into the room, the Boris gun ready. He was fairly hidden behind the scoop, and the technicians and guards were all the way down at the other end of the room, where he had first seen them.

And there it was, all around him, the schematics, the mirror, papers, data, blueprints. He flicked his camera on. Against his chest the camera vibrated, film moving through it. He snatched up a handful of schematics. Perhaps *he* had used these very diagrams, a few weeks before!

He stuffed his pockets with papers. The film came to an end. But he was finished. He squeezed back into the vent, pushing through the mouth and down the tube. The sewerlike corridor was still empty, but there was an insistent drumming sound, the noise of voices and footsteps. So many passages—They were looking for him in a maze of escape corridors.

Jennings ran swiftly. He ran on and on, without regard to direction, trying to keep along the main corridor. On all sides passages flocked off, one after another, countless passages. He was dropping down, lower and lower. Running downhill.

Suddenly he stopped, gasping. The sound behind him had died away for a moment. But there was a new sound, ahead. He went along slowly. The corridor twisted, turning to the right. He advanced slowly, the Boris gun ready.

Two guards were standing a little way ahead, lounging and talking together. Beyond them was a heavy code door. And behind him the sound of voices were coming again, growing louder. They had found the same passage he had taken. They were on the way.

Jennings stepped out, the Boris gun raised. "Put up your hands. Let go of your guns."

The guards gawked at him. Kids, boys with cropped blond hair and shiny uniforms. They moved back, pale and scared.

"The guns. Let them fall."

The two rifles clattered down. Jennings smiled. Boys. Probably this was their first encounter with trouble. Their leather boots shone, brightly polished.

"Open the door," Jennings said. "I want through."

They stared at him. Behind, the noise grew.

"Open it." He became impatient. "Come on." He waved the pistol. "Open it, damn it! Do you want me to—"

"We—we can't."

"What?"

"We can't. It's a code door. We don't have the key. Honest, mister. They don't let us have the key." They were frightened. Jennings felt fear himself now. Behind him the drumming was louder. He was trapped, caught.

Or was he?

Suddenly he laughed. He walked quickly up to the door. "Faith," he murmured, raising his hand. "That's something you should never lose."

"What—what's that?"

"Faith in yourself. Self-confidence."

The door slid back as he held the code key against it. Blinding sunlight streamed in, making him blink. He held the gun steady. He was outside, at the gate. Three guards gaped in amazement at the gun. He was at the gate—and beyond lay the woods.

"Get out of the way." Jennings fired at the metal bars of the gate. The metal burst into flame, melting, a cloud of fire rising.

"Stop him!" From behind, men came pouring, guards, out of the corridor.

Jennings leaped through the smoking gate. The metal tore at him, searing him. He ran through the smoke, rolling and falling. He got to his feet and scurried on, into the trees.

He was outside. *He* had not let him down. The key had worked, all right. He had tried it first on the wrong door.

On and on he ran, sobbing for breath, pushing through the trees. Behind him the Plant and the voices fell away. He had the papers. And he was free.

He found Kelly and gave her the film and everything he had managed to stuff into his pockets. Then he changed back to his regular clothes. Kelly drove him to the edge of Stuartsville and left him off. Jennings watched the cruiser rise up into the air, heading toward New York. Then he went into town and boarded the Intercity rocket.

On the flight he slept, surrounded by dozing businessmen. When he awoke the rocket was settling down, landing at the huge New York spaceport.

Jennings got off, mixing with the flow of people. Now that he was back there was the danger of being picked up by the SP again. Two security officers in their green uniforms watched him impassively as he took a taxi at the field station. The taxi swept him into downtown traffic. Jennings wiped his brow. That was close. Now, to find Kelly.

He ate dinner at a small restaurant, sitting in the back away from the windows. When he emerged the sun was beginning to set. He walked slowly along the sidewalk, deep in thought.

So far so good. He had got the papers and film, and he had got away. The trinkets had worked every step along the way. Without them he would have been helpless. He felt in his pocket. Two left. The serrated half poker chip, and the parcel receipt. He took the receipt out, examining it in the fading evening light.

Suddenly he noticed something. The date on it was today's date. He had caught up with the slip.

He put it away, going on. What did it mean? What was it for? He shrugged. He would know, in time. And the half poker chip. What the hell was it for? No way to tell. In any case, he was certain to get through. *He* had got him by, up to now. Surely there wasn't much left.

He came to Kelly's apartment house and stopped, looking up. Her light was on. She was back; her fast little cruiser had beaten the Intercity rocket. He entered the elevator and rose to her floor.

"Hello," he said, when she opened the door.

"You're all right?"

"Sure. Can I come in?"

He went inside. Kelly closed the door behind him. "I'm glad to see you. The city's swarming with SP men. Almost every block. And the patrols—"

"I know. I saw a couple at the spaceport." Jennings sat down on the couch. "It's good to be back, though."

"I was afraid they might stop all the Intercity flights and check through the passengers."

"They have no reason to assume I'd be coming into the city."

"I didn't think of that." Kelly sat down across from him. "Now, what comes next? Now that you have got away with the material, what are you going to do?"

"Next I meet Rethrick and spring the news on him. The news that the person who escaped from the Plant was myself. He knows that someone got away, but he doesn't know who it was. Undoubtedly, he assumes it was an SP man."

"Couldn't he use the time mirror to find out?"

A shadow crossed Jennings's face. "That's so. I didn't think of that." He rubbed his jaw, frowning. "In any case, I have the material. Or, you have the material."

Kelly nodded.

"All right. We'll go ahead with our plans. Tomorrow we'll see Rethrick. We'll see him here, in New York. Can you get him down to the Office? Will he come if you send for him?"

"Yes. We have a code. If I ask him to come, he'll come."

"Fine. I'll meet him there. When he realizes that we have the picture and schematics he'll have to agree to my demands. He'll have to let me into Rethrick Construction, on my own terms. It's either that, or face the possibility of having the material turned over to the Security Police."

"And once you're in? Once Rethrick agrees to your demands?"

"I saw enough at the Plant to convince me that Rethrick is far bigger than I had realized. How big, I don't know. No wonder *he* was so interested!"

"You're going to demand equal control of the Company?"

Jennings nodded.

"You would never be satisfied to go back as a mechanic, would you? The way you were before."

"No. To get booted out again?" Jennings smiled. "Anyhow, I know *he* intended better things than that. *He* laid careful plans. The trinkets. He must have planned everything long in advance. No, I'm not going back as a mechanic. I saw a lot there, level after level of machines and men. They're doing something. And I want to be in on it."

Kelly was silent.

"See?" Jennings said.

"I see."

He left the apartment, hurrying along the dark street. He had stayed there too long. If the SP found the two of them together it would be all up with Rethrick Construction. He could take no chances, with the end almost in sight.

He looked at his watch. It was past midnight. He would meet Rethrick this morning and present him with the proposition. His spirits rose as he walked. He would be safe. More than safe. Rethrick Construction was aiming at something far larger than mere industrial power. What he had seen had convinced him that a revolution was brewing. Down in the many levels below the ground, down under the fortress of concrete, guarded by guns and armed men, Rethrick was planning a war. Machines were being turned out. The time scoop and the mirror were hard at work, watching, dipping, extracting.

No wonder *he* had worked out such careful plans. *He* had seen all this and understood, begun to ponder. The problem of the mind cleaning. His memory would be gone when he was released. Destruction of all the plans. Destruction? There was the alternate clause in the contract. Others had seen it, used it. But not the way *he* intended!

He was after much more than anyone who had come before. *He* was the first to understand, to plan. The seven trinkets were a bridge to something beyond anything that—

At the end of the block an SP cruiser pulled up to the curb. Its doors slid open.

Jennings stopped, his heart constricting. The night patrol, roaming through the city. It was after eleven, after curfew. He looked quickly around. Everything was dark. The stores and houses were shut up tight, locked for the night. Silent apartment houses, buildings. Even the bars were dark.

He looked back the way he had come. Behind him, a second SP cruiser had stopped. Two SP officers had stepped out onto the curb. They had seen him. They were coming toward him. He stood frozen, looking up and down the street.

Across from him was the entrance of a swank hotel, its neon sign glimmering. He began to walk toward it, his heels echoing against the pavement.

"Stop!" one of the SP men called. "Come back here. What are you doing out? What's your—"

Jennings went up the stairs, into the hotel. He crossed the lobby. The clerk was staring at him. No one else was around. The lobby was deserted. His heart sank. He didn't have a chance. He began to run aimlessly, past the desk, along a carpeted hall. Maybe it led out some back way. Behind him, the SP men had already entered the lobby.

Jennings turned a corner. Two men stepped out, blocking his way.

"Where are you going?"

He stopped, wary. "Let me by." He reached into his coat for the Boris gun. At once the men moved.

"Get him."

His arms were pinned to his sides. Professional hoods. Past them he could see light. Light and sound. Some kind of activity. People.

"All right," one of the hoods said. They dragged him back along the corridor, toward the lobby. Jennings struggled futilely. He had entered a blind alley. Hoods, a joint. The city was dotted with them, hidden in the darkness. The swank hotel a front. They would toss him out, into the hands of the SP.

Some people came along the halls, a man and a woman. Older people. Well dressed. They gazed curiously at Jennings, suspended between the two men.

Suddenly Jennings understood. A wave of relief hit him, blinding him. "Wait," he said thickly. "My pocket."

"Come on."

"Wait. Look. My right pocket. Look for yourselves."

He relaxed, waiting. The hood on his right reached, dipping cautiously into the pocket. Jennings smiled. It was over. *He* had seen even this. There was no possibility of failure. This solved one problem: where to stay until it was time to meet Rethrick. He could stay here.

The hood brought out the half poker chip, examining the serrated edges. "Just a second." From his own coat he took a matching chip, fitting on a gold chain. He touched the edges together.

"All right?" Jennings said.

"Sure." They let him go. He brushed off his coat automatically. "Sure, mister. Sorry. Say, you should have—"

"Take me in the back," Jennings said, wiping his face. "Some people are looking for me. I don't particularly want them to find me."

"Sure." They led him back, into the gambling rooms. The half chip had turned what might have been a disaster into an asset. A gambling and girl joint. One of the few institutions the Police left alone. He was safe. No question of that. Only one thing remained. The struggle with Rethrick!

Rethrick's face was hard. He gazed at Jennings, swallowing rapidly.

"No," he said. "I didn't know it was you. We thought it was the SP."

There was silence. Kelly sat at the chair by her desk, her legs crossed, a cigarette between her fingers. Jennings leaned against the door, his arms folded.

"Why didn't you use the mirror?" he said.

Rethrick's face flickered. "The mirror? You did a good job, my friend. We *tried* to use the mirror."

"Tried?"

"Before you finished your term with us you changed a few leads inside the mirror. When we tried to operate it nothing happened. I left the plant half an hour ago. They were still working on it."

"I did that before I finished my two years?"

"Apparently you had worked out your plans in detail. You knew that with the mirror we would have no trouble tracking you down. You're a good mechanic, Jennings. The best we ever had. We'd like to have you back, sometime. Working for us again. There's not one of us that can operate the mirror the way you could. And right now, we can't use it at all."

Jennings smiled. "I had no idea *he* did anything like that. I underestimated him. *His* protection was even—"

"Who are you talking about?"

"Myself. During the two years. I use the objective. It's easier."

"Well, Jennings. So the two of you worked out an elaborate plan to steal our schematics. Why? What's the purpose? You haven't turned them over to the Police."

"No."

"Then I can assume it's blackmail."

"That's right."

"What for? What do you want?" Rethrick seemed to have aged. He slumped, his eyes small and glassy, rubbing his chin nervously. "You went to a lot of trouble to get us into this position. I'm curious why. While you were working for us you laid the groundwork. Now you've completed it, in spite of our precautions."

"Precautions?"

"Erasing your mind. Concealing the Plant."

"Tell him," Kelly said. "Tell him why you did it."

Jennings took a deep breath. "Rethrick, I did it to get back in. Back to the Company. That's the only reason. No other."

Rethrick stared at him. "To get back into the Company? You can come back in. I told you that." His voice was thin and sharp, edged with strain. "What's the matter with you? You can come back in. For as long as you want to stay."

"As a mechanic."

"Yes. As a mechanic. We employ many—"

"I don't want to come back as a mechanic. I'm not interested in working for you. Listen, Rethrick. The SP picked me up as soon as I left this Office. If it hadn't been for *him* I'd be dead."

"They picked you up?"

"They wanted to know what Rethrick Construction does. They wanted me to tell them."

Rethrick nodded. "That's bad. We didn't know that."

"No, Rethrick. I'm not coming in as an employee you can toss out any time it pleases you. I'm coming in with you, not for you."

"With me?" Rethrick stared at him. Slowly a film settled over his face, an ugly hard film. "I don't understand what you mean."

"You and I are going to run Rethrick Construction together. That'll be the way, from now on. And no one will be burning my memory out, for their own safety."

"That's what you want?"

"Yes."

"And if we don't cut you in?"

"Then the schematics and films go to the SP. It's as simple as that. But I don't want to. I don't want to destroy the Company. I want to get into the Company! I want to be safe. You don't know what it's like, being out there, with no place to go. An individual has no place to turn to, anymore. No one to help him. He's caught between two ruthless forces, a pawn between political and economic powers. And I'm tired of being a pawn."

For a long time Rethrick said nothing. He stared down at the floor, his face dull and blank. At last he looked up. "I know it's that way. That's something I've known for a long time. Longer than you have. I'm a lot older than you. I've seen it come, grow that way, year after year. That's why Rethrick Construction exists. Someday, it'll be all different. Someday, when we have the scoop and the mirror finished. When the weapons are finished."

Jennings said nothing.

"I know very well how it is! I'm an old man. I've been working a long time. When they told me someone had got out of the Plant with schematics, I thought the end had come. We already knew you had damaged the mirror. We knew there was a connection, but we had parts figured wrong.

"We thought, of course, that Security had planted you with us, to find out what we were doing. Then, when you realized you couldn't carry out your information, you damaged the mirror. With the mirror damaged, SP could go ahead and—"

He stopped, rubbing his cheek.

"Go on," Jennings said.

"So you did this alone . . . Blackmail. To get into the Company. You don't know what the Company is for, Jennings! How dare you try to come in! We've been working and building for a long time. You'd wreck us, to save your hide. You'd destroy us, just to save yourself."

"I'm not wrecking you. I can be a lot of help."

"I run the Company alone. It's my Company. I made it, put it together. It's mine."

Jennings laughed. "And what happens when you die? Or is the revolution going to come in your own lifetime?"

Rethrick's head jerked up.

"You'll die, and there won't be anyone to go on. You know I'm a good mechanic. You said so yourself. You're a fool, Rethrick. You want to manage it all yourself. Do everything, decide everything. But you'll die, someday. And then what will happen?"

There was silence.

"You better let me in—for the Company's good, as well as my own. I can do a lot for you. When you're gone the Company will survive in my hands. And maybe the revolution will work."

"You should be glad you're alive at all! If we hadn't allowed you to take your trinkets out with you—"

"What else could you do? How could you let men service your mirror, see their own futures, and not let them lift a finger to help themselves. It's easy to see why you were forced to insert the alternate-payment clause. You had no choice."

"You don't even know what we are doing. Why we exist."

"I have a good idea. After all, I worked for you two years."

Time passed. Rethrick moistened his lips again and again, rubbing his cheek. Perspiration stood out on his forehead. At last he looked up.

"No," he said. "It's no deal. No one will ever run the Company but me. If I die, it dies with me. It's my property."

Jennings became instantly alert. "Then the papers go to the Police."

Rethrick said nothing, but a peculiar expression moved across his face, an expression that gave Jennings a sudden chill.

"Kelly," Jennings said. "Do you have the papers with you?"

Kelly stirred, standing up. She put out her cigarette, her face pale. "No."

"Where are they? Where did you put them?"

"Sorry," Kelly said softly. "I'm not going to tell you."

He stared at her. "What?"

"I'm sorry," Kelly said again. Her voice was small and faint. "They're safe. The SP won't ever get them. But neither will you. When it's convenient, I'll turn them back to my father."

"Your father!"

"Kelly is my daughter," Rethrick said. "That was one thing you didn't count on, Jennings. *He* didn't count on it, either. No one knew that but the two of us. I wanted to keep all positions of trust in the family. I see now that it was a good idea. But it had to be kept secret. If the SP had guessed they would have picked her up at once. Her life wouldn't have been safe."

Jennings let his breath out slowly. "I see."

"It seemed like a good idea to go along with you," Kelly said. "Otherwise you'd have done it alone, anyhow. And you would have had the papers on you. As you said, if the SP caught you with the papers it would be the end of us. So I went along with you. As soon as you gave me the papers I put them in a good safe place." She smiled a little. "No one will find them but me. I'm sorry."

"Jennings, you can come in with us," Rethrick said. "You can work for us forever, if you want. You can have anything you want. Anything except—"

"Except that no one runs the Company but you."

"That's right. Jennings, the Company is old. Older than I am. I didn't bring it into existence. It was—you might say, *willed* to me. I took the burden on. The job of managing it, making it grow, moving it toward the day. The day of revolution, as you put it.

"My grandfather founded the Company, back in the twentieth century. The Company has always been in the family. And it will always be. Someday, when Kelly marries, there'll be an heir to carry it on after me. So that's taken care of. The Company was founded up in Maine, in a small New England town. My grandfather was a little old New Englander, frugal, honest, passionately independent. He had a little repair business of some sort, a little tool and fix-it place. And plenty of knack.

"When he saw government and big business closing in on everyone, he went underground. Rethrick Construction disappeared from the map. It took government quite a while to organize Maine, longer than most places. When the rest of the world had been divided up between international cartels and world-states, there was New England, still alive. Still free. And my grandfather and Rethrick Construction.

"He brought in a few men, mechanics, doctors, lawyers, little once-a-week newspapermen from the Middle West. The Company grew. Weapons appeared, weapons and knowledge. The time scoop and mirror! The Plant was built, secretly, at great cost, over a long period of time. The Plant is big. Big and deep. It goes down many more levels than you saw. *He* saw them, your alter ego. There's a lot of power there. Power, and men who've disappeared, purged all over the world, in fact. We got them first, the best of them.

"Someday, Jennings, we're going to break out. You see, conditions like this can't go on. People can't live this way, tossed back and forth by political and economic powers. Masses of people shoved this way and that according to the needs of this government or that cartel. There's going to be resistance, someday. A strong, desperate resistance. Not by big people, powerful people, but by little people. Bus drivers. Grocers. Vidscreen operators. Waiters. And that's where the Company comes in.

"We're going to provide them with the help they'll need, the tools, weapons, the knowledge. We're going to 'sell' them our services. They'll be able to hire us. And they'll need someone they can hire. They'll have a lot lined up against them. A lot of wealth and power."

There was silence.

"Do you see?" Kelly said. "That's why you mustn't interfere. It's Dad's Company. It's always been that way. That's the way Maine people are. It's part of the family. The Company belongs to the family. It's ours."

"Come in with us," Rethrick said. "As a mechanic. I'm sorry, but that's our limited outlook showing through. Maybe it's narrow, but we've always done things this way."

Jennings said nothing. He walked slowly across the office, his hands in his pockets. After a time he raised the blind and stared out at the street, far below.

Down below, like a tiny black bug, a Security cruiser moved along, drifting silently with the traffic that flowed up and down the street. It joined a second cruiser, already parked. Four SP men were standing by it in their green uniforms, and even as he watched some more could be seen coming from across the street. He let the blind down.

"It's a hard decision to make," he said.

"If you go out there they'll get you," Rethrick said. "They're out there all the time. You haven't got a chance."

"Please—" Kelly said, looking up at him.

Suddenly Jennings smiled. "So you won't tell me where the papers are. Where you put them."

Kelly shook her head.

"Wait." Jennings reached into his pocket. He brought out a small piece of paper. He unfolded it slowly, scanning it. "By any chance did you deposit it with the Dunne National Bank, about three o'clock yesterday afternoon? For safekeeping in their storage vaults?"

Kelly gasped. She grabbed her handbag, unsnapping it. Jennings put the slip of paper, the parcel receipt, back in his pocket. "So *he* saw even that," he murmured. "The last of the trinkets. I wondered what it was for."

Kelly groped frantically in her purse, her face wild. She brought out a slip of paper, waving it.

"You're wrong! Here it is! It's still here." She relaxed a little. "I don't know what *you* have, but this is—"

In the air above them something moved. A dark space formed, a circle. The space stirred. Kelly and Rethrick stared up, frozen.

From the dark circle a claw appeared, a metal claw, joined to a shimmering rod. The claw dropped, swinging in a wide arc. The claw swept the paper from Kelly's fingers. It hesitated for a second. Then it drew itself up again, disappearing with the paper, into the circle of black. Then, silently, the claw and the rod and the circle blinked out. There was nothing. Nothing at all.

"Where—where did it go?" Kelly whispered. "The paper. What was that?"

Jennings patted his pocket. "It's safe. It's safe, right here. I wondered when *he* would show up. I was beginning to worry."

Rethrick and his daughter stood, shocked into silence.

"Don't look so unhappy," Jennings said. He folded his arms. "The paper's safe—and the Company's safe. When the time comes it'll be there, strong and very glad to help out the revolution. We'll see to that, all of us, you, me, and your daughter."

He glanced at Kelly, his eyes twinkling. "All three of us. And maybe by that time there'll be even *more* members to the family!"

SECOND VARIETY

The Russian soldier made his way nervously up the rugged side of the hill, holding his gun ready. He glanced around him, licking his dry lips, his face set. From time to time he reached up a gloved hand and wiped perspiration from his neck, pushing down his coat collar.

Eric turned to Corporal Leone. "Want him? Or can I have him?" He adjusted the view sight so the Russian's features squarely filled the glass, the lines cutting across his hard, somber features.

Leone considered. The Russian was close, moving rapidly, almost running. "Don't fire. Wait." Leone tensed. "I don't think we're needed."

The Russian increased his pace, kicking ash and piles of debris out of his way. He reached the top of the hill and stopped, panting, staring around him. The sky was overcast, with drifting clouds of gray particles. Bare trunks of trees jutted up occasionally; the ground was level and bare, rubble-strewn, with the ruins of buildings standing here and there like yellowing skulls.

The Russian was uneasy. He knew something was wrong. He started down the hill. Now he was only a few paces from the bunker. Eric was getting fidgety. He played with his pistol, glancing at Leone.

"Don't worry," Leone said. "He won't get here. They'll take care of him."

"Are you sure? He's got damn far."

"They hang around close to the bunker. He's getting into the bad part. Get set!"

The Russian began to hurry, sliding down the hill, his boots sinking into the heaps of gray ash, trying to keep his gun up. He stopped for a moment, lifting his field glasses to his face.

"He's looking right at us," Eric said.

The Russian came on. They could see his eyes, like two blue stones. His mouth was open a little. He needed a shave; his chin was stubbled. On one bony cheek was a square of tape, showing blue at the edge. A fungoid spot. His coat was muddy and torn. One glove was missing. As he ran, his belt counter bounced up and down against him.

Leone touched Eric's arm. "Here one comes."

Across the ground something small and metallic came, flashing in the dull sunlight of midday. A metal sphere. It raced up the hill after the Russian, its treads flying. It was small, one of the baby ones. Its claws were out, two razor projections spinning in a blur of white steel. The Russian heard it. He turned instantly, firing. The sphere dissolved into particles. But already a second had emerged and was following the first. The Russian fired again.

A third sphere leaped up the Russian's leg, clicking and whirring. It jumped to the shoulder. The spinning blades disappeared into the Russian's throat.

Eric relaxed. "Well, that's that. God, those damn things give me the creeps. Sometimes I think we were better off before them."

"If we hadn't invented them, they would have." Leone lit a cigarette shakily. "I wonder why a Russian would come all this way alone. I didn't see anyone covering him."

Lieutenant Scott came slipping up the tunnel, into the bunker. "What happened? Something entered the screen."

"An Ivan."

"Just one?"

Eric brought the viewscreen around. Scott peered into it. Now there were numerous metal spheres crawling over the prostrate body, dull metal globes clicking and whirring, sawing up the Russian into small parts to be carried away.

"What a lot of claws," Scott murmured.

"They came like flies. Not much game for them anymore."

Scott pushed the sight away, disgusted. "Like flies. I wonder why he was out there. They know we have claws all around."

A larger robot had joined the smaller spheres. A long blunt tube with projecting eyepieces, it was directing operations. There was not much left of the soldier. What remained was brought down the hillside by the host of claws.

"Sir," Leone said. "If it's all right, I'd like to go out there and take a look at him."

"Why?"

"Maybe he came with something."

Scott considered. He shrugged. "All right. But be careful."

"I have my tab." Leone patted the metal band at his wrist. "I'll be out of bounds."

He picked up his rifle and stepped carefully up to the mouth of the bunker, making his way between blocks of concrete and steel prongs, twisted and bent. The air was cold at the top. He crossed over the ground toward the remains of the soldier, striding across the soft ash. A wind blew around him, swirling gray particles up in his face. He squinted and pushed on.

The claws retreated as he came close, some of them stiffening into immobility. He touched his tab. The Ivan would have given something for that! Short hard radiation emitted from the tab neutralized the claws, put them out of commission. Even the big robot with its two waving eyestalks retreated respectfully as he approached.

He bent down over the remains of the soldier. The gloved hand was closed tightly. There was something in it. Leone pried the fingers apart. A sealed container, aluminum. Still shiny.

He put it in his pocket and made his way back to the bunker. Behind him the claws came back to life, moving into operation again. The procession resumed, metal spheres moving through the gray ash with their loads. He could hear their treads scrabbling against the ground. He shuddered.

Scott watched intently as he brought the shiny tube out of his pocket. "He had that?"

"In his hand." Leone unscrewed the top. "Maybe you should look at it, sir."

Scott took it. He emptied the contents out in the palm of his hand. A small piece of silk paper, carefully folded. He sat down by the light and unfolded it.

"What's it say?" Eric said. Several officers came up the tunnel. Major Hendricks appeared.

"Major," Scott said. "Look at this."

Hendricks read the slip. "This just come?"

"A single runner. Just now."

"Where is he?" Hendricks asked sharply.

"The claws got him."

Major Hendricks grunted. "Here." He passed it to his companions. "I think this is what we've been waiting for. They certainly took their time about it."

"So they want to talk terms," Scott said. "Are we going along with them?"

"That's not for us to decide." Hendricks sat down. "Where's the communications officer? I want the Moon Base."

Leone pondered as the communications officer raised the outside antenna cautiously, scanning the sky above the bunker for any sign of a watching Russian ship.

"Sir," Scott said to Hendricks. "It's sure strange they suddenly came around. We've been using the claws for almost a year. Now all of a sudden they start to fold."

"Maybe claws have been getting down in their bunkers."

"One of the big ones, the kind with stalks, got into an Ivan bunker last week," Eric said. "It got a whole platoon of them before they got their lid shut."

"How do you know?"

"A buddy told me. The thing came back with—with remains."

"Moon Base, sir," the communications officer said.

On the screen the face of the lunar monitor appeared. His crisp uniform contrasted to the uniforms in the bunker. And he was clean-shaven. "Moon Base."

"This is forward command L-Whistle. On Terra. Let me have General Thompson."

The monitor faded. Presently General Thompson's heavy features came into focus. "What is it, Major?"

"Our claws got a single Russian runner with a message. We don't know whether to act on it—there have been tricks like this in the past."

"What's the message?"

"The Russians want us to send a single officer on policy level over to their lines. For a conference. They don't state the nature of the conference.

They say that matters of—" He consulted the slip: "—matters of grave urgency make it advisable that discussion be opened between a representative of the UN forces and themselves."

He held the message up to the screen for the General to scan. Thompson's eyes moved.

"What should we do?" Hendricks said.

"Send out a man."

"You don't think it's a trap?"

"It might be. But the location they give for their forward command is correct. It's worth a try, at any rate."

"I'll send an officer out. And report the results to you as soon as he returns."

"All right, Major." Thompson broke the connection. The screen died. Up above, the antenna came slowly down.

Hendricks rolled up the paper, deep in thought.

"I'll go," Leone said.

"They want somebody at policy level." Hendricks rubbed his jaw. "Policy level. I haven't been outside in months. Maybe I could use a little air."

"Don't you think it's risky?"

Hendricks lifted the view sight and gazed into it. The remains of the Russian were gone. Only a single claw was in sight. It was folding itself back, disappearing into the ash, like a crab. Like some hideous metal crab . . . "That's the only thing that bothers me." Hendricks rubbed his wrist. "I know I'm safe as long as I have this on me. But there's something about them. I hate the damn things. I wish we'd never invented them. There's something wrong with them. Relentless little—"

"If we hadn't invented them, the Ivans would have."

Hendricks pushed the sight back. "Anyhow, it seems to be winning the war. I guess that's good."

"Sounds like you're getting the same jitters as the Ivans."

Hendricks examined his wristwatch. "I guess I had better get started, if I want to be there before dark."

He took a deep breath and then stepped out onto the gray rubbled ground. After a minute he lit a cigarette and stood gazing around him. The landscape was dead. Nothing stirred. He could see for miles, endless ash and slag, ruins of buildings. A few trees without leaves or branches, only the trunks. Above him the eternal rolling clouds of gray, drifting between Terra and the sun.

Major Hendricks went on. Off to the right something scuttled, something round and metallic. A claw, going lickety-split after something. Probably after a small animal, a rat. They got rats, too. As a sort of sideline.

He came to the top of the little hill and lifted his field glasses. The Russian lines were a few miles ahead of him. They had a forward command post there. The runner had come from it.

A squat robot with undulating arms passed by him, its arms weaving inquiringly. The robot went on its way, disappearing under some debris. Hendricks watched it go. He had never seen that type before. There were getting to be more and more types he had never seen, new varieties and sizes coming up from the underground factories.

Hendricks put out his cigarette and hurried on. It was interesting, the use of artificial forms of warfare. How had they got started? Necessity. The Soviet Union had gained great initial success, usual with the side that got the war going. Most of North America had been blasted off the map. Retaliation was quick in coming, of course. The sky was full of circling diskbombers long before the war began; they had been up there for years. The disks began sailing down all over Russia within hours after Washington got it.

But that hadn't helped Washington.

The American bloc governments moved to the Moon Base the first year. There was not much else to do. Europe was gone, a slag heap with dark weeds growing from the ashes and bones. Most of North America was useless; nothing could be planted, no one could live. A few million people kept going up in Canada and down in South America. But during the second year Soviet parachutists began to drop, a few at first, then more and more. They wore the first really effective anti-radiation equipment; what was left of American production moved to the Moon along with the governments.

All but the troops. The remaining troops stayed behind as best they could, a few thousand here, a platoon there. No one knew exactly where they were; they stayed where they could, moving around at night, hiding in ruins, in sewers, cellars, with the rats and snakes. It looked as if the Soviet Union had the war almost won. Except for a handful of projectiles fired off from the Moon daily, there was almost no weapon in use against them. They came and went as they pleased. The war, for all practical purposes, was over. Nothing effective opposed them.

And then the first claws appeared. And overnight the complexion of the war changed.

The claws were awkward, at first. Slow. The Ivans knocked them off almost as fast as they crawled out of their underground tunnels. But then they got better, faster, and more cunning. Factories, all on Terra, turned them out. Factories a long way underground, behind the Soviet lines, factories that had once made atomic projectiles, now almost forgotten.

The claws got faster, and they got bigger. New types appeared, some with feelers, some that flew. There were a few jumping kinds. The best technicians on the Moon were working on designs, making them more and more intricate, more flexible. They became uncanny; the Ivans were having a lot of trouble with them. Some of the little claws were learning to hide themselves, burrowing down into the ash, lying in wait.

And they started getting into the Russian bunkers, slipping down when the lids were raised for air and a look around. One claw inside a bunker, a churning sphere of blades and metal—that was enough. And when one got in others followed. With a weapon like that the war couldn't go on much longer.

Maybe it was already over.

Maybe he was going to hear the news. Maybe the Politburo had decided to throw in the sponge. Too bad it had taken so long. Six years. A long time for war like that, the way they had waged it. The automatic retaliation disks, spinning down all over Russia, hundreds of thousands of them. Bacteria crystals. The Soviet guided missiles, whistling through the air. The chain bombs. And now this, the robots, the claws—

The claws weren't like other weapons. They were *alive*, from any practical standpoint, whether the Governments wanted to admit it or not. They were not machines. They were living things, spinning, creeping, shaking themselves up suddenly from the gray ash and darting toward a man, climbing up him, rushing for his throat. And that was what they had been designed to do. Their job.

They did their job well. Especially lately, with the new designs coming up. Now they repaired themselves. They were on their own. Radiation tabs protected the UN troops, but if a man lost his tab he was fair game for the claws, no matter what his uniform. Down below the surface automatic machinery stamped them out. Human beings stayed a long way off. It was too risky; nobody wanted to be around them. They were left to themselves. And they seemed to be doing all right. The new designs were faster, more complex. More efficient.

Apparently they had won the war.

Major Hendricks lit a second cigarette. The landscape depressed him. Nothing but ash and ruins. He seemed to be alone, the only living thing in the whole world. To the right the ruins of a town rose up, a few walls and heaps of debris. He tossed the dead match away, increasing his pace. Suddenly he stopped, jerking up his gun, his body tense. For a minute it looked like—

From behind the shell of a ruined building a figure came, walking slowly toward him, walking hesitantly.

Hendricks blinked. "Stop!"

The boy stopped. Hendricks lowered his gun. The boy stood silently, looking at him. He was small, not very old. Perhaps eight. But it was hard to tell. Most of the kids who remained were stunted. He wore a faded blue sweater, ragged with dirt, and short pants. His hair was long and matted. Brown hair. It hung over his face and around his ears. He held something in his arms.

"What's that you have?" Hendricks said sharply.

The boy held it out. It was a toy, a bear. A teddy bear. The boy's eyes were large, but without expression.

Hendricks relaxed. "I don't want it. Keep it."

The boy hugged the bear again.

"Where do you live?" Hendricks said.

"In there."

"The ruins?"

"Yes."

"Underground?"

"Yes."

"How many are there?"

"How—how many?"

"How many of you? How big's your settlement?"

The boy did not answer.

Hendricks frowned. "You're not all by yourself, are you?"

The boy nodded.

"How do you stay alive?"

"There's food."

"What kind of food?"

"Different."

Hendricks studied him. "How old are you?"

"Thirteen."

It wasn't possible. Or was it? The boy was thin, stunted. And probably sterile. Radiation exposure, years straight. No wonder he was so small. His arms and legs were like pipe cleaners, knobby and thin. Hendricks touched the boy's arm. His skin was dry and rough; radiation skin. He bent down, looking into the boy's face. There was no expression. Big eyes, big and dark.

"Are you blind?" Hendricks said.

"No. I can see some."

"How do you get away from the claws?"

"The claws?"

"The round things. That run and burrow."

"I don't understand."

Maybe there weren't any claws around. A lot of areas were free. They collected mostly around bunkers, where there were people. The claws had been designed to sense warmth, warmth of living things.

"You're lucky." Hendricks straightened up. "Well? Which way are you going? Back—back there?"

"Can I come with you?"

"With *me*?" Hendricks folded his arms. "I'm going a long way. Miles. I have to hurry." He looked at his watch. "I have to get there by nightfall."

"I want to come."

Hendricks fumbled in his pack. "It isn't worth it. Here." He tossed down the food cans he had with him. "You take these and go back. Okay?"

The boy said nothing.

"I'll be coming back this way. In a day or so. If you're around here when I come back you can come along with me. All right?"

"I want to go with you now."

"It's a long walk."

"I can walk."

Hendricks shifted uneasily. It made too good a target, two people walking along. And the boy would slow him down. But he might not come back this way. And if the boy were really all alone—

"Okay. Come along."

The boy fell in beside him. Hendricks strode along. The boy walked silently, clutching his teddy bear.

"What's your name?" Hendricks said, after a time.

"David Edward Derring."

"David? What—what happened to your mother and father?"

"They died."

"How?"

"In the blast."

"How long ago?"

"Six years."

Hendricks slowed down. "You've been alone six years?"

"No. There were other people for a while. They went away."

"And you've been alone since?"

"Yes."

Hendricks glanced down. The boy was strange, saying very little. Withdrawn. But that was the way they were, the children who had survived. Quiet. Stoic. A strange kind of fatalism gripped them. Nothing came as a surprise. They accepted anything that came along. There was no longer any *normal*, any natural course of things, moral or physical, for them to expect. Custom, habit, all the determining forces of learning were gone; only brute experience remained.

"Am I walking too fast?" Hendricks said.

"No."

"How did you happen to see me?"

"I was waiting."

"Waiting?" Hendricks was puzzled. "What were you waiting for?"

"To catch things."

"What kind of things?"

"Things to eat."

"Oh." Hendricks set his lips grimly. A thirteen-year-old boy, living on rats and gophers and half-rotten canned food. Down in a hole under the ruins of a town. With radiation pools and claws, and Russian dive-mines up above, coasting around in the sky.

"Where are we going?" David asked.

"To the Russian lines."

"Russian?"

"The enemy. The people who started the war. They dropped the first radiation bombs. They began all this."

The boy nodded. His face showed no expression.

"I'm an American," Hendricks said.

There was no comment. On they went, the two of them, Hendricks walking a little ahead, David trailing behind him, hugging his dirty teddy bear against his chest.

About four in the afternoon they stopped to eat. Hendricks built a fire in a hollow between some slabs of concrete. He cleared the weeds away and heaped up bits of wood. The Russians' lines were not very far ahead. Around him was what had once been a long valley, acres of fruit trees and grapes. Nothing remained now but a few bleak stumps and the mountains that stretched across the horizon at the far end. And the clouds of rolling ash that blew and drifted with the wind, settling over the weeds and remains of buildings, walls here and there, once in a while what had been a road.

Hendricks made coffee and heated up some boiled mutton and bread. "Here." He handed bread and mutton to David. David squatted by the edge of the fire, his knees knobby and white. He examined the food and then passed it back, shaking his head.

"No."

"No? Don't you want any?"

"No."

Hendricks shrugged. Maybe the boy was a mutant, used to special food. It didn't matter. When he was hungry he would find something to eat. The boy was strange. But there were many strange changes coming over the world. Life was not the same anymore. It would never be the same again. The human race was going to have to realize that.

"Suit yourself," Hendricks said. He ate the bread and mutton by himself, washing it down with coffee. He ate slowly, finding the food hard to digest. When he was done he got to his feet and stamped the fire out.

David rose slowly, watching him with his young-old eyes.

"We're going," Hendricks said.

"All right."

Hendricks walked along, his gun in his arms. They were close; he was tense, ready for anything. The Russians should be expecting a runner, an answer to their own runner, but they were tricky. There was always the possibility of a slip-up. He scanned the landscape around him. Nothing but slag and ash, a few hills, charred trees. Concrete walls. But some place ahead was the first bunker of the Russian lines, the forward command. Underground, buried deep, with only a periscope showing, a few gun muzzles. Maybe an antenna.

"Will we be there soon?" David asked.

"Yes. Getting tired?"

"No."

"Why, then?"

David did not answer. He plodded carefully along behind, picking his way over the ash. His legs and shoes were gray with dust. His pinched face was streaked, lines of gray ash in rivulets down the pale white of his skin. There was no color to his face. Typical of the new children, growing up in cellars and sewers and underground shelters.

Hendricks slowed down. He lifted his field glasses and studied the ground ahead of him. Were they there, some place, waiting for him? Watching him, the way his men had watched the Russian runner? A chill went up his back. Maybe they were getting their guns ready, preparing to fire, the way his men had prepared, made ready to kill.

Hendricks stopped, wiping perspiration from his face. "Damn." It made him uneasy. But he should be expected. The situation was different.

He strode over the ash, holding his gun tightly with both hands. Behind him came David. Hendricks peered around, tight-lipped. Any second it might happen. A burst of white light, a blast, carefully aimed from inside a deep concrete bunker.

He raised his arm and waved it around in a circle.

Nothing moved. To the right a long ridge ran, topped with dead tree trunks. A few wild vines had grown up around the trees, remains of arbors. And the eternal dark weeds. Hendricks studied the ridge. Was anything up there? Perfect place for a lookout. He approached the ridge warily, David coming silently behind. If it were his command he'd have a sentry up there, watching for troops trying to infiltrate into the command area. Of course, if it were his command there would be the claws around the area for full protection.

He stopped, feet apart, hands on his hips.

"Are we there?" David said.

"Almost."

"Why have we stopped?"

"I don't want to take any chances." Hendricks advanced slowly. Now the ridge lay directly beside him, along his right. Overlooking him. His uneasy feeling increased. If an Ivan were up there he wouldn't have a chance. He waved his arm again. They should be expecting someone in the UN uniform, in response to the note capsule. Unless the whole thing was a trap.

"Keep up with me." He turned toward David. "Don't drop behind."

"With you?"

"Up beside me. We're close. We can't take any chances. Come on."

"I'll be all right." David remained behind him, in the rear, a few paces away, still clutching his teddy bear.

"Have it your way." Hendricks raised his glasses again, suddenly tense. For a moment—had something moved? He scanned the ridge carefully. Everything was silent. Dead. No life up there, only tree trunks and ash. Maybe a few rats. The big black rats that had survived the claws. Mutants— built their own shelters out of saliva and ash. Some kind of plaster. Adaptation. He started forward again.

A tall figure came out on the ridge above him, cloak flapping. Gray-green. A Russian. Behind him a second soldier appeared, another Russian. Both lifted their guns, aiming.

Hendricks froze. He opened his mouth. The soldiers were kneeling, sighting down the side of the slope. A third figure had joined them on the ridge top, a smaller figure in gray-green. A woman. She stood behind the other two.

Hendricks found his voice. "Stop!" He waved up at them frantically. "I'm—"

The two Russians fired. Behind Hendricks there was a faint *pop*. Waves of heat lapped against him, throwing him to the ground. Ash tore at his face, grinding into his eyes and nose. Choking, he pulled himself to his knees. It was all a trap. He was finished. He had come to be killed, like a steer. The soldiers and the woman were coming down the side of the ridge toward him, sliding down through the soft ash. Hendricks was numb. His head throbbed. Awkwardly, he got his rifle up and took aim. It weighed a thousand tons; he could hardly hold it. His nose and cheeks stung. The air was full of the blast smell, a bitter acrid stench.

"Don't fire," the first Russian said, in heavily accented English.

The three of them came up to him, surrounding him. "Put down your rifle, Yank," the other said.

Hendricks was dazed. Everything had happened so fast. He had been caught. And they had blasted the boy. He turned his head. David was gone. What remained of him was strewn across the ground.

The three Russians studied him curiously. Hendricks sat, wiping blood from his nose, picking out bits of ash. He shook his head, trying to clear it. "Why did you do it?" he murmured thickly. "The boy."

"Why?" One of the soldiers helped him roughly to his feet. He turned Hendricks around. "Look."

Hendricks closed his eyes.

"Look!" The two Russians pulled him forward. "See. Hurry up. There isn't much time to spare, Yank!"

Hendricks looked. And gasped.

"See now? Now do you understand?"

From the remains of David a metal wheel rolled. Relays, glinting metal. Parts, wiring. One of the Russians kicked at the heap of remains. Parts popped out, rolling away, wheels and springs and rods. A plastic section fell in, half charred. Hendricks bent shakily down. The front of the head had come off. He could make out the intricate brain, wires and relays, tiny tubes and switches, thousands of minute studs—

"A robot," the soldier holding his arm said. "We watched it tagging you."

"Tagging me?"

"That's their way. They tag along with you. Into the bunker. That's how they get in."

Hendricks blinked, dazed. "But—"

"Come on." They led him toward the ridge. "We can't stay here. It isn't safe. There must be hundreds of them all around here."

The three of them pulled him up the side of the ridge, sliding and slipping on the ash. The woman reached the top and stood waiting for them.

"The forward command," Hendricks muttered. "I came to negotiate with the Soviet—"

"There is no more forward command. *They* got in. We'll explain." They reached the top of the ridge. "We're all that's left. The three of us. The rest were down in the bunker."

"This way. Down this way." The woman unscrewed a lid, a gray manhole cover set in the ground. "Get in."

Hendricks lowered himself. The two soldiers and the woman came behind him, following him down the ladder. The woman closed the lid after them, bolting it tightly into place.

"Good thing we saw you," one of the two soldiers grunted. "It had tagged you about as far as it was going to."

"Give me one of your cigarettes," the woman said. "I haven't had an American cigarette for weeks."

Hendricks pushed the pack to her. She took a cigarette and passed the pack to the two soldiers. In the corner of the small room the lamp gleamed fitfully. The room was low-ceilinged, cramped. The four of them sat around a small wood table. A few dirty dishes were stacked to one side. Behind a ragged curtain a second room was partly visible. Hendricks saw the corner of a coat, some blankets, clothes hung on a hook.

"We were here," the soldier beside him said. He took off his helmet, pushing his blond hair back. "I'm Corporal Rudi Maxer. Polish. Impressed in the Soviet Army two years ago." He held out his hand.

Hendricks hesitated and then shook. "Major Joseph Hendricks."

"Klaus Epstein." The other soldier shook with him, a small dark man with thinning hair. Epstein plucked nervously at his ear. "Austrian. Impressed God knows when. I don't remember. The three of us were here, Rudi and I, with Tasso." He indicated the woman. "That's how we escaped. All the rest were down in the bunker."

"And—and *they* got in?"

Epstein lit a cigarette. "First just one of them. The kind that tagged you. Then it let others in."

Hendricks became alert. "The *kind*? Is there more than one kind?"

"The little boy. David. David holding his teddy bear. That's Variety Three. The most effective."

"What are the other types?"

Epstein reached into his coat. "Here." He tossed a packet of photographs onto the table, tied with a string. "Look for yourself."

Hendricks untied the string.

"You see," Rudi Maxer said, "that was why we wanted to talk terms. The Russians, I mean. We found out about a week ago. Found out that your claws were beginning to make up new designs on their own. New types of their own. Better types. Down in your underground factories behind our lines. You let them stamp themselves, repair themselves. Made them more and more intricate. It's your fault this happened."

Hendricks examined the photos. They had been snapped hurriedly; they were blurred and indistinct. The first few showed—David. David walking along a road, by himself. David and another David. Three Davids. All exactly alike. Each with a ragged teddy bear.

All pathetic.

"Look at the others," Tasso said.

The next pictures, taken at a great distance, showed a towering wounded soldier sitting by the side of a path, his arm in a sling, the stump of one leg extended, a crude crutch on his lap. Then two wounded soldiers, both the same, standing side by side.

"That's Variety One. The Wounded Soldier." Klaus reached out and took the pictures. "You see, the claws were designed to get to human beings. To find them. Each kind was better than the last. They got farther, closer, past most of our defenses, into our lines. But as long as they were merely *machines*, metal spheres with claws and horns, feelers, they could be picked off like any other object. They could be detected as lethal robots as soon as they were seen. Once we caught sight of them—"

"Variety One subverted our whole north wing," Rudi said. "It was a long time before anyone caught on. Then it was too late. They came in, wounded soldiers, knocking and begging to be let in. So we let them in. And as soon as they were in they took over. We were watching out for machines . . ."

"At that time it was thought there was only the one type," Klaus Epstein said. "No one suspected there were other types. The pictures were flashed to us. When the runner was sent to you, we knew of just one type. Variety One. The Wounded Soldier. We thought that was all."

"Your line fell to—"

"To Variety Three. David and his bear. That worked even better." Klaus smiled bitterly. "Soldiers are suckers for children. We brought them in and tried to feed them. We found out the hard way what they were after. At least, those who were in the bunker."

"The three of us were lucky," Rudi said. "Klaus and I were—were visiting Tasso when it happened. This is her place." He waved a big hand around. "This little cellar. We finished and climbed the ladder to start back. From the ridge we saw that they were all around the bunker. Fighting was going on. David and his bear. Hundreds of them. Klaus took the pictures."

Klaus tied up the photographs again.

"And it's going on all along your line?" Hendricks said.

"Yes."

"How about *our* lines?" Without thinking, he touched the tab on his arm. "Can they—"

"They're not bothered by your radiation tabs. It makes no difference to them, Russian, American, Pole, German. It's all the same. They're doing what they were designed to do. Carrying out the original idea. They track down life, wherever they find it."

"They go by warmth," Klaus said. "That was the way you constructed them from the very start. Of course, those you designed were kept back by the radiation tabs you wear. Now they've got around that. These new varieties are lead-lined."

"What's the other variety?" Hendricks asked. "The David type, the Wounded Soldier—what's the other?"

"We don't know." Klaus pointed up at the wall. On the wall were two metal plates, ragged at the edges. Hendricks got up and studied them. They were bent and dented.

"The one on the left came off a Wounded Soldier," Rudi said. "We got one of them. It was going along toward our old bunker. We got it from the ridge, the same way we got the David tagging you."

The plate was stamped: *I-V.* Hendricks touched the other plate. "And this came from the David type?"

"Yes." The plate was stamped: *III-V.*

Klaus took a look at them, leaning over Hendricks's broad shoulder. "You can see what we're up against. There's another type. Maybe it was abandoned. Maybe it didn't work. But there must be a Second Variety. There's One and Three."

"You were lucky," Rudi said. "The David tagged you all the way here and never touched you. Probably thought you'd get it into a bunker, somewhere."

"One gets in and it's all over," Klaus said. "They move fast. One lets all the rest inside. They're inflexible. Machines with one purpose. They were built for only one thing." He rubbed sweat from his lip. "We saw."

They were silent.

"Let me have another cigarette, Yank," Tasso said. "They are good. I almost forgot how they were."

It was night. The sky was black. No stars were visible through the rolling clouds of ash. Klaus lifted the lid cautiously so that Hendricks could look out.

Rudi pointed into the darkness. "Over that way are the bunkers. Where we used to be. Not over half a mile from us. It was just chance that Klaus and I were not there when it happened. Weakness. Saved by our lusts."

"All the rest must be dead," Klaus said in a low voice. "It came quickly. This morning the Politburo reached their decision. They notified us—forward command. Our runner was sent out at once. We saw him start toward the direction of your lines. We covered him until he was out of sight."

"Alex Radrivsky. We both knew him. He disappeared about six o'clock. The sun had just come up. About noon Klaus and I had an hour relief. We crept off, away from the bunkers. No one was watching. We came here. This used to be a town here, a few houses, a street. This cellar was part of a big farmhouse. We knew Tasso would be here, hiding down in her little place. We had come here before. Others from the bunkers came here. Today happened to be our turn."

"So we were saved," Klaus said. "Chance. It might have been others. We—we finished, and then we came up to the surface and started back along the ridge. That was when we saw them, the Davids. We understood right away. We had seen the photos of the First Variety, the Wounded Soldier. Our Commissar distributed them to us with an explanation. If we had gone another step they would have seen us. As it was we had to blast two Davids before we got back. There were hundreds of them, all around. Like ants. We took pictures and slipped back here, bolting the lid tight."

"They're not so much when you catch them alone. We moved faster than they did. But they're inexorable. Not like living things. They came right at us. And we blasted them."

Major Hendricks rested against the edge of the lid, adjusting his eyes to the darkness. "Is it safe to have the lid up at all?"

"If we're careful. How else can you operate your transmitter?"

Hendricks lifted the small belt transmitter slowly. He pressed it against his ear. The metal was cold and damp. He blew against the mike, raising up the short antenna. A faint hum sounded in his ear. "That's true, I suppose."

But he still hesitated.

"We'll pull you under if anything happens," Klaus said.

"Thanks." Hendricks waited a moment, resting the transmitter against his shoulder. "Interesting, isn't it?"

"What?"

"This, the new types. The new varieties of claws. We're completely at their mercy, aren't we? By now they've probably gotten into the UN lines, too. It makes me wonder if we're not seeing the beginning of a new species. *The* new species. Evolution. The race to come after man."

Rudi grunted. "There is no race after man."

"No? Why not? Maybe we're seeing it now, the end of human beings, the beginning of a new society."

"They're not a race. They're mechanical killers. You made them to destroy. That's all they can do. They're machines with a job."

"So it seems now. But how about later on? After the war is over. Maybe, when there aren't any humans to destroy, their real potentialities will begin to show."

"You talk as if they were alive!"

"Aren't they?"

There was silence. "They're machines," Rudi said. "They look like people, but they're machines."

"Use your transmitter, Major," Klaus said. "We can't stay up here forever."

Holding the transmitter tightly, Hendricks called the code of the command bunker. He waited, listening. No response. Only silence. He checked the leads carefully. Everything was in place.

"Scott!" he said into the mike. "Can you hear me?"

Silence. He raised the gain up full and tried again. Only static.

"I don't get anything. They may hear me but they may not want to answer."

"Tell them it's an emergency."

"They'll think I'm being forced to call. Under your direction." He tried again, outlining briefly what he had learned. But still the phone was silent, except for the faint static.

"Radiation pools kill most transmission," Klaus said, after a while. "Maybe that's it."

Hendricks shut the transmitter up. "No use. No answer. Radiation pools? Maybe. Or they hear me, but won't answer. Frankly, that's what I would do, if a runner tried to call from the Soviet lines. They have no reason to believe such a story. They may hear everything I say—"

"Or maybe it's too late."

Hendricks nodded.

"We better get the lid down," Rudi said nervously. "We don't want to take unnecessary chances."

They climbed slowly back down the tunnel. Klaus bolted the lid carefully into place. They descended into the kitchen. The air was heavy and close around them.

"Could they work that fast?" Hendricks said. "I left the bunker this noon. Ten hours ago. How could they move so quickly?"

"It doesn't take them long. Not after the first one gets in. It goes wild. You know what the little claws can do. Even *one* of these is beyond belief. Razors, each finger. Maniacal."

"All right." Hendricks moved away impatiently. He stood with his back to them.

"What's the matter?" Rudi said.

"The Moon Base. God, if they've gotten there—"

"The Moon Base?"

Hendricks turned around. "They couldn't have got to the Moon Base. How would they get there? It isn't possible. I can't believe it."

"What is this Moon Base? We've heard rumors, but nothing definite. What is the actual situation? You seem concerned."

"We're supplied from the Moon. The governments are there, under the lunar surface. All our people and industries. That's what keeps us going. If they should find some way of getting off Terra, onto the Moon—"

"It only takes one of them. Once the first one gets in it admits the others. Hundreds of them, all alike. You should have seen them. Identical. Like ants."

"Perfect socialism," Tasso said. "The ideal of the communist state. All citizens interchangeable."

Klaus grunted angrily. "That's enough. Well? What next?"

Hendricks paced back and forth, around the small room. The air was full of smells of food and perspiration. The others watched him. Presently Tasso pushed through the curtain into the other room. "I'm going to take a nap."

The curtain closed behind her. Rudi and Klaus sat down at the table, still watching Hendricks. "It's up to you," Klaus said. "We don't know your situation."

Hendricks nodded.

"It's a problem." Rudi drank some coffee, filling his cup from a rusty pot. "We're safe here for a while, but we can't stay here forever. Not enough food or supplies."

"But if we go outside—"

"If we go outside they'll get us. Or probably they'll get us. We couldn't go very far. How far is your command bunker, Major?"

"Three or four miles."

"We might make it. The four of us. Four of us could watch all sides. They couldn't slip up behind us and start tagging us. We have three rifles, three blast rifles. Tasso can have my pistol." Rudi tapped his belt. "In the Soviet army we didn't have shoes always, but we had guns. With all four of us armed one of us might get to your command bunker. Preferably you, Major."

"What if they're already there?" Klaus said.

Rudi shrugged. "Well, then we come back here."

Hendricks stopped pacing. "What do you think the chances are they're already in the American lines?"

"Hard to say. Fairly good. They're organized. They know exactly what they're doing. Once they start they go like a horde of locusts. They have to keep moving, and fast. It's secrecy and speed they depend on. Surprise. They push their way in before anyone has any idea."

"I see," Hendricks murmured.

From the other room Tasso stirred. "Major?"

Hendricks pushed the curtain back. "What?"

Tasso looked up at him lazily from the cot. "Have you any more American cigarettes left?"

Hendricks went into the room and sat down across from her, on a wood stool. He felt in his pockets. "No. All gone."

"Too bad."

"What nationality are you?" Hendricks asked after a while.

"Russian."

"How did you get here?"

"Here?"

"This used to be France. This was part of Normandy. Did you come with the Soviet army?"

"Why?"

"Just curious." He studied her. She had taken off her coat, tossing it over the end of the cot. She was young, about twenty. Slim. Her long hair stretched out over the pillow. She was staring at him silently, her eyes dark and large.

"What's on your mind?" Tasso said.

"Nothing. How old are you?"

"Eighteen." She continued to watch him, unblinking, her arms behind her head. She had on Russian army pants and shirt. Gray-green. Thick leather belt with counter and cartridges. Medicine kit.

"You're in the Soviet army?"

"No."

"Where did you get the uniform?"

She shrugged. "It was given to me," she told him.

"How—how old were you when you came here?"

"Sixteen."

"That young?"

Her eyes narrowed. "What do you mean?"

Hendricks rubbed his jaw. "Your life would have been a lot different if there had been no war. Sixteen. You came here at sixteen. To live this way."

"I had to survive."

"I'm not moralizing."

"Your life would have been different, too," Tasso murmured. She reached down and unfastened one of her boots. She kicked the boot off, onto the floor. "Major, do you want to go in the other room? I'm sleepy."

"It's going to be a problem, the four of us here. It's going to be hard to live in these quarters. Are there just the two rooms?"

"Yes."

"How big was the cellar originally? Was it larger than this? Are there other rooms filled up with debris? We might be able to open one of them."

"Perhaps. I really don't know." Tasso loosened her belt. She made herself comfortable on the cot, unbuttoning her shirt. "You're sure you have no more cigarettes?"

"I had only the one pack."

"Too bad. Maybe if we get back to your bunker we can find some." The other boot fell. Tasso reached up for the light cord. "Good night."

"You're going to sleep?"

"That's right."

The room plunged into darkness. Hendricks got up and made his way past the curtain, into the kitchen. And stopped, rigid.

Rudi stood against the wall, his face white and gleaming. His mouth opened and closed but no sounds came. Klaus stood in front of him, the muzzle of his pistol in Rudi's stomach. Neither of them moved. Klaus, his hand tight around the gun, his features set. Rudi, pale and silent, spread-eagled against the wall.

"What—" Hendricks muttered, but Klaus cut him off.

"Be quiet, Major. Come over here. Your gun. Get out your gun."

Hendricks drew his pistol. "What is it?"

"Cover him." Klaus motioned him forward. "Beside me. Hurry!"

Rudi moved a little, lowering his arms. He turned to Hendricks, licking his lips. The whites of his eyes shone wildly. Sweat dripped from his forehead, down his checks. He fixed his gaze on Hendricks. "Major, he's gone insane. Stop him." Rudi's voice was thin and hoarse, almost inaudible.

"What's going on?" Hendricks demanded.

Without lowering his pistol Klaus answered. "Major, remember our discussion? The Three Varieties? We knew about One and Three. But we didn't know about Two. At least, we didn't know before." Klaus's fingers tightened around the gun butt. "We didn't know before, but we know now."

He pressed the trigger. A burst of white heat rolled out of the gun, licking around Rudi.

"Major, this is the Second Variety."

Tasso swept the curtain aside. "Klaus! What did you do?"

Klaus turned from the charred form, gradually sinking down the wall onto the floor. "The Second Variety, Tasso. Now we know. We have all three types identified. The danger is less. I—"

Tasso stared past him at the remains of Rudi, at the blackened, smoldering fragments and bits of cloth. "You killed him."

"Him? *It*, you mean. I was watching. I had a feeling, but I wasn't sure. At least, I wasn't sure before. But this evening I was certain." Klaus rubbed his pistol butt nervously. "We're lucky. Don't you understand? Another hour and it might—"

"You were *certain*?" Tasso pushed past him and bent down, over the steaming remains on the floor. Her face became hard. "Major, see for yourself. Bones. Flesh."

Hendricks bent down beside her. The remains were human remains. Seared flesh, charred bone fragments, part of a skull. Ligaments, viscera, blood. Blood forming a pool against the wall.

"No wheels," Tasso said calmly. She straightened up. "No wheels, no parts, no relays. Not a claw. Not the Second Variety." She folded her arms. "You're going to have to be able to explain this."

Klaus sat down at the table, all the color drained suddenly from his face. He put his head in his hands and rocked back and forth.

"Snap out of it." Tasso's fingers closed over his shoulder. "Why did you do it? Why did you kill him?"

"He was frightened," Hendricks said. "All this, the whole thing, building up around us."

"Maybe."

"What, then. What do you think?"

"I think he may have had a reason for killing Rudi. A good reason."

"What reason?"

"Maybe Rudi learned something."

Hendricks studied her bleak face. "About what?" he asked.

"About him. About Klaus."

Klaus looked up quickly. "You can see what she's trying to say. She thinks I'm the Second Variety. Don't you see, Major? Now she wants you to believe I killed him on purpose. That I'm—"

"Why did you kill him, then?" Tasso said.

"I told you." Klaus shook his head wearily. "I thought he was a claw. I thought I knew."

"Why?"

"I had been watching him. I was suspicious."

"Why?"

"I thought I had seen something. Heard something. I thought I—" He stopped.

"Go on."

"We were sitting at the table. Playing cards. You two were in the other room. It was silent. I thought I heard him—*whirr.*"

There was silence.

"Do you believe that?" Tasso said to Hendricks.

"Yes. I believe what he says."

"I don't. I think he killed Rudi for a good purpose." Tasso touched the rifle, resting in the corner of the room. "Major—"

"No." Hendricks shook his head. "Let's stop it right now. One is enough. We're afraid, the way he was. If we kill him we'll be doing what he did to Rudi."

Klaus looked gratefully up at him. "Thanks. I was afraid. You understand, don't you? Now she's afraid, the way I was. She wants to kill me."

"No more killing." Hendricks moved toward the end of the ladder. "I'm going above and try the transmitter once more. If I can't get them we're moving back toward my lines tomorrow morning."

Klaus rose quickly. "I'll come up with you and give you a hand."

The night air was cold. The earth was cooling off. Klaus took a deep breath, filling his lungs. He and Hendricks stepped onto the ground, out of the tunnel. Klaus planted his feet wide apart, the rifle up, watching and listening. Hendricks crouched by the tunnel mouth, tuning the small transmitter.

"Any luck?" Klaus asked presently.

"Not yet."

"Keep trying. Tell them what happened."

Hendricks kept trying. Without success. Finally he lowered the antenna. "It's useless. They can't hear me. Or they hear me and won't answer. Or—"

"Or they don't exist."

"I'll try once more." Hendricks raised the antenna. "Scott, can you hear me? Come in!"

He listened. There was only static. Then, still very faintly—

"This is Scott."

His fingers tightened. "Scott! Is it you?"

"This is Scott."

Klaus squatted down. "Is it your command?"

"Scott, listen. Do you understand? About them, the claws. Did you get my message? Did you hear me?"

"Yes." Faintly. Almost inaudible. He could hardly make out the word.

"You got my message? Is everything all right at the bunker? None of them got in?"

"Everything is all right."

"Have they tried to get in?"

The voice was weaker.

"No."

Hendricks turned to Klaus. "They're all right."

"Have they been attacked?"

"No." Hendricks pressed the phone tighter to his ear. "Scott I can hardly hear you. Have you notified the Moon Base? Do they know? Are they alerted?"

No answer.

"Scott! Can you hear me?"

Silence.

Hendricks relaxed, sagging. "Faded out. Must be radiation pools."

Hendricks and Klaus looked at each other. Neither of them said anything. After a time Klaus said, "Did it sound like any of your men? Could you identify the voice?"

"It was too faint."

"You couldn't be certain?"

"No."

"Then it could have been—"

"I don't know. Now I'm not sure. Let's go back down and get the lid closed."

They climbed back down the ladder slowly, into the warm cellar. Klaus bolted the lid behind them. Tasso waited for them, her face expressionless.

"Any luck?" she asked.

Neither of them answered. "Well?" Klaus said at last. "What do you think, Major? Was it your officer, or was it one of *them*?"

"I don't know."

"Then we're just where we were before."

Hendricks stared down at the floor, his jaw set. "We'll have to go. To be sure."

"Anyhow, we have food here for only a few weeks. We'd have to go up after that, in any case."

"Apparently so."

"What's wrong?" Tasso demanded. "Did you get across to your bunker? What's the matter?"

"It may have been one of my men," Hendricks said slowly. "Or it may have been one of *them*. But we'll never know standing here." He examined his watch. "Let's turn in and get some sleep. We want to be up early to-morrow."

"Early?"

"Our best chance to get through the claws should be early in the morning," Hendricks said.

The morning was crisp and clear. Major Hendricks studied the countryside through his field glasses.

"See anything?" Klaus said.

"No."

"Can you make out our bunkers?"

"Which way?"

"Here." Klaus took the glasses and adjusted them. "I know where to look." He looked a long time, silently.

Tasso came to the top of the tunnel and stepped up onto the ground. "Anything?"

"No." Klaus passed the glasses back to Hendricks. "They're out of sight. Come on. Let's not stay here."

The three of them made their way down the side of the ridge, sliding in the soft ash. Across a flat rock a lizard scuttled. They stopped instantly, rigid.

"What was it?" Klaus muttered.

"A lizard."

The lizard ran on, hurrying through the ash. It was exactly the same color as the ash.

"Perfect adaptation," Klaus said. "Proves we were right. Lysenko, I mean."

They reached the bottom of the ridge and stopped, standing close together, looking around them.

"Let's go." Hendricks started off. "It's a good long trip, on foot."

Klaus fell in beside him, Tasso walked behind, her pistol held alertly. "Major, I've been meaning to ask you something," Klaus said. "How did you run across the David? The one that was tagging you."

"I met it along the way. In some ruins."

"What did it say?"

"Not much. It said it was alone. By itself."

"You couldn't tell it was a machine? It talked like a living person? You never suspected?"

"It didn't say much. I noticed nothing unusual."

"It's strange, machines so much like people that you can be fooled. Almost alive. I wonder where it'll end."

"They're doing what you Yanks designed them to do," Tasso said. "You designed them to hunt out life and destroy. Human life. Wherever they find it."

Hendricks was watching Klaus intently. "Why did you ask me? What's on your mind?"

"Nothing," Klaus answered.

"Klaus thinks you're the Second Variety," Tasso said calmly, from behind them. "Now he's got his eye on you."

Klaus flushed. "Why not? We sent a runner to the Yank lines and *he* comes back. Maybe he thought he'd find some good game here."

Hendricks laughed harshly. "I came from the UN bunkers. There were human beings all around me."

"Maybe you saw an opportunity to get into the Soviet lines. Maybe you saw your chance. Maybe you—"

"The Soviet lines had already been taken over. Your lines had been invaded before I left my command bunker. Don't forget that."

Tasso came up beside him. "That proves nothing at all, Major."

"Why not?"

"There appears to be little communication between the varieties. Each is made in a different factory. They don't seem to work together. You might have started for the Soviet lines without knowing anything about the work of the other varieties. Or even what the other varieties were like."

"How do you know so much about the claws?" Hendricks said.

"I've seen them. I've observed them take over the Soviet bunkers."

"You know quite a lot," Klaus said. "Actually, you saw very little. Strange that you should have been such an acute observer."

Tasso laughed. "Do you suspect me, now?"

"Forget it," Hendricks said. They walked on in silence.

"Are we going the whole way on foot?" Tasso said, after a while. "I'm not used to walking." She gazed around at the plain of ash, stretching out on all sides of them, as far as they could see. "How dreary."

"It's like this all the way," Klaus said.

"In a way I wish you had been in your bunker when the attack came."

"Somebody else would have been with you, if not me," Klaus muttered.

Tasso laughed, putting her hands in her pockets. "I suppose so."

They walked on, keeping their eyes on the vast plain of silent ash around them.

The sun was setting. Hendricks made his way forward slowly, waving Tasso and Klaus back. Klaus squatted down, resting his gun butt against the ground.

Tasso found a concrete slab and sat down with a sigh. "It's good to rest."

"Be quiet," Klaus said sharply.

Hendricks pushed up to the top of the rise ahead of them. The same rise the Russian runner had come up, the day before. Hendricks dropped down, stretching himself out, peering through his glasses at what lay beyond.

Nothing was visible. Only ash and occasional trees. But there, not more than fifty yards ahead, was the entrance of the forward command bunker. The bunker from which he had come. Hendricks watched silently. No motion. No sign of life. Nothing stirred.

Klaus slithered up beside him. "Where is it?"

"Down there." Hendricks passed him the glasses. Clouds of ash rolled across the evening sky. The world was darkening. They had a couple of hours of light left, at the most. Probably not that much.

"I don't see anything," Klaus said.

"That tree there. The stump. By the pile of bricks. The entrance is to the right of the bricks."

"I'll have to take your word for it."

"You and Tasso cover me from here. You'll be able to sight all the way to the bunker entrance."

"You're going down alone?"

"With my wrist tab I'll be safe. The ground around the bunker is a living field of claws. They collect down in the ash. Like crabs. Without tabs you wouldn't have a chance."

"Maybe you're right."

"I'll walk slowly all the way. As soon as I know for certain—"

"If they're down inside the bunker you won't be able to get back up here. They go fast. You don't realize."

"What do you suggest?"

Klaus considered. "I don't know. Get them to come to the surface. So you can see."

Hendricks brought out his transmitter from his belt, raising the antenna. "Let's get started."

Klaus signaled to Tasso. She crawled expertly up the side of the rise to where they were sitting.

"He's going down alone," Klaus said. "We'll cover him from here. As soon as you see him start back, fire past him at once. They come quick."

"You're not very optimistic," Tasso said.

"No, I'm not."

Hendricks opened the breech of his gun, checking it carefully. "Maybe things are all right."

"You didn't see them. Hundreds of them. All the same. Pouring out like ants."

"I should be able to find out without going down all the way." Hendricks locked his gun, gripping it in one hand, the transmitter in the other. "Well, wish me luck."

Klaus put out his hand. "Don't go down until you're sure. Talk to them from here. Make them show themselves."

Hendricks stood up. He stepped down the side of the rise.

A moment later he was walking slowly toward the pile of bricks and debris beside the dead tree stump. Toward the entrance of the forward command bunker.

Nothing stirred. He raised the transmitter, clicking it on. "Scott? Can you hear me?"

Silence.

"Scott! This is Hendricks. Can you hear me? I'm standing outside the bunker. You should be able to see me in the view sight."

He listened, the transmitter gripped tightly. No sound. Only static. He walked forward. A claw burrowed out of the ash and raced toward him. It halted a few feet away and then slunk off. A second claw appeared, one of the big ones with feelers. It moved toward him, studied him intently, and then fell in behind him, dogging respectfully after him, a few paces away. A moment later a second big claw joined it. Silently, the claws trailed him as he walked slowly toward the bunker.

Hendricks stopped, and behind him, the claws came to a halt. He was close now. Almost to the bunker steps.

"Scott! Can you hear me? I'm standing right above you. Outside. On the surface. Are you picking me up?"

He waited, holding his gun against his side, the transmitter tightly to his ear. Time passed. He strained to hear, but there was only silence. Silence, and faint static.

Then, distantly, metallically—

"This is Scott."

The voice was neutral. Cold. He could not identify it. But the earphone was minute.

"Scott! Listen. I'm standing right above you. I'm on the surface, looking down into the bunker entrance."

"Yes."

"Can you see me?"

"Yes."

"Through the view sight? You have the sight trained on me?"

"Yes."

Hendricks pondered. A circle of claws waited quietly around him, gray-metal bodies on all sides of him. "Is everything all right in the bunker? Nothing unusual has happened?"

"Everything is all right."

"Will you come up to the surface? I want to see you for a moment." Hendricks took a deep breath. "Come up here with me. I want to talk to you."

"Come down."

"I'm giving you an order."

Silence.

"Are you coming?" Hendricks listened. There was no response. "I order you to come to the surface."

"Come down."

Hendricks set his jaw. "Let me talk to Leone."

There was a long pause. He listened to the static. Then a voice came, hard, thin, metallic. The same as the other. "This is Leone."

"Hendricks. I'm on the surface. At the bunker entrance. I want one of you to come up here."

"Come down."

"Why come down? I'm giving you an order!"

Silence. Hendricks lowered the transmitter. He looked carefully around him. The entrance was just ahead. Almost at his feet. He lowered the antenna and fastened the transmitter to his belt. Carefully, he gripped his gun with both hands. He moved forward, a step at a time. If they could see him they knew he was starting toward the entrance. He closed his eyes a moment.

Then he put his foot on the first step that led downward.

Two Davids came up at him, their faces identical and expressionless. He blasted them into particles. More came rushing silently up, a whole pack of them. All exactly the same.

Hendricks turned and raced back, away from the bunker, back toward the rise.

At the top of the rise Tasso and Klaus were firing down. The small claws were already streaking up toward them, shining metal spheres going fast, racing frantically through the ash. But he had no time to think about that. He knelt down, aiming at the bunker entrance, gun against his cheek. The Davids were coming out in groups, clutching their teddy bears, their thin knobby legs pumping as they ran up the steps to the surface. Hendricks fired into the main body of them. They burst apart, wheels and springs flying in all directions. He fired again, through the mist of particles.

A giant lumbering figure rose up in the bunker entrance, tall and swaying. Hendricks paused, amazed. A man, a soldier. With one leg, supporting himself with a crutch.

"Major!" Tasso's voice came. More firing. The huge figure moved forward, Davids swarming around it. Hendricks broke out of his freeze. The First Variety. The Wounded Soldier. He aimed and fired. The soldier burst into bits, parts and relays flying. Now many Davids were out on the flat ground, away from the bunker. He fired again and again, moving slowly back, half-crouching and aiming.

From the rise, Klaus fired down. The side of the rise was alive with claws making their way up. Hendricks retreated toward the rise, running and crouching. Tasso had left Klaus and was circling slowly to the right, moving away from the rise.

A David slipped up toward him, its small white face expressionless, brown hair hanging down in its eyes. It bent over suddenly, opening its arms. Its teddy bear hurtled down and leaped across the ground, bounding toward him. Hendricks fired. The bear and the David both dissolved. He grinned, blinking. It was like a dream.

"Up here!" Tasso's voice. Hendricks made his way toward her. She was over by some columns of concrete, walls of a ruined building. She was firing past him, with the hand pistol Klaus had given her.

"Thanks." He joined her, gasping for breath. She pulled him back, behind the concrete, fumbling at her belt.

"Close your eyes!" She unfastened a globe from her waist. Rapidly, she unscrewed the cap, locking it into place. "Close your eyes and get down."

She threw the bomb. It sailed in an arc, an expert toss, rolling and bouncing to the entrance of the bunker. Two Wounded Soldiers stood uncertainly by the brick pile. More Davids poured from behind them, out onto the plain. One of the Wounded Soldiers moved toward the bomb, stooping awkwardly down to pick it up.

The bomb went off. The concussion whirled Hendricks around, throwing him on his face. A hot wind rolled over him. Dimly he saw Tasso standing behind the columns, firing slowly and methodically at the Davids coming out of the raging clouds of white fire.

Back along the rise Klaus struggled with a ring of claws circling around him. He retreated, blasting at them and moving back, trying to break through the ring.

Hendricks struggled to his feet. His head ached. He could hardly see. Everything was licking at him, raging and whirling. His right arm would not move.

Tasso pulled back toward him. "Come on. Let's go."

"Klaus—he's still up there."

"Come on!" Tasso dragged Hendricks back, away from the columns. Hendricks shook his head, trying to clear it. Tasso led him rapidly away, her eyes intense and bright, watching for claws that had escaped the blast.

One David came out of the rolling clouds of flame. Tasso blasted it. No more appeared.

"But Klaus. What about him?" Hendricks stopped, standing unsteadily. "He—"

"Come on!"

They retreated, moving farther and farther away from the bunker. A few small claws followed them for a little while and then gave up, turning back and going off.

At last Tasso stopped. "We can stop here and get our breaths."

Hendricks sat down on some heaps of debris. He wiped his neck, gasping. "We left Klaus back there."

Tasso said nothing. She opened her gun, sliding a fresh round of blast cartridges into place.

Hendricks stared at her, dazed. "You left him back there on purpose."

Tasso snapped the gun together. She studied the heaps of rubble around them, her face expressionless. As if she were watching for something.

"What is it?" Hendricks demanded. "What are you looking for? Is something coming?" He shook his head, trying to understand. What was she doing? What was she waiting for? He could see nothing. Ash lay all around them, ash and ruins. Occasional stark tree trunks, without leaves or branches. "What—"

Tasso cut him off. "Be still." Her eyes narrowed. Suddenly her gun came up. Hendricks turned, following her gaze.

Back the way they had come a figure appeared. The figure walked unsteadily toward them. Its clothes were torn. It limped as it made its way along, going very slowly and carefully. Stopping now and then, resting and getting its strength. Once it almost fell. It stood for a moment, trying to steady itself. Then it came on.

Klaus.

Hendricks stood up. "Klaus!" He started toward him. "How the hell did you—"

Tasso fired. Hendricks swung back. She fired again, the blast passing him, a searing line of heat. The beam caught Klaus in the chest. He exploded, gears and wheels flying. For a moment he continued to walk. Then he swayed back and forth. He crashed to the ground, his arms flung out. A few more wheels rolled away.

Silence.

Tasso turned to Hendricks. "Now you understand why he killed Rudi."

Hendricks sat down again slowly. He shook his head. He was numb. He could not think.

"Do you see?" Tasso said. "Do you understand?"

Hendricks said nothing. Everything was slipping away from him, faster and faster. Darkness, rolling and plucking at him.

He closed his eyes.

Hendricks opened his eyes slowly. His body ached all over. He tried to sit up but needles of pain shot through his arm and shoulder. He gasped.

"Don't try to get up," Tasso said. She bent down, putting her cold hand against his forehead.

It was night. A few stars glinted above, shining through the drifting clouds of ash. Hendricks lay back, his teeth locked. Tasso watched him impassively. She had built a fire with some wood and weeds. The fire licked feebly, hissing at a metal cup suspended over it. Everything was silent. Unmoving darkness, beyond the fire.

"So he was the Second Variety," Hendricks murmured.

"I had always thought so."

"Why didn't you destroy him sooner?" He wanted to know.

"You held me back." Tasso crossed to the fire to look into the metal cup. "Coffee. It'll be ready to drink in a while."

She came back and sat down beside him. Presently she opened her pistol and began to disassemble the firing mechanism, studying it intently.

"This is a beautiful gun," Tasso said, half aloud. "The construction is superb."

"What about them? The claws."

"The concussion from the bomb put most of them out of action. They're delicate. Highly organized, I suppose."

"The Davids, too?"

"Yes."

"How did you happen to have a bomb like that?"

Tasso shrugged. "We designed it. You shouldn't underestimate our technology, Major. Without such a bomb you and I would no longer exist."

"Very useful."

Tasso stretched out her legs, warming her feet in the heat of the fire. "It surprised me that you did not seem to understand, after he killed Rudi. Why did you think he—"

"I told you. I thought he was afraid."

"Really? You know, Major, for a little while I suspected you. Because you wouldn't let me kill him. I thought you might be protecting him." She laughed.

"Are we safe here?" Hendricks asked presently.

"For a while. Until they get reinforcements from some other area." Tasso began to clean the interior of the gun with a bit of rag. She finished and pushed the mechanism back into place. She closed the gun, running her finger along the barrel.

"We were lucky," Hendricks murmured.

"Yes. Very lucky."

"Thanks for pulling me away."

Tasso did not answer. She glanced up at him, her eyes bright in the fire-light. Hendricks examined his arm. He could not move his fingers. His whole side seemed numb. Down inside him was a dull steady ache.

"How do you feel?" Tasso asked.

"My arm is damaged."

"Anything else?"

"Internal injuries."

"You didn't get down when the bomb went off."

Hendricks said nothing. He watched Tasso pour the coffee from the cup into a flat metal pan. She brought it over to him.

"Thanks." He struggled up enough to drink. It was hard to swallow. His insides turned over and he pushed the pan away. "That's all I can drink now."

Tasso drank the rest. Time passed. The clouds of ash moved across the dark sky above them. Hendricks rested, his mind blank. After a while he became aware that Tasso was standing over him, gazing down at him.

"What is it?" he murmured.

"Do you feel any better?"

"Some."

"You know, Major, if I hadn't dragged you away they would have got you. You would be dead. Like Rudi."

"I know."

"Do you want to know why I brought you out? I could have left you. I could have left you there."

"Why did you bring me out?"

"Because we have to get away from here." Tasso stirred the fire with a stick, peering calmly down into it. "No human being can live here. When their reinforcements come we won't have a chance. I've pondered about it while you were unconscious. We have perhaps three hours before they come."

"And you expect me to get us away?"

"That's right. I expect you to get us out of here."

"Why me?"

"Because I don't know any way." Her eyes shone at him in the half light, bright and steady. "If you can't get us out of here they'll kill us within three hours. I see nothing else ahead. Well, Major? What are you going to do? I've been waiting all night. While you were unconscious I sat here, waiting and listening. It's almost dawn. The night is almost over."

Hendricks considered. "It's curious," he said at last.

"Curious?"

"That you should think I can get us out of here. I wonder what you think I can do."

"Can you get us to the Moon Base?"

"The Moon Base? How?"

"There must be some way."

Hendricks shook his head. "No. There's no way that I know of."

Tasso said nothing. For a moment her steady gaze wavered. She ducked her head, turning abruptly away. She scrambled to her feet. "More coffee?"

"No."

"Suit yourself." Tasso drank silently. He could not see her face. He lay back against the ground, deep in thought, trying to concentrate. It was hard to think. His head still hurt. And the numbing daze still hung over him.

"There might be one way," he said suddenly.

"Oh?"

"How soon is dawn?"

"Two hours. The sun will be coming up shortly."

"There's supposed to be a ship near here. I've never seen it. But I know it exists."

"What kind of a ship?" Her voice was sharp.

"A rocket cruiser."

"Will it take us off? To the Moon Base?"

"It's supposed to. In case of emergency." He rubbed his forehead.

"What's wrong?"

"My head. It's hard to think. I can hardly—hardly concentrate. The bomb."

"Is the ship near here?" Tasso slid over beside him, settling down on her haunches. "How far is it? Where is it?"

"I'm trying to think."

Her fingers dug into his arm. "Nearby?" Her voice was like iron.

"Where would it be? Would they store it underground? Hidden underground?"

"Yes. In a storage locker."

"How do we find it? Is it marked? Is there a code marker to identify it?"

Hendricks concentrated. "No. No markings. No code symbol."

"What then?"

"A sign."

"What sort of sign?"

Hendricks did not answer. In the flickering light his eyes were glazed, two sightless orbs. Tasso's fingers dug into his arm.

"What sort of sign? What is it?"

"I—I can't think. Let me rest."

"All right." She let go and stood up. Hendricks lay back against the ground, his eyes closed. Tasso walked away from him, her hands in her pockets. She kicked a rock out of her way and stood staring up at the sky. The night blackness was already beginning to fade into gray. Morning was coming.

Tasso gripped her pistol and walked around the fire in a circle, back and forth. On the ground Major Hendricks lay, his eyes closed, unmoving. The grayness rose in the sky, higher and higher. The landscape became visible, fields of ash stretching out in all directions. Ash and ruins of buildings, a wall here and there, heaps of concrete, the naked trunk of a tree.

The air was cold and sharp. Somewhere a long way off a bird made a few bleak sounds.

Hendricks stirred. He opened his eyes. "Is it dawn? Already?"

"Yes."

Hendricks sat up a little. "You wanted to know something. You were asking me."

"Do you remember now?"

"Yes."

"What is it?" She tensed. "What?" she repeated sharply.

"A well. A ruined well. It's in a storage locker under a well."

"A well." Tasso relaxed. "Then we'll find a well." She looked at her watch. "We have about an hour, Major. Do you think we can find it in an hour?"

"Give me a hand," Hendricks said.

Tasso put her pistol away and helped him to his feet. "This is going to be difficult."

"Yes it is." Hendricks set his lips tightly. "I don't think we're going to go very far."

They began to walk. The early sun cast a little warmth down on them. The land was flat and barren, stretching out gray and lifeless as far as they could see. A few birds sailed silently, far above them, circling slowly.

"See anything?" Hendricks said. "Any claws?"

"No. Not yet."

They passed through some ruins, upright concrete and bricks. A cement foundation. Rats scuttled away. Tasso jumped back warily.

"This used to be a town," Hendricks said. "A village. Provincial village. This was all grape country, once. Where we are now."

They came onto a ruined street, weeds and cracks crisscrossing it. Over to the right a stone chimney stuck up.

"Be careful," he warned her.

A pit yawned, an open basement. Ragged ends of pipes jutted up, twisted and bent. They passed part of a house, a bathtub turned on its side. A broken chair. A few spoons and bits of china dishes. In the center of the street the ground had sunk away. The depression was filled with weeds and debris and bones.

"Over here," Hendricks murmured.

"This way?"

"To the right."

They passed the remains of a heavy-duty tank. Hendricks's belt counter clicked ominously. The tank had been radiation-blasted. A few feet from the tank a mummified body lay sprawled out, mouth open. Beyond the road was a flat field. Stones and weeds, and bits of broken glass.

"There," Hendricks said.

A stone well jutted up, sagging and broken. A few boards lay across it. Most of the well had sunk into rubble. Hendricks walked unsteadily toward it, Tasso beside him.

"Are you certain about this?" Tasso said. "This doesn't look like any-thing."

"I'm sure." Hendricks sat down at the edge of the well, his teeth locked. His breath came quickly. He wiped perspiration from his face. "This was arranged so the senior command officer could get away. If anything happened. If the bunker fell."

"That was you?"

"Yes."

"Where is the ship? Is it here?"

"We're standing on it." Hendricks ran his hands over the surface of the well stones. "The eye-lock responds to me, not to anybody else. It's my ship. Or it was supposed to be."

There was a sharp click. Presently they heard a low grating sound from below them.

"Step back," Hendricks said. He and Tasso moved away from the well.

A section of the ground slid back. A metal frame pushed slowly up through the ash, shoving bricks and weeds out of the way. The action ceased as the ship nosed into view.

"There it is," Hendricks said.

The ship was small. It rested quietly, suspended in its mesh frame like a blunt needle. A rain of ash sifted down into the dark cavity from which the ship had been raised. Hendricks made his way over to it. He mounted the mesh and unscrewed the hatch, pulling it back. Inside the ship the control banks and the pressure seat were visible.

Tasso came and stood beside him, gazing into the ship. "I'm not accustomed to rocket piloting," she said after a while.

Hendricks glanced at her. "I'll do the piloting."

"Will you? There's only one seat, Major. I can see it's built to carry only a single person."

Hendricks's breathing changed. He studied the interior of the ship intently. Tasso was right. There was only one seat. The ship was built to carry only one person. "I see," he said slowly. "And the one person is you."

She nodded.

"Of course."

"Why?"

"*You* can't go. You might not live through the trip. You're injured. You probably wouldn't get there."

"An interesting point. But you see, I know where the Moon Base is. And you don't. You might fly around for months and not find it. It's well hidden. Without knowing what to look for—"

"I'll have to take my chances. Maybe I won't find it. Not by myself. But I think you'll give me all the information I need. Your life depends on it."

"How?"

"If I find the Moon Base in time, perhaps I can get them to send a ship back to pick you up. *If* I find the Base in time. If not, then you haven't a chance. I imagine there are supplies on the ship. They will last me long enough—"

Hendricks moved quickly. But his injured arm betrayed him. Tasso ducked, sliding lithely aside. Her hand came up, lightning fast. Hendricks saw the gun butt coming. He tried to ward off the blow, but she was too fast. The metal butt struck against the side of his head, just above his ear. Numbing pain rushed through him. Pain and rolling clouds of blackness. He sank down, sliding to the ground.

Dimly, he was aware that Tasso was standing over him, kicking him with her toe.

"Major! Wake up!"

He opened his eyes, groaning.

"Listen to me." She bent down, the gun pointed at his face. "I have to hurry. There isn't much time left. The ship is ready to go, but you must give me the information I need before I leave."

Hendricks shook his head, trying to clear it.

"Hurry up! Where is the Moon Base? How do I find it? What do I look for?"

Hendricks said nothing.

"Answer me!"

"Sorry."

"Major, the ship is loaded with provisions. I can coast for weeks. I'll find the Base eventually. And in a half hour you'll be dead. Your only chance of survival—" She broke off.

Along the slope, by some crumbling ruins, something moved. Something in the ash. Tasso turned quickly, aiming. She fired. A puff of flame leaped. Something scuttled away, rolling across the ash. She fired again. The claw burst apart, wheels flying.

"See?" Tasso said. "A scout. It won't be long."

"You'll bring them back here to get me?"

"Yes. As soon as possible."

Hendricks looked up at her. He studied her intently. "You're telling the truth?" A strange expression had come over his face, an avid hunger. "You will come back for me? You'll get me to the Moon Base?"

"I'll get you to the Moon Base. But tell me where it is! There's only a little time left."

"All right." Hendricks picked up a piece of rock, pulling himself to a sitting position. "Watch."

Hendricks began to scratch in the ash. Tasso stood by him, watching the motion of the rock. Hendricks was sketching a crude lunar map.

"This is the Appenine range. Here is the Crater of Archimedes. The Moon Base is beyond the end of the Appenine, about two hundred miles. I don't know exactly where. No one on Terra knows. But when you're over the Appenine, signal with one red flare and a green flare, followed by two red flares in quick succession. The Base monitor will record your signal. The Base is under the surface, of course. They'll guide you down with magnetic controls."

"And the controls? Can I operate them?"

"The controls are virtually automatic. All you have to do is give the right signal at the right time."

"I will."

"The seat absorbs most of the takeoff shock. Air and temperature are automatically controlled. The ship will leave Terra and pass out into free space. It'll line itself up with the Moon, falling into an orbit around it, about a hundred miles above the surface. The orbit will carry you over the Base. When you're in the region of the Appenine, release the signal rockets."

Tasso slid into the ship and lowered herself into the pressure seat. The arm locks folded automatically around her. She fingered the controls. "Too bad you're not going, Major. All this put here for you, and you can't make the trip."

"Leave me the pistol."

Tasso pulled the pistol from her belt. She held it in her hand, weighing it thoughtfully. "Don't go too far from this location. It'll be hard to find you, as it is."

"No, I'll stay here by the well."

Tasso gripped the takeoff switch, running her fingers over the smooth metal. "A beautiful ship, Major. Well built. I admire your workmanship.

You people have always done good work. You build fine things. Your work, your creations, are your greatest achievement."

"Give me the pistol," Hendricks said impatiently, holding out his hand. He struggled to his feet.

"Good-bye, Major!" Tasso tossed the pistol past Hendricks. The pistol clattered against the ground, bouncing and rolling away. Hendricks hurried after it. He bent down, snatching it up.

The hatch of the ship clanged shut. The bolts fell into place. Hendricks made his way back. The inner door was being sealed. He raised the pistol unsteadily.

There was a shattering roar. The ship burst up from its metal cage, fusing the mesh behind it. Hendricks cringed, pulling back. The ship shot up into the rolling clouds of ash, disappearing into the sky.

Hendricks stood watching a long time, until even the streamer had dissipated. Nothing stirred. The morning air was chill and silent. He began to walk aimlessly back the way they had come. Better to keep moving around. It would be a long time before help came—if it came at all.

He searched his pockets until he found a package of cigarettes. He lit one grimly. They had all wanted cigarettes from him. But cigarettes were scarce.

A lizard slithered by him, through the ash. He halted, rigid. The lizard disappeared. Above, the sun rose higher in the sky. Some flies landed on a flat rock to one side of him. Hendricks kicked at them with his foot.

It was getting hot. Sweat trickled down his face, into his collar. His mouth was dry.

Presently he stopped walking and sat down on some debris. He unfastened his medicine kit and swallowed a few narcotic capsules. He looked around him. Where was he?

Something lay ahead. Stretched out on the ground. Silent and unmoving.

Hendricks drew his gun quickly. It looked like a man. Then he remembered. It was the remains of Klaus. The Second Variety. Where Tasso had blasted him. He could see wheels and relays and metal parts, strewn around on the ash. Glittering and sparkling in the sunlight.

Hendricks got to his feet and walked over. He nudged the inert form with his foot, turning it over a little. He could see the metal hull, the aluminum ribs and struts. More wiring fell out. Like viscera. Heaps of wiring, switches and relays. Endless motors and rods.

He bent down. The brain cage had been smashed by the fall. The artificial brain was visible. He gazed at it. A maze of circuits. Miniature tubes. Wires as fine as hair. He touched the brain cage. It swung aside. The type plate was visible. Hendricks studied the plate.

And blanched.

IV-V.

For a long time he stared at the plate. Fourth Variety. Not the Second. They had been wrong. There were more types. Not just three. Many more, perhaps. At least four. And Klaus wasn't the Second Variety.

But if Klaus wasn't the Second Variety—

Suddenly he tensed. Something was coming, walking through the ash beyond the hill. What was it? He strained to see. Figures. Figures coming slowly along, making their way through the ash.

Coming toward him.

Hendricks crouched quickly, raising his gun. Sweat dripped down into his eyes. He fought down rising panic, as the figures neared.

The first was a David. The David saw him and increased its pace. The others hurried behind it. A second David. A third. Three Davids, all alike, coming toward him silently, without expression, their thin legs rising and falling. Clutching their teddy bears.

He aimed and fired. The first two Davids dissolved into particles. The third came on. And the figure behind it. Climbing silently toward him across the gray ash. A Wounded Soldier, towering over the David. And—

And behind the Wounded Soldier came two Tassos, walking side by side. Heavy belt, Russian army pants, shirt, long hair. The familiar figure, as he had seen her only a little while before. Sitting in the pressure seat of the ship. Two slim, silent figures, both identical.

They were very near. The David bent down suddenly, dropping its teddy bear. The bear raced across the ground. Automatically Hendricks's fingers tightened around the trigger. The bear was gone, dissolved into mist. The two Tasso Types moved on, expressionless, walking side by side, through the gray ash.

When they were almost to him, Hendricks raised the pistol waist high and fired.

The two Tassos dissolved. But already a new group was starting up the rise, five or six Tassos, all identical, a line of them coming rapidly toward him.

And he had given her the ship and the signal code. Because of him she was on her way to the moon, to the Moon Base. He had made it possible.

He had been right about the bomb, after all. It had been designed with knowledge of other types, the David Type and the Wounded Soldier Type. And the Klaus Type. Not designed by human beings. It had been designed by one of the underground factories, apart from all human contact.

The line of Tassos came up to him. Hendricks braced himself, watching them calmly. The familiar face, the belt, the heavy shirt, the bomb carefully in place.

The bomb—

As the Tassos reached for him, a last ironic thought drifted through Hendricks's mind. He felt a little better, thinking about it. The bomb. Made by the Second Variety to destroy the other varieties. Made for that end alone.

They were already beginning to design weapons to use against each other.

IMPOSTER

"One of these days I'm going to take time off," Spence Olham said at first-meal. He looked around at his wife. "I think I've earned a rest. Ten years is a long time."

"And the Project?"

"The war will be won without me. This ball of clay of ours isn't really in much danger." Olham sat down at the table and lit a cigarette. "The news-machines alter dispatches to make it appear the Outspacers are right on top of us. You know what I'd like to do on my vacation? I'd like to take a camping trip to those mountains outside of town, where we went that time. Remember? I got poison oak and you almost stepped on a gopher snake."

"Sutton Wood?" Mary began to clear away the food dishes. "The Wood was burned a few weeks ago. I thought you knew. Some kind of a flash fire."

Olham sagged. "Didn't they even try to find the cause?" His lips twisted. "No one cares anymore. All they can think of is the war." He clamped his jaws together, the whole picture coming up in his mind, the Outspacers, the war, the needle-ships.

"How can we think about anything else?"

Olham nodded. She was right, of course. The dark little ships out of Alpha Centauri had bypassed the Earth cruisers easily, leaving them like helpless turtles. It had been one-way fights, all the way back to Terra.

All the way, until the protec-bubble was demonstrated by Westinghouse Labs. Thrown around the major Earth cities and finally the planet itself, the bubble was the first real defense, the first legitimate answer to the Outspacers—as the news-machines labeled them.

But to win the war, that was another thing. Every lab, every project was working night and day, endlessly, to find something more: a weapon for positive combat. His own project, for example. All day long, year after year.

Olham stood up, putting out his cigarette. "Like the Sword of Damocles. Always hanging over us. I'm getting tired. All I want to do is take a long rest. But I guess everybody feels that way."

He got his jacket from the closet and went out on the front porch. The shoot would be along any moment, the fast little bug that would carry him to the Project.

"I hope Nelson isn't late." He looked at his watch. "It's almost seven."

"Here the bug comes," Mary said, gazing between the rows of houses. The sun glittered behind the roofs, reflecting against the heavy lead plates. The settlement was quiet; only a few people were stirring. "I'll see you later. Try not to work beyond your shift, Spence."

Olham opened the car door and slid inside, leaning back against the seat with a sigh. There was an older man with Nelson.

"Well?" Olham said, as the bug shot ahead. "Heard any interesting news?"

"The usual," Nelson said. "A few Outspace ships hit, another asteroid abandoned for strategic reasons."

"It'll be good when we get the Project into final stage. Maybe it's just the propaganda from the news-machines, but in the last month I've gotten weary of all this. Everything seems so grim and serious, no color to life."

"Do you think the war is in vain?" the older man said suddenly. "You are an integral part of it, yourself."

"This is Major Peters," Nelson said. Olham and Peters shook hands. Olham studied the older man.

"What brings you along so early?" he said. "I don't remember seeing you at the Project before."

"No, I'm not with the Project," Peters said, "but I know something about what you're doing. My own work is altogether different."

A look passed between him and Nelson. Olham noticed it and he frowned. The bug was gaining speed, flashing across the barren, lifeless ground toward the distant rim of the Project building.

"What is your business?" Olham said. "Or aren't you permitted to talk about it?"

"I'm with the government," Peters said. "With FSA, the security organ."

"Oh?" Olham raised an eyebrow. "Is there any enemy infiltration in this region?"

"As a matter of fact I'm here to see you, Mr. Olham."

Olham was puzzled. He considered Peters's words, but he could make nothing of them. "To see me? Why?"

"I'm here to arrest you as an Outspace spy. That's why I'm up so early this morning. *Grab him, Nelson—*"

The gun drove into Olham's ribs. Nelson's hands were shaking, trembling with released emotion, his face pale. He took a deep breath and let it out again.

"Shall we kill him now?" he whispered to Peters. "I think we should kill him now. We can't wait."

Olham stared into his friend's face. He opened his mouth to speak, but no words came. Both men were staring at him steadily, rigid and grim with fright. Olham felt dizzy. His head ached and spun.

"I don't understand," he murmured.

At that moment the shoot car left the ground and rushed up, heading into space. Below them the Project fell away, smaller and smaller, disappearing. Olham shut his mouth.

"We can wait a little," Peters said. "I want to ask him some questions first."

Olham gazed dully ahead as the bug rushed through space.

"The arrest was made all right," Peters said into the vidscreen. On the screen the features of the security chief showed. "It should be a load off everyone's mind."

"Any complications?"

"None. He entered the bug without suspicion. He didn't seem to think my presence was too unusual."

"Where are you now?"

"On our way out, just inside the protec-bubble. We're moving at a maximum speed. You can assume that the critical period is past. I'm glad the takeoff jets in this craft were in good working order. If there had been any failure at that point—"

"Let me see him," the security chief said. He gazed directly at Olham where he sat, his hands in his lap, staring ahead.

"So that's the man." He looked at Olham for a time. Olham said nothing. At last the chief nodded to Peters. "All right. That's enough." A faint trace of disgust wrinkled his features. "I've seen all I want. You've done something that will be remembered for a long time. They're preparing some sort of citation for both of you."

"That's not necessary," Peters said.

"How much danger is there now? Is there still much chance that—"

"There is some chance, but not too much. According to my understanding it requires a verbal key phrase. In any case we'll have to take the risk."

"I'll have the Moon base notified you're coming."

"No." Peters shook his head. "I'll land the ship outside, beyond the base. I don't want it in jeopardy."

"Just as you like." The chief's eyes flickered as he glanced again at Olham. Then his image faded. The screen blanked.

Olham shifted his gaze to the window. The ship was already through the protec-bubble, rushing with greater and greater speed all the time. Peters was in a hurry; below him, rumbling under the floor, the jets were wide open. They were afraid, hurrying frantically, because of him.

Next to him on the seat, Nelson shifted uneasily. "I think we should do it now," he said. "I'd give anything if we could get it over with."

"Take it easy," Peters said. "l want you to guide the ship for a while so I can talk to him."

He slid over beside Olham, looking into his face. Presently he reached out and touched him gingerly, on the arm and then on the cheek.

Olham said nothing. *If I could let Mary know,* he thought again. *If I could find some way of letting her know.* He looked around the ship. How? The vidscreen? Nelson was sitting by the board, holding the gun. There was nothing he could do. He was caught, trapped.

But why?

"Listen," Peters said, "I want to ask you some questions. You know where we're going. We're moving Moonward. In an hour we'll land on the far side, on the desolate side. After we land you'll be turned over immediately to a team of men waiting there. Your body will be destroyed at once. Do you understand that?" He looked at his watch. "Within two hours your parts will be strewn over the landscape. There won't be anything left of you."

Olham struggled out of his lethargy. "Can't you tell me—"

"Certainly, I'll tell you." Peters nodded. "Two days ago we received a report that an Outspace ship had penetrated the protec-bubble. The ship let off a spy in the form of a humanoid robot. The robot was to destroy a particular human being and take his place."

Peters looked calmly at Olham.

"Inside the robot was a U-Bomb. Our agent did not know how the bomb was to be detonated, but he conjectured that it might be by a particular spoken phrase, a certain group of words. The robot would live the life of the person he killed, entering into his usual activities, his job, his social life. He had been constructed to resemble that person. No one would know the difference."

Olham's face went sickly chalk.

"The person whom the robot was to impersonate was Spence Olham, a high-ranking official at one of the research Projects. Because this particular Project was approaching crucial stage, the presence of an animate bomb, moving toward the center of the Project—"

Olham stared down at his hands. "*But I'm Olham!*"

"Once the robot had located and killed Olham it was a simple matter to take over his life. The robot was probably released from the ship eight days ago. The substitution was probably accomplished over the last weekend, when Olham went for a short walk in the hills."

"But I'm Olham." He turned to Nelson, sitting at the controls. "Don't you recognize me? You've known me for twenty years. Don't you remember how we went to college together?" He stood up. "You and I were at the University. We had the same room." He went toward Nelson.

"Stay away from me!" Nelson snarled.

"Listen. Remember our second year? Remember that girl? What was her name—" He rubbed his forehead. "The one with the dark hair. The one we met over at Ted's place."

"Stop!" Nelson waved the gun frantically. "I don't want to hear any more. You killed him! You . . . machine."

Olham looked at Nelson. "You're wrong. I don't know what happened, but the robot never reached me. Something must have gone wrong. Maybe the ship crashed." He turned to Peters. "I'm Olham. I know it. No transfer was made. I'm the same as I've always been."

He touched himself, running his hands over his body. "There must be some way to prove it. Take me back to Earth. An X-ray examination, a neurological study, anything like that will show you. Or maybe we can find the crashed ship."

Neither Peters nor Nelson spoke.

"I am Olham," he said again. "I know I am. But I can't prove it."

"The robot," Peters said, "would be unaware that he was not the real Spence Olham. He would become Olham in mind as well as body. He was given an artificial memory system, false recall. He would look like him, have his memories, his thoughts and interests, perform his job.

"But there would be one difference. Inside the robot is a U-Bomb, ready to explode at the trigger phrase." Peters moved a little away. "That's the one difference. That's why we're taking you to the Moon. They'll disassemble you and remove the bomb. Maybe it will explode, but it won't matter, not there."

Olham sat down slowly.

"We'll be there soon," Nelson said.

He lay back, thinking frantically, as the ship dropped slowly down. Under them was the pitted surface of the Moon, the endless expanse of ruin. What could he do? What would save him?

"Get ready," Peters said.

In a few minutes he would be dead. Down below he could see a tiny dot, a building of some kind. There were men in the building, the demolition team, waiting to tear him to bits. They would rip him open, pull off his arms and legs, break him apart. When they found no bomb they would be surprised; they would know, but it would be too late.

Olham looked around the small cabin. Nelson was still holding the gun. There was no chance there. If he could get to a doctor, have an examination made—that was the only way. Mary could help him. He thought frantically, his mind racing. Only a few minutes, just a little time left. If he could contact her, get word to her some way.

"Easy," Peters said. The ship came down slowly, bumping on the rough ground. There was silence.

"Listen," Olham said thickly. "I can prove I'm Spence Olham. Get a doctor. Bring him here—"

"There's the squad," Nelson pointed. "They're coming." He glanced nervously at Olham. "I hope nothing happens."

"We'll be gone before they start work," Peters said. "We'll be out of here in a moment." He put on his pressure suit. When he had finished he took the gun from Nelson. "I'll watch him for a moment."

Nelson put on his pressure suit, hurrying awkwardly. "How about him?" He indicated Olham. "Will he need one?"

"No." Peters shook his head. "Robots probably don't require oxygen."

The group of men were almost to the ship. They halted, waiting. Peters signaled to them.

"Come on!" He waved his hand and the men approached warily; stiff, grotesque figures in their inflated suits.

"If you open the door," Olham said, "it means my death. It will be murder."

"Open the door," Nelson said. He reached for the handle.

Olham watched him. He saw the man's hand tighten around the metal rod. In a moment the door would swing back, the air in the ship would rush out. He would die, and presently they would realize their mistake. Perhaps at some other time, when there was no war, men might not act this way, hurrying an individual to his death because they were afraid. Everyone was frightened, everyone was willing to sacrifice the individual because of the group fear.

He was being killed because they could not wait to be sure of his guilt. There was not enough time.

He looked at Nelson. Nelson had been his friend for years. They had gone to school together. He had been best man at his wedding. Now Nelson was going to kill him. But Nelson was not wicked; it was not his fault. It was the times. Perhaps it had been the same way during the plagues. When men had shown a spot they probably had been killed, too, without a moment's hesitation, without proof, on suspicion alone. In times of danger there was no other way.

He did not blame them. But he had to live. His life was too precious to be sacrificed. Olham thought quickly. What could he do? Was there anything? He looked around.

"Here goes," Nelson said.

"You're right," Olham said. The sound of his own voice surprised him. It was the strength of desperation. "I have no need of air. Open the door."

They paused, looking at him in curious alarm.

"Go ahead. Open it. It makes no difference." Olham's hand disappeared inside his jacket. "I wonder how far you two can run?"

"Run?"

"You have fifteen seconds to live." Inside his jacket his fingers twisted, his arm suddenly rigid. He relaxed, smiling a little. "You were wrong about the trigger phrase. In that respect you were mistaken. Fourteen seconds, now."

Two shocked faces stared at him from the pressure suits. Then they were struggling, running, tearing the door open. The air shrieked out, spilling into the void. Peters and Nelson bolted out of the ship. Olham came after them. He grasped the door and dragged it shut. The automatic pressure system chugged furiously, restoring the air. Olham let his breath out with a shudder.

One more second—

Beyond the window the two men had joined the group. The group scattered, running in all directions. One by one they threw themselves down, prone on the ground. Olham seated himself at the control board. He moved the dials into place. As the ship rose up into the air the men below scrambled to their feet and stared up, their mouths open.

"Sorry," Olham murmured, "but I've got to get back to Earth."

He headed the ship back the way it had come.

It was night. All around the ship crickets chirped, disturbing the chill darkness. Olham bent over the vidscreen. Gradually the image formed; the call had gone through without trouble. He breathed a sigh of relief.

"Mary," he said. The woman stared at him. She gasped.

"Spence! Where are you? What's happened?"

"I can't tell you. Listen, I have to talk fast. They may break this call off any minute. Go to the Project grounds and get Dr. Chamberlain. If he isn't there, get any doctor. Bring him to the house and have him stay there. Have him bring equipment, X-ray, fluoroscope, everything."

"But—"

"Do as I say. Hurry. Have him get it ready in an hour." Olham leaned toward the screen. "Is everything all right? Are you alone?"

"Alone?"

"Is anyone with you? Has . . . has Nelson or anyone contacted you?"

"No. Spence, I don't understand."

"All right. I'll see you at the house in an hour. And don't tell anyone anything. Get Chamberlain there on any pretext. Say you're very ill."

He broke the connection and looked at his watch. A moment later he left the ship, stepping down into the darkness. He had a half mile to go.

He began to walk.

One light showed in the window, the study light. He watched it, kneeling against the fence. There was no sound, no movement of any kind. He held his watch up and read it by starlight. Almost an hour had passed.

Along the street a shoot bug came. It went on.

Olham looked toward the house. The doctor should have already come. He should be inside, waiting with Mary. A thought struck him. Had she been able to leave the house? Perhaps they had intercepted her. Maybe he was moving into a trap.

But what else could he do?

With a doctor's records, photographs, and reports, there was a chance, a chance of proof. If he could be examined, if he could remain alive long enough for them to study him—

He could prove it that way. It was probably the only way. His one hope lay inside the house. Dr. Chamberlain was a respected man. He was the staff doctor for the Project. He would know, his word on the matter would have meaning. He could overcome their hysteria, their madness, with facts.

Madness—That was what it was. If only they would wait, act slowly, take their time. But they could not wait. He had to die, die at once, without proof, without any kind of trial or examination. The simplest test would tell, but they had no time for the simplest test. They could think only of the danger. Danger, and nothing more.

He stood up and moved toward the house. He came up on the porch. At the door he paused, listening. Still no sound. The house was absolutely still.

Too still.

Olham stood on the porch, unmoving. They were trying to be silent inside. Why? It was a small house; only a few feet away, beyond the door,

Mary and Dr. Chamberlain should be standing. Yet he could hear nothing, no sound of voices, nothing at all. He looked at the door. It was a door he had opened and closed a thousand times, every morning and every night.

He put his hand on the knob. Then, all at once, he reached out and touched the bell instead. The bell pealed, off some place in the back of the house. Olham smiled. He could hear movement.

Mary opened the door. As soon as he saw her face he knew.

He ran, throwing himself into the bushes. A security officer shoved Mary out of the way, firing past her. The bushes burst apart. Olham wriggled around the side of the house. He leaped up and ran, racing frantically into the darkness. A searchlight snapped on, a beam of light circling past him.

He crossed the road and squeezed over a fence. He jumped down and made his way across a backyard. Behind him men were coming, security officers, shouting to each other as they came. Olham gasped for breath, his chest rising and falling.

Her face—He had known at once. The set lips, the terrified, wretched eyes. Suppose he had gone ahead, pushed open the door, and entered! They had tapped the call and come at once, as soon as he had broken off. Probably she believed their account. No doubt she thought he was the robot, too.

Olham ran on and on. He was losing the officers, dropping them behind. Apparently they were not much good at running. He climbed a hill and made his way down the other side. In a moment he would be back at the ship. But where to, this time? He slowed down, stopping. He could see the ship already, outlined against the sky, where he had parked it. The settlement was behind him; he was on the outskirts of the wilderness between the inhabited places, where the forests and desolation began. He crossed a barren field and entered the trees.

As he came toward it, the door of the ship opened.

Peters stepped out, framed against the light. In his arms was a heavy Boris gun. Olham stopped, rigid. Peters stared around him, into the darkness. "I know you're there, someplace," he said. "Come on up here, Olham. There are security men all around you."

Olham did not move.

"Listen to me. We will catch you very shortly. Apparently you still do not believe you're the robot. Your call to the woman indicates that you are still under the illusion created by your artificial memories.

"But you *are* the robot. You are the robot, and inside you is the bomb. Any moment the trigger phrase may be spoken, by you, by someone else, by anyone. When that happens the bomb will destroy everything for miles around. The Project, the woman, all of us will be killed. Do you understand?"

Olham said nothing. He was listening. Men were moving toward him, slipping through the woods.

"If you don't come out, we'll catch you. It will be only a matter of time. We no longer plan to remove you to the Moon base. You will be destroyed on sight, and we will have to take the chance that the bomb will detonate. I have ordered every available security officer into the area. The whole county is being searched, inch by inch. There is no place you can go. Around this wood is a cordon of armed men. You have about six hours left before the last inch is covered."

Olham moved away. Peters went on speaking; he had not seen him at all. It was too dark to see anyone. But Peters was right. There was no place he could go. He was beyond the settlement, on the outskirts where the woods began. He could hide for a time, but eventually they would catch him.

Only a matter of time.

Olham walked quietly through the wood. Mile by mile, each part of the county was being measured off, laid bare, searched, studied, examined. The cordon was coming all the time, squeezing him into a smaller and smaller space.

What was there left? He had lost the ship, the one hope of escape. They were at his home; his wife was with them, believing, no doubt, that the real Olham had been killed. He clenched his fists. Some place there was a wrecked Outspace needle-ship, and in it the remains of the robot. Somewhere nearby the ship had crashed and broken up.

And the robot lay inside, destroyed.

A faint hope stirred him. What if he could find the remains? If he could show them the wreckage, the remains of the ship, the robot—

But where? Where would he find it?

He walked on, lost in thought. Some place, not too far off, probably. The ship would have landed close to the Project; the robot would have expected to go the rest of the way on foot. He went up the side of a hill and looked around. Crashed and burned. Was there some clue, some hint? Had he read anything, heard anything? Some place close by, within walking distance. Some wild place, a remote spot where there would be no people.

Suddenly Olham smiled. Crashed and burned—

Sutton Wood.

He increased his pace.

It was morning. Sunlight filtered down through the broken trees, onto the man crouching at the edge of the clearing. Olham glanced up from time to time, listening. They were not far off, only a few minutes away. He smiled.

Down below him, strewn across the clearing and into the charred stumps that had been Sutton Wood, lay a tangled mass of wreckage. In the sunlight it glittered a little, gleaming darkly. He had not had too much trouble finding it. Sutton Wood was a place he knew well; he had climbed around it many times in his life, when he was younger. He had known where he would find the remains. There was one peak that jutted up suddenly, without a warning.

A descending ship, unfamiliar with the Wood, had little chance of missing it. And now he squatted, looking down at the ship, or what remained of it.

Olham stood up. He could hear them, only a little distance away, coming together, talking in low tones. He tensed himself. Everything depended on who first saw him. If it was Nelson, he had no chance. Nelson would fire at once. He would be dead before they saw the ship. But if he had time to call out, hold them off for a moment—That was all he needed. Once they saw the ship he would be safe.

But if they fired first—

A charred branch cracked. A figure appeared, coming forward uncertainly. Olham took a deep breath. Only a few seconds remained, perhaps the last seconds of his life. He raised his arms, peering intently.

It was Peters.

"Peters!" Olham waved his arms. Peters lifted his gun, aiming. "Don't fire!" His voice shook. "Wait a minute. Look past me, across the clearing."

"I've found him," Peters shouted. Security men came pouring out of the burned woods around him.

"Don't shoot. Look past me. The ship, the needle-ship. The Outspace ship. Look!"

Peters hesitated. The gun wavered.

"It's down there," Olham said rapidly. "I knew I'd find it here. The burned wood. Now you believe me. You'll find the remains of the robot in the ship. Look, will you?"

"There is something down there," one of the men said nervously.

"Shoot him!" a voice said. It was Nelson.

"Wait." Peters turned sharply. "I'm in charge. Don't anyone fire. Maybe he's telling the truth."

"Shoot him," Nelson said. "He killed Olham. Any minute he may kill us all. If the bomb goes off—"

"Shut up." Peters advanced toward the slope. He stared down. "Look at that." He waved two men up to him. "Go down there and see what that is."

The men raced down the slope, across the clearing. They bent down, poking in the ruins of the ship.

"Well?" Peters called.

Olham held his breath. He smiled a little. It must be there; he had not had time to look, himself, but it had to be there. Suddenly doubt assailed him. Suppose the robot had lived long enough to wander away? Suppose his body had been completely destroyed, burned to ashes by the fire?

He licked his lips. Perspiration came out on his forehead. Nelson was staring at him, his face still livid. His chest rose and fell.

"Kill him," Nelson said. "Before he kills us."

The two men stood up.

"What have you found?" Peters said. He held the gun steady. "Is there anything there?"

"Looks like something. It's a needle-ship, all right. There's something beside it."

"I'll look." Peters strode past Olham. Olham watched him go down the hill and up to the men. The others were following after him, peering to see.

"It's a body of some sort," Peters said. "Look at it!"

Olham came along with them. They stood around in a circle, staring down.

On the ground, bent and twisted in a strange shape, was a grotesque form. It looked human, perhaps; except that it was bent so strangely, the arms and legs flung off in all directions. The mouth was open; the eyes stared glassily.

"Like a machine that's run down," Peters murmured. Olham smiled feebly. "Well?" he said.

Peters looked at him. "I can't believe it. You were telling the truth all the time."

"The robot never reached me," Olham said. He took out a cigarette and lit it. "It was destroyed when the ship crashed. You were all too busy with the war to wonder why an out-of-the-way woods would suddenly catch fire and burn. Now you know."

He stood smoking, watching the men. They were dragging the grotesque remains from the ship. The body was stiff, the arms and legs rigid.

"You'll find the bomb now," Olham said. The men laid the body on the ground. Peters bent down.

"I think I see the corner of it." He reached out, touching the body.

The chest of the corpse had been laid open. Within the gaping tear something glinted, something metal. The men stared at the metal without speaking.

"That would have destroyed us all, if it had lived," Peters said. "That metal box there."

There was silence.

"I think we owe you something," Peters said to Olham. "This must have been a nightmare to you. If you hadn't escaped, we would have—" He broke off.

Olham put out his cigarette. "I knew, of course, that the robot had never reached me. But I had no way of proving it. Sometimes it isn't possible to prove a thing right away. That was the whole trouble. There wasn't any way I could demonstrate that I was myself."

"How about a vacation?" Peters said. "I think we might work out a month's vacation for you. You could take it easy, relax."

"I think right now I want to go home," Olham said.

"All right, then," Peters said. "Whatever you say."

Nelson had squatted down on the ground, beside the corpse. He reached out toward the glint of metal visible within the chest.

"Don't touch it," Olham said. "It might still go off. We better let the demolition squad take care of it later on."

Nelson said nothing. Suddenly he grabbed hold of the metal, reaching his hand inside the chest. He pulled.

"What are you doing?" Olham cried.

Nelson stood up. He was holding on to the metal object. His face was blank with terror. It was a metal knife, an Outspace needle-knife, covered with blood.

"This killed him," Nelson whispered. "My friend was killed with this." He looked at Olham. "You killed him with this and left him beside the ship."

Olham was trembling. His teeth chattered. He looked from the knife to the body. "This can't be Olham," he said. His mind spun, everything was whirling. "Was I wrong?"

He gaped.

"But if that's Olham, then I must be—"

He did not complete the sentence, only the first phrase. The blast was visible all the way to Alpha Centauri.

THE KING OF THE ELVES

It was raining and getting dark. Sheets of water blew along the row of pumps at the edge of the filling station; the tree across the highway bent against the wind.

Shadrach Jones stood just inside the doorway of the little building, leaning against an oil drum. The door was open and gusts of rain blew in onto the wood floor. It was late; the sun had set, and the air was turning cold. Shadrach reached into his coat and brought out a cigar. He bit the end off it and lit it carefully, turning away from the door. In the gloom, the cigar burst into life, warm and glowing. Shadrach took a deep draw. He buttoned his coat around him and stepped out onto the pavement.

"Darn," he said. "What a night!" Rain buffeted him, wind blew at him. He looked up and down the highway, squinting. There were no cars in sight. He shook his head, locked up the gasoline pumps.

He went back into the building and pulled the door shut behind him. He opened the cash register and counted the money he'd taken in during the day. It was not much.

Not much, but enough for one old man. Enough to buy him tobacco and firewood and magazines, so that he could be comfortable as he waited for the occasional cars to come by. Not very many cars came along the highway anymore. The highway had begun to fall into disrepair; there were many cracks in its dry, rough surface, and most cars preferred to take the big state highway that ran beyond the hills. There was nothing in Derryville to attract them, to make them turn toward it. Derryville was a small town, too small to bring in any of the major industries, too small to be very important to anyone. Sometimes hours went by without—

Shadrach tensed. His fingers closed over the money. From outside came a sound, the melodic ring of the signal wire stretched along the pavement.

Dinggg!

Shadrach dropped the money into the till and pushed the drawer closed. He stood up slowly and walked toward the door, listening. At the door, he snapped off the light and waited in the darkness, staring out.

He could see no car there. The rain was pouring down, swirling with the wind; clouds of mist moved along the road. And something was standing beside the pumps.

He opened the door and stepped out. At first, his eyes could make nothing out. Then the old man swallowed uneasily.

Two tiny figures stood in the rain, holding a kind of platform between them. Once, they might have been gaily dressed in bright garments, but now their clothes hung limp and sodden, dripping in the rain. They glanced halfheartedly at Shadrach. Water streaked their tiny faces, great drops of water. Their robes blew about them with the wind, lashing and swirling.

On the platform, something stirred. A small head turned wearily, peering at Shadrach. In the dim light, a rain-streaked helmet glinted dully.

"Who are you?" Shadrach said.

The figure on the platform raised itself up. "I'm the King of the Elves and I'm wet."

Shadrach stared in astonishment.

"That's right," one of the bearers said. "We're all wet."

A small group of Elves came straggling up, gathering around their king. They huddled together forlornly, silently.

"The King of the Elves," Shadrach repeated. "Well, I'll be darned."

Could it be true? They were very small, all right, and their dripping clothes were strange and oddly colored.

But *Elves*?

"I'll be darned. Well, whatever you are, you shouldn't be out on a night like this."

"Of course not," the king murmured. "No fault of our own. No fault . . ." His voice trailed off into a choking cough. The Elf soldiers peered anxiously at the platform.

"Maybe you better bring him inside," Shadrach said. "My place is up the road. He shouldn't be out in the rain."

"Do you think we like being out on a night like this?" one of the bearers muttered. "Which way is it? Direct us."

Shadrach pointed up the road. "Over there. Just follow me. I'll get a fire going."

He went down the road, feeling his way onto the first of the flat stone steps that he and Phineas Judd had laid during the summer. At the top of the steps, he looked back. The platform was coming slowly along, swaying a little from side to side. Behind it, the Elf soldiers picked their way, a tiny column of silent dripping creatures, unhappy and cold.

"I'll get the fire started," Shadrach said. He hurried them into the house.

Wearily, the Elf King lay back against the pillow. After sipping hot chocolate, he had relaxed and his heavy breathing sounded suspiciously like a snore.

Shadrach shifted in discomfort.

"I'm sorry," the Elf King said suddenly, opening his eyes. He rubbed his forehead. "I must have drifted off. Where was I?"

"You should retire, Your Majesty," one of the soldiers said sleepily. "It is late and these are hard times."

"True," the Elf King said, nodding. "Very true." He looked up at the towering figure of Shadrach, standing before the fireplace, a glass of beer in his hand. "Mortal, we thank you for your hospitality. Normally, we do not impose on human beings."

"It's those Trolls," another of the soldiers said, curled up on a cushion of the couch.

"Right," another soldier agreed. He sat up, groping for his sword. "Those reeking Trolls, digging and croaking—"

"You see," the Elf King went on, "as our party was crossing from the Great Low Steps toward the Castle, where it lies in the hollow of the Towering Mountains—"

"You mean Sugar Ridge," Shadrach supplied helpfully.

"The Towering Mountains. Slowly we made our way. A rainstorm came up. We became confused. All at once a group of Trolls appeared, crashing through the underbrush. We left the woods and sought safety on the Endless Path—"

"The highway. Route Twenty."

"So that is why we're here." The Elf King paused a moment. "Harder and harder it rained. The wind blew around us, cold and bitter. For an endless time we toiled along. We had no idea where we were going or what would become of us."

The Elf King looked up at Shadrach. "We knew only this: Behind us, the Trolls were coming, creeping through the woods, marching through the rain, crushing everything before them."

He put his hand to his mouth and coughed, bending forward. All the Elves waited anxiously until he was done. He straightened up.

"It was kind of you to allow us to come inside. We will not trouble you for long. It is not the custom of the Elves—"

Again he coughed, covering his face with his hand. The Elves drew toward him apprehensively. At last the king stirred. He sighed.

"What's the matter?" Shadrach asked. He went over and took the cup of chocolate from the fragile hand. The Elf King lay back, his eyes shut.

"He has to rest," one of the soldiers said. "Where's your room? The sleeping room."

"Upstairs," Shadrach said. "I'll show you where."

Late that night, Shadrach sat by himself in the dark, deserted living room, deep in meditation. The Elves were asleep above him, upstairs in the bedroom, the Elf King in the bed, the others curled up together on the rug.

The house was silent. Outside, the rain poured down endlessly, blowing against the house. Shadrach could hear the tree branches slapping in the wind. He clasped and unclasped his hands. What a strange business it was—all these Elves, with their old, sick king, their piping voices. How anxious and peevish they were!

But pathetic, too; so small and wet, with water dripping down from them, and all their gay robes limp and soggy.

The Trolls—what were they like? Unpleasant and not very clean. Something about digging, breaking, and pushing through the woods . . .

Suddenly, Shadrach laughed in embarrassment. What was the matter with him, believing all this? He put his cigar out angrily, his ears red. What was going on? What kind of joke was this?

Elves? Shadrach grunted in indignation. Elves in Derryville? In the middle of Colorado? Maybe there were Elves in Europe. Maybe in Ireland. He had heard of that. But here? Upstairs in his own house, sleeping in his own bed?

"I've heard just about enough of this," he said. "I'm not an idiot, you know."

He turned toward the stairs, feeling for the banister in the gloom. He began to climb.

Above him, a light went on abruptly. A door opened.

Two Elves came slowly out onto the landing. They looked down at him. Shadrach halted halfway up the stairs. Something on their faces made him stop.

"What's the matter?" he asked hesitantly.

They did not answer. The house was turning cold, cold and dark, with the chill of the rain outside and the chill of the unknown inside.

"What is it?" he said again. "What's the matter?"

"The King is dead," one of the Elves said. "He died a few moments ago."

Shadrach stared up, wide-eyed. "He did? But—"

"He was very cold and very tired." The Elves turned away, going back into the room, slowly and quietly shutting the door.

Shadrach stood, his fingers on the banister, hard, lean fingers, strong and thin.

He nodded his head blankly.

"I see," he said to the closed door. "He's dead."

The Elf soldiers stood around him in a solemn circle. The living room was bright with sunlight, the cold white glare of early morning.

"But wait," Shadrach said. He plucked at his necktie. "I have to get to the filling station. Can't you talk to me when I come home?"

The faces of the Elf soldiers were serious and concerned.

"Listen," one of them said. "Please hear us out. It is very important to us."

Shadrach looked past them. Through the window he saw the highway, steaming in the heat of day, and down a little way was the gas station, glittering brightly. And even as he watched, a car came up to it and honked thinly, impatiently. When nobody came out of the station, the car drove off again down the road.

"We beg you," a soldier said.

Shadrach looked down at the ring around him, the anxious faces, scored with concern and trouble. Strangely, he had always thought of Elves as carefree beings, flitting without worry or sense—

"Go ahead," he said. "I'm listening." He went over to the big chair and sat down. The Elves came up around him. They conversed among themselves for a moment, whispering, murmuring distantly. Then they turned toward Shadrach.

The old man waited, his arms folded.

"We cannot be without a king," one of the soldiers said. "We could not survive. Not these days."

"The Trolls," another added. "They multiply very fast. They are terrible beasts. They're heavy and ponderous, crude, bad-smelling—"

"The odor of them is awful. They come up from the dark wet places, under the earth, where the blind, groping plants feed in silence, far below the surface, far from the sun."

"Well, you ought to elect a king, then," Shadrach suggested. "I don't see any problem there."

"We do not elect the King of the Elves," a soldier said. "The old king must name his successor."

"Oh," Shadrach replied. "Well, there's nothing wrong with that method."

"As our old king lay dying, a few distant words came forth from his lips," a soldier said. "We bent closer, frightened and unhappy, listening."

"Important, all right," agreed Shadrach. "Not something you'd want to miss."

"He spoke the name of him who will lead us."

"Good. You caught it, then. Well, where's the difficulty?"

"The name he spoke was—was your name."

Shadrach stared. "*Mine?*"

"The dying king said: 'Make him, the towering mortal, your king. Many things will come if he leads the Elves into battle against the Trolls. I see the rising once again of the Elf Empire, as it was in the old days, as it was before—"

"Me!" Shadrach leaped up. "Me? King of the Elves?"

Shadrach walked about the room, his hands in his pockets. "Me, Shadrach Jones, King of the Elves." He grinned a little. "I sure never thought of it before."

He went to the mirror over the fireplace and studied himself. He saw his thin, graying hair, his bright eyes, dark skin, his big Adam's apple.

"King of the Elves," he said. "King of the Elves. Wait till Phineas Judd hears about this. Wait till I tell him!"

Phineas Judd would certainly be surprised!

Above the filling station, the sun shown, high in the clear blue sky.

Phineas Judd sat playing with the accelerator of his old Ford truck. The motor raced and slowed. Phineas reached over and turned the ignition key off, then rolled the window all the way down.

"What did you say?" he asked. He took off his glasses and began to polish them, steel rims between slender, deft fingers that were patient from years of practice. He restored his glasses to his nose and smoothed what remained of his hair into place.

"What was it, Shadrach?" he said. "Let's hear that again."

"I'm King of the Elves," Shadrach repeated. He changed position, bringing his other foot up on the running board. "Who would have thought it? Me, Shadrach Jones, King of the Elves."

Phineas gazed at him. "How long have you been—King of the Elves, Shadrach?"

"Since the night before last."

"I see. The night before last." Phineas nodded. "I see. And what, may I ask, occurred the night before last?"

"The Elves came to my house. When the old king died, he told them that—"

A truck came rumbling up and the driver leaped out. "Water!" he said. "Where the hell is the hose?"

Shadrach turned reluctantly. "I'll get it." He turned back to Phineas.

"Maybe I can talk to you tonight when you come back from town. I want to tell you the rest. It's very interesting."

"Sure," Phineas said, starting up his little truck. "Sure, Shadrach. I'm very interested to hear."

He drove off down the road.

Later in the day, Dan Green ran his flivver up to the filling station.

"Hey, Shadrach," he called. "Come over here! I want to ask you something."

Shadrach came out of the little house, holding a waste-rag in his hand. "What is it?"

"Come here." Dan leaned out the window, a wide grin on his face, splitting his face from ear to ear. "Let me ask you something, will you?"

"Sure."

"Is it true? Are you really the King of the Elves?"

Shadrach flushed a little. "I guess I am," he admitted, looking away. "That's what I am, all right."

Dan's grin faded. "Hey, you trying to kid me? What's the gag?"

Shadrach became angry. "What do you mean? Sure, I'm the King of the Elves. And anyone who says I'm not—"

"All right, Shadrach," Dan said, starting up the flivver quickly. "Don't get mad. I was just wondering."

Shadrach looked very strange.

"All right," Dan said. "You don't hear me arguing, do you?"

By the end of the day, everyone around knew about Shadrach and how he had suddenly become the King of the Elves. Pop Richey, who ran the Lucky Store in Derryville, claimed Shadrach was doing it to drum up trade for the filling station.

"He's a smart old fellow," Pop said. "Not very many cars go along there anymore. He knows what he's doing."

"I don't know," Dan Green disagreed. "You should hear him, I think he really believes it."

"King of the Elves?" They all began to laugh. "Wonder what he'll say next."

Phineas Judd pondered. "I've known Shadrach for years. I can't figure it out." He frowned, his face wrinkled and disapproving. "I don't like it."

Dan looked at him. "Then you think he believes it?"

"Sure," Phineas said. "Maybe I'm wrong, but I really think he does."

"But how could he believe it?" Pop asked. "Shadrach is no fool. He's been in business for a long time. He must be getting something out of it, the way I see it. But what, if it isn't to build up the filling station?"

"Why, don't you know what he's getting?" Dan said, grinning. His gold tooth shone.

"What?" Pop demanded.

"He's got a whole kingdom to himself, that's what—to do with like he wants. How would you like that, Pop? Wouldn't you like to be King of the Elves and not have to run this old store anymore?"

"There isn't anything wrong with my store," Pop said. "I ain't ashamed to run it. Better than being a clothing salesman."

Dan flushed. "Nothing wrong with that, either." He looked at Phineas. "Isn't that right? Nothing wrong with selling clothes, is there, Phineas?"

Phineas was staring down at the floor. He glanced up. "What? What was that?"

"What you thinking about?" Pop wanted to know. "You look worried."

"I'm worried about Shadrach," Phineas said. "He's getting old. Sitting out there by himself all the time, in the cold weather, with the rainwater running over the floor—it blows something awful in the winter, along the highway—"

"Then you *do* think he believes it?" Dan persisted. "You *don't* think he's getting something out of it?"

Phineas shook his head absently and did not answer.

The laughter died down. They all looked at one another.

That night, as Shadrach was locking up the filling station, a small figure came toward him from the darkness.

"Hey!" Shadrach called out. "Who are you?"

An Elf soldier came into the light, blinking. He was dressed in a little gray robe, buckled at the waist with a band of silver. On his feet were little leather boots. He carried a short sword at his side.

"I have a serious message for you," the Elf said. "Now, where did I put it?"

He searched his robe while Shadrach waited. The Elf brought out a tiny scroll and unfastened it, breaking the wax expertly. He handed it to Shadrach.

"What's it say?" Shadrach asked. He bent over, his eyes close to the vellum. "I don't have my glasses with me. Can't quite make out these little letters."

"The Trolls are moving. They've heard that the old king is dead, and they're rising, in all the hills and valleys around. They will try to break the Elf Kingdom into fragments, scatter the Elves—"

"I see," Shadrach said. "Before your new king can really get started."

"That's right." The Elf soldier nodded. "This is a crucial moment for the Elves. For centuries, our existence has been precarious. There are so many Trolls, and Elves are very frail and often take sick—"

"Well, what should I do? Are there any suggestions?"

"You're supposed to meet with us under the Great Oak tonight. We'll take you into the Elf Kingdom, and you and your staff will plan and map the defense of the Kingdom."

"What?" Shadrach looked uncomfortable. "But I haven't eaten dinner. And my gas station—tomorrow is Saturday, and a lot of cars—"

"But you are King of the Elves," the soldier said.

Shadrach put his hand to his chin and rubbed it slowly.

"That's right," he replied. "I am, ain't I?"

The Elf soldier bowed.

"I wish I'd known this sort of thing was going to happen," Shadrach said. "I didn't suppose being King of the Elves—"

He broke off, hoping for an interruption. The Elf soldier watched him calmly, without expression.

"Maybe you ought to have someone else as your king," Shadrach decided. "I don't know very much about war and things like that, fighting and all that sort of business." He paused, shrugged his shoulders. "It's nothing I've ever mixed in. They don't have wars here in Colorado. I mean they don't have wars between human beings."

Still the Elf soldier remained silent.

"Why was I picked?" Shadrach went on helplessly, twisting his hands.

"I don't know anything about it. What made him go and pick me? Why didn't he pick somebody else?"

"He trusted you," the Elf said. "You brought him inside your house, out of the rain. He knew that you expected nothing for it, that there was nothing you wanted. He had known few who gave and asked nothing back."

"Oh." Shadrach thought it over. At last he looked up. "But what about my gas station? And my house? And what will they say, Dan Green and Pop down at the store—"

The Elf soldier moved away, out of the light. "I have to go. It's getting late, and at night the Trolls come out. I don't want to be too far away from the others."

"Sure," Shadrach said.

"The Trolls are afraid of nothing, now that the old king is dead. They forage everywhere. No one is safe."

"Where did you say the meeting is to be? And what time?"

"At the Great Oak. When the moon sets tonight, just as it leaves the sky."

"I'll be there, I guess," Shadrach said. "I suppose you're right. The King of the Elves can't afford to let his kingdom down when it needs him most."

He looked around, but the Elf soldier was already gone.

Shadrach walked up the highway, his mind full of doubts and wonderings. When he came to the first of the flat stone steps, he stopped.

"And the old oak tree is on Phineas's farm! What'll Phineas say?"

But he was the Elf King and the Trolls were moving in the hills. Shadrach stood listening to the rustle of the wind as it moved through the trees beyond the highway, and along the far slopes and hills.

Trolls? Were there really Trolls there, rising up, bold and confident in the darkness of the night, afraid of nothing, afraid of no one?

And this business of being Elf King . . .

Shadrach went on up the steps, his lips pressed tight. When he reached the top of the stone steps, the last rays of sunlight had already faded. It was night.

Phineas Judd stared out the window. He swore and shook his head. Then he went quickly to the door and ran out onto the porch. In the cold moonlight a dim figure was walking slowly across the lower field, coming toward the house along the cow trail.

"Shadrach!" Phineas cried. "What's wrong? What are you doing out this time of night?"

Shadrach stopped and put his fists stubbornly on his hips.

"You go back home," Phineas said. "What's got into you?"

"I'm sorry, Phineas," Shadrach answered. "I'm sorry I have to go over your land. But I have to meet somebody at the old oak tree."

"At this time of night?"

Shadrach bowed his head.

"What's the matter with you, Shadrach? Who in the world you going to meet in the middle of the night on my farm?"

"I have to meet with the Elves. We're going to plan out the war with the Trolls."

"Well, I'll be damned," Phineas Judd said. He went back inside the house and slammed the door. For a long time he stood thinking. Then he went back out on the porch again. "What did you say you were doing? You don't have to tell me, of course, but I just—"

"I have to meet the Elves at the old oak tree. We must have a general council of war against the Trolls."

"Yes, indeed. The Trolls. Have to watch for the Trolls all the time."

"Trolls are everywhere," Shadrach stated, nodding his head. "I never realized it before. You can't forget them or ignore them. They never forget you. They're always planning, watching you—"

Phineas gaped at him, speechless.

"Oh, by the way," Shadrach said. "I may be gone for some time. It depends on how long this business is going to take. I haven't had much experience in fighting Trolls, so I'm not sure. But I wonder if you'd mind looking after the gas station for me, about twice a day, maybe once in the morning and once at night, to make sure no one's broken in or anything like that."

"You're going away?" Phineas came quickly down the stairs. "What's all this about Trolls? Why are you going?"

Shadrach patiently repeated what he had said.

"But what for?"

"Because I'm the Elf King. I have to lead them."

There was silence. "I see," Phineas said, at last. "That's right, you *did* mention it before, didn't you? But, Shadrach, why don't you come inside for a while and you can tell me about the Trolls and drink some coffee and—"

"Coffee?" Shadrach looked up at the pale moon above him, the moon and the bleak sky. The world was still and dead and the night was very cold and the moon would not be setting for some time.

Shadrach shivered.

"It's a cold night," Phineas urged. "Too cold to be out. Come on in—"

"I guess I have a little time," Shadrach admitted. "A cup of coffee wouldn't do any harm. But I can't stay very long . . ."

Shadrach stretched his legs out and sighed. "This coffee sure tastes good, Phineas."

Phineas sipped a little and put his cup down. The living room was quiet and warm. It was a very neat little living room with solemn pictures on the walls, gray uninteresting pictures that minded their own business. In the corner was a small reed organ with sheet music carefully arranged on top of it.

Shadrach noticed the organ and smiled. "You still play, Phineas?"

"Not much anymore. The bellows don't work right. One of them won't come back up."

"I suppose I could fix it sometime. If I'm around, I mean."

"That would be fine," Phineas said. "I was thinking of asking you."

"Remember how you used to play 'Vilia' and Dan Green came up with that lady who worked for Pop during the summer? The one who wanted to open a pottery shop?"

"I sure do," Phineas said.

Presently, Shadrach set down his coffee cup and shifted in his chair.

"You want more coffee?" Phineas asked quickly. He stood up. "A little more?"

"Maybe a little. But I have to be going pretty soon."

"It's a bad night to be outside."

Shadrach looked through the window. It was darker; the moon had almost gone down. The fields were stark. Shadrach shivered. "I wouldn't disagree with you," he said.

Phineas turned eagerly. "Look, Shadrach. You go on home where it's warm. You can come out and fight Trolls some other night. There'll always be Trolls. You said so yourself. Plenty of time to do that later, when the weather's better. When it's not so cold."

Shadrach rubbed his forehead wearily. "You know, it all seems like some sort of a crazy dream. When did I start talking about Elves and Trolls? When did it all begin?" His voice trailed off. "Thank you for the coffee." He got slowly to his feet. "It warmed me up a lot. And I appreciated the talk. Like old times, you and me sitting here the way we used to."

"Are you going?" Phineas hesitated. "*Home?*"

"I think I better. It's late."

Phineas got quickly to his feet. He led Shadrach to the door, one arm around his shoulder.

"All right, Shadrach, you go on home. Take a good hot bath before you go to bed. It'll fix you up. And maybe just a little snort of brandy to warm the blood."

Phineas opened the front door and they went slowly down the porch steps, onto the cold, dark ground.

"Yes, I guess I'll be going," Shadrach said. "Good night—"

"You go on home." Phineas patted him on the arm. "You run along home and take a good hot bath. And then go straight to bed."

"That's a good idea. Thank you, Phineas. I appreciate your kindness." Shadrach looked down at Phineas's hand on his arm. He had not been that close to Phineas for years.

Shadrach contemplated the hand. He wrinkled his brow, puzzled.

Phineas's hand was huge and rough and his arms were short. His fingers were blunt; his nails broken and cracked. Almost black, or so it seemed in the moonlight.

Shadrach looked up at Phineas. "Strange," he murmured.

"What's strange, Shadrach?"

In the moonlight, Phineas's face seemed oddly heavy and brutal. Shadrach had never noticed before how the jaw bulged, what a great protruding jaw it was. The skin was yellow and coarse, like parchment. Behind the glasses, the eyes were like two stones, cold and lifeless. The ears were immense, the hair stringy and matted.

Odd that he never noticed before. But he had never seen Phineas in the moonlight.

Shadrach stepped away, studying his old friend. From a few feet off, Phineas Judd seemed unusually short and squat. His legs were slightly bowed. His feet were enormous. And there was something else—

"What is it?" Phineas demanded, beginning to grow suspicious. "Is there something wrong?"

Something was completely wrong. And he had never noticed it, not in all the years they had been friends. All around Phineas Judd was an odor, a faint, pungent stench of rot, of decaying flesh, damp and moldy.

Shadrach glanced slowly about him. "Something wrong?" he echoed. "No, I wouldn't say that."

By the side of the house was an old rain barrel, half fallen apart. Shadrach walked over to it.

"No, Phineas. I wouldn't say there's something wrong."

"What are you doing?"

"Me?" Shadrach took hold of one of the barrel staves and pulled it loose. He walked back to Phineas, carrying the barrel stave carefully. "I'm King of the Elves. Who—or what—are you?"

Phineas roared and attacked with his great murderous shovel hands.

Shadrach smashed him over the head with the barrel stave. Phineas bellowed with rage and pain.

At the shattering sound, there was a clatter and from underneath the house came a furious horde of bounding, leaping creatures, dark bent-over things, their bodies heavy and squat, their feet and heads immense. Shadrach took one look at the flood of dark creatures pouring out from Phineas's basement. He knew what they were.

"Help!" Shadrach shouted. "Trolls! Help!"

The Trolls were all around him, grabbing hold of him, tugging at him, climbing up him, pummeling his face and body.

Shadrach fell to with the barrel stave, swung again and again, kicking Trolls with his feet, whacking them with the barrel stave. There seemed to be hundreds of them. More and more poured out from under Phineas's house, a surging black tide of pot-shaped creatures, their great eyes and teeth gleaming in the moonlight.

"Help!" Shadrach cried again, more feebly now. He was getting winded. His heart labored painfully. A Troll bit his wrist, clinging to his arm. Shadrach flung it away, pulling loose from the horde clutching his trouser legs, the barrel stave rising and falling.

One of the Trolls caught hold of the stave. A whole group of them helped, wrenching furiously, trying to pull it away. Shadrach hung on desperately. Trolls were all over him, on his shoulders, clinging to his coat, riding his arms, his legs, pulling his hair—

He heard a high-pitched clarion call from a long way off, the sound of some distant golden trumpet, echoing in the hills.

The Trolls suddenly stopped attacking. One of them dropped off Shadrach's neck. Another let go of his arm.

The call came again, this time more loudly.

"Elves!" a Troll rasped. He turned and moved toward the sound, grinding his teeth and spitting with fury.

"Elves!"

The Trolls swarmed forward, a growing wave of gnashing teeth and nails, pushing furiously toward the Elf columns. The Elves broke formation and joined battle, shouting with wild joy in their shrill, piping voices. The tide of Trolls rushed against them, Troll against Elf, shovel nails against golden sword, biting jaw against dagger.

"Kill the Elves!"

"Death to the Trolls!"

"Onward!"

"Forward!"

Shadrach fought desperately with the Trolls that were still clinging to him. He was exhausted, panting and gasping for breath. Blindly, he whacked on and on, kicking and jumping, throwing Trolls away from him, through the air and across the ground.

How long the battle raged, Shadrach never knew. He was lost in a sea of dark bodies, round and evil-smelling, clinging to him, tearing, biting, fastened to his nose and hair and fingers. He fought silently, grimly.

All around him, the Elf legions clashed with the Troll horde, little groups of struggling warriors on all sides.

Suddenly Shadrach stopped fighting. He raised his head, looking uncertainly around him. Nothing moved. Everything was silent. The fighting had ceased.

A few Trolls still clung to his arms and legs. Shadrach whacked one with the barrel stave. It howled and dropped to the ground. He staggered back, struggling with the last Troll, who hung tenaciously to his arm.

"Now you!" Shadrach gasped. He pried the Troll loose and flung it into the air. The Troll fell to the ground and scuttled off into the night.

There was nothing more. No Troll moved anywhere. All was silent across the bleak moon-swept fields.

Shadrach sank down on a stone. His chest rose and fell painfully. Red specks swam before his eyes. Weakly, he got out his pocket handkerchief and wiped his neck and face. He closed his eyes, shaking his head from side to side.

When he opened his eyes again, the Elves were coming toward him, gathering their legion together again. The Elves were disheveled and bruised. Their golden armor was gashed and torn. Their helmets were bent or missing. Most of their scarlet plumes were gone. Those that still remained were drooping and broken.

But the battle was over. The war was won. The Troll hordes had been put to flight.

Shadrach got slowly to his feet. The Elf warriors stood around him in a circle, gazing up at him with silent respect. One of them helped steady him as he put his handkerchief away in his pocket.

"Thank you," Shadrach murmured. "Thank you very much."

"The Trolls have been defeated," an Elf stated, still awed by what had happened.

Shadrach gazed around at the Elves. There were many of them, more than he had ever seen before. All the Elves had turned out for the battle. They were grim-faced, stern with the seriousness of the moment, weary from the terrible struggle.

"Yes, they're gone, all right," Shadrach said. He was beginning to get his breath. "That was a close call. I'm glad you fellows came when you did. I was just about finished, fighting them all by myself."

"All alone, the King of the Elves held off the entire Troll army," an Elf announced shrilly.

"Eh?" Shadrach said, taken aback. Then he smiled. "That's true, I *did* fight them alone for a while. I *did* hold off the Trolls all by myself. The whole darn Troll army."

"There is more," an Elf said.

Shadrach blinked. "More?"

"Look over here, O King, mightiest of all the Elves. This way. To the right."

The Elves led Shadrach over.

"What is it?" Shadrach murmured, seeing nothing at first. He gazed down, trying to pierce the darkness. "Could we have a torch over here?"

Some Elves brought little pine torches.

There, on the frozen ground, lay Phineas Judd, on his back. His eyes were blank and staring, his mouth half open. He did not move. His body was cold and stiff.

"He is dead," an Elf said solemnly.

Shadrach gulped in sudden alarm. Cold sweat stood out abruptly on his forehead. "My gosh! My old friend! What have I done?"

"You have slain the Great Troll."

Shadrach paused.

"I *what*?"

"You have slain the Great Troll, leader of all the Trolls."

"This has never happened before," another Elf exclaimed excitedly. "The Great Troll has lived for centuries. Nobody imagined he could die. This is our most historic moment."

All the Elves gazed down at the silent form with awe, awe mixed with more than a little fear.

"Oh, go on!" Shadrach said. "That's just Phineas Judd."

But as he spoke, a chill moved up his spine. He remembered what he had seen a little while before, as he stood close by Phineas, as the dying moonlight crossed his old friend's face.

"Look." One of the Elves bent over and unfastened Phineas's blue-serge vest. He pushed the coat and vest aside. "See?"

Shadrach bent down to look.

He gasped.

Underneath Phineas Judd's blue-serge vest was a suit of mail, an encrusted mesh of ancient, rusting iron, fastened tightly around the squat body. On the mail stood an engraved insignia, dark and timeworn, embedded with dirt and rust. A moldering half-obliterated emblem. The emblem of a crossed owl leg and toadstool.

The emblem of the Great Troll.

"Golly," Shadrach said. "And *I* killed him."

For a long time he gazed silently down. Then, slowly, realization began to grow in him. He straightened up, a smile forming on his face.

"What is it, O King?" an Elf piped.

"I just thought of something," Shadrach said. "I just realized that—that since the Great Troll is dead and the Troll army has been put to flight—"

He broke off. All the Elves were waiting.

"I thought maybe I—that is, maybe if you don't need me anymore—"

The Elves listened respectfully. "What is it, Mighty King? Go on."

"I thought maybe now I could go back to the filling station and not be king any more." Shadrach glanced hopefully around at them. "Do you think so? With the war over and all. With him dead. What do you say?"

For a time, the Elves were silent. They gazed unhappily down at the ground. None of them said anything. At last they began moving away, collecting their banners and pennants.

"Yes, you may go back," an Elf said quietly. "The war is over. The Trolls have been defeated. You may return to your filling station, if that is what you want."

A flood of relief swept over Shadrach. He straightened up, grinning from ear to ear. "Thanks! That's fine. That's really fine. That's the best news I've heard in my life."

He moved away from the Elves, rubbing his hands together and blowing on them.

"Thanks an awful lot." He grinned around at the silent Elves. "Well, I guess I'll be running along, then. It's late. Late and cold. It's been a hard night. I'll—I'll see you around."

The Elves nodded silently.

"Fine. Well, good night." Shadrach turned and started along the path. He stopped for a moment, waving back at the Elves. "It was quite a battle, wasn't it? We really licked them." He hurried on along the path. Once again he stopped, looking back and waving. "Sure glad I could help out. Well, good night!"

One or two of the Elves waved, but none of them said anything.

———

Shadrach Jones walked slowly toward his place. He could see it from the rise, the highway that few cars traveled, the filling station falling to ruin, the house that might not last as long as himself, and not enough money coming in to repair them or buy a better location.

He turned around and went back.

The Elves were still gathered there in the silence of the night. They had not moved away.

"I was hoping you hadn't gone," Shadrach said, relieved.

"And we were hoping you would not leave," said a soldier.

Shadrach kicked a stone. It bounced through the tight silence and stopped. The Elves were still watching him.

"Leave?" Shadrach asked. "And me King of the Elves?"

"Then you will remain our king?" an Elf cried.

"It's a hard thing for a man of my age to change. To stop selling gasoline and suddenly be a king. It scared me for a while. But it doesn't anymore."

"You will? You *will*?"

"Sure," said Shadrach Jones.

The little circle of Elf torches closed in joyously. In their light, he saw a platform like the one that had carried the old King of the Elves. But this one was much larger, big enough to hold a man, and dozens of the soldiers waited with proud shoulders under the shafts.

A soldier gave him a happy bow. "For you, Sire."

Shadrach climbed aboard. It was less comfortable than walking, but he knew this was how they wanted to take him to the Kingdom of the Elves.

ADJUSTMENT TEAM

It was bright morning. The sun shone down on the damp lawns and sidewalks, reflecting off the sparkling parked cars. The Clerk came walking hurriedly, leafing through his instructions, flipping pages and frowning. He stopped in front of the small green stucco house for a moment, and then turned up the walk, entering the backyard.

The dog was asleep inside his shed, his back turned to the world. Only his thick tail showed.

"For heaven's sake," the Clerk exclaimed, hands on his hips. He tapped his mechanical pencil noisily against his clipboard. "Wake up, you in there."

The dog stirred. He came slowly out of his shed, head first, blinking and yawning in the morning sunlight. "Oh, it's you. Already?" He yawned again.

"Big doings." The Clerk ran his expert finger down the traffic-control sheet. "They're adjusting Sector T137 this morning. Starting at exactly nine o'clock." He glanced at his pocket watch. "Three-hour alteration. Will finish by noon."

"T137? That's not far from here."

The Clerk's thin lips twisted with contempt. "Indeed. You're showing astonishing perspicacity, my black-haired friend. Maybe you can divine why I'm here."

"We overlap with T137."

"Exactly. Elements from this Sector are involved. We must make sure they're properly placed when the adjustment begins." The Clerk glanced toward the small green stucco house. "Your particular task concerns the man in there. He is employed by a business establishment lying within Sector T137. It's essential that he be there before nine o'clock."

The dog studied the house. The shades had been let up. The kitchen light was on. Beyond the lace curtains dim shapes could be seen, stirring around the table. A man and woman. They were drinking coffee.

"There they are," the dog murmured. "The man, you say? He's not going to be harmed, is he?"

"Of course not. But he must be at his office early. Usually he doesn't leave until after nine. Today he must leave at eight-thirty. He must be within Sector T137 before the process begins, or he won't be altered to coincide with the new adjustment."

The dog sighed. "That means I have to summon."

"Correct." The Clerk checked his instruction sheet. "You're to summon at precisely eight-fifteen. You've got that? Eight-fifteen. No later."

"What will an eight-fifteen summons bring?"

The Clerk flipped open his instruction book, examining the code columns. "It will bring A Friend with a Car. To drive him to work early." He closed the book and folded his arms, preparing to wait. "That way he'll get to his office almost an hour ahead of time. Which is vital."

"Vital," the dog murmured. He lay down, half inside his shed. His eyes closed. "Vital."

"Wake up! This must be done exactly on time. If you summon too soon or too late—"

The dog nodded sleepily. "I know. I'll do it right. I *always* do it right."

Ed Fletcher poured more cream in his coffee. He sighed, leaning back in his chair. Behind him the oven hissed softly, filling the kitchen with warm fumes. The yellow overhead light beamed down.

"Another roll?" Ruth asked.

"I'm full." Ed sipped his coffee. "You can have it."

"Have to go." Ruth got to her feet, unfastening her robe. "Time to go to work."

"Already?"

"Sure. You lucky bum! Wish I could sit around." Ruth moved toward the bathroom, running her fingers through her long black hair. "When you work for the Government you start early."

"But you get off early," Ed pointed out. He unfolded the *Chronicle,* examining the sporting green. "Well, have a good time today. Don't type any wrong words, any double entendres."

The bathroom door closed, as Ruth shed her robe and began dressing.

Ed yawned and glanced up at the clock over the sink. Plenty of time. Not even eight. He sipped more coffee and then rubbed his stubbled chin. He would have to shave. He shrugged lazily. Ten minutes, maybe.

Ruth came bustling out in her nylon slip, hurrying into the bedroom. "I'm late." She rushed rapidly around, getting into her blouse and skirt, her stockings, her little white shoes. Finally she bent over and kissed him. "Good-bye, honey. I'll do the shopping tonight."

"Good-bye." Ed lowered his newspaper and put his arm around his wife's trim waist, hugging her affectionately. "You smell nice. Don't flirt with the boss."

Ruth ran out the front door, clattering down the steps. He heard the click of her heels diminish down the sidewalk.

She was gone. The house was silent. He was alone.

Ed got to his feet, pushing his chair back. He wandered lazily into the bathroom, and got his razor down. Eight-ten. He washed his face, rubbing it down with shaving cream, and began to shave. He shaved leisurely. He had plenty of time.

The Clerk bent over his round pocket watch, licking his lips nervously. Sweat stood out on his forehead. The second hand ticked on. Eight-fourteen. Almost time.

"Get ready!" the Clerk snapped. He tensed, his small body rigid. "Ten seconds to go!

"*Time!*" the Clerk cried.

Nothing happened.

The Clerk turned, eyes wide with horror. From the little shed a thick black tail showed. The dog had gone back to sleep.

"TIME!" the Clerk shrieked. He kicked wildly at the furry rump. "In the name of God—"

The dog stirred. He thumped around hastily, backing out of the shed. "My goodness." Embarrassed, he made his way quickly to the fence. Standing up on his hind paws, he opened his mouth wide. "Woof!" he summoned. He glanced apologetically at the Clerk. "I beg your pardon. I can't understand how—"

The Clerk gazed fixedly down at his watch. Cold terror knotted his stomach. The hands showed eight-sixteen. "You failed," he grated. "You failed! You miserable flea-bitten rag-bag of a worn-out old mutt! You failed!"

The dog dropped and came anxiously back. "I failed, you say? You mean the summons time was—?"

"You summoned too late." The Clerk put his watch away slowly, a glazed expression on his face. "You summoned too late. We won't get A Friend with a Car. There's no telling what will come instead. I'm afraid to see what eight-sixteen brings."

"I hope he'll be in Sector T137 in time."

"He won't," the Clerk wailed. "He won't be there. We've made a mistake. We've made things go wrong!"

Ed was rinsing the shaving cream from his face when the muffled sound of the dog's bark echoed through the silent house.

"Damn," Ed muttered. "Wake up the whole block." He dried his face, listening. Was somebody coming?

A vibration. Then—

The doorbell rang.

Ed came out of the bathroom. Who could it be? Had Ruth forgotten something? He tossed on a white shirt and opened the front door.

A bright young man, face bland and eager, beamed happily at him. "Good morning, sir." He tipped his hat. "I'm sorry to bother you so early—"

"What do you want?"

"I'm from the Federal Life Insurance Company. I'm here to see you about—"

Ed pushed the door closed. "Don't want any. I'm in a rush. Have to get to work."

"Your wife said this was the only time I could catch you." The young man picked up his briefcase, easing the door open again. "She especially asked me to come this early. We don't usually begin our work at this time, but since she asked me, I made a special note about it."

"OK." Sighing wearily, Ed admitted the young man. "You can explain your policy while I get dressed."

The young man opened his briefcase on the couch, laying out heaps of pamphlets and illustrated folders. "I'd like to show you some of these figures, if I may. It's of great importance to you and your family to—"

Ed found himself sitting down, going over the pamphlets. He purchased a ten-thousand-dollar policy on his own life and then eased the young man out. He looked at the clock. Practically nine-thirty!

"Damn." He'd be late to work. He finished fastening his tie, grabbed his coat, turned off the oven and the lights, dumped the dishes in the sink, and ran out on the porch.

As he hurried toward the bus stop he was cursing inwardly. Life insurance salesmen. Why did the jerk have to come just as he was getting ready to leave?

Ed groaned. No telling what the consequences would be, getting to the office late. He wouldn't get there until almost ten. He set himself in anticipation. A sixth sense told him he was in for it. Something bad. It was the wrong day to be late.

If only the salesman hadn't come.

Ed hopped off the bus a block from his office. He began walking rapidly. The huge clock in front of Stein's Jewelry Store told him it was almost ten.

His heart sank. Old Douglas would give him hell for sure. He could see it now. Douglas puffing and blowing, red-faced, waving his thick finger at him; Miss Evans, smiling behind her typewriter; Jackie, the office boy, grinning and snickering; Earl Hendricks; Joe and Tom; Mary, dark-eyed, full bosom and long lashes. All of them, kidding him the whole rest of the day.

He came to the corner and stopped for the light. On the other side of the street rose a big white concrete building, the towering column of steel and cement, girders and glass windows—the office building. Ed flinched. Maybe he could say the elevator got stuck. Somewhere between the second and third floor.

The streetlight changed. Nobody else was crossing. Ed crossed alone. He hopped up on the curb on the far side—

And stopped, rigid.

The sun had winked off. One moment it was beaming down. Then it was gone. Ed looked up sharply. Gray clouds swirled above him. Huge, formless clouds. Nothing more. An ominous, thick haze that made every-thing waver and dim. Uneasy chills plucked at him. *What was it?*

He advanced cautiously, feeling his way through the mist. Everything was silent. No sounds—not even the traffic sounds. Ed peered frantically around, trying to see through the rolling haze. No people. No cars. No sun. Nothing.

The office building loomed up ahead, ghostly. It was an indistinct gray. He put out his hand uncertainly—

A section of the building fell away. It rained down, a torrent of parti-cles. Like sand. Ed gaped foolishly. A cascade of gray debris, spilling around his feet. And where he had touched the building, a jagged cavity yawned— an ugly pit marring the concrete.

Dazed, he made his way to the front steps. He mounted them. The steps gave way underfoot. His feet sank down. He was wading through shifting sand, weak, rotted stuff that broke under his weight.

He got into the lobby. The lobby was dim and obscure. The overhead lights flickered feebly in the gloom. An unearthly pall hung over every-thing.

He spied the cigar stand. The seller leaned silently, resting on the counter, toothpick between his teeth, his face vacant. *And gray.* He was gray all over.

"Hey," Ed croaked. "What's going on?"

The seller did not answer. Ed reached out toward him. His hand touched the seller's gray arm—and passed right through.

"Good God," Ed said.

The seller's arm came loose. It fell to the lobby floor, disintegrating into fragments. Bits of gray fiber. Like dust. Ed's senses reeled.

"Help!" he shouted, finding his voice.

No answer. He peered around. A few shapes stood here and there: a man reading a newspaper, two women waiting at the elevator.

Ed made his way over to the man. He reached out and touched him.

The man slowly collapsed. He settled into a heap, a loose pile of gray ash. Dust. Particles. The two women dissolved when he touched them. Silently. They made no sound as they broke apart.

Ed found the stairs. He grabbed hold of the banister and climbed. The stairs collapsed under him. He hurried faster. Behind him lay a broken path—his footprints clearly visible in the concrete. Clouds of ash blew around him as he reached the second floor.

He gazed down the silent corridor. He saw more clouds of ash. He heard no sound. There was just darkness—rolling darkness.

He climbed unsteadily to the third floor. Once, his shoe broke completely through the stair. For a sickening second he hung, poised over a yawning hole that looked down into a bottomless nothing.

Then he climbed on, and emerged in front of his own office: DOUGLAS AND BLAKE, REAL ESTATE.

The hall was dim, gloomy with clouds of ash. The overhead lights flickered fitfully. He reached for the door handle. The handle came off in his hand. He dropped it and dug his fingernails into the door. The plate glass crashed past him, breaking into bits. He tore the door open and stepped over it, into the office.

Miss Evans sat at her typewriter, fingers resting quietly on the keys. She did not move. She was gray, her hair, her skin, her clothing. She was without color. Ed touched her. His fingers went through her shoulder, into dry flakiness.

He drew back, sickened. Miss Evans did not stir.

He moved on. He pushed against a desk. The desk collapsed into rotting dust. Earl Hendricks stood by the water cooler, a cup in his hand. He was a gray statue, unmoving. Nothing stirred. No sound. No life. The whole office was gray dust—without life or motion.

Ed found himself out in the corridor again. He shook his head, dazed. What did it mean? Was he going out of his mind? Was he—?

A sound.

Ed turned, peering into the gray mist. A creature was coming, hurrying rapidly. A man—a man in a white robe. Behind him others came. Men in white, with equipment. They were lugging complex machinery.

"Hey—" Ed gasped weakly.

The men stopped. Their mouths opened. Their eyes popped.

"Look!"

"Something's gone wrong!"

"One's still charged."

"Get the de-energizer."

"We can't proceed until—"

The men came toward Ed, moving around him. One lugged a long hose with some sort of nozzle. A portable cart came wheeling up. Instructions were rapidly shouted.

Ed broke out of his paralysis. Fear swept over him. Panic. Something hideous was happening. He had to get out. Warn people. Get away.

He turned and ran, back down the stairs. The stairs collapsed under him. He fell half a flight, rolling in heaps of dry ash. He got to his feet and hurried on, down to the ground floor.

The lobby was lost in the clouds of gray ash. He pushed blindly through, toward the door. Behind him, the white-clad men were coming, dragging their equipment and shouting to each other, hurrying quickly after him.

He reached the sidewalk. Behind him the office building wavered and sagged, sinking to one side, torrents of ash raining down in heaps. He raced toward the corner, the men just behind him. Gray clouds swirled around him. He groped his way across the street, hands outstretched. He gained the opposite curb—

The sun winked on. Warm yellow sunlight streamed down on him. Cars honked. Traffic lights changed. On all sides men and women in bright spring clothes hurried and pushed: shoppers, a blue-clad cop, salesmen with briefcases. Stores, windows, signs . . . noisy cars moving up and down the street. . . .

And overhead was the bright sun and familiar blue sky.

Ed halted, gasping for breath. He turned and looked back the way he had come. Across the street was the office building—as it had always been. Firm and distinct. Concrete and glass and steel.

He stepped back a pace and collided with a hurrying citizen. "Hey," the man grunted. "Watch it."

"Sorry." Ed shook his head, trying to clear it. From where he stood, the office building looked like always, big and solemn and substantial, rising up imposingly on the other side of the street.

But a minute ago—

Maybe he was out of his mind. He had seen the building crumbling into dust. Building—and people. They had fallen into gray clouds of dust. And the men in white—they had chased him. Men in white robes, shouting orders, wheeling complex equipment.

He was out of his mind. There was no other explanation. Weakly, Ed turned and stumbled along the sidewalk, his mind reeling. He moved blindly, without purpose, lost in a haze of confusion and terror.

The Clerk was brought into the top-level Administrative chambers and told to wait.

He paced back and forth nervously, clasping and wringing his hands in an agony of apprehension. He took off his glasses and wiped them shakily.

Lord. All the trouble and grief. And it wasn't his fault. But he would have to take the rap. It was his responsibility to get the Summoners routed out and their instructions followed. The miserable flea-infested Summoner had gone back to sleep—and *he* would have to answer for it.

The doors opened. "All right," a voice murmured, preoccupied. It was a tired, care-worn voice. The Clerk trembled and entered slowly, sweat dripping down his neck into his celluloid collar.

The Old Man glanced up, laying aside his book. He studied the Clerk calmly, his faded blue eyes mild—a deep, ancient mildness that made the Clerk tremble even more. He took out his handkerchief and mopped his brow.

"I understand there was a mistake," the Old Man murmured. "In connection with Sector T137. Something to do with an element from an adjoining area."

"That's right." The Clerk's voice was faint and husky. "Very unfortunate."

"What exactly occurred?"

"I started out this morning with my instruction sheets. The material relating to T137 had top priority, of course. I served notice on the Summoner in my area that an eight-fifteen summons was required."

"Did the Summoner understand the urgency?"

"Yes, sir." The Clerk hesitated. "But—"

"But what?"

The Clerk twisted miserably. "While my back was turned the Summoner crawled back in his shed and went to sleep. I was occupied, checking the exact time with my watch. I called the moment—but there was no response."

"You called at eight-fifteen exactly?"

"Yes, sir! Exactly eight-fifteen. But the Summoner was asleep. By the time I managed to arouse him it was eight-*sixteen*. He summoned, but instead of A Friend with a Car we got—A Life Insurance Salesman." The Clerk's face screwed up with disgust. "The Salesman kept the element there until almost nine-thirty. Therefore he was late to work instead of early."

For a moment the Old Man was silent. "Then the element was not within T137 when the adjustment began."

"No. He arrived about ten o'clock."

"During the middle of the adjustment." The Old Man got to his feet and paced slowly back and forth, face grim, hands behind his back. His long robe flowed out behind him. "A serious matter. During a Sector Adjustment all related elements from other Sectors must be included. Otherwise, their orientations remain out of phase. When this element entered T137 the adjustment had been in progress fifty minutes. The element encountered the Sector at its most de-energized stage. He wandered about until one of the adjustment teams met him."

"Did they catch him?"

"Unfortunately, no. He fled, out of the Sector. Into a nearby fully energized area."

"What—what then?"

The Old Man stopped pacing, his lined face grim. He ran a heavy hand through his long white hair. "We do not know. We lost contact with him. We will reestablish contact soon, of course. But for the moment he is out of control."

"What are you going to do?"

"He must be contacted and contained. He must be brought up here. There's no other solution."

"Up *here*!"

"It is too late to de-energize him. By the time he is regained he will have told others. To wipe his mind clean would only complicate matters. Usual methods will not suffice. I must deal with this problem myself."

"I hope he's located quickly," the Clerk said.

"He will be. Every Watcher is alerted. Every Watcher and every Summoner." The Old Man's eyes twinkled. "Even the Clerks, although we hesitate to count on them."

The Clerk flushed. "I'll be glad when this thing is over," he muttered.

Ruth came tripping down the stairs and out of the building, into the hot noonday sun. She lit a cigarette and hurried along the walk, her small bosom rising and falling as she breathed in the spring air.

"Ruth." Ed stepped up behind her.

"Ed!" She spun, gasping in astonishment. "What are you doing away from—?"

"Come on." Ed grabbed her arm, pulling her along. "Let's keep moving."

"But what—?"

"I'll tell you later." Ed's face was pale and grim. "Let's go where we can talk. In private."

"I was going down to have lunch at Louie's. We can talk there." Ruth hurried along breathlessly. "What is it? What's happened? You look so strange. And why aren't you at work? Did you—did you get fired?"

They crossed the street and entered a small restaurant. Men and women milled around, getting their lunch. Ed found a table in the back, secluded in a corner. "Here." He sat down abruptly. "This will do." She slid into the other chair.

Ed ordered a cup of coffee. Ruth had salad and creamed tuna on toast, coffee and peach pie. Silently, Ed watched her as she ate, his face dark and moody.

"Please tell me," Ruth begged him.

"You really want to know?"

"Of course I want to know!" Ruth put her small hand anxiously on his. "I'm your wife."

"Something happened today. This morning. I was late to work. A damn insurance man came by and held me up. I was half an hour late."

Ruth caught her breath. "Douglas fired you."

"No." Ed ripped a paper napkin slowly into bits. He stuffed the bits in the half-empty water glass. "I was worried as hell. I got off the bus and hurried down the street. I noticed it when I stepped up on the curb in front of the office."

"Noticed what?"

Ed told her. The whole works. Everything.

When he had finished, Ruth sat back, her face white, hands trembling. "I see," she murmured. "No wonder you're upset." She drank a little cold coffee, the cup rattling against the saucer. "What a terrible thing."

Ed leaned intently toward his wife. "Ruth. Do you think I'm going crazy?"

Ruth's red lips twisted. "I don't know what to say. It's so strange. . . ."

"Yeah. Strange is hardly the word for it. I poked my hands right through them. Like they were clay. Old dry clay. Dust. Dust figures." Ed lit a cigarette from Ruth's pack. "When I got out I looked back and there it was. The office building. Like always."

"You were afraid Mr. Douglas would bawl you out, weren't you?"

"Sure. I was afraid—and guilty." Ed's eyes flickered. "I know what you're thinking. I was late and I couldn't face him. So I had some sort of protective psychotic fit. Retreat from reality." He stubbed the cigarette out savagely. "Ruth, I've been wandering around town since. Two and a half hours. Sure, I'm afraid. I'm afraid like hell to go back."

"Of Douglas?"

"No! The men in white." Ed shuddered. "God. Chasing me. With their damn hoses and—and equipment."

Ruth was silent. Finally she looked up at her husband, her dark eyes bright. "You have to go back, Ed."

"Back? Why?"

"To prove something."

"Prove what?"

"Prove it's all right." Ruth's hand pressed against his. "You have to, Ed. You have to go back and face it. To show yourself there's nothing to be afraid of."

"The hell with it! After what I saw? Listen, Ruth. I saw the fabric of reality split open. I saw—*behind*. Underneath. I saw what was really there. And I don't want to go back. I don't want to see dust people again. Ever."

Ruth's eyes were fixed intently on him. "I'll go back with you," she said.

"For God's sake."

"For *your* sake. For your sanity. So you'll know." Ruth got abruptly to her feet, pulling her coat around her. "Come on, Ed. I'll go with you. We'll go up there together. To the office of Douglas and Blake, Real Estate. I'll even go in with you to see Mr. Douglas."

Ed got up slowly, staring hard at his wife. "You think I blacked out. Cold feet. Couldn't face the boss." His voice was low and strained. "Don't you?"

Ruth was already threading her way toward the cashier. "Come on. You'll see. It'll all be there. Just like it always was."

"OK," Ed said. He followed her slowly. "We'll go back there—and see which of us is right."

They crossed the street together, Ruth holding on tight to Ed's arm. Ahead of them was the building, the towering structure of concrete and metal and glass.

"There it is," Ruth said. "See?"

There it was, all right. The big building rose up, firm and solid, glittering in the early afternoon sun, its windows sparkling brightly.

Ed and Ruth stepped up onto the curb. Ed tensed himself, his body rigid. He winced as his foot touched the pavement—

But nothing happened: the street noises continued; cars, people hurrying past; a kid selling papers. There were sounds, smells, the noise of a city in the middle of the day. And overhead was the sun and the bright blue sky.

"See?" Ruth said. "I was right."

They walked up the front steps, into the lobby. Behind the cigar stand the seller stood, arms folded, listening to the ball game. "Hi, Mr. Fletcher," he called to Ed. His face lit up good-naturedly. "Who's the dame? Your wife know about this?"

Ed laughed unsteadily. They passed on toward the elevator. Four or five businessmen stood waiting. They were middle-aged men, well dressed, waiting impatiently in a bunch. "Hey, Fletcher," one said. "Where you been all day? Douglas is yelling his head off."

"Hello, Earl," Ed muttered. He gripped Ruth's arm. "Been a little sick."

The elevator came. They got in. The elevator rose. "Hi, Ed," the elevator operator said. "Who's the good-looking gal? Why don't you introduce her around?"

Ed grinned mechanically. "My wife."

The elevator let them off at the third floor. Ed and Ruth got out, heading toward the glass door of Douglas and Blake, Real Estate.

Ed halted, breathing shallowly. "Wait." He licked his lips. "I—"

Ruth waited calmly as Ed wiped his forehead and neck with his handkerchief. "All right now?"

"Yeah." Ed moved forward. He pulled open the glass door.

Miss Evans glanced up, ceasing her typing. "Ed Fletcher! Where on earth have you been?"

"I've been sick. Hello, Tom."

Tom glanced up from his work. "Hi, Ed. Say, Douglas is yelling for your scalp. Where have you been?"

"I know." Ed turned wearily to Ruth. "I guess I better go in and face the music."

Ruth squeezed his arm. "You'll be all right. I know." She smiled, a relieved flash of white teeth and red lips. "OK? Call me if you need me."

"Sure." Ed kissed her briefly on the mouth. "Thanks, honey. Thanks a lot. I don't know what the hell went wrong with me. I guess it's over."

"Forget it. So long." Ruth skipped back out of the office, the door closing after her. Ed listened to her race down the hall to the elevator.

"Nice little gal," Jackie said appreciatively.

"Yeah." Ed nodded, straightening his necktie. He moved unhappily toward the inner office, steeling himself. Well, he had to face it. Ruth was right. But he was going to have a hell of a time explaining it to the boss. He could see Douglas now, thick red wattles, big bull roar, face distorted with rage—

Ed stopped abruptly at the entrance to the inner office. He froze rigid. The inner office—it was *changed*.

The hackles of his neck rose. Cold fear gripped him, clutching at his windpipe. The inner office was different. He turned his head slowly, taking in the sight: the desks, chairs, fixtures, file cabinets, pictures.

Changes. Little changes. Subtle. Ed closed his eyes and opened them slowly. He was alert, breathing rapidly, his pulse racing. It was changed, all right. No doubt about it.

"What's the matter, Ed?" Tom asked. The staff watched him curiously, pausing in their work.

Ed said nothing. He advanced slowly into the inner office. The office had been *gone over*. He could tell. Things had been altered. Rearranged. Nothing obvious—nothing he could put his finger on. But he could tell.

Joe Kent greeted him uneasily. "What's the matter, Ed? You look like a wild dog. Is something—?"

Ed studied Joe. He was different. Not the same. What was it?

Joe's face. It was a little fuller. His shirt was blue-striped. Joe never wore blue stripes. Ed examined Joe's desk. He saw papers and accounts. The desk—it was too far to the right. And it was bigger. It wasn't the same desk.

The picture on the wall. It wasn't the same. It was a different picture entirely. And the things on top of the file cabinet—some were new, others were gone.

He looked back through the door. Now that he thought about it, Miss Evans's hair was different, done a different way. And it was lighter.

In here, Mary, filing her nails, over by the window—she was taller, fuller. Her purse, lying on the desk in front of her—a red purse, red knit.

"You always . . . have that purse?" Ed demanded.

Mary glanced up. "What?"

"That purse. You always have that?"

Mary laughed. She smoothed her skirt coyly around her shapely thighs, her long lashes blinking modestly. "Why, Mr. Fletcher. What do you mean?"

Ed turned away. *He knew.* Even if she didn't. She had been redone—changed: her purse, her clothes, her figure, everything about her. None of them knew—but him. His mind spun dizzily. They were all changed. All of them were different. They had all been remolded, recast. Subtly—but it was there.

The wastebasket. It was smaller, not the same. The window shades—white, not ivory. The wallpaper was not the same pattern. The lighting fixtures . . .

Endless, subtle changes.

Ed made his way back to the inner office. He lifted his hand and knocked on Douglas's door.

"Come in."

Ed pushed the door open. Nathan Douglas looked up impatiently.

"Mr. Douglas—" Ed began. He came into the room unsteadily—and stopped.

Douglas was not the same. Not at all. His whole office was changed: the rugs, the drapes. The desk was oak, not mahogany. And Douglas himself. . . .

Douglas was younger, thinner. His hair, brown. His skin not so red. His face smoother. No wrinkles. Chin reshaped. Eyes green, not black. He was a different man. But still Douglas—a different Douglas. A different version!

"What is it?" Douglas demanded impatiently. "Oh, it's you, Fletcher. Where were you this morning?"

Ed backed out. Fast.

He slammed the door and hurried back through the inner office. Tom and Miss Evans glanced up, startled. Ed passed them by, grabbing the hall door open.

"Hey!" Tom called. "What—?"

Ed hurried down the hall. Terror leaped through him. He had to hurry. He had *seen*. There wasn't much time. He came to the elevator and stabbed the button.

No time.

He ran to the stairs and started down. He reached the second floor. His terror grew. It was a matter of seconds.

Seconds!

The public phone. Ed ran into the phone booth. He dragged the door shut after him. Wildly, he dropped a dime in the slot and dialed. He had to call the police. He held the receiver to his ear, his heart pounding.

Warn them. Changes. Somebody tampering with reality. Altering it. He had been right. The white-clad men . . . their equipment . . . going through the building.

"Hello!" Ed shouted hoarsely. There was no answer. No hum. Nothing.

Ed peered frantically out the door.

And he sagged, defeated. Slowly he hung up the telephone receiver.

He was no longer on the second floor. The phone booth was rising, leaving the second floor behind, carrying him up, faster and faster. It rose floor by floor, moving silently, swiftly.

The phone booth passed through the ceiling of the building and out into the bright sunlight. It gained speed. The ground fell away below.

Buildings and streets were getting smaller each moment. Tiny specks hurried along, far below, cars and people, dwindling rapidly.

Clouds drifted between him and the earth. Ed shut his eyes, dizzy with fright. He held on desperately to the door handles of the phone booth.

Faster and faster the phone booth climbed. The earth was rapidly being left behind, far below.

Ed peered up wildly. *Where?* Where was he going? Where was it taking him?

He stood gripping the door handles, waiting.

The Clerk nodded curtly. "That's him, all right. The element in question."

Ed Fletcher looked around him. He was in a huge chamber. The edges fell away into indistinct shadows. In front of him stood a man with notes and ledgers under his arm, peering at him through steel-rimmed glasses. He was a nervous little man, sharp-eyed, with celluloid collar, blue-serge suit, vest, watch chain. He wore black shiny shoes.

And beyond him—

An old man sat quietly, in an immense modern chair. He watched Fletcher calmly, his blue eyes mild and tired. A strange thrill shot through Fletcher. It was not fear. Rather it was a vibration, rattling his bones—a deep sense of awe, tinged with fascination.

"Where—what is this place?" he asked faintly. He was still dazed from his quick ascent.

"Don't ask questions!" the nervous little man snapped angrily, tapping his pencil against his ledgers. "You're here to answer, not ask."

The Old Man moved a little. He raised his hand. "I will speak to the element alone," he murmured. His voice was low. It vibrated and rumbled through the chamber. Again the waver of fascinated awe swept Ed.

"Alone?" The little fellow backed away, gathering his books and papers in his arms. "Of course." He glanced hostilely at Ed Fletcher. "I'm glad he's finally in custody. All the work and trouble just for—"

He disappeared through a door. The door closed softly behind him. Ed and the Old Man were alone.

"Please sit down," the Old Man said.

Ed found a seat. He sat down awkwardly, nervously. He got out his cigarettes and then put them away again.

"What's wrong?" the Old Man asked.

"I'm just beginning to understand."

"Understand what?"

"That I'm dead."

The Old Man smiled briefly. "Dead? No, you're not dead. You're . . . visiting. An unusual event, but necessitated by circumstances." He leaned toward Ed. "Mr. Fletcher, you have got yourself involved with something."

"Yeah," Ed agreed. "I wish I knew what it was. Or how it happened."

"It was not your fault. You were a victim of a clerical error. A mistake was made—not by you. But involving you."

"What mistake?" Ed rubbed his forehead wearily. "I—I got in on something. I saw *through*. I saw something I wasn't supposed to see."

The Old Man nodded. "That's right. You saw something you were not supposed to see—something few elements have been aware of, let alone witnessed."

"Elements?"

"An official term. Let it pass. A mistake was made, but we hope to rectify it. It is my hope that—"

"Those people," Ed interrupted. "Heaps of dry ash. And gray. Like they were dead. Only it was everything: the stairs and walls and floor. No color or life."

"That Sector had been temporarily de-energized. So the adjustment team could enter and effect changes."

"Changes." Ed nodded. "That's right. When I went back later, everything was alive again. But not the same. It was all different."

"The adjustment was complete by noon. The team finished its work and re-energized the Sector."

"I see," Ed muttered.

"You were supposed to have been in the Sector when the adjustment began. Because of an error you were not. You came into the Sector late—during the adjustment itself. You fled, and when you returned it was over. You saw, and you should not have seen. Instead of a witness you should have been part of the adjustment. Like the others, you should have undergone changes."

Sweat came out on Ed Fletcher's head. He wiped it away. His stomach turned over. Weakly, he cleared his throat. "I get the picture." His voice was almost inaudible. A chilling premonition moved through him. "I was supposed to be changed like the others. But I guess something went wrong."

"Something went wrong. An error occurred. And now a serious problem exists. You have seen these things. You know a great deal. And you are not coordinated with the new configuration."

"Gosh," Ed muttered. "Well, I won't tell anybody." Cold sweat poured off him. "You can count on that. I'm as good as changed."

"You have already told someone," the Old Man said coldly.

"Me?" Ed blinked. "Who?"

"Your wife."

Ed trembled. The color drained from his face, leaving it sickly white. "That's right. I did."

"Your wife knows." The Old Man's face twisted angrily. "A woman. Of all the things to tell—"

"I didn't know." Ed retreated, panic leaping through him. "But I know *now*. You can count on me. Consider me changed."

The ancient blue eyes bored keenly into him, peering far into his depths. "And you were going to call the police. You wanted to inform the authorities."

"But I didn't know *who* was doing the changing."

"Now you know. The natural process must be supplemented—adjusted here and there. Corrections must be made. We are fully licensed to make such corrections. Our adjustment teams perform vital work."

Ed plucked up a measure of courage. "This particular adjustment. Douglas. The office. What was it for? I'm sure it was some worthwhile purpose."

The Old Man waved his hand. Behind him in the shadows an immense map glowed into existence. Ed caught his breath. The edges of the map faded off in obscurity. He saw an infinite web of detailed sections, a network of squares and ruled lines. Each square was marked. Some glowed with a blue light. The lights altered constantly.

"The Sector Board," the Old Man said. He sighed wearily. "A staggering job. Sometimes we wonder how we can go on another period. But it must be done. For the good of all. For *your* good."

"The change. In our—our Sector."

"Your office deals in real estate. The old Douglas was a shrewd man, but rapidly becoming infirm. His physical health was waning. In a few days Douglas will be offered a chance to purchase a large unimproved forest area in western Canada. It will require most of his assets. The older, less virile Douglas would have hesitated. It is imperative he not hesitate. He must purchase the area and clear the land at once. Only a younger man—a younger Douglas—would undertake this.

"When the land is cleared, certain anthropological remains will be discovered. They have already been placed there. Douglas will lease his land to the Canadian Government for scientific study. The remains found there will cause international excitement in learned circles.

"A chain of events will be set in motion. Men from numerous countries will come to Canada to examine the remains. Soviet, Polish, and Czech scientists will make the journey.

"The chain of events will draw these scientists together for the first time in years. National research will be temporarily forgotten in the excitement of these nonnational discoveries. One of the leading Soviet scientists will make friends with a Belgian scientist. Before they depart they will agree to correspond—without the knowledge of their governments, of course.

"The circle will widen. Other scientists on both sides will be drawn in. A society will be founded. More and more educated men will transfer an increasing amount of time to this international society. Purely national research will suffer a slight but extremely critical eclipse. The war tension will somewhat wane.

"This alteration is vital. And it is dependent on the purchase and clearing of the section of wilderness in Canada. The old Douglas would not have dared take the risk. But the altered Douglas, and his altered, more youthful staff, will pursue this work with wholehearted enthusiasm. And from this, the vital chain of widening events will come about. The beneficiaries will be *you*. Our methods may seem strange and indirect. Even incomprehensible. But I assure you we know what we're doing."

"I know that now," Ed said.

"So you do. You know a great deal. Much too much. No element should possess such knowledge. I should perhaps call an adjustment team in here. . . ."

A picture formed in Ed's mind: swirling gray clouds, gray men and women. He shuddered. "Look," he croaked. "I'll do anything. Anything at all. Only don't de-energize me." Sweat ran down his face. "OK?"

The Old Man pondered. "Perhaps some alternative could be found. There is another possibility. . . ."

"What?" Ed asked eagerly. "What is it?"

The Old Man spoke slowly, thoughtfully. "If I allow you to return, you will swear never to speak of the matter? Will you swear not to reveal to anyone the things you saw? The things you know?"

"Sure!" Ed gasped eagerly, blinding relief flooding over him. "I swear!"

"Your wife. She must know nothing more. She must think it was only a passing psychological fit—retreat from reality."

"She thinks that already."

"She must continue to."

Ed set his jaw firmly. "I'll see that she continues to think it was a mental aberration. She'll never know what really happened."

"You are certain you can keep the truth from her?"

"Sure," Ed said confidently. "I know I can."

"All right." The Old Man nodded slowly. "I will send you back. But you must tell no one." He swelled visibly. "Remember: you will eventually come back to me—everyone does, in the end—and your fate will not be enviable."

"I won't tell her," Ed said, sweating. "I promise. You have my word on that. I can handle Ruth. Don't give it a second thought."

Ed arrived home at sunset.

He blinked, dazed from the rapid descent. For a moment he stood on the pavement, regaining his balance and catching his breath. Then he walked quickly up the path.

He pushed the door open and entered the little green stucco house.

"Ed!" Ruth came flying, face distorted with tears. She threw her arms around him, hugging him tight. "Where the hell have you been?"

"Been?" Ed murmured. "At the office, of course."

Ruth pulled back abruptly. "No, you haven't."

Vague tendrils of alarm plucked at Ed. "Of course I have. Where else—?"

"I called Douglas about three. He said you left. You walked out, practically as soon as I turned my back. Eddie—"

Ed patted her nervously. "Take it easy, honey." He began unbuttoning his coat. "Everything's OK. Understand? Things are perfectly all right."

Ruth sat down on the arm of the couch. She blew her nose, dabbing at her eyes. "If you knew how much I've worried." She put her handkerchief away and folded her arms. "I want to know where you were."

Uneasily, Ed hung his coat in the closet. He came over and kissed her. Her lips were ice cold. "I'll tell you all about it. But what do you say we have something to eat? I'm starved."

Ruth studied him intently. She got down from the arm of the couch. "I'll change and fix dinner."

She hurried into the bedroom and slipped off her shoes and nylons. Ed followed her. "I didn't mean to worry you," he said carefully. "After you left me today I realized you were right."

"Oh?" Ruth unfastened her blouse and skirt, arranging them over a hanger. "Right about what?"

"About me." He manufactured a grin and made it glow across his face. "About . . . what happened."

Ruth hung her slip over the hanger. She studied her husband intently as she struggled into her tight-fitting jeans. "Go on."

The moment had come. It was now or never. Ed Fletcher braced himself and chose his words carefully. "I realized," he stated, "that the whole darn thing was in my mind. You were right, Ruth. Completely right. And I even realize what caused it."

Ruth rolled her cotton T-shirt down and tucked it in her jeans. "What was the cause?"

"Overwork."

"Overwork?"

"I need a vacation. I haven't had a vacation in years. My mind isn't on the job. I've been daydreaming." He said it firmly, but his heart was in his mouth. "I need to get away. To the mountains. Bass fishing. Or—" He searched his mind frantically. "Or—"

Ruth came toward him ominously. "Ed!" she said sharply. "Look at me!"

"What's the matter?" Panic shot through him. "Why are you looking at me like that?"

"Where were you this afternoon?"

Ed's grin faded. "I told you. I went for a walk. Didn't I tell you? A walk. To think things over."

"Don't lie to me, Eddie Fletcher! I can tell when you're lying!" Fresh tears welled up in Ruth's eyes. Her breasts rose and fell excitedly under her cotton shirt. "Admit it! You didn't go for a walk!"

Ed stammered weakly. Sweat poured off him. He sagged helplessly against the door. "What do you mean?"

Ruth's black eyes flashed with anger. "Come on! I want to know where you were! Tell me! I have a right to know. What really happened?"

Ed retreated in terror, his resolve melting like wax. It was going all wrong. "Honest. I went out for a—"

"Tell me!" Ruth's sharp fingernails dug into his arm. "I want to know where you were—and who you were with!"

Ed opened his mouth. He tried to grin, but his face failed to respond. "I don't know what you mean."

"You know what I mean. Who were you with? Where did you go? Tell me! I'll find out sooner or later."

There was no way out. He was licked—and he knew it. He couldn't keep it from her. Desperately he stalled, praying for time. If he could only distract her, get her mind on something else. If she would only let up, even for a second. He could invent something—a better story. Time—he needed more time. "Ruth, you've got to—"

Suddenly there was a sound: the bark of a dog, echoing through the dark house.

Ruth let go, cocking her head alertly. "That was Dobbie. I think somebody's coming."

The doorbell rang.

"You stay here. I'll be right back." Ruth ran out of the room, to the front door. "Darn it." She pulled the front door open.

"Good evening!" The young man stepped quickly inside, loaded down with objects, grinning broadly at Ruth. "I'm from the Sweep-Rite Vacuum Cleaner Company."

Ruth scowled impatiently. "Really, we're about to sit down at the table."

"Oh, this will only take a moment." The young man set down the vacuum cleaner and its attachments with a metallic crash. Rapidly, he unrolled a long illustrated banner, showing the vacuum cleaner in action. "Now, if you'll just hold this while I plug in the cleaner—"

He bustled happily about, unplugging the TV set, plugging in the cleaner, pushing the chairs out of his way.

"I'll show you the drape scraper first." He attached a hose and nozzle to the big gleaming tank. "Now, if you'll just sit down I'll demonstrate each of these easy-to-use attachments." His happy voice rose over the roar of the cleaner. "You'll notice—"

Ed Fletcher sat down on the bed. He groped in his pocket until he found his cigarettes. Shakily he lit one and leaned back against the wall, weak with relief.

He gazed up, a look of gratitude on his face. "Thanks," he said softly. "I think we'll make it—after all. Thanks a lot."

FOSTER, YOU'RE DEAD

School was agony, as always. Only today it was worse. Mike Foster finished weaving his two watertight baskets and sat rigid, while all around him the other children worked. Outside the concrete-and-steel building the late-afternoon sun shone cool. The hills sparkled green and brown in the crisp autumn air. In the overhead sky a few NATS circled lazily above the town.

The vast, ominous shape of Mrs. Cummings, the teacher, silently approached his desk. "Foster, are you finished?"

"Yes, ma'am," he answered eagerly. He pushed the baskets up. "Can I leave now?"

Mrs. Cummings examined his baskets critically. "What about your trap-making?" she demanded.

He fumbled in his desk and brought out his intricate small-animal trap. "All finished, Mrs. Cummings. And my knife, it's done, too." He showed her the razor-edged blade of his knife, glittering metal he had shaped from a discarded gasoline drum. She picked up the knife and ran her expert finger doubtfully along the blade.

"Not strong enough," she stated. "You've oversharpened it. It'll lose its edge the first time you use it. Go down to the main weapons-lab and examine the knives they've got there. Then hone it back some and get a thicker blade."

"Mrs. Cummings," Mike Foster pleaded, "could I fix it *tomorrow*? Could I leave right now, please?"

Everybody in the classroom was watching with interest. Mike Foster flushed; he hated to be singled out and made conspicuous, but he *had* to get away. He couldn't stay in school one minute more.

Inexorable, Mrs. Cummings rumbled, "Tomorrow is digging day. You won't have time to work on your knife."

"I will," he assured her quickly. "After the digging."

"No, you're not too good at digging." The old woman was measuring the boy's spindly arms and legs. "I think you better get your knife finished today. And spend all day tomorrow down at the field."

"What's the use of digging?" Mike Foster demanded, in despair.

"Everybody has to know how to dig," Mrs. Cummings answered patiently. Children were snickering on all sides; she shushed them with a hostile glare. "You all know the importance of digging. When the war begins the whole surface will be littered with debris and rubble. If we hope to survive we'll have to dig down, won't we? Have any of you ever watched a gopher digging around the roots of plants? The gopher knows he'll find something valuable down there under the surface of the ground. We're all going to be little brown gophers. We'll all have to learn to dig down in the rubble and find the good things, because that's where they'll be."

Mike Foster sat miserably plucking his knife, as Mrs. Cummings moved away from his desk and up the aisle. A few children grinned contemptuously at him, but nothing penetrated his haze of wretchedness. Digging wouldn't do him any good. When the bombs came he'd be killed instantly. All the vaccination shots up and down his arms, on his thighs and buttocks, would be of no use. He had wasted his allowance money: Mike Foster wouldn't be alive to catch any of the bacterial plagues. Not unless—

He sprang up and followed Mrs. Cummings to her desk. In an agony of desperation he blurted, "Please, I have to leave. I have to do something."

Mrs. Cummings's tired lips twisted angrily. But the boy's fearful eyes stopped her. "What's wrong?" she demanded. "Don't you feel well?"

The boy stood frozen, unable to answer her. Pleased by the tableau, the class murmured and giggled until Mrs. Cummings rapped angrily on her desk with a writer. "Be quiet," she snapped. Her voice softened a shade. "Michael, if you're not functioning properly, go downstairs to the psyche clinic. There's no point trying to work when your reactions are conflicted. Miss Groves will be glad to optimum you."

"No," Foster said.

"Then what is it?"

The class stirred. Voices answered for Foster; his tongue was stuck with misery and humiliation. "His father's an anti-P," the voices explained. "They don't have a shelter and he isn't registered in Civic Defense. His father hasn't even contributed to the NATS. They haven't done anything."

Mrs. Cummings gazed up in amazement at the mute boy. "You don't have a shelter?"

He shook his head.

A strange feeling filled the woman. "But—" She had started to say, *But you'll die up here.* She changed it to "But where'll you go?"

"Nowhere," the mild voices answered for him. "Everybody else'll be down in their shelters and he'll be up here. He doesn't even have a permit for the school shelter."

Mrs. Cummings was shocked. In her dull, scholastic way she had assumed every child in the school had a permit to the elaborate subsurface chambers under the building. But of course not. Only children whose parents were part of CD, who contributed to arming the community. And if Foster's father was an anti-P . . .

"He's afraid to sit here," the voices chimed in calmly. "He's afraid it'll come while he's sitting here, and everybody else will be safe down in the shelter."

He wandered slowly along, hands deep in his pockets, kicking at dark stones on the sidewalk. The sun was setting. Snub-nosed commuter rockets were unloading tired people, glad to be home from the factory strip a hundred miles to the west. On the distant hills something flashed: a radar tower revolving silently in the evening gloom. The circling NATS had increased in number. The twilight hours were the most dangerous; visual observers couldn't spot high-speed missiles coming in close to the ground. Assuming the missiles came.

A mechanical news-machine shouted at him excitedly as he passed. War, death, amazing new weapons developed at home and abroad. He hunched his shoulders and continued on, past the little concrete shells that served as houses, each exactly alike, sturdy reinforced pillboxes. Ahead of him bright neon signs glowed in the settling gloom: the business district, alive with traffic and milling people.

Half a block from the bright cluster of neons he halted. To his right was a public shelter, a dark tunnel-like entrance with a mechanical turnstile glowing dully. Fifty cents admission. If he was here, on the street, and he had fifty cents, he'd be all right. He had pushed down into public shelters many times, during the practice raids. But other times, hideous, nightmare times that never left his mind, he hadn't had the fifty cents. He had stood mute and terrified, while people pushed excitedly past him; and the shrill shrieks of the sirens thundered everywhere.

He continued slowly, until he came to the brightest blotch of light, the great, gleaming showrooms of General Electronics, two blocks long, illuminated on all sides, a vast square of pure color and radiation. He halted and examined for the millionth time the fascinating shapes, the display that always drew him to a hypnotized stop whenever he passed.

In the center of the vast room was a single object. An elaborate pulsing blob of machinery and support struts, beams and walls and sealed locks. All spotlights were turned on it; huge signs announced its hundred and one advantages—as if there could be any doubt.

THE NEW 1972 BOMBPROOF RADIATION-SEALED SUBSURFACE SHELTER IS HERE! CHECK THESE STAR-STUDDED FEATURES:

- automatic descent-lift—jam-proof, self-powered, e-z locking
- triple-layer hull guaranteed to withstand 5*g* pressure without buckling
- A-powered heating and refrigeration system—self-servicing air-purification network
- three decontamination stages for food and water
- four hygienic stages for pre-burn exposure
- complete antibiotic processing
- e-z payment plan

He gazed at the shelter a long time. It was mostly a big tank, with a neck at one end that was the descent tube, and an emergency escape-hatch at the other. It was completely self-contained: a miniature world that supplied its own light, heat, air, water, medicines, and almost inexhaustible food. When fully stocked there were visual and audio tapes, entertainment, beds, chairs, vidscreen, everything that made up the above-surface home. It was, actually, a home below the ground. Nothing was missing that might be needed or enjoyed. A family would be safe, even comfortable, during the most severe H-bomb and bacterial-spray attack.

It cost twenty thousand dollars.

While he was gazing silently at the massive display, one of the salesmen stepped out onto the dark sidewalk, on his way to the cafeteria. "Hi, sonny," he said automatically, as he passed Mike Foster. "Not bad, is it?"

"Can I go inside?" Foster asked quickly. "Can I go down in it?"

The salesman stopped, as he recognized the boy. "You're that kid," he said slowly, "that damn kid who's always pestering us."

"I'd like to go down in it. Just for a couple minutes. I won't bust any-thing—I promise. I won't even touch anything."

The salesman was young and blond, a good-looking man in his early twenties. He hesitated, his reactions divided. The kid was a pest. But he had a family, and that meant a reasonable prospect. Business was bad; it was late September and the seasonal slump was still on. There was no profit in telling the boy to go peddle his newstapes; but on the other hand it was bad business encouraging small fry to crawl around the merchandise. They wasted time; they broke things; they pilfered small stuff when nobody was looking.

"No dice," the salesman said. "Look, send your old man down here. Has he seen what we've got?"

"Yes," Mike Foster said tightly.

"What's holding him back?" The salesman waved expansively up at the great gleaming display. "We'll give him a good trade-in on his old one, allowing for depreciation and obsolescence. What model has he got?"

"We don't have any," Mike Foster said.

The salesman blinked. "Come again?"

"My father says it's a waste of money. He says they're trying to scare people into buying things they don't need. He says—"

"Your father's an anti-P?"

"Yes," Mike Foster answered unhappily.

The salesman let out his breath. "Okay, kid. Sorry we can't do business. It's not your fault." He lingered. "What the hell's wrong with him? Does he put on the NATS?"

"No."

The salesman swore under his breath. A coaster, sliding along, safe because the rest of the community was putting up thirty percent of its income to keep a constant-defense system going. There were always a few of them, in every town. "How's your mother feel?" the salesman demanded. "She go along with him?"

"She says—" Mike Foster broke off. "Couldn't I go down in it for a little while? I won't bust anything. Just *once*."

"How'd we ever sell it if we let kids run through it? We're not marking it down as a demonstration model—we've got roped into that too often." The salesman's curiosity was aroused. "How's a guy get to be anti-P? He always feel this way, or did he get stung with something?"

"He says they sold people as many cars and washing machines and television sets as they could use. He says NATS and bomb shelters aren't good for anything, so people never get all they can use. He says factories can keep turning out guns and gas masks forever, and as long as people are afraid they'll keep paying for them because they think if they don't they might get killed, and maybe a man gets tired of paying for a new car every year and stops, but he's never going to stop buying shelters to protect his children."

"You believe that?" the salesman asked.

"I wish we had that shelter," Mike Foster answered. "If we had a shelter like that I'd go down and sleep in it every night. It'd be there when we needed it."

"Maybe there won't be a war," the salesman said. He sensed the boy's misery and fear, and he grinned good-naturedly down at him. "Don't worry all the time. You probably watch too many vidtapes—get out and play, for a change."

"Nobody's safe on the surface," Mike Foster said. "We have to be down below. And there's no place I can go."

"Send your old man around," the salesman muttered uneasily. "Maybe we can talk him into it. We've got a lot of time-payment plans. Tell him to ask for Bill O'Neill. Okay?"

Mike Foster wandered away, down the black evening street. He knew he was supposed to be home, but his feet dragged and his body was heavy and dull. His fatigue made him remember what the athletic coach had said the day before, during exercises. They were practicing breath suspension, holding a lungful of air and running. He hadn't done well; the others were still redfaced and racing when he halted, expelled his air, and stood gasping frantically for breath.

"Foster," the coach said angrily, "you're dead. You know that? If this had been a gas attack—" He shook his head wearily. "Go over there and practice by yourself. You've got to do better, if you expect to survive."

But he didn't expect to survive.

When he stepped up onto the porch of his home, he found the living room lights already on. He could hear his father's voice, and more faintly his mother's from the kitchen. He closed the door after him and began unpeeling his coat.

"Is that you?" his father demanded. Bob Foster sat sprawled out in his chair, his lap full of tapes and report sheets from his retail furniture store. "Where have you been? Dinner's been ready half an hour." He had taken off his coat and rolled up his sleeves. His arms were pale and thin, but muscular. He was tired; his eyes were large and dark, his hair thinning. Restlessly, he moved the tapes around, from one stack to another.

"I'm sorry," Mike Foster said.

His father examined his pocket watch; he was surely the only man who still carried a watch. "Go wash your hands. What have you been doing?" He scrutinized his son. "You look odd. Do you feel all right?"

"I was downtown," Mike Foster said.

"What were you doing?"

"Looking at the shelters."

Wordless, his father grabbed up a handful of reports and stuffed them into a folder. His thin lips set; hard lines wrinkled his forehead. He snorted furiously as tapes spilled everywhere; he bent stiffly to pick them up. Mike Foster made no move to help him. He crossed to the closet and gave his coat to the hanger. When he turned away his mother was directing the table of food into the dining room.

They ate without speaking, intent on their food and not looking at each other. Finally his father said, "What'd you see? Same old dogs, I suppose."

"There's the new '72 models," Mike Foster answered.

"They're the same as the '71 models." His father threw down his fork savagely; the table caught and absorbed it. "A few new gadgets, some more chrome. That's all." Suddenly he was facing his son defiantly. "Right?"

Mike Foster toyed wretchedly with his creamed chicken. "The new ones have a jam-proof descent-lift. You can't get stuck halfway down. All you have to do is get in it, and it does the rest."

"There'll be one next year that'll pick you up and carry you down. This one'll be obsolete as soon as people buy it. That's what they want—they want you to keep buying. They keep putting out new ones as fast as they can. This isn't 1972, it's still 1971. What's that thing doing out already? Can't they wait?"

Mike Foster didn't answer. He had heard it all before, many times. There was never anything new, only chrome and gadgets; yet the old ones became obsolete, anyhow. His father's argument was loud, impassioned, almost frenzied, but it made no sense. "Let's get an old one, then," he blurted out. "I don't care, any one'll do. Even a secondhand one."

"No, you want the *new* one. Shiny and glittery to impress the neighbors. Lots of dials and knobs and machinery. How much do they want for it?"

"Twenty thousand dollars."

His father let his breath out. "Just like that."

"They've easy time-payment plans."

"Sure. You pay for it the rest of your life. Interest, carrying charges, and how long is it guaranteed for?"

"Three months."

"What happens when it breaks down? It'll stop purifying and decontaminating. It'll fall apart as soon as the three months are over."

Mike Foster shook his head. "No. It's big and sturdy."

His father flushed. He was a small man, slender and light, brittle-boned. He thought suddenly of his lifetime of lost battles, struggling up the hard way, carefully collecting and holding on to something, a job, money, his retail store, bookkeeper to manager, finally owner. "They're scaring us to keep the wheels going," he yelled desperately at his wife and son. "They don't want another depression."

"Bob," his wife said, slowly and quietly, "you have to stop this. I can't stand any more."

Bob Foster blinked. "What're you talking about?" he muttered. "I'm tired. These goddamn taxes. It isn't possible for a little store to keep open, not with the big chains. There ought to be a law." His voice trailed off. "I guess I'm through eating." He pushed away from the table and got to his feet. "I'm going to lie down on the couch and take a nap."

His wife's thin face blazed. "You have to get one! I can't stand the way they talk about us. All the neighbors and the merchants, everybody who knows. I can't go anywhere or do anything without hearing about it. Ever since that day they put up the flag. *Anti-P.* The last in the whole town. Those things circling around up there, and everybody paying for them but us."

"No," Bob Foster said. "I can't get one."

"Why not?"

"Because," he answered simply, "I can't afford it."

There was silence.

"You've put everything in that store," Ruth said finally. "And it's failing anyhow. You're just like a pack rat, hoarding everything down at that ratty little hole-in-the-wall. Nobody wants wood furniture anymore. You're a relic—a curiosity." She slammed at the table and it leaped wildly to gather the empty dishes, like a startled animal. It dashed furiously from the room and back into the kitchen, the dishes churning in its washtank as it raced.

Bob Foster sighed wearily. "Let's not fight. I'll be in the living room. Let me take a nap for an hour or so. Maybe we can talk about it later."

"Always later," Ruth said bitterly.

Her husband disappeared into the living room, a small, hunched-over figure, hair scraggly and gray, shoulder blades like broken wings.

Mike got to his feet. "I'll go study my homework," he said. He followed after his father, a strange look on his face.

The living room was quiet; the vidset was off and the lamp was down low. Ruth was in the kitchen setting the controls on the stove for the next month's meals. Bob Foster lay stretched out on the couch, his shoes off, his head on a pillow. His face was gray with fatigue. Mike hesitated for a moment and then said, "Can I ask you something?"

His father grunted and stirred, opened his eyes. "What?"

Mike sat down facing him. "Tell me again how you gave advice to the President."

His father pulled himself up. "I didn't give any advice to the President. I just talked to him."

"Tell me about it."

"I've told you a million times. Every once in a while, since you were a baby. You were with me." His voice softened, as he remembered. "You were just a toddler—we had to carry you."

"What did he look like?"

"Well," his father began, slipping into a routine he had worked out and petrified over the years, "he looked about like he does in the vidscreen. Smaller, though."

"Why was he here?" Mike demanded avidly, although he knew every detail. The President was his hero, the man he most admired in all the world. "Why'd he come all the way out here to *our* town?"

"He was on a tour." Bitterness crept into his father's voice. "He happened to be passing through."

"What kind of a tour?"

"Visiting towns all over the country." The harshness increased. "Seeing how we were getting along. Seeing if we had bought enough NATS and bomb shelters and plague shots and gas masks and radar networks to repel attack. The General Electronics Corporation was just beginning to put up its big showrooms and displays—everything bright and glittering and expensive. The first defense equipment available for home purchase." His lips twisted. "All on easy-payment plans. Ads, posters, searchlights, free gardenias and dishes for the ladies."

Mike Foster's breath panted in his throat. "That was the day we got our Preparedness Flag," he said hungrily. "That was the day he came to give us our flag. And they ran it up on the flagpole in the middle of the town, and everybody was there yelling and cheering."

"You remember that?"

"I—think so. I remember people and sounds. And it was hot. It was June, wasn't it?"

"June 10, 1965. Quite an occasion. Not many towns had the big green flag, then. People were still buying cars and TV sets. They hadn't discovered those days were over. TV sets and cars are good for something—you can only manufacture and sell so many of them."

"He gave *you* the flag, didn't he?"

"Well, he gave it to all us merchants. The Chamber of Commerce had it arranged. Competition between towns, see who can buy the most the soonest. Improve our town and at the same time stimulate business. Of course, the way they put it, the idea was if we had to *buy* our gas masks and bomb shelters we'd take better care of them. As if we ever damaged telephones and sidewalks. Or highways, because the whole state provided them. Or armies. Haven't there always been armies? Hasn't the government always organized its people for defense? I guess defense costs too much. I guess they save a lot of money, cut down the national debt by this."

"Tell me what he said," Mike Foster whispered.

His father fumbled for his pipe and lit it with trembling hands. "He said, *'Here's your flag, boys. You've done a good job.'*" Bob Foster choked, as acrid pipe fumes guzzled up. "He was red-faced, sunburned, not embarrassed. Perspiring and grinning. He knew how to handle himself. He knew a lot of first names. Told a funny joke."

The boy's eyes were wide with awe. "He came all the way out here, and you talked to him."

"Yeah," his father said. "I talked to him. They were all yelling and cheering. The flag was going up, the big green Preparedness Flag."

"You said—"

"I said to him, *'Is that all you brought us? A strip of green cloth?'*" Bob Foster dragged tensely on his pipe. "That was when I became an anti-P. Only I didn't know it at the time. All I knew was we were on our own, except for a strip of green cloth. We should have been a country, a whole nation, one hundred and seventy million people working together to defend ourselves. And instead, we're a lot of separate little towns, little walled forts. Sliding and slipping back to the Middle Ages. Raising our separate armies—"

"Will the President ever come back?" Mike asked.

"I doubt it. He was—just passing through."

"If he comes back," Mike whispered, tense and not daring to hope, "can we go *see* him? Can we *look* at him?"

Bob Foster pulled himself up to a sitting position. His bony arms were bare and white; his lean face was drab with weariness. And resignation. "How much was the damn thing you saw?" he demanded hoarsely. "That bomb shelter?"

Mike's heart stopped beating. "Twenty thousand dollars."

"This is Thursday. I'll go down with you and your mother next Saturday." Bob Foster knocked out his smoldering, half-lit pipe. "I'll get it on the easy-payment plan. The fall buying season is coming up soon. I usually do good—people buy wood furniture for Christmas gifts." He got up abruptly from the couch. "Is it a deal?"

Mike couldn't answer; he could only nod.

"Fine," his father said, with desperate cheerfulness. "Now you won't have to go down and look at it in the window."

The shelter was installed—for an additional two hundred dollars—by a fast-working team of laborers in brown coats with the words GENERAL ELECTRONICS stitched across their backs. The backyard was quickly restored, dirt and shrubs spaded in place, the surface smoothed over, and the bill respectfully slipped under the front door. The lumbering delivery truck, now empty, clattered off down the street and the neighborhood was again silent.

Mike Foster stood with his mother and a small group of admiring neighbors on the back porch of the house. "Well," Mrs. Carlyle said finally, "now you've got a shelter. The best there is."

"That's right," Ruth Foster agreed. She was conscious of the people around her; it had been some time since so many had shown up at once. Grim satisfaction filled her gaunt frame, almost resentment. "It certainly makes a difference," she said harshly.

"Yes," Mr. Douglas from down the street agreed. "Now you have some place to go." He had picked up the thick book of instructions the laborers had left. "It says here you can stock it for a whole year. Live down there twelve months without coming up once." He shook his head admiringly. "Mine's an old '69 model. Good for only six months. I guess maybe—"

"It's still good enough for us," his wife cut in, but there was a longing wistfulness in her voice. "Can we go down and peek at it, Ruth? It's all ready, isn't it?"

Mike made a strangled noise and moved jerkily forward. His mother smiled understandingly. "He has to go down there first. He gets first look at it—it's really for him, you know."

Their arms folded against the chill September wind, the group of men and women stood waiting and watching, as the boy approached the neck of the shelter and halted a few steps in front of it.

He entered the shelter carefully, almost afraid to touch anything. The neck was big for him; it was built to admit a full-grown man. As soon as his weight was on the descent-lift it dropped beneath him. With a breathless *whoosh* it plummeted down the pitch-black tube to the body of the shelter. The lift slammed hard against its shock absorbers and the boy stumbled from it. The lift shot back to the surface, simultaneously sealing off the sub-surface shelter, an impassable steel-and-plastic cork in the narrow neck.

Lights had come on around him automatically. The shelter was bare and empty; no supplies had yet been carried down. It smelled of varnish and motor grease: below him the generators were throbbing dully. His presence activated the purifying and decontamination systems; on the blank concrete wall meters and dials moved into sudden activity.

He sat down on the floor, knees drawn up, face solemn, eyes wide. There was no sound but that of the generators; the world above was completely cut off. He was in a little self-contained cosmos; everything needed was here—or would be here, soon: food, water, air, things to do. Nothing else was wanted. He could reach out and touch—whatever he needed. He could stay here forever, through all time, without stirring. Complete and entire. Not lacking, not fearing, with only the sound of the generators purring below him, and the sheer, ascetic walls around and above him on all sides, faintly warm, completely friendly, like a living container.

Suddenly he shouted, a loud jubilant shout that echoed and bounced from wall to wall. He was deafened by the reverberation. He shut his eyes tight and clenched his fists. Joy filled him. He shouted again—and let the roar of sound lap over him, his own voice reinforced by the near walls, close and hard and incredibly powerful.

The kids in school knew even before he showed up the next morning. They greeted him as he approached, all of them grinning and nudging each other. "Is it true your folks got a new General Electronics Model S-72ft?" Earl Peters demanded.

"That's right," Mike answered. His heart swelled with a peaceful confidence he had never known. "Drop around," he said, as casually as he could. "I'll show it to you."

He passed on, conscious of their envious faces.

"Well, Mike," Mrs. Cummings said, as he was leaving the classroom at the end of the day. "How does it feel?"

He halted by her desk, shy and full of quiet pride. "It feels good," he admitted.

"Is your father contributing to the NATS?"

"Yes."

"And you've got a permit for our school shelter?"

He happily showed her the small blue seal clamped around his wrist. "He mailed a check to the city for everything. He said, 'As long as I've gone this far I might as well go the rest of the way.'"

"Now you have everything everybody else has." The elderly woman smiled across at him. "I'm glad of that. You're now a pro-P, except there's no such term. You're just—like everyone else."

The next day the news-machines shrilled out the news. The first revelation of the new Soviet bore-pellets.

Bob Foster stood in the middle of the living room, the newstape in his hands, his thin face flushed with fury and despair. "Goddamn it, it's a plot!" His voice rose in baffled frenzy. "We just bought the thing and now look. *Look!*" He shoved the tape at his wife. "You see? I told you!"

"I've seen it," Ruth said wildly. "I suppose you think the whole world was just waiting with you in mind. They're always improving weapons, Bob. Last week it was those grain-impregnation flakes. This week it's bore-pellets. You don't expect them to stop the wheels of progress because you finally broke down and bought a shelter, do you?"

The man and woman faced each other. "What the hell are we going to do?" Bob Foster asked quietly.

Ruth paced back into the kitchen. "I heard they were going to turn out adaptors."

"Adaptors! What do you mean?"

"So people won't have to buy new shelters. There was a commercial on the vidscreen. They're going to put some kind of metal grill on the market, as soon as the government approves it. They spread it over the ground and it intercepts the bore-pellets. It screens them, makes them explode on the surface, so they can't burrow down to the shelter."

"How much?"

"They didn't say."

Mike Foster sat crouched on the sofa, listening. He had heard the news at school. They were taking their test on berry-identification, examining encased samples of wild berries to distinguish the harmless ones from the toxic, when the bell had announced a general assembly. The principal read them the news about the bore-pellets and then gave a routine lecture on emergency treatment of a new variant of typhus, recently developed.

His parents were still arguing. "We'll have to get one," Ruth Foster said calmly. "Otherwise it won't make any difference whether we've got a shelter or not. The bore-pellets were specifically designed to penetrate the surface and seek out warmth. As soon as the Russians have them in production—"

"I'll get one," Bob Foster said. "I'll get an anti-pellet grill and whatever else they have. I'll buy everything they put on the market. I'll never stop buying."

"It's not as bad as that."

"You know, this game has one real advantage over selling people cars and TV sets. With something like this we *have* to buy. It isn't a luxury, something big and flashy to impress the neighbors, something we could do without. If we don't buy this we die. They always said the way to sell something was create anxiety in people. Create a sense of insecurity—tell them they smell bad or look funny. But this makes a joke out of deodorant and hair oil. You can't escape this. If you don't buy, *they'll kill you.* The perfect sales-pitch. Buy or die—new slogan. Have a shiny new General Electronics H-bomb shelter in your backyard or be slaughtered."

"Stop talking like that!" Ruth snapped.

Bob Foster threw himself down at the kitchen table. "All right. I give up. I'll go along with it."

"You'll get one? I think they'll be on the market by Christmas."

"Oh, yes," Foster said. "They'll be out by Christmas." There was a strange look on his face. "I'll buy one of the damn things for Christmas, and so will everybody else."

The GEC grill-screen adaptors were a sensation.

Mike Foster walked slowly along the crowd-packed December street, through the late-afternoon twilight. Adaptors glittered in every store window. All shapes and sizes, for every kind of shelter. All prices, for every pocketbook. The crowds of people were gay and excited, typical Christmas crowds, shoving good-naturedly, loaded down with packages and heavy overcoats. The air was white with gusts of sweeping snow. Cars nosed cautiously along the jammed streets. Lights and neon displays, immense glowing store windows gleamed on all sides.

His own house was dark and silent. His parents weren't home yet. Both of them were down at the store working; business had been bad and his mother was taking the place of one of the clerks. Mike held his hand up to the code-key, and the front door let him in. The automatic furnace had kept the house warm and pleasant. He removed his coat and put away his schoolbooks.

He didn't stay in the house long. His heart pounding with excitement, he felt his way out the back door and started onto the back porch.

He forced himself to stop, turn around, and reenter the house. It was better if he didn't hurry things. He had worked out every moment of the process, from the first instant he saw the low hinge of the neck reared up hard and firm against the evening sky. He had made a fine art of it; there was no wasted motion. His procedure had been shaped, molded until it was a beautiful thing. The first overwhelming sense of *presence* as the neck of the shelter came around him. Then the blood-freezing rush of air as the descent-lift hurtled down all the way to the bottom.

And the grandeur of the shelter itself.

Every afternoon, as soon as he was home, he made his way down into it, below the surface, concealed and protected in its steel silence, as he had done since the first day. Now the chamber was full, not empty. Filled with endless cans of food, pillows, books, vidtapes, audiotapes, prints on the walls, bright fabrics, textures and colors, even vases of flowers. The shelter was his place, where he crouched curled up, surrounded by everything he needed.

Delaying things as long as possible, he hurried back through the house and rummaged in the audiotape file. He'd sit down in the shelter until dinner, listening to *Wind in the Willows*. His parents knew where to find him; he was always down there. Two hours of uninterrupted happiness, alone by himself in the shelter. And then when dinner was over he would hurry back down, to stay until time for bed. Sometimes late at night, when his parents were sound asleep, he got quietly up and made his way outside, to the shelter-neck, and down into its silent depths. To hide until morning.

He found the audiotape and hurried through the house, out onto the back porch and into the yard. The sky was a bleak gray, shot with streamers of ugly black clouds. The lights of the town were coming on here and there. The yard was cold and hostile. He made his way uncertainly down the steps—and froze.

A vast yawning cavity loomed. A gaping mouth, vacant and toothless, fixed open to the night sky. There was nothing else. The shelter was gone.

He stood for an endless time, the tape clutched in one hand, the other hand on the porch railing. Night came on; the dead hole dissolved in darkness. The whole world gradually collapsed into silence and abysmal gloom. Weak stars came out; lights in nearby houses came on fitfully, cold and faint. The boy saw nothing. He stood unmoving, his body rigid as stone, still facing the great pit where the shelter had been.

Then his father was standing beside him. "How long have you been here?" his father was saying. "How long, Mike? Answer me!"

With a violent effort Mike managed to drag himself back. "You're home early," he muttered.

"I left the store early on purpose. I wanted to be here when you—got home."

"It's gone."

"Yes." His father's voice was cold, without emotion. "The shelter's gone. I'm sorry, Mike. I called them and told them to take it back."

"Why?"

"I couldn't pay for it. Not this Christmas, with those grills everyone's getting. I can't compete with them." He broke off and then continued wretchedly, "They were damn decent. They gave me back half the money I put in." His voice twisted ironically. "I knew if I made a deal with them before Christmas I'd come out better. They can resell it to somebody else."

Mike said nothing.

"Try to understand," his father went on harshly. "I had to throw what capital I could scrape together into the store. I have to keep it running. It was either give up the shelter or the store. And if I gave up the store—"

"Then we wouldn't have anything."

His father caught hold of his arm. "Then we'd have to give up the shelter, too." His thin, strong fingers dug in spasmodically. "You're growing up—you're old enough to understand. We'll get one later, maybe not the biggest, the most expensive, but something. It was a mistake, Mike. I couldn't swing it, not with the goddamn adaptor things to buck. I'm keeping up the NAT payments, though. And your school tab. I'm keeping that going. This isn't a matter of principle," he finished desperately. "I can't help it. Do you understand, Mike? *I had to do it.*"

Mike pulled away.

"Where are you going?" His father hurried after him. "Come back here!" He grabbed for his son frantically, but in the gloom he stumbled and fell. Stars blinded him as his head smashed into the edge of the house; he pulled himself up painfully and groped for some support.

When he could see again, the yard was empty. His son was gone.

"Mike!" he yelled. "Where are you?"

There was no answer. The night wind blew clouds of snow around him, a thin bitter gust of chilled air. Wind and darkness, nothing else.

Bill O'Neill wearily examined the clock on the wall. It was nine-thirty: he could finally close the doors and lock up the big dazzling store. Push the milling, murmuring throngs of people outside and on their way home.

"Thank God," he breathed, as he held the door open for the last old lady, loaded down with packages and presents. He threw the code bolt in place and pulled down the shade. "What a mob. I never saw so many people."

"All done," Al Conners said, from the cash register. "I'll count the money—you go around and check everything. Make sure we got all of them out."

O'Neill pushed his blond hair back and loosened his tie. He lit a cigarette gratefully, then moved around the store, checking light switches, turning off the massive GEC displays and appliances. Finally he approached the huge bomb shelter that took up the center of the floor.

He climbed the ladder to the neck and stepped onto the lift. The lift dropped with a *whoosh* and a second later he stepped out in the cavelike interior of the shelter.

In one corner Mike Foster sat curled up in a tight heap, his knees drawn up against his chin, his skinny arms wrapped around his ankles. His face was pushed down; only his ragged brown hair showed. He didn't move as the salesman approached him, astounded.

"Jesus!" O'Neill exclaimed. "It's that kid."

Mike said nothing. He hugged his legs tighter and buried his head as far down as possible.

"What the hell are you doing down here?" O'Neill demanded, surprised and angry. His outrage increased. "I thought your folks got one of these." Then he remembered. "That's right. We had to repossess it."

Al Conners appeared from the descent-lift. "What's holding you up? Let's get out of here and—" He saw Mike and broke off. "What's he doing down here? Get him out and let's go."

"Come on, kid," O'Neill said gently. "Time to go home."

Mike didn't move.

The two men looked at each other. "I guess we're going to have to drag him out," Conners said grimly. He took off his coat and tossed it over a decontamination fixture. "Come on. Let's get it over with."

It took both of them. The boy fought desperately, without sound, clawing and struggling and tearing at them with his fingernails, kicking them, slashing at them, biting them when they grabbed him. They half-dragged, half-carried him to the descent-lift and pushed him into it long enough to activate the mechanism. O'Neill rode up with him; Conners came immediately after. Grimly, efficiently, they bundled the boy to the front door, threw him out, and locked the bolts after him.

"Wow," Conners gasped, sinking down against the counter. His sleeve was torn and his cheek was cut and gashed. His glasses hung from one ear; his hair was rumpled and he was exhausted. "Think we ought to call the cops? There's something wrong with that kid."

O'Neill stood by the door, panting for breath and gazing out into the darkness. He could see the boy sitting on the pavement. "He's still out there," he muttered. People pushed by the boy on both sides. Finally one of them stopped and got him up. The boy struggled away, and then disappeared into the darkness. The larger figure picked up its packages, hesitated a moment, and then went on. O'Neill turned away. "What a hell of a thing." He wiped his face with his handkerchief. "He sure put up a fight."

"What was the matter with him? He never said anything, not a goddamn word."

"Christmas is a hell of a time to repossess something," O'Neill said. He reached shakily for his coat. "It's too bad. I wish they could have kept it."

Conners shrugged. "No tickie, no laundry."

"Why the hell can't we give them a deal? Maybe—" O'Neill struggled to get the word out. "Maybe sell the shelter wholesale, to people like that."

Conners glared at him angrily. "*Wholesale?* And then everybody wants it wholesale. It wouldn't be fair—and how long would we stay in business? How long would GEC last that way?"

"I guess not very long," O'Neill admitted moodily.

"Use your head." Conners laughed sharply. "What you need is a good stiff drink. Come on in the back closet—I've got a fifty of Haig and Haig in a drawer back there. A little something to warm you up, before you go home. That's what you need."

Mike Foster wandered aimlessly along the dark street, among the crowds of shoppers hurrying home. He saw nothing; people pushed against him but he was unaware of them. Lights, laughing people, the honking of car horns, the clang of signals. He was blank, his mind empty and dead. He walked automatically, without consciousness or feeling.

To his right a garish neon sign winked and glowed in the deepening night shadows. A huge sign, bright and colorful.

PEACE ON EARTH   GOOD WILL TO MEN
PUBLIC SHELTER   ADMISSION 50¢

UPON THE DULL EARTH

Silvia ran laughing through the night brightness, between the roses and cosmos and Shasta daisies, down the gravel path and beyond the heaps of sweet-tasting grass swept from the lawns. Stars, caught in pools of water, glittered everywhere, as she brushed through them to the slope beyond the brick wall. Cedars supported the sky and ignored the slim shape squeezing past, her brown hair flying, her eyes flashing.

"Wait for me," Rick complained, as he cautiously threaded his way after her, along the half-familiar path. Silvia danced on without stopping. "Slow down!" he shouted angrily.

"Can't—we're late." Without warning, Silvia appeared in front of him, blocking the path. "Empty your pockets," she gasped, her gray eyes sparkling. "Throw away all metal. You know they can't stand metal."

Rick searched his pockets. In his overcoat were two dimes and a fifty-cent piece. "Do these count?"

"*Yes!*" Silvia snatched the coins and threw them into the dark heaps of calla lilies. The bits of metal hissed into the moist depths and were gone. "Anything else?" She caught hold of his arm anxiously. "They're already on their way. Anything else, Rick?"

"Just my watch." Rick pulled his wrist away as Silvia's wild fingers snatched for the watch. "*That's* not going in the bushes."

"Then lay it on the sundial—or the wall. Or in a hollow tree." Silvia raced off again. Her excited, rapturous voice danced back to him. "Throw away your cigarette case. And your keys, your belt buckle—everything metal. You know how they hate metal. Hurry, we're late!"

Rick followed sullenly after her. "All right, *witch*."

Silvia snapped at him furiously from the darkness. "Don't *say* that! It isn't true. You've been listening to my sisters and my mother and—"

Her words were drowned out by the sound. Distant flapping, a long way off, like vast leaves rustling in a winter storm. The night sky was alive with the frantic poundings; they were coming very quickly this time. They were too greedy, too desperately eager to wait. Flickers of fear touched the man and he ran to catch up with Silvia.

Silvia was a tiny column of green skirt and blouse in the center of the thrashing mass. She was pushing them away with one arm and trying to manage the faucet with the other. The churning activity of wings and bodies twisted her like a reed. For a time she was lost from sight.

"Rick!" she called faintly. "Come here and help!" She pushed them away and struggled up. "They're suffocating me!"

Rick fought his way through the wall of flashing white to the edge of the trough. They were drinking greedily at the blood that spilled from the wooden faucet. He pulled Silvia close against him; she was terrified and trembling. He held her tight until some of the violence and fury around them had died down.

"They're hungry," Silvia gasped feebly.

"You're a little cretin for coming ahead. They can sear you to ash!"

"I know. They can do anything." She shuddered, excited and frightened. "Look at them," she whispered, her voice husky with awe. "Look at the size of them—their wing-spread. And they're *white*, Rick. Spotless—perfect. There's nothing in our world as spotless as that. Great and clean and wonderful."

"They certainly wanted the lamb's blood."

Silvia's soft hair blew against his face as the wings fluttered on all sides. They were leaving now, roaring up into the sky. Not up, really—away. Back to their own world whence they had scented the blood. But it was not only the blood—they had come because of Silvia. *She* had attracted them.

The girl's gray eyes were wide. She reached up toward the rising white creatures. One of them swooped close. Grass and flowers sizzled as blinding white flames roared in a brief fountain. Rick scrambled away. The flaming figure hovered momentarily over Silvia and then there was a hollow *pop.* The last of the white-winged giants was gone. The air, the ground, gradually cooled into darkness and silence.

"I'm sorry," Silvia whispered.

"Don't do it again," Rick managed. He was numb with shock. "It isn't safe."

"Sometimes I forget. I'm sorry, Rick. I didn't mean to draw them so close." She tried to smile. "I haven't been that careless in months. Not since that other time, when I first brought you out here." The avid, wild look slid across her face. "Did you *see* him? Power and flames! And he didn't even touch us. He just—looked at us. That was all. And everything's burned up, all around."

Rick grabbed hold of her. "Listen," he grated. "You mustn't call them again. It's wrong. This isn't their world."

"It's not wrong—it's beautiful."

"It's not safe!" His fingers dug into her flesh until she gasped. "Stop tempting them down here!"

Silvia laughed hysterically. She pulled away from him, out into the blasted circle that the horde of angels had seared behind them as they rose into the sky. "I can't *help* it," she cried. "I belong with them. They're my family, my people. Generations of them, back into the past."

"What do you mean?"

"They're my ancestors. And some day I'll join them."

"You are a little witch!" Rick shouted furiously.

"No," Silvia answered. "Not a witch, Rick. Don't you see? I'm a saint."

The kitchen was warm and bright. Silvia plugged in the Silex and got a big red can of coffee down from the cupboards over the sink. "You mustn't listen to them," she said, as she set out plates and cups and got cream from the refrigerator. "You know they don't understand. Look at them in there."

Silvia's mother and her sisters, Betty Lou and Jean, stood huddled together in the living room, fearful and alert, watching the young couple in the kitchen. Walter Everett was standing by the fireplace, his face blank, remote.

"Listen to *me*," Rick said. "You have this power to attract them. You mean you're not—isn't Walter your real father?"

"Oh, yes—of course he is. I'm completely human. Don't I look human?"

"But you're the only one who has the power."

"I'm not physically different," Silvia said thoughtfully. "I have the ability to see, that's all. Others have had it before me—saints, martyrs. When I was a child, my mother read to me about St. Bernadette. Remember where her cave was? Near a hospital. They were hovering there and she saw one of them."

"But the blood! It's grotesque. There never was anything like that."

"Oh, yes. The blood draws them, lamb's blood especially. They hover over battlefields. Valkyries—carrying off the dead to Valhalla. That's why saints and martyrs cut and mutilate themselves. You know where I got the idea?"

Silvia fastened a little apron around her waist and filled the Silex with coffee. "When I was nine years old, I read of it in Homer, in the *Odyssey*. Ulysses dug a trench in the ground and filled it with blood to attract the spirits. The shades from the nether world."

"That's right," Rick admitted reluctantly. "I remember."

"The ghosts of people who died. They had lived once. Everybody lives here, then dies and goes there." Her face glowed. "We're all going to have wings! We're all going to fly. We'll all be filled with fire and power. We won't be worms anymore."

"Worms! That's what you always call me."

"Of course you're a worm. We're all worms—grubby worms creeping over the crust of the Earth, through dust and dirt."

"Why should blood bring them?"

"Because it's life and they're attracted by life. Blood is *uisge beatha*— the water of life."

"Blood means death! A trough of spilled blood . . ."

"It's *not* death. When you see a caterpillar crawl into its cocoon, do you think it's dying?"

Walter Everett was standing in the doorway. He stood listening to his daughter, his face dark. "One day," he said hoarsely, "they're going to grab her and carry her off. She wants to go with them. She's waiting for that day."

"You see?" Silvia said to Rick. "He doesn't understand either." She shut off the Silex and poured coffee. "Coffee for you?" she asked her father.

"No," Everett said.

"Silvia," Rick said, as if speaking to a child, "if you went away with them, you know you couldn't come back to us."

"We all have to cross sooner or later. It's all part of our life."

"But you're only nineteen," Rick pleaded. "You're young and healthy and beautiful. And our marriage—what about our marriage?" He half rose from the table. "Silvia, you've got to stop this!"

"I *can't* stop it. I was seven when I saw them first." Silvia stood by the sink, gripping the Silex, a faraway look in her eyes. "Remember, Daddy? We were living back in Chicago. It was winter. I fell, walking home from school." She held up a slim arm. "See the scar? I fell and cut myself on the gravel and slush. I came home crying—it was sleeting and the wind was howling around me. My arm was bleeding and my mitten was soaked with blood. And then I looked up and saw them."

There was silence.

"They want you," Everett said wretchedly. "They're flies—bluebottles, hovering around, waiting for you. Calling you to come along with them."

"Why not?" Silvia's gray eyes were shining and her cheeks radiated joy and anticipation. "You've seen them, Daddy. You know what it means. Transfiguration—from clay into gods!"

Rick left the kitchen. In the living room, the two sisters stood together, curious and uneasy. Mrs. Everett stood by herself, her face granite-hard, eyes bleak behind her steel-rimmed glasses. She turned away as Rick passed them.

"What happened out there?" Betty Lou asked him in a taut whisper. She was fifteen, skinny and plain, hollow cheeked, with mousy, sand-colored hair. "Silvia never lets us come out with her."

"Nothing happened," Rick answered.

Anger stirred the girl's barren face. "That's not true. You were both out in the garden, in the dark, and—"

"Don't talk to him!" her mother snapped. She yanked the two girls away and shot Rick a glare of hatred and misery. Then she turned quickly from him.

Rick opened the door to the basement and switched on the light. He descended slowly into the cold, damp room of concrete and dirt, with its unwinking yellow light hanging from the dust-covered wires overhead.

In one corner loomed the big floor furnace with its mammoth hot-air pipes. Beside it stood the water heater and discarded bundles, boxes of books, newspapers and old furniture, thick with dust, encrusted with strings of spiderwebs.

At the far end were the washing machine and spin dryer. And Silvia's pump and refrigeration system.

From the workbench Rick selected a hammer and two heavy pipe wrenches. He was moving toward the elaborate tanks and pipes when Silvia appeared abruptly at the top of the stairs, her coffee cup in one hand.

She hurried quickly down to him. "What are you doing down here?" she asked, studying him intently. "Why that hammer and those two wrenches?"

Rick dropped the tools back onto the bench. "I thought maybe this could be solved on the spot."

Silvia moved between him and the tanks. "I thought you understood. They've always been a part of my life. When I brought you with me the first time, you seemed to see what—"

"I don't want to lose you," Rick said harshly, "to anybody or anything—in this world or any other. *I'm not going to give you up.*"

"It's not giving me up!" Her eyes narrowed. "You came down here to destroy and break everything. The moment I'm not looking you'll smash all this, won't you?"

"That's right."

Fear replaced anger on the girl's face. "Do you want me to be chained here? I have to go on—I'm through with this part of the journey. I've stayed here long enough."

"Can't you wait?" Rick demanded furiously. He couldn't keep the ragged edge of despair out of his voice. "Doesn't it come soon enough anyhow?"

Silvia shrugged and turned away, her arms folded, her red lips tight together. "You want to be a worm always. A fuzzy, little creeping caterpillar."

"I want *you.*"

"You can't *have* me!" She whirled angrily. "I don't have any time to waste with this."

"You have higher things in mind," Rick said savagely.

"Of course." She softened a little. "I'm sorry, Rick. Remember Icarus? You want to fly, too. I know it."

"In my time."

"Why not now? Why wait? You're afraid." She slid lithely away from him, cunning twisting her red lips. "Rick, I want to show you something. Promise me first—you won't tell anybody."

"What is it?"

"Promise?" She put her hand to his mouth. "I have to be careful. It cost a lot of money. Nobody knows about it. It's what they do in China—everything goes toward it."

"I'm curious," Rick said. Uneasiness flicked at him. "Show it to me."

Trembling with excitement, Silvia disappeared behind the huge lumbering refrigerator, back into the darkness behind the web of frost-hard freezing coils. He could hear her tugging and pulling at something. Scraping sounds, sounds of something large being dragged out.

"See?" Silvia gasped. "Give me a hand, Rick. It's heavy. Hardwood and brass—and metal lined. It's hand-stained and polished. And the carving—see the carving! Isn't it beautiful?"

"What is it?" Rick demanded huskily.

"It's my cocoon," Silvia said simply. She settled down in a contented heap on the floor, and rested her head happily against the polished oak coffin.

Rick grabbed her by the arm and dragged her to her feet. "You can't sit with that coffin, down here in the basement with—" He broke off. "What's the matter?"

Silvia's face was twisting with pain. She backed away from him and put her finger quickly to her mouth. "I cut myself—when you pulled me up— on a nail or something." A thin trickle of blood oozed down her fingers. She groped in her pocket for a handkerchief.

"Let me see it." He moved toward her, but she avoided him. "Is it bad?" he demanded.

"Stay away from me," Silvia whispered.

"What's wrong? Let me see it!"

"Rick," Silvia said in a low intense voice, "get some water and adhesive tape. As quickly as possible!" She was trying to keep down her rising terror. "I have to stop the bleeding."

"Upstairs?" He moved awkwardly away. "It doesn't look too bad. Why don't you . . ."

"Hurry." The girl's voice was suddenly bleak with fear. "Rick, *hurry*!"

Confused, he ran a few steps.

Silvia's terror poured after him. "No, it's too late," she called thinly. "Don't come back—keep away from me. It's my own fault. I trained them to come. *Keep away!* I'm sorry, Rick. *Oh*—" Her voice was lost to him, as the wall of the basement burst and shattered. A cloud of luminous white forced its way through and blazed out into the basement.

It was Silvia they were after. She ran a few hesitant steps toward Rick, halted uncertainly, then the white mass of bodies and wings settled around her. She shrieked once. Then a violent explosion blasted the basement into a shimmering dance of furnace heat.

He was thrown to the floor. The cement was hot and dry—the whole basement crackled with heat. Windows shattered as pulsing white shapes pushed out again. Smoke and flames licked up the walls. The ceiling sagged and rained plaster down.

Rick struggled to his feet. The furious activity was dying away. The basement was a littered chaos. All surfaces were scorched black, seared and crusted with smoking ash. Splintered wood, torn cloth, and broken concrete were strewn everywhere. The furnace and washing machine were in ruins. The elaborate pumping and refrigeration system now was a glittering mass of slag. One whole wall had been twisted aside. Plaster was rubbled over everything.

Silvia was a twisted heap, arms and legs doubled grotesquely. Shriveled, carbonized remains of fire-scorched ash, settling in a vague mound. What had been left were charred fragments, a brittle burned-out husk.

It was a dark night, cold and intense. A few stars glittered like ice from above his head. A faint, dank wind stirred through the dripping calla lilies and whipped gravel up in a frigid mist along the path between the black roses.

He crouched for a long time, listening and watching. Behind the cedars, the big house loomed against the sky. At the bottom of the slope a few cars slithered along the highway. Otherwise, there was no sound. Ahead of him jutted the squat outline of the porcelain trough and the pipe that had carried blood from the refrigerator in the basement. The trough was empty and dry, except for a few leaves that had fallen in it.

Rick took a deep breath of thin night air and held it. Then he got stiffly to his feet. He scanned the sky, but saw no movement. They were there, though, watching and waiting—dim shadows, echoing into the legendary past, a line of god-figures.

He picked up the heavy gallon drums, dragged them to the trough, and poured blood from a New Jersey abattoir, cheap-grade steer refuse, thick and clotted. It splashed against his clothes and he backed away nervously. But nothing stirred in the air above. The garden was silent, drenched with night fog and darkness.

He stood beside the trough, waiting and wondering if they were coming. They had come for Silvia, not merely for the blood. Without her there was no attraction but the raw food. He carried the empty metal cans over to the bushes and kicked them down the slope. He searched his pockets carefully, to make sure there was no metal in them.

Over the years, Silvia had nourished their habit of coming. Now she was on the other side. Did that mean they wouldn't come? Somewhere in the damp bushes something rustled. An animal or a bird?

In the trough the blood glistened, heavy and dull, like old lead. It was their time to come, but nothing stirred the great trees above. He picked out the rows of nodding black roses, the gravel path down which he and Silvia had run—violently he shut out the recent memory of her flashing eyes and deep red lips. The highway beyond the slope—the empty, deserted garden—the silent house in which her family huddled and waited. After a time, there was a dull, swishing sound. He tensed, but it was only a diesel truck lumbering along the highway, headlights blazing.

He stood grimly, his feet apart, his heels dug into the soft black ground. He wasn't leaving. He was staying there until they came. He wanted her back—at any cost.

Overhead, foggy webs of moisture drifted across the moon. The sky was a vast barren plain, without life or warmth. The deathly cold of deep space, away from suns and living things. He gazed up until his neck ached. Cold stars, sliding in and out of the matted layer of fog. Was there anything else? Didn't they want to come, or weren't they interested in him? It had been Silvia who had interested them—now they had her.

Behind him there was a movement without sound. He sensed it and started to turn, but suddenly, on all sides, the trees and undergrowth shifted. Like cardboard props they wavered and ran together, blending dully in the night shadows. Something moved through them, rapidly, silently, then was gone.

They had come. He could feel them. They had shut off their power and flame. Cold, indifferent statues, rising among the trees, dwarfing the cedars—remote from him and his world, attracted by curiosity and mild habit.

"Silvia," he said clearly. "Which are you?"

There was no response. Perhaps she wasn't among them. He felt foolish. A vague flicker of white drifted past the trough, hovered momentarily, and then went on without stopping. The air above the trough vibrated, then died into immobility, as another giant inspected briefly and withdrew.

Panic breathed through him. They were leaving again, receding back into their own world. The trough had been rejected; they weren't interested.

"Wait," he muttered thickly.

Some of the white shadows lingered. He approached them slowly, wary of their flickering immensity. If one of them touched him, he would sizzle briefly and puff into a dark heap of ash. A few feet away he halted.

"You know what I want," he said. "I want her back. She shouldn't have been taken yet."

Silence.

"You were too greedy," he said. "You did the wrong thing. She was going to come over to you, eventually. She had it all worked out."

The dark fog rustled. Among the trees the flickering shapes stirred and pulsed, responsive to his voice. "*True*," came a detached impersonal sound. The sound drifted around him, from tree to tree, without location or direction. It was swept off by the night wind to die into dim echoes.

Relief settled over him. They had paused—they were aware of him—listening to what he had to say.

"You think it's right?" he demanded. "She had a long life here. We were to marry, have children."

There was no answer, but he was conscious of a growing tension. He listened intently, but he couldn't make out anything. Presently he realized a struggle was taking place, a conflict among them. The tension grew—more shapes flickered—the clouds, the icy stars, were obscured by the vast presence swelling around him.

"Rick!" A voice spoke close by. Wavering, drifting back into the dim regions of the trees and dripping plants. He could hardly hear it—the words were gone as soon as they were spoken. "Rick—help me get back."

"Where are you?" He couldn't locate her. "What can I do?"

"I don't know." Her voice was wild with bewilderment and pain. "I don't understand. Something went wrong. They must have thought I—wanted to come right away. I *didn't*!"

"I know," Rick said. "It was an accident."

"They were waiting. The cocoon, the trough—but it was too soon." Her terror came across to him, from the vague distances of another universe. "Rick, I've changed my mind. I want to come back."

"It's not as simple as that."

"I know. Rick, time is different on this side. I've been gone so long—your world seems to creep along. It's been years, hasn't it?"

"One week," Rick said.

"It was their fault. You don't blame me, do you? They know they did the wrong thing. Those who did it have been punished, but that doesn't help me." Misery and panic distorted her voice so he could hardly understand her. "How can I come back?"

"Don't they know?"

"They say it can't be done." Her voice trembled. "They say they destroyed the clay part—it was incinerated. There's nothing for me to go back to."

Rick took a deep breath. "Make them find some other way. It's up to them. Don't they have the power? They took you over too soon—they must send you back. It's *their* responsibility."

The white shapes shifted uneasily. The conflict rose sharply; they couldn't agree. Rick warily moved back a few paces.

"They say it's dangerous," Silvia's voice came from no particular spot. "They say it was attempted once." She tried to control her voice. "The nexus between this world and yours is unstable. There are vast amounts of free-floating energy. The power we—on this side—have isn't really our own. It's a universal energy, tapped and controlled."

"Why can't they . . ."

"This is a higher continuum. There's a natural process of energy from lower to higher regions. But the reverse process is risky. The blood—it's a sort of guide to follow—a bright marker."

"Like moths around a lightbulb," Rick said bitterly.

"If they send me back and something goes wrong—" She broke off and then continued, "If they make a mistake, I might be lost between the two regions. I might be absorbed by the free energy. It seems to be partly alive. It's not understood. Remember Prometheus and the fire . . ."

"I see," Rick said, as calmly as he could.

"Darling, if they try to send me back, I'll have to find some shape to enter. You see, I don't exactly have a shape anymore. There's no real material form on this side. What you see, the wings and the whiteness, are not really there. If I succeeded in making the trip back to your side . . ."

"You'd have to mold something," Rick said.

"I'd have to take something there—something of clay. I'd have to enter it and reshape it. As He did a long time ago, when the original form was put on your world."

"If they did it once, they can do it again."

"The One who did that is gone. He passed on upward." There was unhappy irony in her voice. "There are regions beyond this. The ladder doesn't stop here. Nobody knows where it ends, it just seems to keep on going up and up. World after world."

"Who decides about you?" Rick demanded.

"It's up to me," Silvia said faintly. "They say, if I want to take the chance, they'll try it."

"What do you think you'll do?" he asked.

"I'm afraid. What if something goes wrong? You haven't seen it, the region between. The possibilities there are incredible—they terrify me. He was the only one with enough courage. Everyone else has been afraid."

"It was their fault. They have to take responsibility."

"They know that." Silvia hesitated miserably. "Rick, darling, please tell me what to do."

"Come back!"

Silence. Then her voice, thin and pathetic. "All right, Rick. If you think that's the right thing."

"It is," he said firmly. He forced his mind not to think, not to picture or imagine anything. *He had to have her back.* "Tell them to get started now. Tell them—"

A deafening crack of heat burst in front of him. He was lifted up and tossed into a flaming sea of pure energy. They were leaving and the scalding lake of sheer power bellowed and thundered around him. For a split second he thought he glimpsed Silvia, her hands reaching imploringly toward him.

Then the fire cooled and he lay blinded in dripping, night-moistened darkness. Alone in the silence.

Walter Everett was helping him up. "You damn fool!" he was saying, again and again. "You shouldn't have brought them back. They've got enough from us."

Then he was in the big, warm living room. Mrs. Everett stood silently in front of him, her face hard and expressionless. The two daughters hovered anxiously around him, fluttering and curious, eyes wide with morbid fascination.

"I'll be all right," Rick muttered. His clothing was charred and blackened. He rubbed black ash from his face. Bits of dried grass stuck to his hair—they had seared a circle around him as they'd ascended. He lay back against the couch and closed his eyes. When he opened them, Betty Lou Everett was forcing a glass of water into his hands.

"Thanks," he muttered.

"You should never have gone out there," Walter Everett repeated. "Why? Why'd you do it? You know what happened to her. You want the same thing to happen to you?"

"I want her back," Rick said quietly.

"Are you mad? You can't get her back. She's gone." His lips twitched convulsively. "You saw her."

Betty Lou was gazing at Rick intently. "What happened out there?" she demanded. "You saw her."

Rick got heavily to his feet and left the living room. In the kitchen he emptied the water in the sink and poured himself a drink. While he was leaning wearily against the sink, Betty Lou appeared in the doorway.

"What do you want?" Rick demanded.

The girl's face was flushed an unhealthy red. "I know something happened out there. You were feeding them, weren't you?" She advanced toward him. "You're trying to get her back?"

"That's right," Rick said.

Betty Lou giggled nervously. "But you can't. She's dead—her body's been cremated—I saw it." Her face worked excitedly. "Daddy always said that something bad would happen to her, and it did." She leaned close to Rick. "She was a witch! She got what she deserved!"

"She's coming back," Rick said.

"*No!*" Panic stirred the girl's drab features. "She *can't* come back. She's dead—like she always said—worm into butterfly—she's a butterfly!"

"Go inside," Rick said.

"You can't order me around," Betty Lou answered. Her voice rose hysterically. "This is *my* house. We don't want you around here anymore. Daddy's going to tell you. He doesn't want you and I don't want you and my mother and sister . . ."

The change came without warning. Like a film gone dead, Betty Lou froze, her mouth half open, one arm raised, her words dead on her tongue. She was suspended, an instantly lifeless thing raised off the floor, as if caught between two slides of glass. A vacant insect, without speech or sound, inert and hollow. Not dead, but abruptly thinned back to primordial inanimacy.

Into the captured shell filtered new potency and being. It settled over her, a rainbow of life that poured into place eagerly—like hot fluid—into every part of her. The girl stumbled and moaned; her body jerked violently and pitched against the wall. A china teacup tumbled from an overhead shelf and smashed on the floor. The girl retreated numbly, one hand to her mouth, her eyes wide with pain and shock.

"Oh!" she gasped. "I cut myself." She shook her head and gazed up mutely at him, appealing to him. "On a nail or something."

"*Silvia!*" He caught hold of her and dragged her to her feet, away from the wall. It was *her* arm he gripped, warm and full and mature. Stunned gray eyes, brown hair, quivering breasts—she was now as she had been those last moments in the basement.

"Let's see it," he said. He tore her hand from her mouth and shakily examined her finger. There was no cut, only a thin white line rapidly dimming. "It's all right, honey. You're all right. There's nothing wrong with you!"

"Rick, I was over *there*." Her voice was husky and faint. "They came and dragged me across with them." She shuddered violently. "Rick, am I actually *back*?"

He crushed her tight. "Completely back."

"It was so long. I was over there a century. Endless ages. I thought—" Suddenly she pulled away. "Rick . . ."

"What is it?"

Silvia's face was wild with fear. "There's something wrong."

"There's nothing wrong. You've come back home and that's all that matters."

Silvia retreated from him. "But they took a living form, didn't they? Not discarded clay. They don't have the power, Rick. They altered His work instead." Her voice rose in panic. "A mistake—they should have known better than to alter the balance. It's unstable and none of them can control the . . ."

Rick blocked the doorway. "Stop talking like that!" he said fiercely. "It's worth it—*anything's* worth it. If they set things out of balance, it's their own fault."

"We can't turn it back!" Her voice rose shrilly, thin and hard, like drawn wire. "We've set it in motion, started the waves lapping out. The balance He set up is *altered*."

"Come on, darling," Rick said. "Let's go and sit in the living room with your family. You'll feel better. You'll have to try to recover from this."

They approached the three seated figures, two on the couch, one in the straight chair by the fireplace. The figures sat motionless, their faces blank, their bodies limp and waxen, dulled forms that did not respond as the couple entered the room.

Rick halted, uncomprehending. Walter Everett was slumped forward, newspaper in one hand, slippers on his feet; his pipe was still smoking in the deep ashtray on the arm of his chair. Mrs. Everett sat with a lapful of sewing, her face grim and stern, but strangely vague. An unformed face, as if the material were melting and running together. Jean sat huddled in a shapeless heap, a ball of clay wadded up, more formless each moment.

Abruptly Jean collapsed. Her arms fell loose beside her. Her head sagged. Her body, her arms and legs filled out. Her features altered rapidly. Her clothing changed. Colors flowed in her hair, her eyes, her skin. The waxen pallor was gone.

Pressing her fingers to her lips she gazed up at Rick mutely. She blinked and her eyes focused. "Oh," she gasped. Her lips moved awkwardly; the voice was faint and uneven, like a poor soundtrack. She struggled up jerkily, with uncoordinated movements that propelled her stiffly to her feet and toward him—one awkward step at a time—like a wire dummy.

"Rick, I cut myself," she said. "On a nail or something."

What had been Mrs. Everett stirred. Shapeless and vague, it made dull sounds and flopped grotesquely. Gradually it hardened and shaped itself. "My finger," its voice gasped feebly. Like mirror echoes dimming off into darkness, the third figure in the easy chair took up the words. Soon, they were all of them repeating the phrase, four fingers, their lips moving in unison.

"My finger. I cut myself, Rick."

Parrot reflections, receding mimicries of words and movement. And the settling shapes were familiar in every detail. Again and again, repeated around him, twice on the couch, in the easy chair, close beside him—so close he could hear her breath and see her trembling lips.

"What is it?" the Silvia beside him asked.

On the couch one Silvia resumed its sewing—she was sewing methodically, absorbed in her work. In the deep chair another took up its newspapers, its pipe and continued reading. One huddled, nervous and afraid. The one beside him followed as he retreated to the door. She was panting with uncertainty, her gray eyes wide, her nostrils flaring.

"Rick . . ."

He pulled the door open and made his way out onto the dark porch. Machine-like, he felt his way down the steps, through the pools of night collected everywhere, toward the driveway. In the yellow square of light behind him, Silvia was outlined, peering unhappily after him. And behind her, the other figures, identical, pure repetitions, nodding over their tasks.

He found his coupe and pulled out onto the road.

Gloomy trees and houses flashed past. He wondered how far it would go. Lapping waves spreading out—a widening circle as the imbalance spread.

He turned onto the main highway; there were soon more cars around him. He tried to see into them, but they moved too swiftly. The car ahead was a red Plymouth. A heavyset man in a blue business suit was driving, laughing merrily with the woman beside him. He pulled his own coupe up close behind the Plymouth and followed it. The man flashed gold teeth, grinned, waved his plump hands. The girl was dark-haired, pretty. She smiled at the man, adjusted her white gloves, smoothed down her hair, then rolled up the window on her side.

He lost the Plymouth. A heavy diesel truck cut in between them. Desperately he swerved around the truck and nosed in beyond the swift-moving red sedan. Presently it passed him and, for a moment, the two occupants were clearly framed. The girl resembled Silvia. The same delicate line of her small chin—the same deep lips, parting slightly when she smiled—the same slender arms and hands. It was Silvia. The Plymouth turned off and there was no other car ahead of him.

He drove for hours through the heavy night darkness. The gas gauge dropped lower and lower. Ahead of him dismal rolling countryside spread out, blank fields between towns and unwinking stars suspended in the bleak sky. Once, a cluster of red and yellow lights gleamed. An intersection—filling stations and a big neon sign. He drove on past it.

At a single-pump stand, he pulled the car off the highway, onto the oil-soaked gravel. He climbed out, his shoes crunching the stone underfoot, as he grabbed the gas hose and unscrewed the cap of his car's tank. He had the tank almost full when the door of the drab station building opened and a slim woman in white overalls and navy shirt, with a little cap lost in her brown curls, stepped out.

"Good evening, Rick," she said quietly.

He put back the gas hose. Then he was driving out onto the highway. Had he screwed the cap back on again? He didn't remember. He gained speed. He had gone over a hundred miles. He was nearing the state line.

At a little roadside cafe, warm, yellow light glowed in the chill gloom of early morning. He slowed the car down and parked at the edge of the highway in the deserted parking lot. Bleary-eyed he pushed the door open and entered.

Hot, thick smells of cooking ham and black coffee surrounded him, the comfortable sight of people eating. A jukebox blared in the corner. He threw himself onto a stool and hunched over, his head in his hands. A thin farmer next to him glanced at him curiously and then returned to his newspaper. Two hard-faced women across from him gazed at him momentarily. A handsome youth in denim jacket and jeans was eating red beans and rice, washing it down with steaming coffee from a heavy mug.

"What'll it be?" the pert blond waitress asked, a pencil behind her ear, her hair tied back in a tight bun. "Looks like you've got some hangover, mister."

He ordered coffee and vegetable soup. Soon he was eating, his hands working automatically. He found himself devouring a ham-and-cheese sandwich; had he ordered it? The jukebox blared and people came and went. There was a little town sprawled beside the road, set back in some gradual hills. Gray sunlight, cold and sterile, filtered down as morning came. He ate hot apple pie and sat wiping dully at his mouth with a napkin.

The cafe was silent. Outside nothing stirred. An uneasy calm hung over everything. The jukebox had ceased. None of the people at the counter stirred or spoke. An occasional truck roared past, damp and lumbering, windows rolled up tight.

When he looked up, Silvia was standing in front of him. Her arms were folded and she gazed vacantly past him. A bright yellow pencil was behind her ear. Her brown hair was tied back in a hard bun. At the corner others were sitting, other Silvias, dishes in front of them, half dozing or eating, some of them reading. Each the same as the next, except for their clothing.

He made his way back to his parked car. In half an hour he had crossed the state line. Cold, bright sunlight sparkled off dew-moist roofs and pavements as he sped through tiny unfamiliar towns.

Along the shiny morning streets he saw them moving—early risers, on their way to work. In twos and threes they walked, their heels echoing in sharp silence. At bus stops he saw groups of them collected together. In the houses, rising from their beds, eating breakfast, bathing, dressing, were more of them—hundreds of them, legions without number. A town of them preparing for the day, resuming their regular tasks, as the circle widened and spread.

He left the town behind. The car slowed under him as his foot slid heavily from the gas pedal. Two of them walked across a level field together. They carried books—children on their way to school. Repetition, unvarying and identical. A dog circled excitedly after them, unconcerned, his joy untainted.

He drove on. Ahead a city loomed, its stern columns of office buildings sharply outlined against the sky. The streets swarmed with noise and activity as he passed through the main business section. Somewhere, near the center of the city, he overtook the expanding periphery of the circle and emerged beyond. Diversity took the place of the endless figures of Silvia. Gray eyes and brown hair gave way to countless varieties of men and women, children and adults, of all ages and appearances. He increased his speed and raced out on the far side, onto the wide four-lane highway.

He finally slowed down. He was exhausted. He had driven for hours; his body was shaking with fatigue.

Ahead of him a carrot-haired youth was cheerfully thumbing a ride, a thin bean-pole in brown slacks and light camel's-hair sweater. Rick pulled to a halt and opened the front door. "Hop in," he said.

"Thanks, buddy." The youth hurried to the car and climbed in as Rick gathered speed. He slammed the door and settled gratefully back against the seat. "It was getting hot, standing there."

"How far are you going?" Rick demanded.

"All the way to Chicago." The youth grinned shyly. "Of course, I don't expect you to drive me that far. Anything at all is appreciated." He eyed Rick curiously. "Which way you going?"

"Anywhere," Rick said. "I'll drive you to Chicago."

"It's two hundred miles!"

"Fine," Rick said. He steered over into the left lane and gained speed. "If you want to go to New York, I'll drive you there."

"You feel all right?" The youth moved away uneasily. "I sure appreciate a lift, but . . ." He hesitated. "I mean, I don't want to take you out of your way."

Rick concentrated on the road ahead, his hands gripping hard around the rim of the wheel. "I'm going fast. I'm not slowing down or stopping."

"You better be careful," the youth warned, in a troubled voice. "I don't want to get in an accident."

"I'll do the worrying."

"But it's dangerous. What if something happens? It's too risky."

"You're wrong," Rick muttered grimly, eyes on the road. "It's worth the risk."

"But if something goes wrong—" The voice broke off uncertainly and then continued, "I might be lost. It would be easy. It's all so unstable." The voice trembled with worry and fear. "Rick, please . . ."

Rick whirled. "How do you know my name?"

The youth was crouched in a heap against the door. His face had a soft, molten look, as if it were losing its shape and sliding together in an unformed mass. "I want to come back," he was saying, from within himself, "but I'm afraid. You haven't seen it—the region between. It's nothing but energy, Rick. He tapped it a long time ago, but nobody else knows how."

The voice lightened, became clear and treble. The hair faded to a rich brown. Gray, frightened eyes flickered up at Rick. Hands frozen, he hunched over the wheel and forced himself not to move. Gradually he decreased speed and brought the car over into the right-hand lane.

"Are we stopping?" the shape beside him asked. It was Silvia's voice now. Like a new insect, drying in the sun, the shape hardened and locked into firm reality. Silvia struggled up on the seat and peered out. "Where are we? We're between towns."

He jammed on the brakes, reached past her, and threw open the door. "Get out!"

Silvia gazed at him uncomprehendingly. "What do you mean?" she faltered. "Rick, what is it? What's wrong?"

"*Get out!*"

"Rick, I don't understand." She slid over a little. Her toes touched the pavement. "Is there something wrong with the car? I thought everything was all right."

He gently shoved her out and slammed the door. The car leaped ahead, out into the stream of mid-morning traffic. Behind him the small, dazed figure was pulling itself up, bewildered and injured. He forced his eyes from the rearview mirror and crushed down the gas pedal with all his weight.

The radio buzzed and clicked in vague static when he snapped it briefly on. He turned the dial and, after a time, a big network station came in. A faint, puzzled voice, a woman's voice. For a time he couldn't make out the words. Then he recognized it and, with a pang of panic, switched the thing off.

Her voice. Murmuring plaintively. Where was the station? Chicago. The circle had already spread that far.

He slowed down. There was no point hurrying. It had already passed him by and gone on. Kansas farms—sagging stores in little old Mississippi towns—along the bleak streets of New England manufacturing cities swarms of brown-haired gray-eyed women would be hurrying.

It would cross the ocean. Soon it would take in the whole world. Africa would be strange—kraals of white-skinned young women, all exactly alike, going about the primitive chores of hunting and fruit-gathering, mashing grain, skinning animals. Building fires and weaving cloth and carefully shaping razor-sharp knives.

In China . . . he grinned inanely. She'd look strange there, too. In the austere high-collar suit, the almost monastic robe of the young communist cadres. Parade marching up the main streets of Peiping. Row after row of slim-legged full-breasted girls, with heavy Russian-made rifles. Carrying spades, picks, shovels. Columns of cloth-booted soldiers. Fast-moving workers with their precious tools. Reviewed by an identical figure on the elaborate stand overlooking the street, one slender arm raised, her gentle, pretty face expressionless and wooden.

He turned off the highway onto a side road. A moment later he was on his way back, driving slowly, listlessly, the way he had come.

At an intersection a traffic cop waded out through traffic to his car. He sat rigid, hands on the wheel, waiting numbly.

"Rick," she whispered pleadingly as she reached the window. "Isn't everything all right?"

"Sure," he answered dully.

She reached in through the open window and touched him imploringly on the arm. Familiar figures, red nails, the hand he knew so well. "I want to be with you so badly. Aren't we together again? Aren't I back?"

"Sure."

She shook her head miserably. "I don't understand," she repeated. "I thought it was all right again."

Savagely he put the car into motion and hurtled ahead. The intersection was left behind.

It was afternoon. He was exhausted, riddled with fatigue. He guided the car toward his own town automatically. Along the streets she hurried everywhere, on all sides. She was omnipresent. He came to his apartment building and parked.

The janitor greeted him in the empty hall. Rick identified him by the greasy rag clutched in one hand, the big push broom, the bucket of wood shavings. "Please," she implored, "tell me what it is, Rick. Please tell me."

He pushed past her, but she caught at him desperately. "Rick, *I'm back*. Don't you understand? They took me too soon and then they sent me back again. It was a mistake. I won't ever call them again—that's all in the past." She followed after him, down the hall to the stairs. "I'm never going to call them again."

He climbed the stairs. Silvia hesitated, then settled down on the bottom step in a wretched, unhappy heap, a tiny figure in thick workman's clothing and huge cleated boots.

He unlocked his apartment door and entered.

The late afternoon sky was a deep blue beyond the windows. The roofs of nearby apartment buildings sparkled white in the sun.

His body ached. He wandered clumsily into the bathroom—it seemed alien and unfamiliar, a difficult place to find. He filled the bowl with hot water, rolled up his sleeves, and washed his face and hands in the swirling hot steam. Briefly, he glanced up.

It was a terrified reflection that showed out of the mirror above the bowl, a face, tear-stained and frantic. The face was difficult to catch—it seemed to waver and slide. Gray eyes, bright with terror. Trembling red mouth, pulse-fluttering throat, soft brown hair. The face gazed out pathetically—and then the girl at the bowl bent to dry herself.

She turned and moved wearily out of the bathroom into the living room.

Confused, she hesitated, then threw herself onto a chair and closed her eyes, sick with misery and fatigue.

"Rick," she murmured pleadingly. "Try to help me. I'm back, aren't I?" She shook her head, bewildered. "Please, Rick, I thought everything was all right."

AUTOFAC

I

Tension hung over the three waiting men. They smoked, paced back and forth, kicked aimlessly at weeds growing by the side of the road. A hot noonday sun glared down on brown fields, rows of neat plastic houses, the distant line of mountains to the west.

"Almost time," Earl Perine said, knotting his skinny hands together. "It varies according to the load, a half second for every additional pound."

Bitterly, Morrison answered, "You've got it plotted? You're as bad as it is. Let's pretend it just *happens* to be late."

The third man said nothing. O'Neill was visiting from another settlement; he didn't know Perine and Morrison well enough to argue with them. Instead, he crouched down and arranged the papers clipped to his aluminum checkboard. In the blazing sun, O'Neill's arms were tanned, furry, glistening with sweat. Wiry, with tangled gray hair, horn-rimmed glasses, he was older than the other two. He wore slacks, a sports shirt, and crepe-soled shoes. Between his fingers, his fountain pen glittered, metallic and efficient.

"What're you writing?" Perine grumbled.

"I'm laying out the procedure we're going to employ," O'Neill said mildly. "Better to systematize it now, instead of trying at random. We want to know what we tried and what didn't work. Otherwise we'll go around in a circle. The problem we have here is one of communication; that's how I see it."

"Communication," Morrison agreed in his deep, chesty voice. "Yes, we can't get in touch with the damn thing. It comes, leaves off its load, and goes on—there's no contact between us and it."

"It's a machine," Perine said excitedly. "It's dead—blind and deaf."

"But it's in contact with the outside world," O'Neill pointed out. "There has to be some way to get to it. Specific semantic signals are meaningful to it; all we have to do is find those signals. Rediscover, actually. Maybe half a dozen out of a billion possibilities."

A low rumble interrupted the three men. They glanced up, wary and alert. The time had come.

"Here it is," Perine said. "Okay, wise guy, let's see you make one single change in its routine."

The truck was massive, rumbling under its tightly packed load. In many ways, it resembled conventional human-operated transportation vehicles, but with one exception—there was no driver's cabin. The horizontal surface was a loading stage, and the part that would normally be the headlights and radiator grill was a fibrous spongelike mass of receptors, the limited sensory apparatus of this mobile utility extension.

Aware of the three men, the truck slowed to a halt, shifted gears, and pulled on its emergency brake. A moment passed as relays moved into action; then a portion of the loading surface tilted and a cascade of heavy cartons spilled down onto the roadway. With the objects fluttered a detailed inventory sheet.

"You know what to do," O'Neill said rapidly. "Hurry up, before it gets out of here."

Expertly, grimly, the three men grabbed up the deposited cartons and ripped the protective wrappers from them. Objects gleamed: a binocular microscope, a portable radio, heaps of plastic dishes, medical supplies, razor blades, clothing, food. Most of the shipment, as usual, was food. The three men systematically began smashing objects. In a few minutes, there was nothing but a chaos of debris littered around them.

"That's that," O'Neill panted, stepping back. He fumbled for his check-sheet. "Now let's see what it does."

The truck had begun to move away; abruptly it stopped and backed toward them. Its receptors had taken in the fact that the three men had demolished the dropped-off portion of the load. It spun in a grinding half circle and came around to face its receptor bank in their direction. Up went its antenna; it had begun communicating with the factory. Instructions were on the way.

A second, identical load was tilted and shoved off the truck.

"We failed," Perine groaned as a duplicate inventory sheet fluttered after the new load. "We destroyed all that stuff for nothing."

"What now?" Morrison asked O'Neill. "What's the next stratagem on our board?"

"Give me a hand." O'Neill grabbed up a carton and lugged it back to the truck. Sliding the carton onto the platform, he turned for another. The other two men followed clumsily after him. They put the load back onto the truck. As the truck started forward, the last square box was again in place.

The truck hesitated. Its receptors registered the return of its load. From within its works came a low sustained buzzing.

"This may drive it crazy," O'Neill commented, sweating. "It went through its operation and accomplished nothing."

The truck made a short, abortive move toward going on. Then it swung purposefully around and, in a blur of speed, again dumped the load onto the road.

"Get them!" O'Neill yelled. The three men grabbed up the cartons and feverishly reloaded them. But as fast as the cartons were shoved back on the horizontal stage, the truck's grapples tilted them down its far-side ramps and onto the road.

"No use," Morrison said, breathing hard. "Water through a sieve."

"We're licked," Perine gasped in wretched agreement, "like always. We humans lose every time."

The truck regarded them calmly, its receptors blank and impassive. It was doing its job. The planetwide network of automatic factories was smoothly performing the task imposed on it five years before, in the early days of the Total Global Conflict.

"There it goes," Morrison observed dismally. The truck's antenna had come down; it shifted into low gear and released its parking brake.

"One last try," O'Neill said. He swept up one of the cartons and ripped it open. From it he dragged a ten-gallon milk tank and unscrewed the lid. "Silly as it seems."

"This is absurd," Perine protested. Reluctantly, he found a cup among the littered debris and dipped it into the milk. "A kid's game!"

The truck had paused to observe them.

"Do it," O'Neill ordered sharply. "Exactly the way we practiced it."

The three of them drank quickly from the milk tank, visibly allowing the milk to spill down their chins; there had to be no mistaking what they were doing.

As planned, O'Neill was the first. His face twisting in revulsion, he hurled the cup away and violently spat the milk into the road.

"God's sake!" he choked.

The other two did the same; stamping and loudly cursing, they kicked over the milk tank and glared accusingly at the truck.

"It's no good!" Morrison roared.

Curious, the truck came slowly back. Electronic synapses clicked and whirred, responding to the situation; its antenna shot up like a flagpole.

"I think this is it," O'Neill said, trembling. As the truck watched, he dragged out a second milk tank, unscrewed its lid, and tasted the contents. "The same!" he shouted at the truck. "It's just as bad!"

From the truck popped a metal cylinder. The cylinder dropped at Morrison's feet; he quickly snatched it up and tore it open.

STATE NATURE OF DEFECT

The instruction sheets listed rows of possible defects, with neat boxes by each; a punch-stick was included to indicate the particular deficiency of the product.

"What'll I check?" Morrison asked. "Contaminated? Bacterial? Sour? Rancid? Incorrectly labeled? Broken? Crushed? Cracked? Bent? Soiled?"

Thinking rapidly, O'Neill said, "Don't check any of them. The factory's undoubtedly ready to test and resample. It'll make its own analysis and then ignore us." His face glowed as frantic inspiration came. "Write in that blank at the bottom. It's an open space for further data."

"Write what?"

O'Neill said, "Write: *the product is thoroughly pizzled.*"

"What's that?" Perine demanded, baffled.

"Write it! It's a semantic garble—the factory won't be able to understand it. Maybe we can jam the works."

With O'Neill's pen, Morrison carefully wrote that the milk was pizzled. Shaking his head, he resealed the cylinder and returned it to the truck. The truck swept up the milk tanks and slammed its railing tidily into place.

With a shriek of tires, it hurtled off. From its slot, a final cylinder bounced; the truck hurriedly departed, leaving the cylinder lying in the dust.

O'Neill got it open and held up the paper for the others to see.

A FACTORY REPRESENTATIVE
WILL BE SENT OUT.
BE PREPARED TO SUPPLY COMPLETE DATA
ON PRODUCT DEFICIENCY.

For a moment, the three men were silent. Then Perine began to giggle. "We did it. We contacted it. We got across."

"We sure did," O'Neill agreed. "It never heard of a product being pizzled."

Cut into the base of the mountains lay the vast metallic cube of the Kansas City factory. Its surface was corroded, pitted with radiation pox, cracked and scarred from the five years of war that had swept over it. Most of the factory was buried subsurface, only its entrance stages visible. The truck was a speck rumbling at high speed toward the expanse of black metal. Presently an opening formed in the uniform surface; the truck plunged into it and disappeared inside. The entrance snapped shut.

"Now the big job remains," O'Neill said. "Now we have to persuade it to close down operations—to shut itself off."

II

Judith O'Neill served hot black coffee to the people sitting around the living room. Her husband talked while the others listened. O'Neill was as close to being an authority on the autofac system as could still be found.

In his own area, the Chicago region, he had shorted out the protective fence of the local factory long enough to get away with data tapes stored in its posterior brain. The factory, of course, had immediately reconstructed a better type of fence. But he had shown that the factories were not infallible.

"The Institute of Applied Cybernetics," O'Neill explained, "had complete control over the network. Blame the war. Blame the big noise along the lines of communication that wiped out the knowledge we need. In any case, the Institute failed to transmit its information to us, so we can't transmit our information to the factories—the news that the war is over and we're ready to resume control of industrial operations."

"And meanwhile," Morrison added sourly, "the damn network expands and consumes more of our natural resources all the time."

"I get the feeling," Judith said, "that if I stamped hard enough, I'd fall right down into a factory tunnel. They must have mines everywhere by now."

"Isn't there some limiting injunction?" Perine asked nervously. "Were they set up to expand indefinitely?"

"Each factory is limited to its own operational area," O'Neill said, "but the network itself is unbounded. It can go on scooping up our resources forever. The Institute decided it gets top priority; we mere people come second."

"Will there be *anything* left for us?" Morrison wanted to know.

"Not unless we can stop the network's operations. It's already used up half a dozen basic minerals. Its search teams are out all the time, from every factory, looking everywhere for some last scrap to drag home."

"What would happen if tunnels from two factories crossed each other?"

O'Neill shrugged. "Normally, that won't happen. Each factory has its own special section of our planet, its own private cut of the pie for its exclusive use."

"But it *could* happen."

"Well, they're raw material-tropic; as long as there's anything left, they'll hunt it down." O'Neill pondered the idea with growing interest. "It's something to consider. I suppose as things get scarcer—"

He stopped talking. A figure had come into the room; it stood silently by the door, surveying them all.

In the dull shadows, the figure looked almost human. For a brief moment, O'Neill thought it was a settlement latecomer. Then, as it moved forward, he realized that it was only quasi-human: a functional upright biped chassis, with data-receptors mounted at the top, effectors and proprioceptors mounted in a downward worm that ended in floor-grippers. Its resemblance to a human being was testimony to nature's efficiency; no sentimental imitation was intended.

The factory representative had arrived.

It began without preamble. "This is a data-collecting machine capable of communicating on an oral basis. It contains both broadcasting and receiving apparatus and can integrate facts relevant to its line of inquiry."

The voice was pleasant, confident. Obviously it was a tape, recorded by some Institute technician before the war. Coming from the quasi-human shape, it sounded grotesque; O'Neill could vividly imagine the dead young man whose cheerful voice now issued from the mechanical mouth of this upright construction of steel and wiring.

"One word of caution," the pleasant voice continued. "It is fruitless to consider this receptor human and to engage it in discussions for which it is not equipped. Although purposeful, it is not capable of conceptual thought; it can only reassemble material already available to it."

The optimistic voice clicked out and a second voice came on. It resembled the first, but now there were no intonations or personal mannerisms. The machine was utilizing the dead man's phonetic speech-pattern for its own communication.

"Analysis of the rejected product," it stated, "shows no foreign elements or noticeable deterioration. The product meets the continual testing-standards employed throughout the network. Rejection is therefore on a basis outside the test area; standards not available to the network are being employed."

"That's right," O'Neill agreed. Weighing his words with care, he continued, "We found the milk substandard. We want nothing to do with it. We insist on more careful output."

The machine responded presently. "The semantic content of the term 'pizzled' is unfamiliar to the network. It does not exist in the taped vocabulary. Can you present a factual analysis of the milk in terms of specific elements present or absent?"

"No," O'Neill said warily; the game he was playing was intricate and dangerous. "'Pizzled' is an overall term. It can't be reduced to chemical constituents."

"What does 'pizzled' signify?" the machine asked. "Can you define it in terms of alternate semantic symbols?"

O'Neill hesitated. The representative had to be steered from its special inquiry to more general regions, to the ultimate problem of closing down the network. If he could pry it open at any point, get the theoretical discussion started . . .

"'Pizzled,'" he stated, "means the condition of a product that is manufactured when no need exists. It indicates the rejection of objects on the grounds that they are no longer wanted."

The representative said, "Network analysis shows a need of high-grade pasteurized milk-substitute in this area. There is no alternate source; the network controls all the synthetic mammary-type equipment in existence." It added, "Original taped instructions describe milk as an essential to human diet."

O'Neill was being outwitted; the machine was returning the discussion to the specific. "We've decided," he said desperately, "that we don't *want* any more milk. We'd prefer to go without it, at least until we can locate cows."

"That is contrary to the network tapes," the representative objected. "There are no cows. All milk is produced synthetically."

"Then we'll produce it synthetically ourselves," Morrison broke in impatiently. "Why can't we take over the machines? My God, we're not children! We can run our own lives!"

The factory representative moved toward the door. "Until such time as your community finds other sources of milk supply, the network will continue to supply you. Analytical and evaluating apparatus will remain in this area, conducting the customary random sampling."

Perine shouted futilely, "How can we find other sources? You have the whole setup! You're running the whole show!" Following after it, he bellowed, "You say we're not ready to run things—you claim we're not capable. How do you know? You don't give us a chance! We'll never have a chance!"

O'Neill was petrified. The machine was leaving; its one-track mind had completely triumphed.

"Look," he said hoarsely, blocking its way. "We want you to shut down, understand. We want to take over your equipment and run it ourselves. The war's over with. Damn it, you're not needed anymore!"

The factory representative paused briefly at the door. "The inoperative cycle," it said, "is not geared to begin until network production merely duplicates outside production. There is at this time, according to our continual sampling, no outside production. Therefore network production continues."

Without warning, Morrison swung the steel pipe in his hand. It slashed against the machine's shoulder and burst through the elaborate network of sensory apparatus that made up its chest. The tank of receptors shattered; bits of glass, wiring, and minute parts showered everywhere.

"It's a paradox!" Morrison yelled. "A word game—a semantic game they're pulling on us. The Cyberneticists have it rigged." He raised the pipe and again brought it down savagely on the unprotesting machine. "They've got us hamstrung. We're completely helpless."

The room was in uproar. "It's the only way," Perine gasped as he pushed past O'Neill. "We'll have to destroy them—it's the network or us." Grabbing down a lamp, he hurled it in the "face" of the factory representative. The lamp and the intricate surface of plastic burst; Perine waded in, groping blindly for the machine. Now all the people in the room were closing furiously around the upright cylinder, their impotent resentment boiling over. The machine sank down and disappeared as they dragged it to the floor.

Trembling, O'Neill turned away. His wife caught hold of his arm and led him to the side of the room.

"The idiots," he said dejectedly. "They can't destroy it; they'll only teach it to build more defenses. They're making the whole problem worse."

Into the living room rolled a network repair team. Expertly, the mechanical units detached themselves from the half-track mother-bug and scurried toward the mound of struggling humans. They slid between people and rapidly burrowed. A moment later, the inert carcass of the factory representative was dragged into the hopper of the mother-bug. Parts were collected, torn remnants gathered up and carried off. The plastic strut and gear was located. Then the units restationed themselves on the bug and the team departed.

Through the open door came a second factory representative, an exact duplicate of the first. And outside in the hall stood two more upright machines. The settlement had been combed at random by a corps of representatives. Like a horde of ants, the mobile data-collecting machines had filtered through the town until, by chance, one of them had come across O'Neill.

"Destruction of network mobile data-gathering equipment is detrimental to best human interests," the factory representative informed the roomful of people. "Raw material intake is at a dangerously low ebb; what

basic materials still exist should be utilized in the manufacture of consumer commodities."

O'Neill and the machine stood facing each other.

"Oh?" O'Neill said softly. "That's interesting. I wonder what you're
lowest on—and what you'd really be willing to fight for."

Helicopter rotors whined tinnily above O'Neill's head; he ignored
them and peered through the cabin window at the ground not far below.

Slag and ruins stretched everywhere. Weeds poked their way up, sickly
stalks among which insects scuttled. Here and there, rat colonies were visible: matted hovels constructed of bone and rubble. Radiation had mutated
the rats, along with most insects and animals. A little farther, O'Neill identified a squadron of birds pursuing a ground squirrel. The squirrel dived
into a carefully prepared crack in the surface of slag and the birds turned,
thwarted.

"You think we'll ever have it rebuilt?" Morrison asked. "It makes me
sick to look at it."

"In time," O'Neill answered. "Assuming, of course, that we get industrial control back. And assuming that anything remains to work with. At
best, it'll be slow. We'll have to inch out from the settlements."

To the right was a human colony, tattered scarecrows, gaunt and ema-
ciated, living among the ruins of what had once been a town. A few acres of
barren soil had been cleared; drooping vegetables wilted in the sun, chick-
ens wandered listlessly here and there, and a fly-bothered horse lay panting
in the shade of a crude shed.

"Ruins-squatters," O'Neill said gloomily. "Too far from the network—
not tangent to any of the factories."

"It's their own fault," Morrison told him angrily. "They could come
into one of the settlements."

"That was their town. They're trying to do what *we're* trying to do—
build up things again on their own. But they're starting now, without tools
or machines, with their bare hands, nailing together bits of rubble. And it
won't work. We need machines. We can't repair ruins; we've got to start
industrial production."

Ahead lay a series of broken hills, chipped remains that had once been a ridge. Beyond stretched out the titanic ugly sore of an H-bomb crater, half filled with stagnant water and slime, a disease-ridden inland sea.

And beyond that—a glitter of busy motion.

"There," O'Neill said tensely. He lowered the helicopter rapidly. "Can you tell which factory they're from?"

"They all look alike to me," Morrison muttered, leaning over to see. "We'll have to wait and follow them back, when they get a load."

"*If* they get a load," O'Neill corrected.

The autofac exploring crew ignored the helicopter buzzing overhead and concentrated on its job. Ahead of the main truck scuttled two tractors; they made their way up mounds of rubble, probes burgeoning like quills, shot down the far slope, and disappeared into a blanket of ash that lay spread over the slag. The two scouts burrowed until only their antennas were visible. They burst up to the surface and scuttled on, their treads whirring and clanking.

"What are they after?" Morrison asked.

"God knows." O'Neill leafed intently through the papers on his clipboard. "We'll have to analyze all our back-order slips."

Below them, the autofac exploring crew disappeared behind. The helicopter passed over a deserted stretch of sand and slag on which nothing moved. A grove of scrub-brush appeared and then, far to the right, a series of tiny moving dots.

A procession of automatic ore carts was racing over the bleak slag, a string of rapidly moving metal trucks that followed one another nose to tail. O'Neill turned the helicopter toward them and a few minutes later it hovered above the mine itself.

Masses of squat mining equipment had made their way to the operations. Shafts had been sunk; empty carts waited in patient rows. A steady stream of loaded carts hurled toward the horizon, dribbling ore after them. Activity and the noise of machines hung over the area, an abrupt center of industry in the bleak wastes of slag.

"Here comes that exploring crew," Morrison observed, peering back the way they had come. "You think maybe they'll tangle?" He grinned. "No, I guess it's too much to hope for."

"It is this time," O'Neill answered. "They're looking for different substances, probably. And they're normally conditioned to ignore each other."

The first of the exploring bugs reached the line of ore carts. It veered slightly and continued its search; the carts traveled in their inexorable line as if nothing had happened.

Disappointed, Morrison turned away from the window and swore. "No use. It's like each doesn't exist for the other."

Gradually the exploring crew moved away from the line of carts, past the mining operations and over a ridge beyond. There was no special hurry; they departed without having reacted to the ore-gathering syndrome.

"Maybe they're from the same factory," Morrison said hopefully.

O'Neill pointed to the antennas visible on the major mining equipment. "Their vanes are turned at a different vector, so these represent two factories. It's going to be hard; we'll have to get it exactly right or there won't be any reaction." He clicked on the radio and got hold of the monitor at the settlement. "Any results on the consolidated back-order sheets?"

The operator put him through to the settlement governing offices.

"They're starting to come in," Perine told him. "As soon as we get sufficient samplings, we'll try to determine which raw materials which factories lack. It's going to be risky, trying to extrapolate from complex products. There may be a number of basic elements common to the various sublots."

"What happens when we've identified the missing element?" Morrison asked O'Neill. "What happens when we've got two tangent factories short on the same material?"

"Then," O'Neill said grimly, "we start collecting the material ourselves—even if we have to melt down every object in the settlements."

III

In the moth-ridden darkness of night, a dim wind stirred, chill and faint. Dense underbrush rattled metallically. Here and there a nocturnal rodent prowled, its senses hyper-alert, peering, planning, seeking food.

The area was wild. No human settlements existed for miles; the entire region had been seared flat, cauterized by repeated H-bomb blasts. Somewhere in the murky darkness, a sluggish trickle of water made its way among slag and weeds, dripping thickly into what had once been an elaborate labyrinth of sewer mains. The pipes lay cracked and broken, jutting up into the night darkness, overgrown with creeping vegetation. The wind raised clouds of black ash that swirled and danced among the weeds. Once an enormous mutant wren stirred sleepily, pulled its crude protective night coat of rags around it, and dozed off.

For a time, there was no movement. A streak of stars showed in the sky overhead, glowing starkly, remotely. Earl Perine shivered, peered up, and huddled closer to the pulsing heat-element placed on the ground between the three men.

"Well?" Morrison challenged, teeth chattering.

O'Neill didn't answer. He finished his cigarette, crushed it against a mound of decaying slag, and, getting out his lighter, lit another. The mass of tungsten—the bait—lay a hundred yards directly ahead of them.

During the last few days, both the Detroit and Pittsburgh factories had run short of tungsten. And in at least one sector, their apparatus overlapped. This sluggish heap represented precision cutting tools, parts ripped from electrical switches, high-quality surgical equipment, sections of permanent magnets, measuring devices—tungsten from every possible source, gathered feverishly from all the settlements.

Dark mist lay spread over the tungsten mound. Occasionally, a night moth fluttered down, attracted by the glow of reflected starlight. The moth hung momentarily, beat its elongated wings futilely against the interwoven tangle of metal, and then drifted off, into the shadows of the thick-packed vines that rose up from the stumps of sewer pipes.

"Not a very damn pretty spot," Perine said wryly.

"Don't kid yourself," O'Neill retorted. "This is the prettiest spot on Earth. This is the spot that marks the grave of the autofac network. People are going to come around here looking for it someday. There's going to be a plaque here a mile high."

"You're trying to keep your morale up," Morrison snorted. "You don't believe they're going to slaughter themselves over a heap of surgical tools and lightbulb filaments. They've probably got a machine down in the bottom level that sucks tungsten out of rock."

"Maybe," O'Neill said, slapping at a mosquito. The insect dodged cannily and then buzzed over to annoy Perine. Perine swung viciously at it and squatted sullenly down against the damp vegetation.

And there was what they had come to see.

O'Neill realized with a start that he had been looking at it for several minutes without recognizing it. The search-bug lay absolutely still. It rested at the crest of a small rise of slag, its anterior end slightly raised, receptors fully extended. It might have been an abandoned hulk; there was no activity of any kind, no sign of life or consciousness. The search-bug fitted perfectly into the wasted, fire-drenched landscape. A vague tub of metal sheets and gears and flat treads, it rested and waited. And watched.

It was examining the heap of tungsten. The bait had drawn its first bite.

"Fish," Perine said thickly. "The line moved. I think the sinker dropped."

"What the hell are you mumbling about?" Morrison grunted. And then he, too, saw the search-bug. "Jesus," he whispered. He half rose to his feet, massive body arched forward. "Well, there's *one* of them. Now all we need is a unit from the other factory. Which do you suppose it is?"

O'Neill located the communication vane and traced its angle. "Pittsburgh, so pray for Detroit . . . pray like mad."

Satisfied, the search-bug detached itself and rolled forward. Cautiously approaching the mound, it began a series of intricate maneuvers, rolling first one way and then another. The three watching men were mystified—until they glimpsed the first probing stalks of other search-bugs.

"Communication," O'Neill said softly. "Like bees."

Now five Pittsburgh search-bugs were approaching the mound of tungsten products. Receptors waving excitedly, they increased their pace, scurrying in a sudden burst of discovery up the side of the mound to the top. A bug burrowed and rapidly disappeared. The whole mound shuddered; the bug was down inside, exploring the extent of the find.

Ten minutes later, the first Pittsburgh ore carts appeared and began industriously hurrying off with their haul.

"Damn it!" O'Neill said, agonized. "They'll have it all before Detroit shows up."

"Can't we do anything to slow them down?" Perine demanded helplessly. Leaping to his feet, he grabbed up a rock and heaved it at the nearest cart. The rock bounced off and the cart continued its work, unperturbed.

O'Neill got to his feet and prowled around, body rigid with impotent fury. Where were they? The autofacs were equal in all respects and the spot was the exact same linear distance from each center. Theoretically, the parties should have arrived simultaneously. Yet there was no sign of Detroit—and the final pieces of tungsten were being loaded before his eyes.

But then something streaked past him.

He didn't recognize it, for the object moved too quickly. It shot like a bullet among the tangled vines, raced up the side of the hill-crest, poised for an instant to aim itself, and hurtled down the far side. It smashed directly into the lead cart. Projectile and victim shattered in an abrupt burst of sound.

Morrison leaped up. "What the hell?"

"That's it!" Perine screamed, dancing around and waving his skinny arms. "It's Detroit!"

A second Detroit search-bug appeared, hesitated as it took in the situation, and then flung itself furiously at the retreating Pittsburgh carts. Fragments of tungsten scattered everywhere—parts, wiring, broken plates, gears and springs and bolts of the two antagonists flew in all directions. The remaining carts wheeled screechingly; one of them dumped its load and rattled off at top speed. A second followed, still weighed down with tungsten. A Detroit search-bug caught up with it, spun directly in its path, and neatly overturned it. Bug and cart rolled down a shallow trench, into a stagnant pool of water. Dripping and glistening, the two of them struggled, half submerged.

"Well," O'Neill said unsteadily, "we did it. We can start back home." His legs felt weak. "Where's our vehicle?"

As he gunned the truck motor, something flashed a long way off, something large and metallic, moving over the dead slag and ash. It was a dense clot of carts, a solid expanse of heavy-duty ore carriers racing to the scene. Which factory were they from?

It didn't matter, for out of the thick tangle of black dripping vines, a web of counter-extensions was creeping to meet them. Both factories were assembling their mobile units. From all directions, bugs slithered and crept, closing in around the remaining heap of tungsten. Neither factory was going to let needed raw material get away; neither was going to give up its find. Blindly, mechanically, in the grip of inflexible directives, the two opponents labored to assemble superior forces.

"Come on," Morrison said urgently. "Let's get out of here. All hell is bursting loose."

O'Neill hastily turned the truck in the direction of the settlement. They began rumbling through the darkness on their way back. Every now and then, a metallic shape shot by them, going in the opposite direction.

"Did you see the load in that last cart?" Perine asked, worried. "It wasn't empty."

Neither were the carts that followed it, a whole procession of bulging supply carriers directed by an elaborate high-level surveying unit.

"Guns," Morrison said, eyes wide with apprehension. "They're taking in weapons. But who's going to use them?"

"They are," O'Neill answered. He indicated a movement to their right. "Look over there. This is something we hadn't expected."

They were seeing the first factory representative move into action.

As the truck pulled into the Kansas City settlement, Judith hurried breathlessly toward them. Fluttering in her hand was a strip of metal-foil paper.

"What is it?" O'Neill demanded, grabbing it from her.

"Just come." His wife struggled to catch her breath. "A mobile car— raced up, dropped it off—and left. Big excitement. Golly, the factory's—a blaze of lights. You can see it for miles."

O'Neill scanned the paper. It was a factory certification for the last group of settlement-placed orders, a total tabulation of requested and factory-analyzed needs. Stamped across the list in heavy black type were six foreboding words:

ALL SHIPMENTS SUSPENDED UNTIL FURTHER NOTICE

Letting out his breath harshly, O'Neill handed the paper over to Perine. "No more consumer goods," he said ironically, a nervous grin twitching across his face. "The network's going on a wartime footing."

"Then we did it?" Morrison asked haltingly.

"That's right," O'Neill said. Now that the conflict had been sparked, he felt a growing, frigid terror. "Pittsburgh and Detroit are in it to the finish. It's too late for us to change our minds now—they're lining up allies."

IV

Cool morning sunlight lay across the ruined plain of black metallic ash. The ash smoldered a dull, unhealthy red; it was still warm.

"Watch your step," O'Neill cautioned. Grabbing hold of his wife's arm, he led her from the rusty, sagging truck, up onto the top of a pile of strewn concrete blocks, the scattered remains of a pillbox installation. Earl Perine followed, making his way carefully, hesitantly.

Behind them, the dilapidated settlement lay spread out, a disorderly checkerboard of houses, buildings, and streets. Since the autofac network had closed down its supply and maintenance, the human settlements had fallen into semibarbarism. The commodities that remained were broken and only partly usable. It had been over a year since the last mobile factory truck had appeared, loaded with food, tools, clothing, and repair parts. From the flat expanse of dark concrete and metal at the foot of the mountains, nothing had emerged in their direction.

Their wish had been granted—they were cut off, detached from the network.

On their own.

Around the settlement grew ragged fields of wheat and tattered stalks of sun-baked vegetables. Crude handmade tools had been distributed, primitive artifacts hammered out with great labor by the various settlements. The settlements were linked only by horse-drawn carts and by the slow stutter of the telegraph key.

They had managed to keep their organization, though. Goods and services were exchanged on a slow, steady basis. Basic commodities were produced and distributed. The clothing that O'Neill and his wife and Earl Perine wore was coarse and unbleached, but sturdy. And they had managed to convert a few of the trucks from gasoline to wood.

"Here we are," O'Neill said. "We can see from here."

"Is it worth it?" Judith asked, exhausted. Bending down, she plucked aimlessly at her shoe, trying to dig a pebble from the soft hide sole. "It's a long way to come, to see something we've seen every day for thirteen months."

"True," O'Neill admitted, his hand briefly resting on his wife's limp shoulder. "But this may be the last. And that's what we want to see."

In the gray sky above them, a swift circling dot of opaque black moved. High, remote, the dot spun and darted, following an intricate and wary course. Gradually, its gyrations moved it toward the mountains and the bleak expanse of bomb-rubbled structure sunk in their base.

"San Francisco," O'Neill explained. "One of those long-range hawk projectiles, all the way from the West Coast."

"And you think it's the last?" Perine asked.

"It's the only one we've seen this month." O'Neill seated himself and began sprinkling dried bits of tobacco into a trench of brown paper. "And we used to see hundreds."

"Maybe they have something better," Judith suggested. She found a smooth rock and tiredly seated herself. "Could it be?"

Her husband smiled ironically. "No. They don't have anything better."

The three of them were tensely silent. Above them, the circling dot of black drew closer. There was no sign of activity from the flat surface of metal and concrete; the Kansas City factory remained inert, totally unresponsive. A few billows of warm ash drifted across it and one end was partly submerged in rubble. The factory had taken numerous direct hits. Across the plain, the furrows of its subsurface tunnels lay exposed, clogged with debris and the dark, water-seeking tendrils of tough vines.

"Those damn vines," Perine grumbled, picking at an old sore on his unshaven chin. "They're taking over the world."

Here and there around the factory, the demolished ruin of a mobile extension rusted in the morning dew. Carts, trucks, search-bugs, factory representatives, weapons carriers, guns, supply trains, subsurface projectiles, indiscriminate parts of machinery mixed and fused together in shapeless piles. Some had been destroyed returning to the factory; others had been contacted as they emerged, fully loaded, heavy with equipment. The factory itself—what remained of it—seemed to have settled more deeply into the earth. Its upper surface was barely visible, almost lost in drifting ash.

In four days, there had been no known activity, no visible movement of any sort.

"It's dead," Perine said. "You can see it's dead."

O'Neill didn't answer. Squatting down, he made himself comfortable and prepared to wait. In his own mind, he was sure that some fragment of automation remained in the eroded factory. Time would tell. He examined his wristwatch; it was eight-thirty. In the old days, the factory would be starting its daily routine. Processions of trucks and varied mobile units would be coming to the surface, loaded with supplies, to begin their expeditions to the human settlement.

Off to the right, something stirred. He quickly turned his attention to it.

A single battered ore-gathering cart was creeping clumsily toward the factory. One last damaged mobile unit trying to complete its task. The cart was virtually empty; a few meager scraps of metal lay strewn in its hold. A scavenger . . . the metal was sections ripped from destroyed equipment encountered on the way. Feebly, like a blind metallic insect, the cart approached the factory. Its progress was incredibly jerky. Every now and then, it halted, bucked and quivered, and wandered aimlessly off the path.

"Control is bad," Judith said, with a touch of horror in her voice. "The factory's having trouble guiding it back."

Yes, he had seen that. Around New York, the factory had lost its high-frequency transmitter completely. Its mobile units had floundered in crazy gyrations, racing in random circles, crashing against rocks and trees, sliding into gullies, overturning, finally unwinding and becoming reluctantly inanimate.

The ore cart reached the edge of the ruined plain and halted briefly. Above it, the dot of black still circled the sky. For a time, the cart remained frozen.

"The factory's trying to decide," Perine said. "It needs the material, but it's afraid of that hawk up there."

The factory debated and nothing stirred. Then the ore cart again resumed its unsteady crawl. It left the tangle of vines and started out across the blasted open plain. Painfully, with infinite caution, it headed toward the slab of dark concrete and metal at the base of the mountains.

The hawk stopped circling.

"Get down!" O'Neill said sharply. "They've got those rigged with the new bombs."

His wife and Perine crouched down beside him and the three of them peered warily at the plain and the metal insect crawling laboriously across it. In the sky, the hawk swept in a straight line until it hung directly over the cart. Then, without a sound or warning, it came down in a straight dive. Hands to her face, Judith shrieked, "I can't watch! It's awful! Like wild animals!"

"It's not after the cart," O'Neill grated.

As the airborne projectile dropped, the cart put on a burst of desperate speed. It raced noisily toward the factory, clanking and rattling, trying in a last futile attempt to reach safety. Forgetting the menace above, the frantically eager factory opened up and guided its mobile unit directly inside. And the hawk had what it wanted.

Before the barrier could close, the hawk swooped down in a long glide parallel with the ground. As the cart disappeared into the depths of the factory, the hawk shot after it, a swift shimmer of metal that hurtled past the clanking cart. Suddenly aware, the factory snapped the barrier shut. Grotesquely, the cart struggled; it was caught fast in the half-closed entrance.

But whether it freed itself didn't matter. There was a dull rumbling stir. The ground moved, billowed, then settled back. A deep shock wave passed beneath the three watching human beings. From the factory rose a single column of black smoke. The surface of concrete split like a dried pod; it shriveled and broke, and dribbled shattered bits of itself in a shower of ruin. The smoke hung for a while, drifting aimlessly away with the morning wind.

The factory was a fused, gutted wreck. It had been penetrated and destroyed.

O'Neill got stiffly to his feet. "That's all. All over with. We've got what we set out after—we've destroyed the autofac network." He glanced at Perine. "Or was that what we were after?"

They looked toward the settlement that lay behind them. Little remained of the orderly rows of houses and streets of the previous years. Without the network, the settlement had rapidly decayed. The original prosperous neatness had dissipated; the settlement was shabby, ill-kept.

"Of course," Perine said haltingly. "Once we get into the factories and start setting up our own assembly lines . . ."

"Is there anything left?" Judith inquired.

"There must be something left. My God, there were levels going down miles!"

"Some of those bombs they developed toward the end were awfully big," Judith pointed out. "Better than anything we had in our war."

"Remember that camp we saw? The ruins-squatters?"

"I wasn't along," Perine said.

"They were like wild animals. Eating roots and larvae. Sharpening rocks, tanning hides. Savagery, bestiality."

"But that's what people like that want," Perine answered defensively.

"Do they? Do we want this?" O'Neill indicated the straggling settlement. "Is this what we set out looking for, that day we collected the tungsten? Or that day we told the factory truck its milk was—" He couldn't remember the word.

"Pizzled," Judith supplied.

"Come on," O'Neill said. "Let's get started. Let's see what's left of that factory—left for us."

They approached the ruined factory late in the afternoon. Four trucks rumbled shakily up to the rim of the gutted pit and halted, motors steaming, tailpipes dripping. Wary and alert, workmen scrambled down and stepped gingerly across the hot ash.

"Maybe it's too soon," one of them objected.

O'Neill had no intention of waiting. "Come on," he ordered. Grabbing up a flashlight, he stepped down into the crater.

The sheltered hull of the Kansas City factory lay directly ahead. In its gutted mouth, the ore cart still hung caught, but it was no longer struggling. Beyond the cart was an ominous pool of gloom. O'Neill flashed his light through the entrance; the tangled, jagged remains of upright supports were visible.

"We want to get down deep," he said to Morrison, who prowled cautiously beside him. "If there's anything left, it's at the bottom."

Morrison grunted. "Those boring moles from Atlanta got most of the deep layers."

"Until the others got their mines sunk." O'Neill stepped carefully through the sagging entrance, climbed a heap of debris that had been tossed against the slit from inside, and found himself within the factory—an expanse of confused wreckage, without pattern or meaning.

"Entropy," Morrison breathed, oppressed. "The thing it always hated. The thing it was built to fight. Random particles everywhere. No purpose to it."

"Down underneath," O'Neill said stubbornly, "we may find some sealed enclaves. I know they got so they were dividing up into autonomous sections, trying to preserve repair units intact, to re-form the composite factory."

"The moles got most of them, too," Morrison observed, but he lumbered after O'Neill.

Behind them, the workmen came slowly. A section of wreckage shifted ominously and a shower of hot fragments cascaded down.

"You men get back to the trucks," O'Neill said. "No sense endangering any more of us than we have to. If Morrison and I don't come back, forget us—don't risk sending a rescue party." As they left, he pointed out to Morrison a descending ramp still partially intact. "Let's get below."

Silently, the two men passed one dead level after another. Endless miles of dark ruin stretched out, without sound or activity. The vague shapes of darkened machinery, unmoving belts, and conveyer equipment were partially visible, and the partially completed husks of war projectiles, bent and twisted by the final blast.

"We can salvage some of that," O'Neill said, but he didn't actually believe it. The machinery was fused, shapeless. Everything in the factory had run together, molten slag without form or use. "Once we get it to the surface . . ."

"We can't," Morrison contradicted bitterly. "We don't have hoists or winches." He kicked at a heap of charred supplies that had stopped along its broken belt and spilled halfway across the ramp.

"It seemed like a good idea at the time," O'Neill said as the two of them continued past vacant levels of machines. "But now that I look back, I'm not so sure."

They had penetrated a long way into the factory. The final level lap spread out ahead of them. O'Neill flashed the light here and there, trying to locate undestroyed sections, portions of the assembly process still intact.

It was Morrison who felt it first. He suddenly dropped to his hands and knees; heavy body pressed against the floor, he lay listening, face hard, eyes wide. "For God's sake—"

"What is it?" O'Neill cried. Then he, too, felt it. Beneath them, a faint, insistent vibration hummed through the floor, a steady hum of activity. They had been wrong; the hawk had not been totally successful. Below, in a deeper level, the factory was still alive. Closed, limited operations still went on.

"On its own," O'Neill muttered, searching for an extension of the descent-lift. "Autonomous activity, set to continue after the rest is gone. How do we get down?"

The descent-lift was broken off, sealed by a thick section of metal. The still-living layer beneath their feet was completely cut off; there was no entrance.

Racing back the way they had come, O'Neill reached the surface and hailed the first truck. "Where the hell's the torch? Give it here!"

The precious blowtorch was passed to him and he hurried back, puffing, into the depths of the ruined factory where Morrison waited. Together, the two of them began frantically cutting through the warped metal flooring, burning apart the sealed layers of protective mesh.

"It's coming," Morrison gasped, squinting in the glare of the torch. The plate fell with a clang, disappearing into the level below. A blaze of white light burst up around them and the two men leaped back.

In the sealed chamber, furious activity boomed and echoed, a steady process of moving belts, whirring machine-tools, fast-moving mechanical supervisors. At one end, a steady flow of raw materials entered the line; at the far end, the final product was whipped off, inspected, and crammed into a conveyer tube.

All this was visible for a split second; then the intrusion was discovered. Robot relays came into play. The blaze of lights flickered and dimmed. The assembly line froze to a halt, stopped in its furious activity.

The machines clicked off and became silent.

At one end, a mobile unit detached itself and sped up the wall toward the hole O'Neill and Morrison had cut. It slammed an emergency seal in place and expertly welded it tight. The scene below was gone. A moment later the floor shivered as activity resumed.

Morrison, white-faced and shaking, turned to O'Neill. "What are they doing? What are they making?"

"Not weapons," O'Neill said.

"That stuff is being sent up"—Morrison gestured convulsively—"to the surface."

Shakily, O'Neill climbed to his feet. "Can we locate the spot?"

"I—think so."

"We better." O'Neill swept up the flashlight and started toward the ascent ramp. "We're going to have to see what those pellets are that they're shooting up."

The exit valve of the conveyer tube was concealed in a tangle of vines and ruins a quarter of a mile beyond the factory. In a slot of rock at the base of the mountains the valve poked up like a nozzle. From ten yards away, it was invisible; the two men were almost on top of it before they noticed it.

Every few moments, a pellet burst from the valve and shot up into the sky. The nozzle revolved and altered its angle of deflection; each pellet was launched in a slightly varied trajectory.

"How far are they going?" Morrison wondered.

"Probably varies. It's distributing them at random." O'Neill advanced cautiously, but the mechanism took no note of him. Plastered against the towering wall of rock was a crumpled pellet; by accident, the nozzle had released it directly at the mountainside. O'Neill climbed up, got it, and jumped down.

The pellet was a smashed container of machinery, tiny metallic elements too minute to be analyzed without a microscope.

"Not a weapon," O'Neill said.

The cylinder had split. At first he couldn't tell if it had been the impact or deliberate internal mechanisms at work. From the rent, an ooze of metal bits was sliding. Squatting down, O'Neill examined them.

The bits were in motion. Microscopic machinery, smaller than ants, smaller than pins, working energetically, purposefully—constructing something that looked like a tiny rectangle of steel.

"They're building," O'Neill said, awed. He got up and prowled on. Off to the side, at the far edge of the gully, he came across a downed pellet far advanced on its construction. Apparently it had been released some time ago.

This one had made great enough progress to be identified. Minute as it was, the structure was familiar. The machinery was building a miniature replica of the demolished factory.

"Well," O'Neill said thoughtfully, "we're back where we started from. For better or worse . . . I don't know."

"I guess they must be all over Earth by now," Morrison said, "landing everywhere and going to work."

A thought struck O'Neill. "Maybe some of them are geared to escape velocity. That would be neat—autofac networks throughout the whole universe."

Behind him, the nozzle continued to spurt out its torrent of metal seeds.

THE MINORITY REPORT

I

The first thought Anderton had when he saw the young man was: *I'm getting bald. Bald and fat and old.* But he didn't say it aloud. Instead, he pushed back his chair, got to his feet, and came resolutely around the side of his desk, his right hand rigidly extended. Smiling with forced amiability, he shook hands with the young man.

"Witwer?" he asked, managing to make this query sound gracious.

"That's right," the young man said. "But the name's Ed to you, of course. That is, if you share my dislike for needless formality." The look on his blond, overly confident face showed that he considered the matter settled. It would be Ed and John: Everything would be agreeably cooperative right from the start.

"Did you have much trouble finding the building?" Anderton asked guardedly, ignoring the too-friendly overture. *Good God, he had to hold on to something.* Fear touched him and he began to sweat. Witwer was moving around the office as if he already owned it—as if he were measuring it for size. Couldn't he wait a couple of days—a decent interval?

"No trouble," Witwer answered blithely, his hands in his pockets. Eagerly, he examined the voluminous files that lined the wall. "I'm not coming into your agency blind, you understand. I have quite a few ideas of my own about the way Precrime is run."

Shakily, Anderton lit his pipe. "How is it run? I should like to know."

"Not badly," Witwer said. "In fact, quite well."

Anderton regarded him steadily. "Is that your private opinion? Or is it just cant?"

Witwer met his gaze guilelessly. "Private and public. The Senate's pleased with your work. In fact, they're enthusiastic." He added, "As enthusiastic as very old men can be."

Anderton winced, but outwardly he remained impassive. It cost him an effort, though. He wondered what Witwer *really* thought. What was actually going on in that close-cropped skull? The young man's eyes were blue, bright—and disturbingly clever. Witwer was nobody's fool. And obviously he had a great deal of ambition.

"As I understand it," Anderton said cautiously, "you're going to be my assistant until I retire."

"That's my understanding, too," the other replied, without an instant's hesitation.

"Which may be this year, or next year—or ten years from now." The pipe in Anderton's hand trembled. "I'm under no compulsion to retire. I founded Precrime and I can stay on here as long as I want. It's purely *my* decision."

Witwer nodded, his expression still guileless. "Of course."

With an effort, Anderton cooled down a trifle. "I merely wanted to get things straight."

"From the start," Witwer agreed. "You're the boss. What you say goes." With every evidence of sincerity, he asked: "Would you care to show me the organization? I'd like to familiarize myself with the general routine as soon as possible."

As they walked along the busy, yellow-lit tiers of offices, Anderton said: "You're acquainted with the theory of precrime, of course. I presume we can take that for granted."

"I have the information publicly available," Witwer replied. "With the aid of your precog mutants, you've boldly and successfully abolished the post-crime punitive system of jails and fines. As we all realize, punishment was never much of a deterrent, and could scarcely have afforded comfort to a victim already dead."

They had come to the descent lift. As it carried them swiftly downward, Anderton said: "You've probably grasped the basic legalistic drawback to pre-crime methodology. We're taking in individuals who have broken no law."

"But they surely will," Witwer affirmed with conviction.

"Happily they *don't*—because we get them first, before they can commit an act of violence. So the commission of the crime itself is absolute metaphysics. We claim they're culpable. They, on the other hand, eternally claim they're innocent. And, in a sense, they *are* innocent."

The lift let them out, and they again paced down a yellow corridor. "In our society we have no major crimes," Anderton went on, "but we do have a detention camp full of would-be criminals."

Doors opened and closed, and they were in the analytical wing. Ahead of them rose impressive banks of equipment—the data-receptors, and the computing mechanisms that studied and restructured the incoming material. And beyond the machinery sat the three precogs, almost lost to view in the maze of wiring.

"There they are," Anderton said dryly. "What do you think of them?"

In the gloomy half-darkness the three idiots sat babbling. Every incoherent utterance, every random syllable, was analyzed, compared, reassembled in the form of visual symbols, transcribed on conventional punchcards, and ejected into various coded slots. All day long the idiots babbled, imprisoned in their special high-backed chairs, held in one rigid position by metal bands, and bundles of wiring, clamps. Their physical needs were taken care of automatically. They had no spiritual needs. Vegetable-like, they muttered and dozed and existed. Their minds were dull, confused, lost in shadows.

But not the shadows of today. The three gibbering, fumbling creatures, with their enlarged heads and wasted bodies, were contemplating the future. The analytical machinery was recording prophecies, and as the three precog idiots talked, the machinery carefully listened.

For the first time Witwer's face lost its breezy confidence. A sick, dismayed expression crept into his eyes, a mixture of shame and moral shock. "It's not—pleasant," he murmured. "I didn't realize they were so—" He groped in his mind for the right word, gesticulating. "So—deformed."

"Deformed and retarded," Anderton instantly agreed. "Especially the girl, there. Donna is forty-five years old. But she looks about ten. The talent absorbs everything; the esp-lobe shrivels the balance of the frontal area. But what do we care? We get their prophecies. They pass on what we need. They don't understand any of it, but *we* do."

Subdued, Witwer crossed the room to the machinery. From a slot he collected a stack of cards. "Are these names that have come up?" he asked.

"Obviously." Frowning, Anderton took the stack from him. "I haven't had a chance to examine them," he explained, impatiently concealing his annoyance.

Fascinated, Witwer watched the machinery pop a fresh card into the now empty slot. It was followed by a second—and a third. From the whirring disks came one card after another. "The precogs must see quite far into the future," Witwer exclaimed.

"They see a quite limited span," Anderton informed him. "One week or two ahead at the very most. Much of their data is worthless to us—simply not relevant to our line. We pass it on to the appropriate agencies. And they in turn trade data with us. Every important bureau has its cellar of treasured *monkeys*."

"Monkeys?" Witwer stared at him uneasily. "Oh, yes, I understand. See no evil, speak no evil, et cetera. Very amusing."

"Very *apt*." Automatically, Anderton collected the fresh cards which had been turned up by the spinning machinery. "Some of these names will be totally discarded. And most of the remainder record petty crimes: thefts, income tax evasion, assault, extortion. As I'm sure you know, Precrime has cut down felonies by ninety-nine and decimal point eight percent. We seldom get actual murder or treason. After all, the culprit knows we'll confine him in the detention camp a week before he gets a chance to commit the crime."

"When was the last time an actual murder was committed?" Witwer asked.

"Five years ago," Anderton said, pride in his voice.

"How did it happen?"

"The criminal escaped our teams. We had his name—in fact, we had all the details of the crime, including the victim's name. We knew the exact moment, the location of the planned act of violence. But in spite of us he was able to carry it out." Anderton shrugged. "After all, we can't get all of them." He riffled the cards. "But we do get most."

"One murder in five years." Witwer's confidence was returning. "Quite an impressive record . . . something to be proud of."

Quietly Anderton said: "I *am* proud. Thirty years ago I worked out the theory—back in the days when the self-seekers were thinking in terms of quick raids on the stock market. I saw something legitimate ahead—something of tremendous social value."

He tossed the packet of cards to Wally Page, his subordinate in charge of the monkey block. "See which ones we want," he told him. "Use your own judgment."

As Page disappeared with the cards, Witwer said thoughtfully: "It's a big responsibility."

"Yes, it is," agreed Anderton. "If we let one criminal escape—as we did five years ago—we've got a human life on our conscience. We're solely responsible. If we slip up, somebody dies." Bitterly, he jerked three new cards from the slot. "It's a public trust."

"Are you ever tempted to—" Witwer hesitated. "I mean, some of the men you pick up must offer you plenty."

"It wouldn't do any good. A duplicate file of cards pops out at Army GHQ. It's check and balance. They can keep their eye on us as continuously as they wish." Anderton glanced briefly at the top card. "So even if we wanted to accept a—"

He broke off, his lips tightening.

"What's the matter?" Witwer asked curiously.

Carefully, Anderton folded up the top card and put it away in his pocket. "Nothing," he muttered. "Nothing at all."

The harshness in his voice brought a flush to Witwer's face. "You really don't like me," he observed.

"True," Anderton admitted. "I don't. But—"

He couldn't believe he disliked the young man that much. It didn't seem possible: it *wasn't* possible. Something was wrong. Dazed, he tried to steady his tumbling mind.

On the card was his name. Line one—an already accused future murderer! According to the coded punches, Precrime Commissioner John A. Anderton was going to kill a man—and within the next week.

With absolute, overwhelming conviction, he didn't believe it.

II

In the outer office, talking to Page, stood Anderton's slim and attractive young wife, Lisa. She was engaged in a sharp, animated discussion of policy, and barely glanced up as Witwer and her husband entered.

"Hello, darling," Anderton said.

Witwer remained silent. But his pale eyes flickered slightly as they rested on the brown-haired woman in her trim police uniform. Lisa was now an executive official of Precrime but once, Witwer knew, she had been Anderton's secretary.

Noticing the interest on Witwer's face, Anderton paused and reflected. To plant the card in the machines would require an accomplice on the inside—someone who was closely connected with Precrime and had access to the analytical equipment. Lisa was an improbable element. But the possibility did exist.

Of course, the conspiracy could be large-scale and elaborate, involving far more than a "rigged" card inserted somewhere along the line. The original data itself might have been tampered with. Actually, there was no telling how far back the alteration went. A cold fear touched him as he began to see the possibilities. His original impulse—to tear open the machines and remove all the data—was uselessly primitive. Probably the tapes agreed with the card: He would only incriminate himself further.

He had approximately twenty-four hours. Then, the Army people would check over their cards and discover the discrepancy. They would find in their files a duplicate of the card he had appropriated. He had only one of two copies, which meant that the folded card in his pocket might just as well be lying on Page's desk in plain view of everyone.

From outside the building came the drone of police cars starting out on their routine round-ups. How many hours would elapse before one of them pulled up in front of *his* house?

"What's the matter, darling?" Lisa asked him uneasily. "You look as if you've just seen a ghost. Are you all right?"

"I'm fine," he assured her.

Lisa suddenly seemed to become aware of Ed Witwer's admiring scrutiny. "Is this gentleman your new co-worker, darling?" she asked.

Warily, Anderton introduced his new associate. Lisa smiled in friendly greeting. Did a covert awareness pass between them? He couldn't tell. God, he was beginning to suspect everybody—not only his wife and Witwer, but a dozen members of his staff.

"Are you from New York?" Lisa asked.

"No," Witwer replied. "I've lived most of my life in Chicago. I'm staying at a hotel—one of the big downtown hotels. Wait—I have the name written on a card somewhere."

While he self-consciously searched his pockets, Lisa suggested: "Per-

haps you'd like to have dinner with us. We'll be working in close coopera-
tion, and I really think we ought to get better acquainted."

Startled, Anderton backed off. What were the chances of his wife's
friendliness being benign, accidental? Witwer would be present the balance
of the evening, and would now have an excuse to trail along to Anderton's
private residence. Profoundly disturbed, he turned impulsively, and moved
toward the door.

"Where are you going?" Lisa asked, astonished.

"Back to the monkey block," he told her. "I want to check over some
rather puzzling data tapes before the Army sees them." He was out in the
corridor before she could think of a plausible reason for detaining him.

Rapidly, he made his way to the ramp at its far end. He was striding
down the outside stairs toward the public sidewalk, when Lisa appeared
breathlessly behind him.

"What on earth has come over you?" Catching hold of his arm, she
moved quickly in front of him. "I *knew* you were leaving," she exclaimed,
blocking his way. "What's wrong with you? Everybody thinks you're—" She
checked herself. "I mean, you're acting so erratically."

People surged by them—the usual afternoon crowd. Ignoring them,
Anderton pried his wife's fingers from his arm. "I'm getting out," he told
her. "While there's still time."

"But—*why*?"

"I'm being framed—deliberately and maliciously. This creature is out
to get my job. The Senate is getting at me *through* him."

Lisa gazed up at him, bewildered. "But he seems like such a nice young
man."

"Nice as a water moccasin."

Lisa's dismay turned to disbelief. "I don't believe it. Darling, all this
strain you've been under—" Smiling uncertainly, she faltered: "It's not
really credible that Ed Witwer is trying to frame you. How could he, even if
he wanted to? Surely Ed wouldn't—"

"Ed?"

"That's his name, isn't it?"

Her brown eyes flashed in startled, wildly incredulous protest. "Good
heavens, you're suspicious of everybody. You actually believe I'm mixed up
with it in some way, don't you?"

He considered. "I'm not sure."

She drew closer to him, her eyes accusing. "That's not true. You really believe it. Maybe you *ought* to go away for a few weeks. You desperately need a rest. All this tension and trauma, a younger man coming in. You're acting paranoiac. Can't you see that? People plotting against you. Tell me, do you have any actual proof?"

Anderton removed his wallet and took out the folded card. "Examine this carefully," he said, handing it to her.

The color drained out of her face, and she gave a little harsh, dry gasp.

"The setup is fairly obvious," Anderton told her, as levelly as he could. "This will give Witwer a legal pretext to remove me right now. He won't have to wait until I resign." Grimly, he added: "They know I'm good for a few years yet."

"But—"

"It will end the check and balance system. Precrime will no longer be an independent agency. The Senate will control the police, and after that—" His lips tightened. "They'll absorb the Army too. Well, it's outwardly logical enough. *Of course* I feel hostility and resentment toward Witwer—*of course* I have a motive.

"Nobody likes to be replaced by a younger man, and find himself turned out to pasture. It's all really quite plausible—except that I haven't the remotest intention of killing Witwer. But I can't prove that. So what can I do?"

Mutely, her face very white, Lisa shook her head. "I—I don't know. Darling, if only—"

"Right now," Anderton said abruptly, "I'm going home to pack my things. That's about as far ahead as I can plan."

"You're really going to—to try to hide out?"

"I am. As far as the Centaurian-colony planets, if necessary. It's been done successfully before, and I have a twenty-four-hour start." He turned resolutely. "Go back inside. There's no point in your coming with me."

"Did you imagine I would?" Lisa asked huskily.

Startled, Anderton stared at her. "Wouldn't you?" Then with amazement, he murmured: "No, I can see you don't believe me. You still think I'm imagining all this." He jabbed savagely at the card. "Even with that evidence you still aren't convinced."

"No," Lisa agreed quickly, "I'm not. You didn't look at it closely enough, darling. Ed Witwer's name isn't on it."

Incredulous, Anderton took the card from her.

"Nobody says you're going to kill Ed Witwer," Lisa continued rapidly, in a thin, brittle voice. "The card *must* be genuine, understand? And it has nothing to do with Ed. He's not plotting against you and neither is anybody else."

Too confused to reply, Anderton stood studying the card. She was right. Ed Witwer was not listed as his victim. On line five, the machine had neatly stamped another name.

LEOPOLD KAPLAN

Numbly, he pocketed the card. He had never heard of the man in his life.

III

The house was cool and deserted, and almost immediately Anderton began making preparations for his journey. While he packed, frantic thoughts passed through his mind.

Possibly he was wrong about Witwer—but how could he be sure? In any event, the conspiracy against him was far more complex than he had realized. Witwer, in the overall picture, might be merely an insignificant puppet animated by someone else—by some distant, indistinct figure only vaguely visible in the background.

It had been a mistake to show the card to Lisa. Undoubtedly, she would describe it in detail to Witwer. He'd never get off Earth, never have an opportunity to find out what life on a frontier planet might be like.

While he was thus preoccupied, a board creaked behind him. He turned from the bed, clutching a weather-stained winter sports jacket, to face the muzzle of a gray-blue A-pistol.

"It didn't take you long," he said, staring with bitterness at the tight-lipped, heavyset man in a brown overcoat who stood holding the gun in his gloved hand. "Didn't she even hesitate?"

The intruder's face registered no response. "I don't know what you're talking about," he said. "Come along with me."

Startled, Anderton laid down the sports jacket. "You're not from my agency? You're not a police officer?"

Protesting and astonished, he was hustled outside the house to a waiting limousine. Instantly three heavily armed men closed in behind him. The door slammed and the car shot off down the highway, away from the city. Impassive and remote, the faces around him jogged with the motion of the speeding vehicle as open fields, dark and somber, swept past.

Anderton was still trying futilely to grasp the implications of what had happened, when the car came to a rutted side road, turned off, and descended into a gloomy sub-surface garage. Someone shouted an order. The heavy metal lock grated shut and overhead lights blinked on. The driver turned off the car motor.

"You'll have reason to regret this," Anderton warned hoarsely, as they dragged him from the car. "Do you realize who I am?"

"We realize," the man in the brown overcoat said.

At gunpoint, Anderton was marched upstairs, from the clammy silence of the garage into a deep-carpeted hallway. He was, apparently, in a luxurious private residence, set out in the war-devoured rural area. At the far end of the hallway he could make out a room—a book-lined study simply but tastefully furnished. In a circle of lamplight, his face partly in shadows, a man he had never met sat waiting for him.

As Anderton approached, the man nervously slipped a pair of rimless glasses in place, snapped the case shut, and moistened his dry lips. He was elderly, perhaps seventy or older, and under his arm was a slim silver cane. His body was thin, wiry, his attitude curiously rigid. What little hair he had was dusty brown—a carefully smoothed sheen of neutral color above his pale, bony skull. Only his eyes seemed really alert.

"Is this Anderton?" he inquired querulously, turning to the man in the brown overcoat. "Where did you pick him up?"

"At his home," the other replied. "He was packing—as we expected."

The man at the desk shivered visibly. "Packing." He took off his glasses and jerkily returned them to their case. "Look here," he said bluntly to Anderton, "what's the matter with you? Are you hopelessly insane? How could you kill a man you've never met?"

The old man, Anderton suddenly realized, was Leopold Kaplan.

"First, I'll ask you a question," Anderton countered rapidly. "Do you realize what you've done? I'm Commissioner of Police. I can have you sent up for twenty years."

He was going to say more, but a sudden wonder cut him short.

"*How did you find out?*" he demanded. Involuntarily, his hand went to his pocket, where the folded card was hidden. "It won't be for another—"

"I wasn't notified through your agency," Kaplan broke in, with angry impatience. "The fact that you've never heard of me doesn't surprise me too much. Leopold Kaplan, General of the Army of the Federated Westbloc Alliance." Begrudgingly, he added, "Retired, since the end of the Anglo-Chinese War, and the abolishment of AFWA."

It made sense. Anderton had suspected that the Army processed its duplicate cards immediately, for its own protection. Relaxing somewhat, he demanded: "Well? You've got me here. What next?"

"Evidently," Kaplan said, "I'm not going to have you destroyed, or it would have shown up on one of those miserable little cards. I'm curious about you. It seemed incredible to me that a man of your stature could contemplate the cold-blooded murder of a total stranger. There must be something more here. Frankly, I'm puzzled. If it represented some kind of Police strategy—" He shrugged his thin shoulders. "Surely you wouldn't have permitted the duplicate card to reach us."

"Unless," one of his men suggested, "it's a deliberate plant."

Kaplan raised his bright, bird-like eyes and scrutinized Anderton. "What do you have to say?"

"That's exactly what it is," Anderton said, quick to see the advantage of stating frankly what he believed to be the simple truth. "The prediction on the card was deliberately fabricated by a clique inside the police agency. The card is prepared and I'm netted. I'm relieved of my authority automatically. My assistant steps in and claims he prevented the murder in the usual efficient Precrime manner. Needless to say, there is no murder or intent to murder."

"I agree with you that there will be no murder," Kaplan affirmed grimly. "You'll be in police custody. I intend to make certain of that."

Horrified, Anderton protested: "You're taking me back there? If I'm in custody I'll never be able to prove—"

"I don't care what you prove or don't prove," Kaplan interrupted. "All I'm interested in is having you out of the way." Frigidly, he added: "For my own protection."

"He was getting ready to leave," one of the men asserted.

"That's right," Anderton said, sweating. "As soon as they get hold of me I'll be confined in the detention camp. Witwer will take over—lock, stock, and barrel." His face darkened. "And my wife. They're acting in concert, apparently."

For a moment Kaplan seemed to waver. "It's possible," he conceded, regarding Anderton steadily. Then he shook his head. "I can't take the chance. If this is a frame against you, I'm sorry. But it's simply not my affair." He smiled slightly. "However, I wish you luck." To the men he said: "Take him to the police building and turn him over to the highest authority." He mentioned the name of the acting commissioner, and waited for Anderton's reaction.

"Witwer!" Anderton echoed, incredulous.

Still smiling slightly, Kaplan turned and clicked on the console radio in the study. "Witwer has already assumed authority. Obviously, he's going to create quite an affair out of this."

There was a brief static hum, and then, abruptly, the radio blared out into the room—a noisy professional voice, reading a prepared announcement.

". . . all citizens are warned not to shelter or in any fashion aid or assist this dangerous marginal individual. The extraordinary circumstance of an escaped criminal at liberty and in a position to commit an act of violence is unique in modern times. All citizens are hereby notified that legal statutes still in force implicate any and all persons failing to cooperate fully with the police in their task of apprehending John Allison Anderton. To repeat: The Precrime Agency of the Federal Westbloc Government is in the process of locating and neutralizing its former Commissioner, John Allison Anderton, who, through the methodology of the Precrime system, is hereby declared a potential murderer and as such forfeits his rights to freedom and all its privileges."

"It didn't take him long," Anderton muttered, appalled. Kaplan snapped off the radio and the voice vanished.

"Lisa must have gone directly to him," Anderton speculated bitterly.

"Why should he wait?" Kaplan asked. "You made your intentions clear."

He nodded to his men. "Take him back to town. I feel uneasy having him so close. In that respect I concur with Commissioner Witwer. I want him neutralized as soon as possible."

IV

Cold, light rain beat against the pavement, as the car moved through the dark streets of New York City toward the police building.

"You can see his point," one of the men said to Anderton. "If you were in his place you'd act just as decisively."

Sullen and resentful, Anderton stared straight ahead.

"Anyhow," the man went on, "you're just one of many. Thousands of people have gone to that detention camp. You won't be lonely. As a matter of fact, you may not want to leave."

Helplessly, Anderton watched pedestrians hurrying along the rain-swept sidewalks. He felt no strong emotion. He was aware only of an overpowering fatigue. Dully, he checked off the street numbers: they were getting near the police station.

"This Witwer seems to know how to take advantage of an opportunity," one of the men observed conversationally. "Did you ever meet him?"

"Briefly," Anderton answered.

"He wanted your job—so he framed you. Are you sure of that?"

Anderton grimaced. "Does it matter?"

"I was just curious." The man eyed him languidly. "So you're the ex-Commissioner of Police. People in the camp will be glad to see you coming. They'll remember you."

"No doubt," Anderton agreed.

"Witwer sure didn't waste any time. Kaplan's lucky—with an official like that in charge." The man looked at Anderton almost pleadingly. "You're really convinced it's a plot, eh?"

"Of course."

"You wouldn't harm a hair of Kaplan's head? For the first time in history, Precrime goes wrong? An innocent man is framed by one of those cards. Maybe there've been other innocent people—right?"

"It's quite possible," Anderton admitted listlessly.

"Maybe the whole system can break down. Sure, you're not going to commit a murder—and maybe none of them were. Is that why you told Kaplan you wanted to keep yourself outside? Were you hoping to prove the system wrong? I've got an open mind, if you want to talk about it."

Another man leaned over, and asked, "Just between the two of us, is there really anything to this plot stuff? Are you really being framed?"

Anderton sighed. At that point he wasn't certain, himself. Perhaps he was trapped in a closed, meaningless time-circle with no motive and no beginning. In fact, he was almost ready to concede that he was the victim of a weary, neurotic fantasy, spawned by growing insecurity. Without a fight, he was willing to give himself up. A vast weight of exhaustion lay upon him. He was struggling against the impossible—and all the cards were stacked against him.

The sharp squeal of tires roused him. Frantically, the driver struggled to control the car, tugging at the wheel and slamming on the brakes, as a massive bread truck loomed up from the fog and ran directly across the lane ahead. Had he gunned the motor instead he might have saved himself. But too late he realized his error. The car skidded, lurched, hesitated for a brief instant, and then smashed head-on into the bread truck.

Under Anderton the seat lifted up and flung him face-forward against the door. Pain, sudden, intolerable, seemed to burst in his brain as he lay gasping and trying feebly to pull himself to his knees. Somewhere the crackle of fire echoed dismally, a patch of hissing brilliance winking in the swirls of mist making their way into the twisted hulk of the car.

Hands from outside the car reached for him. Slowly he became aware that he was being dragged through the rent that had been the door. A heavy seat cushion was shoved brusquely aside, and all at once he found himself on his feet, leaning heavily against a dark shape and being guided into the shadows of an alley a short distance from the car.

In the distance, police sirens wailed.

"You'll live," a voice grated in his ear, low and urgent. It was a voice he had never heard before, as unfamiliar and harsh as the rain beating into his face. "Can you hear what I'm saying?"

"Yes," Anderton acknowledged. He plucked aimlessly at the ripped sleeve of his shirt. A cut on his cheek was beginning to throb. Confused, he tried to orient himself. "You're not—"

"Stop talking and listen." The man was heavyset, almost fat. Now his big hands held Anderton propped against the wet brick wall of the building, out of the rain and the flickering light of the burning car. "We had to do it that way," he said. "It was the only alternative. We didn't have much time. We thought Kaplan would keep you at his place longer."

"Who are you?" Anderton managed.

The moist, rain-streaked face twisted into a humorless grin. "My name's Fleming. You'll see me again. We have about five seconds before the police get here. Then we're back where we started." A flat packet was stuffed into Anderton's hands. "That's enough loot to keep you going. And there's a full set of identification in there. We'll contact you from time to time." His grin increased and became a nervous chuckle. "Until you've proved your point."

Anderton blinked. "It is a frameup, then?"

"Of course." Sharply, the man swore. "You mean they got you to believe it, too?"

"I thought—" Anderton had trouble talking; one of his front teeth seemed to be loose. "Hostility toward Witwer . . . replaced, my wife and a younger man, natural resentment. . . ."

"Don't kid yourself," the other said. "You know better than that. This whole business was worked out carefully. They had every phase of it under control. The card was set to pop the day Witwer appeared. They've already got the first part wrapped up. Witwer is Commissioner, and you're a hunted criminal."

"Who's behind it?"

"Your wife."

Anderton's head spun. "You're positive?"

The man laughed. "You bet your life." He glanced quickly around. "Here come the police. Take off down this alley. Grab a bus, get yourself into the slum section, rent a room and buy a stack of magazines to keep you busy. Get other clothes—You're smart enough to take care of yourself. Don't try to leave Earth. They've got all the intersystem transports screened. If you can keep low for the next seven days, you're made."

"Who are you?" Anderton demanded.

Fleming let go of him. Cautiously, he moved to the entrance of the alley and peered out. The first police car had come to rest on the damp pavement; its motor spinning tinnily, it crept suspiciously toward the smouldering ruin that had been Kaplan's car. Inside the wreck the squad of men were stirring feebly, beginning to creep painfully through the tangle of steel and plastic out into the cold rain.

"Consider us a protective society," Fleming said softly, his plump, expressionless face shining with moisture. "A sort of police force that watches the police. To see," he added, "that everything stays on an even keel."

His thick hand shot out. Stumbling, Anderton was knocked away from him, half-falling into the shadows and damp debris that littered the alley.

"Get going," Fleming told him sharply. "And don't discard that packet." As Anderton felt his way hesitantly toward the far exit of the alley, the man's last words drifted to him. "Study it carefully and you may still survive."

V

The identification cards described him as Ernest Temple, an unemployed electrician, drawing a weekly subsistence from the State of New York, with a wife and four children in Buffalo and less than a hundred dollars in assets. A sweat-stained green card gave him permission to travel and to maintain no fixed address. A man looking for work needed to travel. He might have to go a long way.

As he rode across town in the almost empty bus, Anderton studied the description of Ernest Temple. Obviously, the cards had been made out with him in mind, for all the measurements fitted. After a time he wondered about the fingerprints and the brain-wave pattern. They couldn't possibly stand comparison. The walletful of cards would get him past only the most cursory examinations.

But it was something. And with the ID cards came ten thousand dollars in bills. He pocketed the money and cards, then turned to the neatly typed message in which they had been enclosed.

At first he could make no sense of it. For a long time he studied it, perplexed.

The existence of a majority logically implies a corresponding minority.

The bus had entered the vast slum region, the tumbled miles of cheap hotels and broken-down tenements that had sprung up after the mass destruction of the war. It slowed to a stop, and Anderton got to his feet. A few passengers idly observed his cut cheek and damaged clothing. Ignoring them, he stepped down onto the rain-swept curb.

Beyond collecting the money due him, the hotel clerk was not interested. Anderton climbed the stairs to the second floor and entered the narrow, musty-smelling room that now belonged to him. Gratefully, he locked the door and pulled down the window shades. The room was small but clean. Bed, dresser, scenic calendar, chair, lamp, a radio with a slot for the insertion of quarters.

He dropped a quarter into it and threw himself heavily down on the bed. All main stations carried the police bulletin. It was novel, exciting, something unknown to the present generation. An escaped criminal! The public was avidly interested.

". . . this man has used the advantage of his high position to carry out an initial escape," the announcer was saying, with professional indignation. "Because of his high office he had access to the previewed data and the trust placed in him permitted him to evade the normal process of detection and relocation. During the period of his tenure he exercised his authority to send countless potentially guilty individuals to their proper confinement, thus sparing the lives of innocent victims. This man, John Allison Anderton, was instrumental in the original creation of the Precrime system, the prophylactic pre-detection of criminals through the ingenious use of mutant precogs, capable of previewing future events and transferring orally that data to analytical machinery. These three precogs, in their vital function. . . ."

The voice faded out as he left the room and entered the tiny bathroom. There, he stripped off his coat and shirt, and ran hot water in the wash bowl. He began bathing the cut on his cheek. At the drugstore on the corner he had bought iodine and Band-Aids, a razor, comb, toothbrush, and other small things he would need. The next morning he intended to find a secondhand clothing store and buy more suitable clothing. After all, he was now an unemployed electrician, not an accident-damaged Commissioner of Police.

In the other room the radio blared on. Only subconsciously aware of it, he stood in front of the cracked mirror, examining a broken tooth.

". . . the system of three precogs finds its genesis in the computers of the middle decades of this century. How are the results of an electronic computer checked? By feeding the data to a second computer of identical design. But two computers are not sufficient. If each computer arrived at a different answer it is impossible to tell *a priori* which is correct. The solution, based on a careful study of statistical method, is to utilize a third computer to check the results of the first two. In this manner, a so-called majority report is obtained. It can be assumed with fair probability that the agreement of two out of three computers indicates which of the alternative results is accurate. It would not be likely that two computers would arrive at identically incorrect solutions—"

Anderton dropped the towel he was clutching and raced into the other room. Trembling, he bent to catch the blaring words of the radio.

". . . unanimity of all three precogs is a hoped-for but seldom-achieved phenomenon, acting-Commissioner Witwer explains. It is much more common to obtain a collaborative majority report of two precogs, plus a minority report of some slight variation, usually with reference to time and place, from the third mutant. This is explained by the theory of *multiple-futures*. If only one time-path existed, precognitive information would be of no importance, since no possibility would exist, in possessing this information, of altering the future. In the Precrime Agency's work we must first of all assume—"

Frantically, Anderton paced around the tiny room. Majority report— only two of the precogs had concurred on the material underlying the card. That was the meaning of the message enclosed with the packet. The report of the third precog, the minority report, was somehow of importance.

Why?

His watch told him that it was after midnight. Page would be off duty. He wouldn't be back in the monkey block until the next afternoon. It was a slim chance, but worth taking. Maybe Page would cover for him, and maybe not. He would have to risk it.

He had to see the minority report.

VI

Between noon and one o'clock the rubbish-littered streets swarmed with people. He chose that time, the busiest part of the day, to make his call. Selecting a phone booth in a patron-teeming super drugstore, he dialed the familiar police number and stood holding the cold receiver to his ear. Deliberately, he had selected the aud, not the vid line: in spite of his secondhand clothing and seedy, unshaven appearance, he might be recognized.

The receptionist was new to him. Cautiously, he gave Page's extension. If Witwer were removing the regular staff and putting in his satellites, he might find himself talking to a total stranger.

"Hello," Page's gruff voice came.

Relieved, Anderton glanced around. Nobody was paying any attention to him. The shoppers wandered among the merchandise, going about their daily routines. "Can you talk?" he asked. "Or are you tied up?"

There was a moment of silence. He could picture Page's mild face torn with uncertainty as he wildly tried to decide what to do. At last came halting words. "Why—are you calling here?"

Ignoring the question, Anderton said, "I didn't recognize the receptionist. New personnel?"

"Brand-new," Page agreed, in a thin, strangled voice. "Big turnovers, these days."

"So I hear." Tensely, Anderton asked, "How's your job? Still safe?"

"Wait a minute." The receiver was put down and the muffled sound of steps came in Anderton's ear. It was followed by the quick slam of a door being hastily shut. Page returned. "We can talk better now," he said hoarsely.

"How much better?"

"Not a great deal. Where are you?"

"Strolling through Central Park," Anderton said. "Enjoying the sunlight." For all he knew, Page had gone to make sure the line-tap was in place. Right now, an airborne police team was probably on its way. But he had to take the chance. "I'm in a new field," he said curtly. "I'm an electrician these days."

"Oh?" Page said, baffled.

"I thought maybe you had some work for me. If it can be arranged, I'd like to drop by and examine your basic computing equipment. Especially the data and analytical banks in the monkey block."

After a pause, Page said, "It—might be arranged. If it's really important."

"It is," Anderton assured him. "When would be best for you?"

"Well," Page said, struggling. "I'm having a repair team come in to look at the intercom equipment. The acting-Commissioner wants it improved, so he can operate quicker. You might trail along."

"I'll do that. About when?"

"Say four o'clock. Entrance B, level 6. I'll—meet you."

"Fine," Anderton agreed, already starting to hang up. "I hope you're still in charge, when I get there."

He hung up and rapidly left the booth. A moment later he was pushing through the dense pack of people crammed into the nearby cafeteria. Nobody would locate him there.

He had three and a half hours to wait. And it was going to seem a lot longer. It proved to be the longest wait of his life before he finally met Page as arranged.

The first thing Page said was: "You're out of your mind. Why in hell did you come back?"

"I'm not back for long." Tautly, Anderton prowled around the monkey block, systematically locking one door after another. "Don't let anybody in. I can't take chances."

"You should have quit when you were ahead." In an agony of apprehension, Page followed after him. "Witwer is making hay, hand over fist. He's got the whole country screaming for your blood."

Ignoring him, Anderton snapped open the main control bank of the analytical machinery. "Which of the three monkeys gave the minority report?"

"Don't question me—I'm getting out." On his way to the door Page halted briefly, pointed to the middle figure, and then disappeared. The door closed; Anderton was alone.

The middle one. He knew that one well. The dwarfed, hunched-over figure had sat buried in its wiring and relays for fifteen years. As Anderton approached, it didn't look up. With eyes glazed and blank, it contemplated a world that did not yet exist, blind to the physical reality that lay around it.

"Jerry" was twenty-four years old. Originally, he had been classified as a hydrocephalic idiot but when he reached the age of six the psych testers had identified the precog talent, buried under the layers of tissue corrosion.

Placed in a government-operated training school, the latent talent had been cultivated. By the time he was nine the talent had advanced to a useful stage. "Jerry," however, remained in the aimless chaos of idiocy; the burgeoning faculty had absorbed the totality of his personality.

Squatting down, Anderton began disassembling the protective shields that guarded the tape reels stored in the analytical machinery. Using schematics, he traced the leads back from the final stages of the integrated computers, to the point where "Jerry's" individual equipment branched off. Within minutes he was shakily lifting out two half-hour tapes: recent rejected data not fused with majority reports. Consulting the code chart, he selected the section of tape which referred to his particular card.

A tape scanner was mounted nearby. Holding his breath, he inserted the tape, activated the transport, and listened. It took only a second. From the first statement of the report it was clear what had happened. He had what he wanted; he could stop looking.

"Jerry's" vision was misphased. Because of the erratic nature of precognition, he was examining a time-area slightly different from that of his companions. For him, the report that Anderton would commit a murder was an event to be integrated along with everything else. That assertion— and Anderton's reaction—was one more piece of datum.

Obviously, "Jerry's" report superseded the majority report. Having been informed that he would commit a murder, Anderton would change his mind and not do so. The preview of the murder had canceled out the murder; prophylaxis had occurred simply in his being informed. Already, a new time-path had been created. But "Jerry" was outvoted.

Trembling, Anderton rewound the tape and clicked on the recording head. At high speed he made a copy of the report, restored the original, and removed the duplicate from the transport. Here was the proof that the card was invalid: *obsolete*. All he had to do was show it to Witwer. . . .

His own stupidity amazed him. Undoubtedly, Witwer had seen the report; and in spite of it, had assumed the job of Commissioner, had kept the police teams out. Witwer didn't intend to back down; he wasn't concerned with Anderton's innocence.

What, then, could he do? Who else would be interested?

"You damn fool!" a voice behind him grated, wild with anxiety.

Quickly, he turned. His wife stood at one of the doors, in her police uniform, her eyes frantic with dismay. "Don't worry," he told her briefly, displaying the reel of tape. "I'm leaving."

Her face distorted, Lisa rushed frantically up to him. "Page said you were here, but I couldn't believe it. He shouldn't have let you in. He just doesn't understand what you are."

"What am I?" Anderton inquired caustically. "Before you answer, maybe you better listen to this tape."

"I don't want to listen to it! I just want you to get out of here! Ed Witwer knows somebody's down here. Page is trying to keep him occupied, but—" She broke off, her head turned stiffly to one side. "He's here now! He's going to force his way in."

"Haven't you got any influence? Be gracious and charming. He'll probably forget about me."

Lisa looked at him in bitter reproach. "There's a ship parked on the roof. If you want to get away. . . ." Her voice choked and for an instant she was silent. Then she said, "I'll be taking off in a minute or so. If you want to come—"

"I'll come," Anderton said. He had no other choice. He had secured his tape, his proof, but he hadn't worked out any method of leaving. Gladly, he hurried after the slim figure of his wife as she strode from the block, through a side door, and down a supply corridor, her heels clicking loudly in the deserted gloom.

"It's a good fast ship," she told him over her shoulder. "It's emergency-fueled—ready to go. I was going to supervise some of the teams."

VII

Behind the wheel of the high-velocity police cruiser, Anderton outlined what the minority report tape contained. Lisa listened without comment, her face pinched and strained, her hands clasped tensely in her lap. Below the ship, the war-ravaged rural countryside spread out like a relief map, the vacant regions between cities crater-pitted and dotted with the ruins of farms and small industrial plants.

"I wonder," she said, when he had finished, "how many times this has happened before."

"A minority report? A great many times."

"I mean, one precog misphased. Using the report of the others as data—superseding them." Her eyes dark and serious, she added, "Perhaps a lot of the people in the camps are like you."

"No," Anderton insisted. But he was beginning to feel uneasy about it, too. "I was in a position to see the card, to get a look at the report. That's what did it."

"But—" Lisa gestured significantly. "Perhaps all of them would have reacted that way. We could have told them the truth."

"It would have been too great a risk," he answered stubbornly.

Lisa laughed sharply. "Risk? Chance? Uncertainty? With precogs around?"

Anderton concentrated on steering the fast little ship. "This is a unique case," he repeated. "And we have an immediate problem. We can tackle the theoretical aspects later on. I have to get this tape to the proper people— before your bright young friend demolishes it."

"You're taking it to Kaplan?"

"I certainly am." He tapped the reel of tape which lay on the seat between them. "He'll be interested. Proof that his life isn't in danger ought to be of vital concern to him."

From her purse, Lisa shakily got out her cigarette case. "And you think he'll help you."

"He may—or he may not. It's a chance worth taking."

"How did you manage to go underground so quickly?" Lisa asked. "A completely effective disguise is difficult to obtain."

"All it takes is money," he answered evasively.

As she smoked, Lisa pondered. "Probably Kaplan will protect you," she said. "He's quite powerful."

"I thought he was only a retired general."

"Technically—that's what he is. But Witwer got out the dossier on him. Kaplan heads an unusual kind of exclusive veterans' organization. It's actually a kind of club, with a few restricted members. High officers only—an international class from both sides of the war. Here in New York they maintain a great mansion of a house, three glossy-paper publications, and occasional TV coverage that costs them a small fortune."

"What are you trying to say?"

"Only this. You've convinced me that you're innocent. I mean, it's obvious that you *won't* commit a murder. But you must realize now that the original report, the majority report, *was not a fake.* Nobody falsified it. Ed Witwer didn't create it. There's no plot against you, and there never was. If you're going to accept this minority report as genuine you'll have to accept the majority one, also."

Reluctantly, he agreed. "I suppose so."

"Ed Witwer," Lisa continued, "is acting in complete good faith. He really believes you're a potential criminal—and why not? He's got the majority report sitting on his desk, but you have that card folded up in your pocket."

"I destroyed it," Anderton said, quietly.

Lisa leaned earnestly toward him. "Ed Witwer isn't motivated by any desire to get your job," she said. "He's motivated by the same desire that has always dominated you. He believes in Precrime. He wants the system to continue. I've talked to him and I'm convinced he's telling the truth."

Anderton asked, "Do you want me to take this reel to Witwer? If I do— he'll destroy it."

"Nonsense," Lisa retorted. "The originals have been in his hands from the start. He could have destroyed them any time he wished."

"That's true," Anderton conceded. "Quite possibly he didn't know."

"Of course he didn't. Look at it this way. If Kaplan gets hold of that tape, the police will be discredited. Can't you see why? It would prove that the majority report was an error. Ed Witwer is absolutely right. You have to be taken in—if Precrime is to survive. You're thinking of your own safety. But think, for a moment, about the system." Leaning over, she stubbed out her cigarette and fumbled in her purse for another. "Which means more to you—your own personal safety or the existence of the system?"

"My safety," Anderton answered, without hesitation.

"You're positive?"

"If the system can survive only by imprisoning innocent people, then it deserves to be destroyed. My personal safety is important because I'm a human being. And furthermore—"

From her purse, Lisa got out an incredibly tiny pistol. "I believe," she told him huskily, "that I have my finger on the firing release. I've never used a weapon like this before. But I'm willing to try."

After a pause, Anderton asked: "You want me to turn the ship around? Is that it?"

"Yes, back to the police building. I'm sorry. If you could put the good of the system above your own selfish—"

"Keep your sermon," Anderton told her. "I'll take the ship back. But I'm not going to listen to your defense of a code of behavior no intelligent man could subscribe to."

Lisa's lips pressed into a thin, bloodless line. Holding the pistol tightly, she sat facing him, her eyes fixed intently on him as he swung the ship in a broad arc. A few loose articles rattled from the glove compartment as the little craft turned on a radical slant, one wing rising majestically until it pointed straight up.

Both Anderton and his wife were supported by the constraining metal arms of their seats. But not so the third member of the party.

Out of the corner of his eye, Anderton saw a flash of motion. A sound came simultaneously, the clawing struggle of a large man as he abruptly lost his footing and plunged into the reinforced wall of the ship. What followed happened quickly. Fleming scrambled instantly to his feet, lurching and wary, one arm lashing out for the woman's pistol. Anderton was too startled to cry out. Lisa turned, saw the man—and screamed. Fleming knocked the gun from her hand, sending it clattering to the floor.

Grunting, Fleming shoved her aside and retrieved the gun. "Sorry," he gasped, straightening up as best he could. "I thought she might talk more. That's why I waited."

"You were here when—" Anderton began—and stopped. It was obvious that Fleming and his men had kept him under surveillance. The existence of Lisa's ship had been duly noted and factored in, and while Lisa had debated whether it would be wise to fly him to safety, Fleming had crept into the storage compartment of the ship.

"Perhaps," Fleming said, "you'd better give me that reel of tape." His moist, clumsy fingers groped for it. "You're right—Witwer would have melted it down to a puddle."

"Kaplan, too?" Anderton asked numbly, still dazed by the appearance of the man.

"Kaplan is working directly with Witwer. That's why his name showed on line five of the card. Which one of them is the actual boss, we can't tell. Possibly neither." Fleming tossed the tiny pistol away and got out his own heavy-duty military weapon. "You pulled a real flub in taking off with this woman. I told you she was back of the whole thing."

"I can't believe that," Anderton protested. "If she—"

"You've got no sense. This ship was warmed up by Witwer's order. They wanted to fly you out of the building so that we couldn't get to you. With you on your own, separated from us, you didn't stand a chance."

A strange look passed over Lisa's stricken features. "It's not true," she whispered. "Witwer never saw this ship. I was going to supervise—"

"You almost got away with it," Fleming interrupted inexorably. "We'll be lucky if a police patrol ship isn't hanging on us. There wasn't time to check." He squatted down as he spoke, directly behind the woman's chair. "The first thing is to get this woman out of the way. We'll have to drag you completely out of this area. Page tipped off Witwer on your new disguise, and you can be sure it has been widely broadcast."

Still crouching, Fleming seized hold of Lisa. Tossing his heavy gun to Anderton, he expertly tilted her chin up until her temple was shoved back against the seat. Lisa clawed frantically at him; a thin, terrified wail rose in her throat. Ignoring her, Fleming closed his great hands around her neck and began relentlessly to squeeze.

"No bullet wound," he explained, gasping. "She's going to fall out—natural accident. It happens all the time. But in this case, her neck will be broken *first*."

It seemed strange that Anderton waited so long. As it was, Fleming's thick fingers were cruelly embedded in the woman's pale flesh before he lifted the butt of the heavy-duty pistol and brought it down on the back of Fleming's skull. The monstrous hands relaxed. Staggered, Fleming's head fell forward and he sagged against the wall of the ship. Trying feebly to collect himself, he began dragging his body upward. Anderton hit him again, this time above the left eye. He fell back, and lay still.

Struggling to breathe, Lisa remained for a moment huddled over, her body swaying back and forth. Then, gradually, the color crept back into her face.

"Can you take the controls?" Anderton asked, shaking her, his voice urgent.

"Yes, I think so." Almost mechanically she reached for the wheel. "I'll be all right. Don't worry about me."

"This pistol," Anderton said, "is Army ordnance issue. But it's not from the war. It's one of the useful new ones they've developed. I could be a long way off but there's just a chance—"

He climbed back to where Fleming lay spread out on the deck. Trying not to touch the man's head, he tore open his coat and rummaged in his pockets. A moment later Fleming's sweat-sodden wallet rested in his hands.

Tod Fleming, according to his identification, was an Army Major attached to the Internal Intelligence Department of Military Information. Among the various papers was a document signed by General Leopold Kaplan, stating that Fleming was under the special protection of his own group—the International Veterans' League.

Fleming and his men were operating under Kaplan's orders. The bread truck, the accident, had been deliberately rigged.

It meant that Kaplan had deliberately kept him out of police hands. The plan went back to the original contact in his home, when Kaplan's men had picked him up as he was packing. Incredulous, he realized what had really happened. Even then, they were making sure they got him before the police. From the start, it had been an elaborate strategy to make certain that Witwer would fail to arrest him.

"You were telling the truth," Anderton said to his wife, as he climbed back in the seat. "Can we get hold of Witwer?"

Mutely, she nodded. Indicating the communications circuit of the dashboard, she asked: "What—did you find?"

"Get Witwer for me. I want to talk to him as soon as I can. It's very urgent."

Jerkily, she dialed, got the closed-channel mechanical circuit, and raised police headquarters in New York. A visual panorama of petty police officials flashed by before a tiny replica of Ed Witwer's features appeared on the screen.

"Remember me?" Anderton asked him.

Witwer blanched. "Good God. What happened? Lisa, are you bringing him in?" Abruptly his eyes fastened on the gun in Anderton's hands. "Look," he said savagely, "don't do anything to her. Whatever you may think, she's not responsible."

"I've already found that out," Anderton answered. "Can you get a fix on us? We may need protection getting back."

"*Back!*" Witwer gazed at him unbelievingly. "You're coming in? You're giving yourself up?"

"I am, yes." Speaking rapidly, urgently, Anderton added, "There's something you must do immediately. Close off the monkey block. Make certain nobody gets it—Page or anyone else. *Especially Army people.*"

"Kaplan," the miniature image said.

"What about him?"

"He was here. He—he just left."

Anderton's heart stopped beating. "What was he doing?"

"Picking up data. Transcribing duplicates of our precog reports on you. He insisted he wanted them solely for his protection."

"Then he's already got it," Anderton said. "It's too late."

Alarmed, Witwer almost shouted: "Just what do you mean? What's happening?"

"I'll tell you," Anderton said heavily, "when I get back to my office."

VIII

Witwer met him on the roof of the police building. As the small ship came to rest, a cloud of escort ships dipped their fins and sped off. Anderton immediately approached the blond-haired young man.

"You've got what you wanted," he told him. "You can lock me up, and send me to the detention camp. But that won't be enough."

Witwer's blue eyes were pale with uncertainty. "I'm afraid I don't understand—"

"It's not my fault. I should never have left the police building. Where's Wally Page?"

"We've already clamped down on him," Witwer replied. "He won't give us any trouble."

Anderton's face was grim.

"You're holding him for the wrong reason," he said. "Letting me into the monkey block was no crime. But passing information to Army is. You've had an Army plant working here." He corrected himself, a little lamely, "I mean, I have."

"I've called back the order on you. Now the teams are looking for Kaplan."

"Any luck?"

"He left here in an Army truck. We followed him, but the truck got into a militarized Barracks. Now they've got a big wartime R-3 tank blocking the street. It would be civil war to move it aside."

Slowly, hesitantly, Lisa made her way from the ship. She was still pale and shaken and on her throat an ugly bruise was forming.

"What happened to you?" Witwer demanded. Then he caught sight of Fleming's inert form lying spread out inside. Facing Anderton squarely, he said: "Then you've finally stopped pretending this is some conspiracy of mine."

"I have."

"You don't think I'm—" He made a disgusted face. "*Plotting* to get your job."

"Sure you are. Everybody is guilty of that sort of thing. And I'm plotting to keep it. But this is something else—and you're not responsible."

"Why do you assert," Witwer inquired, "that it's too late to turn yourself in? My God, we'll put you in the camp. The week will pass and Kaplan will still be alive."

"He'll be alive, yes," Anderton conceded. "But he can prove he'd be just as alive if I were walking the streets. He has the information that proves the majority report obsolete. He can break the Precrime system." He finished, "Heads or tails, he wins—and we lose. The Army discredits us; their strategy paid off."

"But why are they risking so much? What exactly do they want?"

"After the Anglo-Chinese War, the Army lost out. It isn't what it was in the good old AFWA days. They ran the complete show, both military and domestic. And they did their own police work."

"Like Fleming," Lisa said faintly.

"After the war, the Westbloc was demilitarized. Officers like Kaplan were retired and discarded. Nobody likes that." Anderton grimaced. "I can sympathize with him. He's not the only one. But we couldn't keep on running things that way. We had to divide up the authority."

"You say Kaplan has won," Witwer said. "Isn't there anything we can do?"

"I'm not going to kill him. We know it and he knows it. Probably he'll come around and offer us some kind of deal. We'll continue to function, but the Senate will abolish our real pull. You wouldn't like that, would you?"

"I should say not," Witwer answered emphatically. "One of these days I'm going to be running this agency." He flushed. "Not immediately, of course."

Anderton's expression was somber. "It's too bad you publicized the majority report. If you had kept it quiet, we could cautiously draw it back in. But everybody's heard about it. We can't retract it now."

"I guess not," Witwer admitted awkwardly. "Maybe I—don't have this job down as neatly as I imagined."

"You will, in time. You'll be a good police officer. You believe in the status quo. But learn to take it easy." Anderton moved away from them. "I'm going to study the data tapes of the majority report. I want to find out exactly how I was supposed to kill Kaplan." Reflectively, he finished: "It might give me some ideas."

The data tapes of the precogs "Donna" and "Mike" were separately stored. Choosing the machinery responsible for the analysis of "Donna," he opened the protective shield and laid out the contents. As before, the code informed him which reels were relevant and in a moment he had the tape-transport mechanism in operation.

It was approximately what he had suspected. This was the material utilized by "Jerry"—the superseded time-path. In it Kaplan's Military Intelligence agents kidnapped Anderton as he drove home from work. Taken to Kaplan's villa, the organization GHQ of the International Veterans' League. Anderton was given an ultimatum: voluntarily disband the Precrime system or face open hostilities with Army.

In this discarded time-path, Anderton, as Police Commissioner, had turned to the Senate for support. No support was forthcoming. To avoid civil war, the Senate had ratified the dismemberment of the police system, and decreed a return to military law "to cope with the emergency." Taking a corps of fanatic police, Anderton had located Kaplan and shot him, along with other officials of the Veterans' League. Only Kaplan had died. The others had been patched up. And the coup had been successful.

This was "Donna." He rewound the tape and turned to the material previewed by "Mike." It would be identical; both precogs had combined to present a unified picture. "Mike" began as "Donna" had begun: Anderton had become aware of Kaplan's plot against the police. But something was wrong. Puzzled, he ran the tape back to the beginning. Incomprehensibly, it didn't jibe. Again he relayed the tape, listening intently.

The "Mike" report was quite different from the "Donna" report.

An hour later, he had finished his examination, put away the tapes, and left the monkey block. As soon as he emerged, Witwer asked, "What's the matter? I can see something's wrong."

"No," Anderton answered slowly, still deep in thought. "Not exactly wrong." A sound came to his ears. He walked vaguely over to the window and peered out.

The street was crammed with people. Moving down the center lane was a four-column line of uniformed troops. Rifles, helmets . . . marching soldiers in their dingy wartime uniforms, carrying the cherished pennants of AFWA flapping in the cold afternoon wind.

"An Army rally," Witwer explained bleakly. "I was wrong. They're not going to make a deal with us. Why should they? Kaplan's going to make it public."

Anderton felt no surprise. "He's going to read the minority report?"

"Apparently. They're going to demand the Senate disband us, and take away our authority. They're going to claim we've been arresting innocent men—nocturnal police raids, that sort of thing. Rule by terror."

"You suppose the Senate will yield?"

Witwer hesitated. "I wouldn't want to guess."

"I'll guess," Anderton said. "They will. That business out there fits with what I learned downstairs. We've got ourselves boxed in and there's only one direction we can go. Whether we like it or not, we'll have to take it." His eyes had a steely glint.

Apprehensively, Witwer asked: "What is it?"

"Once I say it, you'll wonder why you didn't invent it. Very obviously, I'm going to have to fulfill the publicized report. I'm going to have to kill Kaplan. That's the only way we can keep them from discrediting us."

"But," Witwer said, astonished, "the majority report has been superseded."

"I can do it," Anderton informed him, "but it's going to cost. You're familiar with the statutes governing first-degree murder?"

"Life imprisonment."

"At least. Probably, you could pull a few wires and get it commuted to exile. I could be sent to one of the colony planets, the good old frontier."

"Would you—prefer that?"

"Hell, no," Anderton said heartily. "But it would be the lesser of the two evils. And it's got to be done."

"I don't see how you can kill Kaplan."

Anderton got out the heavy-duty military weapon Fleming had tossed to him. "I'll use this."

"They won't stop you?"

"Why should they? They've got that minority report that says I've changed my mind."

"Then the minority report is incorrect?"

"No," Anderton said, "it's absolutely correct. But I'm going to murder Kaplan anyhow."

IX

He had never killed a man. He had never even seen a man killed. And he had been Police Commissioner for thirty years. For this generation, deliberate murder had died out. It simply didn't happen.

A police car carried him to within a block of the Army rally. There, in the shadows of the back seat, he painstakingly examined the pistol Fleming had provided him. It seemed to be intact. Actually, there was no doubt of the outcome. He was absolutely certain of what would happen within the next half hour. Putting the pistol back together, he opened the door of the parked car and stepped warily out.

Nobody paid the slightest attention to him. Surging masses of people pushed eagerly forward, trying to get within hearing distance of the rally. Army uniforms predominated and at the perimeter of the cleared area, a line of tanks and major weapons was displayed—formidable armament still in production.

Army had erected a metal speaker's stand and ascending steps. Behind the stand hung the vast AFWA banner, emblem of the combined powers that had fought in the war. By a curious corrosion of time, the AFWA Veterans' League included officers from the wartime enemy. But a general was a general and fine distinctions had faded over the years.

Occupying the first rows of seats sat the high brass of the AFWA command. Behind them came junior commissioned officers. Regimental banners swirled in a variety of colors and symbols. In fact, the occasion had taken on the aspect of a festive pageant. On the raised stand itself sat stern-faced dignitaries of the Veterans' League, all of them tense with expectancy. At the extreme edges, almost unnoticed, waited a few police units, ostensibly to keep order. Actually, they were informants making observations. If order were kept, the Army would maintain it.

The late-afternoon wind carried the muffled booming of many people packed tightly together. As Anderton made his way through the dense mob he was engulfed by the solid presence of humanity. An eager sense of anticipation held everybody rigid. The crowd seemed to sense that something spectacular was on the way. With difficulty, Anderton forced his way past the rows of seats and over to the tight knot of Army officials at the edge of the platform.

Kaplan was among them. But he was now General Kaplan.

The vest, the gold pocket watch, the cane, the conservative business suit—all were gone. For this event, Kaplan had got his old uniform from its mothballs. Straight and impressive, he stood surrounded by what had been his general staff. He wore his service bars, his medals, his boots, his decorative short-sword, and his visored cap. It was amazing how transformed a bald man became under the stark potency of an officer's peaked and visored cap.

Noticing Anderton, General Kaplan broke away from the group and strode to where the younger man was standing. The expression on his thin, mobile countenance showed how incredulously glad he was to see the Commissioner of Police.

"This is a surprise," he informed Anderton, holding out his small gray-gloved hand. "It was my impression you had been taken in by the acting Commissioner."

"I'm still out," Anderton answered shortly, shaking hands. "After all, Witwer has that same reel of tape." He indicated the package Kaplan clutched in his steely fingers and met the man's gaze confidently.

In spite of his nervousness, General Kaplan was in good humor. "This is a great occasion for the Army," he revealed. "You'll be glad to hear I'm going to give the public a full account of the spurious charge brought against you."

"Fine," Anderton answered noncommittally.

"It will be made clear that you were unjustly accused." General Kaplan was trying to discover what Anderton knew. "Did Fleming have an opportunity to acquaint you with the situation?"

"To some degree," Anderton replied. "You're going to read only the minority report? That's all you've got there?"

"I'm going to compare it to the majority report." General Kaplan signaled an aide and a leather briefcase was produced. "Everything is here—all the evidence we need," he said. "You don't mind being an example, do you? Your case symbolizes the unjust arrests of countless individuals." Stiffly, General Kaplan examined his wristwatch. "I must begin. Will you join me on the platform?"

"Why?"

Coldly, but with a kind of repressed vehemence, General Kaplan said: "So they can see the living proof. You and I together—the killer and his victim. Standing side by side, exposing the whole sinister fraud which the police have been operating."

"Gladly," Anderton agreed. "What are we waiting for?"

Disconcerted, General Kaplan moved toward the platform. Again, he glanced uneasily at Anderton, as if visibly wondering why he had appeared and what he really knew. His uncertainty grew as Anderton willingly mounted the steps of the platform and found himself a seat directly beside the speaker's podium.

"You fully comprehend what I'm going to be saying?" General Kaplan demanded. "The exposure will have considerable repercussions. It may cause the Senate to reconsider the basic validity of the Precrime system."

"I understand," Anderton answered, arms folded. "Let's go."

A hush had descended on the crowd. But there was a restless, eager stirring when General Kaplan obtained the briefcase and began arranging his material in front of him.

"The man sitting at my side," he began, in a clean, clipped voice, "is familiar to you all. You may be surprised to see him, for until recently he was described by the police as a dangerous killer."

The eyes of the crowd focused on Anderton. Avidly, they peered at the only potential killer they had ever been privileged to see at close range.

"Within the last few hours, however," General Kaplan continued, "the police order for his arrest has been canceled; because former Commissioner Anderton voluntarily gave himself up? No, that is not strictly accurate. He is sitting here. He has not given himself up, but the police are no longer interested in him. John Allison Anderton is innocent of any crime in the past, present, and future. The allegations against him were patent frauds, diabolical distortions of a contaminated penal system based on a false premise—a vast, impersonal engine of destruction grinding men and women to their doom."

Fascinated, the crowd glanced from Kaplan to Anderton. Everyone was familiar with the basic situation.

"Many men have been seized and imprisoned under the so-called prophylactic Precrime structure," General Kaplan continued, his voice gaining feeling and strength. "Accused not of crimes they have committed, *but of crimes they will commit*. It is asserted that these men, if allowed to remain free, will at some future time commit felonies.

"But there can be no valid knowledge about the future. As soon as precognitive information is obtained, *it cancels itself out*. The assertion that this man will commit a future crime is paradoxical. The very act of possessing this data renders it spurious. In every case, without exception, the report of the three police precogs has invalidated their own data. If no arrests had been made, there would still have been no crimes committed."

Anderton listened idly, only half-hearing the words. The crowd, however, listened with great interest. General Kaplan was now gathering up a summary made from the minority report. He explained what it was and how it had come into existence.

From his coat pocket, Anderton slipped out his gun and held it in his lap. Already, Kaplan was laying aside the minority report, the precognitive material obtained from "Jerry." His lean, bony fingers groped for the summary of first, "Donna," and after that, "Mike."

"This was the original majority report," he explained. "The assertion, made by the first two precogs, that Anderton would commit a murder. Now here is the automatically invalidated material. I shall read it to you." He whipped out his rimless glasses, fitted them to his nose, and started slowly to read.

A queer expression appeared on his face. He halted, stammered, and abruptly broke off. The papers fluttered from his hands. Like a cornered animal, he spun, crouched, and dashed from the speaker's stand.

For an instant his distorted face flashed past Anderton. On his feet now, Anderton raised the gun, stepped quickly forward, and fired. Tangled up in the rows of feet projecting from the chairs that filled the platform, Kaplan gave a single shrill shriek of agony and fright. Like a ruined bird, he tumbled, fluttering and flailing, from the platform to the ground below. Anderton stepped to the railing, but it was already over.

Kaplan, as the majority report had asserted, was dead. His thin chest was a smoking cavity of darkness, crumbling ash that broke loose as the body lay twitching.

Sickened, Anderton turned away, and moved quickly between the rising figures of stunned Army officers. The gun, which he still held, guaranteed that he would not be interfered with. He leaped from the platform and edged into the chaotic mass of people at its base. Stricken, horrified, they struggled to see what had happened. The incident, occurring before their very eyes, was incomprehensible. It would take time for acceptance to replace blind terror.

At the periphery of the crowd, Anderton was seized by the waiting police. "You're lucky to get out," one of them whispered to him as the car crept cautiously ahead.

"I guess I am," Anderton replied remotely. He settled back and tried to compose himself. He was trembling and dizzy. Abruptly, he leaned forward and was violently sick.

"The poor devil," one of the cops murmured sympathetically.

Through the swirls of misery and nausea, Anderton was unable to tell whether the cop was referring to Kaplan or to himself.

X

Four burly policemen assisted Lisa and John Anderton in the packing and loading of their possessions. In fifty years, the ex-Commissioner of Police had accumulated a vast collection of material goods. Somber and pensive, he stood watching the procession of crates on their way to the waiting trucks.

By truck they would go directly to the field—and from there to Centaurus X by inter-system transport. A long trip for an old man. But he wouldn't have to make it back.

"There goes the second from the last crate," Lisa declared, absorbed and preoccupied by the task. In sweater and slacks, she roamed through the barren rooms, checking on last-minute details. "I suppose we won't be able to use these new atronic appliances. They're still using electricity on Centten."

"I hope you don't care too much," Anderton said.

"We'll get used to it," Lisa replied, and gave him a fleeting smile. "Won't we?"

"I hope so. You're positive you'll have no regrets. If I thought—"

"No regrets," Lisa assured him. "Now suppose you help me with this crate."

As they boarded the lead truck, Witwer drove up in a patrol car. He leaped out and hurried up to them, his face looking strangely haggard. "Before you take off," he said to Anderton, "you'll have to give me a breakdown on the situation with the precogs. I'm getting inquiries from the Senate. They want to find out if the middle report, the retraction, was an error—or what." Confusedly, he finished: "I still can't explain it. The minority report was wrong, wasn't it?"

"Which minority report?" Anderton inquired, amused.

Witwer blinked. "Then that *is* it. I might have known."

Seated in the cabin of the truck, Anderton got out his pipe and shook tobacco into it. With Lisa's lighter he ignited the tobacco and began operations. Lisa had gone back to the house, wanting to be sure nothing vital had been overlooked.

"There were three minority reports," he told Witwer, enjoying the young man's confusion. Someday, Witwer would learn not to wade into situations he didn't fully understand. Satisfaction was Anderton's final emotion. Old and worn out as he was, he had been the only one to grasp the real nature of the problem.

"The three reports were consecutive," he explained. "The first was 'Donna.' In that time-path, Kaplan told me of the plot, and I promptly murdered him. 'Jerry,' phased slightly ahead of 'Donna,' used her report as data. He factored in my knowledge of the report. In that, the second time-path, all I wanted to do was to keep my job. It wasn't Kaplan I wanted to kill. It was my own position and life I was interested in."

"And 'Mike' was the third report? That came *after* the minority report?" Witwer corrected himself. "I mean, it came last?"

"'Mike' was the last of the three, yes. Faced with the knowledge of the first report, I had decided *not* to kill Kaplan. That produced report two. But faced with *that* report, I changed my mind back. Report two, situation two, was the situation Kaplan wanted to create. It was to the advantage of the police to re-create position one. And by that time I was thinking of the police. I had figured out what Kaplan was doing. The third report invalidated the second one in the same way the second one invalidated the first. That brought us back where we started from."

Lisa came over, breathless and gasping. "Let's go—we're all finished here." Lithe and agile, she ascended the metal rungs of the truck and squeezed in beside her husband and the driver. The latter obediently started up his truck and the others followed.

"Each report was different," Anderton concluded. "Each was unique. But two of them agreed on one point. If left free, *I would kill Kaplan.* That created the illusion of a majority report. Actually, that's all it was—an illusion. 'Donna' and 'Mike' previewed the same event—but in two totally different time-paths, occurring under totally different situations. 'Donna' and 'Jerry,' the so-called minority report and half of the majority report, were incorrect. Of the three, 'Mike' was correct—since no report came after his, to invalidate him. That sums it up."

Anxiously, Witwer trotted along beside the truck, his smooth, blond face creased with worry. "Will it happen again? Should we overhaul the setup?"

"It can happen in only one circumstance," Anderton said. "My case was unique, since I had access to the data. It *could* happen again—but only to the next Police Commissioner. So watch your step." Briefly, he grinned, deriving no inconsiderable comfort from Witwer's strained expression. Beside him, Lisa's red lips twitched and her hand reached out and closed over his.

"Better keep your eyes open," he informed young Witwer. "It might happen to you at any time."

THE DAYS OF PERKY PAT

At ten in the morning a terrific horn, familiar to him, hooted Sam Regan out of his sleep, and he cursed the careboy upstairs; he knew the racket was deliberate. The careboy, circling, wanted to be certain that flukers—and not merely wild animals—got the care parcels that were to be dropped.

We'll get them, we'll get them, Sam Regan said to himself as he zipped his dust-proof overalls, put his feet into boots, and then grumpily sauntered as slowly as possible toward the ramp. Several other flukers joined him, all showing similar irritation.

"He's early today," Tod Morrison complained. "And I'll bet it's all staples, sugar and flour and lard—nothing interesting like say candy."

"We ought to be grateful," Norman Schein said.

"Grateful!" Tod halted to stare at him. "GRATEFUL?"

"Yes," Schein said. "What do you think we'd be eating without them: If they hadn't seen the clouds ten years ago."

"Well," Tod said sullenly, "I just don't like them to come *early;* I actually don't exactly mind their coming, as such."

As he put his shoulders against the lid at the top of the ramp, Schein said genially, "That's mighty tolerant of you, Tod boy. I'm sure the careboys would be pleased to hear your sentiments."

Of the three of them, Sam Regan was the last to reach the surface; he did not like the upstairs at all, and he did not care who knew it. And anyhow, no one could compel him to leave the safety of the Pinole Fluke-pit; it was entirely his business, and he noted now that a number of his fellow flukers had elected to remain below in their quarters, confident that those who did answer the horn would bring them back something.

"It's bright," Tod murmured, blinking in the sun.

The care ship sparkled close overhead, set against the gray sky as if hanging from an uneasy thread. Good pilot, this drop, Tod decided. He, or rather *it*, just lazily handles it, in no hurry. Tod waved at the care ship, and once more the huge horn burst out its din, making him clap his hands to his ears. Hey, a joke's a joke, he said to himself. And then the horn ceased; the careboy had relented.

"Wave to him to drop," Norm Schein said to Tod. "You've got the wigwag."

"Sure," Tod said, and began laboriously flapping the red flag, which the Martian creatures had long ago provided, back and forth, back and forth.

A projectile slid from the underpart of the ship, tossed out stabilizers, spiraled toward the ground.

"Sheoot," Sam Regan said with disgust. "It is staples; they don't have the parachute." He turned away, not interested.

How miserable the upstairs looked today, he thought as he surveyed the scene surrounding him. There, to the right, the uncompleted house which someone—not far from their pit—had begun to build out of lumber salvaged from Vallejo, ten miles to the north. Animals or radiation dust had gotten the builder, and so his work remained where it was; it would never be put to use. And, Sam Regan saw, an unusually heavy precipitate had formed since last he had been up here, Thursday morning or perhaps Friday; he had lost exact track. The darn dust, he thought. Just rocks, pieces of rubble, and the dust. World's becoming a dusty object with no one to whisk it off regularly. How about you? he asked silently of the Martian careboy flying in slow circles overhead. Isn't your technology limitless? Can't you appear some morning with a dust rag a million miles in surface area and restore our planet to pristine newness?

Or rather, he thought, to pristine *oldness,* the way it was in the "oldays," as the children call it. We'd like that. While you're looking for something to give to us in the way of further aid, try that.

The careboy circled once more, searching for signs of writing in the dust: a message from the flukers below. I'll write that, Sam thought. BRING DUST RAG, RESTORE OUR CIVILIZATION. Okay, careboy?

All at once the care ship shot off, no doubt on its way back home to its base on Luna or perhaps all the way to Mars.

From the open fluke-pit hole, up which the three of them had come, a further head poked, a woman. Jean Regan, Sam's wife, appeared, shielded by a bonnet against the gray, blinding sun, frowning and saying, "Anything important? Anything *new*?"

" 'Fraid not," Sam said. The care parcel projectile had landed and he walked toward it, scuffing his boots in the dust. The hull of the projectile had cracked open from the impact and he could see the canisters already. It looked to be five thousand pounds of salt—might as well leave it up here so the animals wouldn't starve, he decided. He felt despondent.

How peculiarly anxious the careboys were. Concerned all the time that the mainstays of existence be ferried from their own planet to Earth. They must think we eat all day long, Sam thought. My God . . . the pit was filled to capacity with stored foods. But of course it had been one of the smallest public shelters in Northern California.

"Hey," Schein said, stooping down by the projectile and peering into the crack opened along its side. "I believe I see something we can use." He found a rusted metal pole—once it had helped reinforce the concrete side of an ol-days public building—and poked at the projectile, stirring its release mechanism into action. The mechanism, triggered off, popped the rear half of the projectile open . . . and there lay the contents.

"Looks like radios in that box," Tod said. "Transistor radios." Thoughtfully stroking his short black beard he said, "Maybe we can use them for something new in our layouts."

"Mine's already got a radio," Schein pointed out.

"Well, build an electronic self-directing lawn mower with the parts," Tod said. "You don't have that, do you?" He knew the Scheins' Perky Pat layout fairly well; the two couples, he and his wife with Schein and his, had played together a good deal, being almost evenly matched.

Sam Regan said, "Dibs on the radios, because I can use them." His layout lacked the automatic garage-door opener that both Schein and Tod had; he was considerably behind them.

"Let's get to work," Schein agreed. "We'll leave the staples here and just cart back the radios. If anybody wants the staples, let them come here and get them. Before the do-cats do."

Nodding, the other two men fell to the job of carting the useful contents of the projectile to the entrance of their fluke-pit ramp. For use in their precious, elaborate Perky Pat layouts.

Seated cross-legged with his whetstone, Timothy Schein, ten years old and aware of his many responsibilities, sharpened his knife, slowly and expertly. Meanwhile, disturbing him, his mother and father noisily quarreled with Mr. and Mrs. Morrison, on the far side of the partition. They were playing Perky Pat again. As usual.

How many times today they have to play that dumb game? Timothy asked himself. Forever, I guess. He could see nothing in it, but his parents played on anyhow. And they weren't the only ones; he knew from what other kids said, even from other fluke-pits, that their parents, too, played Perky Pat most of the day, and sometimes even on into the night.

His mother said loudly, "Perky Pat's going to the grocery store and it's got one of those electric eyes that opens the door. Look." A pause. "See, it opened for her, and now she's inside."

"She pushes a cart," Timothy's dad added, in support.

"No, she doesn't," Mrs. Morrison contradicted. "That's wrong. She gives her list to the grocer and he fills it."

"That's only in little neighborhood stores," his mother explained. "And this is a supermarket, you can tell because of the electric eye door."

"I'm sure all grocery stores had electric eye doors," Mrs. Morrison said stubbornly, and her husband chimed in with his agreement. Now the voices rose in anger; another squabble had broken out. As usual.

Aw, cung to them, Timothy said to himself, using the strongest word which he and his friends knew. What's a supermarket anyhow? He tested the blade of his knife—he had made it himself, originally, out of a heavy metal pan—and then hopped to his feet. A moment later he had sprinted silently down the hall and was rapping his special rap on the door of the Chamberlains' quarters.

Fred, also ten years old, answered. "Hi. Ready to go? I see you got that ol' knife of yours sharpened; what do you think we'll catch?"

"Not a do-cat," Timothy said. "A lot better than that; I'm tired of eating do-cat. Too peppery."

"Your parents playing Perky Pat?"

"Yeah."

Fred said, "My mom and dad have been gone for a long time, off playing with the Benteleys." He glanced sideways at Timothy, and in an instant they had shared their mute disappointment regarding their parents. Gosh, and maybe the darn game was all over the world, by now; that would not have surprised either of them.

"How come your parents play it?" Timothy asked.

"Same reason yours do," Fred said.

Hesitating, Timothy said, "Well, why? I don't know why they do; I'm asking you, can't you say?"

"It's because—" Fred broke off. "Ask them. Come on; let's get upstairs and start hunting." His eyes shone. "Let's see what we can catch and kill today."

Shortly, they had ascended the ramp, popped open the lid, and were crouching amidst the dust and rocks, searching the horizon. Timothy's heart pounded; this moment always overwhelmed him, the first instant of reaching the upstairs. The thrilling initial sight of the expanse. Because it was never the same. The dust, heavier today, had a darker gray color to it than before; it seemed denser, more mysterious.

Here and there, covered by many layers of dust, lay parcels dropped from past relief ships—dropped and left to deteriorate. Never to be claimed. And, Timothy saw, an additional new projectile which had arrived that morning. Most of its cargo could be seen within; the grown-ups had not had any use for the majority of the contents, today.

"Look," Fred said softly.

Two do-cats—mutant dogs or cats; no one knew for sure—could be seen, lightly sniffing at the projectile. Attracted by the unclaimed contents.

"We don't want them," Timothy said.

"That one's sure nice and fat," Fred said longingly. But it was Timothy who had the knife; all he himself had was a string with a metal bolt on the end, a bull-roarer that could kill a bird or a small animal at a distance—but useless against a do-cat, which generally weighed fifteen to twenty pounds and sometimes more.

High up in the sky a dot moved at immense speed, and Timothy knew that it was a care ship heading for another fluke-pit, bringing supplies to it. Sure are busy, he thought to himself. Those careboys always coming and going; they never stop, because if they did, the grown-ups would die. Wouldn't that be too bad? he thought ironically. Sure be sad.

Fred said, "Wave to it and maybe it'll drop something." He grinned at Timothy, and then they both broke out laughing.

"Sure," Timothy said. "Let's see; what do I want?" Again the two of them laughed at the idea of them wanting something. The two boys had the entire upstairs, as far as the eye could see . . . they had even more than the careboys had, and that was plenty, more than plenty.

"Do you think they know," Fred said, "that our parents play Perky Pat with furniture made out of what they drop? I bet they don't know about Perky Pat; they never have seen a Perky Pat doll, and if they did they'd be really mad."

"You're right," Timothy said. "They'd be so sore they'd probably stop dropping stuff." He glanced at Fred, catching his eye.

"Aw no," Fred said. "We shouldn't tell them; your dad would beat you again if you did that, and probably me, too."

Even so, it was an interesting idea. He could imagine first the surprise and then the anger of the careboys; it would be fun to see that, see the reaction of the eight-legged Martian creatures who had so much charity inside their warty bodies, the cephalopodic univalve mollusk-like organisms who had voluntarily taken it upon themselves to supply succor to the waning remnants of the human race . . . this was how they got paid back for their charity, this utterly wasteful, stupid purpose to which their goods were being put. This stupid Perky Pat game that all the adults played.

And anyhow it would be very hard to tell them; there was almost no communication between humans and careboys. They were too different. Acts, deeds, could be done, conveying something . . . but not mere words, not mere *signs*. And anyhow—

A great brown rabbit bounded by to the right, past the half-completed house. Timothy whipped out his knife. "Oh boy!" he said aloud in excitement. "Let's go!" He set off across the rubbly ground, Fred a little behind him. Gradually they gained on the rabbit; swift running came easy to the two boys: they had done much practicing.

"Throw the knife!" Fred panted, and Timothy, skidding to a halt, raised his right arm, paused to take aim, and then hurled the sharpened, weighted knife. His most valuable, self-made possession.

It cleaved the rabbit straight through its vitals. The rabbit tumbled, slid, raising a cloud of dust.

"I bet we can get a dollar for that!" Fred exclaimed, leaping up and down. "The hide alone—I bet we can get fifty cents just for the darn hide!"

Together, they hurried toward the dead rabbit, wanting to get there before a red-tailed hawk or a day-owl swooped on it from the gray sky above.

Bending, Norman Schein picked up his Perky Pat doll and said sullenly, "I'm quitting; I don't want to play anymore."

Distressed, his wife protested, "But we've got Perky Pat all the way downtown in her new Ford hardtop convertible and parked and a dime in the meter and she's shopped and now she's in the analyst's office reading *Fortune*—we're way ahead of the Morrisons! Why do you want to quit, Norm?"

"We just don't agree," Norman grumbled. "You say analysts charged twenty dollars an hour and I distinctly remember them charging only ten; nobody could charge twenty. So you're penalizing our side, and for what? The Morrisons agree it was only ten. Don't you?" he said to Mr. and Mrs. Morrison, who squatted on the far side of the layout which combined both couples' Perky Pat sets.

Helen Morrison said to her husband, "You went to the analyst more than I did; are you sure he charged only ten?"

"Well, I went mostly to group therapy," Tod said. "At the Berkeley State Mental Hygiene Clinic, and they charged according to your ability to pay. And Perky Pat is at a *private* psychoanalyst."

"We'll have to ask someone else," Helen said to Norman Schein. "I guess all we can do now this minute is suspend the game." He found himself being glared at by her, too, now, because by his insistence on the one point he had put an end to their game for the whole afternoon.

"Shall we leave it all set up?" Fran Schein asked. "We might as well; maybe we can finish tonight after dinner."

Norman Schein gazed down at their combined layout, the swanky shops, the well-lit streets with the parked new-model cars, all of them shiny, the split-level house itself, where Perky Pat lived and where she entertained Leonard, her boyfriend. It was the *house* that he perpetually yearned for; the house was the real focus of the layout—of all the Perky Pat layouts, however much they might otherwise differ.

Perky Pat's wardrobe, for instance, there in the closet of the house, the big bedroom closet. Her capri pants, her white cotton short-shorts, her two-piece polka-dot swimsuit, her fuzzy sweaters . . . and there, in her bedroom, her hi-fi set, her collection of long-playing records . . .

It had been this way, once, really been like this in the ol-days. Norm Schein could remember his own l-p record collection, and he had once had clothes almost as swanky as Perky Pat's boyfriend Leonard, cashmere jackets and tweed suits and Italian sportshirts and shoes made in England. He hadn't owned a Jaguar XKE sports car, like Leonard did, but he had owned a fine-looking old 1963 Mercedes-Benz, which he had used to drive to work.

We lived then, Norm Schein said to himself, *like Perky Pat and Leonard do now.* This is how it actually was.

To his wife he said, pointing to the clock radio which Perky Pat kept beside her bed, "Remember our G.E. clock radio? How it used to wake us up in the morning with classical music from that FM station, KSFR? The 'Wolf-gangers,' the program was called. From six A.M. to nine every morning."

"Yes," Fran said, nodding soberly. "And you used to get up before me; I knew I should have gotten up and fixed bacon and hot coffee for you, but it was so much fun just indulging myself, not stirring for half an hour longer, until the kids woke up."

"Woke up, hell; they were awake before we were," Norm said. "Don't you remember? They were in the back watching 'The Three Stooges' on TV until eight. Then I got up and fixed hot cereal for them, and then I went on to my job at Ampex down at Redwood City."

"Oh yes," Fran said. "The TV." Their Perky Pat did not have a TV set; they had lost it to the Regans in a game a week ago, and Norm had not yet been able to fashion another one realistic-looking enough to substitute. So, in a game, they pretended now that "the TV repairman had come for it." That was how they explained their Perky Pat not having something she really would have had.

Norm thought, Playing this game . . . it's like being back there, back in the world before the war. That's why we play it, I suppose. He felt shame, but only fleetingly; the shame, almost at once, was replaced by the desire to play a little longer.

"Let's not quit," he said suddenly. "I'll agree the psychoanalyst would have charged Perky Pat twenty dollars. Okay?"

"Okay," both the Morrisons said together, and they settled back down once more to resume the game.

Tod Morrison had picked up their Perky Pat; he held it, stroking its blond hair—theirs was blond, whereas the Scheins' was a brunette—and fiddling with the snaps of its skirt.

"Whatever are you doing?" his wife inquired.

"Nice skirt she has," Tod said. "You did a good job sewing it."

Norm said, "Ever know a girl, back in the ol-days, that looked like Perky Pat?"

"No," Tod Morrison said somberly. "Wish I had, though. I *saw* girls like Perky Pat, especially when I was living in Los Angeles during the Korean War. But I just could never manage to know them personally. And of course there were really terrific girl singers, like Peggy Lee and Julie London . . . they looked a lot like Perky Pat."

"Play," Fran said vigorously. And Norm, whose turn it was, picked up the spinner and spun.

"Eleven," he said. "That gets my Leonard out of the sports car repair garage and on his way to the racetrack." He moved the Leonard doll ahead.

Thoughtfully, Tod Morrison said, "You know, I was out the other day hauling in perishables which the careboys had dropped . . . Bill Ferner was there, and he told me something interesting. He met a fluker from a fluke-pit down where Oakland used to be. And at that fluke-pit you know what they play? Not Perky Pat. They never have heard of Perky Pat."

"Well, what do they play, then?" Helen asked.

"They have another doll entirely." Frowning, Tod continued, "Bill says the Oakland fluker called it a Connie Companion doll. Ever hear of that?"

"A 'Connie Companion' doll," Fran said thoughtfully. "How strange. I wonder what she's like. Does she have a boyfriend?"

"Oh sure," Tod said. "His name is Paul. Connie and Paul. You know, we ought to hike down there to that Oakland Fluke-pit one of these days and see what Connie and Paul look like and how they live. Maybe we could learn a few things to add to our own layouts."

Norm said, "Maybe we could play them."

Puzzled, Fran said, "Could a Perky Pat play a Connie Companion? Is that possible? I wonder what would happen?"

There was no answer from any of the others. Because none of them knew.

As they skinned the rabbit, Fred said to Timothy, "Where did the name 'fluker' come from? It's sure an ugly word; why do they use it?"

"A fluker is a person who lived through the hydrogen war," Timothy explained. "You know, by a fluke. A fluke of fate? See? Because almost everyone was killed; there used to be thousands of people."

"But what's a 'fluke,' then? When you say a 'fluke of fate—'"

"A fluke is when fate has decided to spare you," Timothy said, and that was all he had to say on the subject. That was all he knew.

Fred said thoughtfully, "But you and I, we're not flukers because we weren't alive when the war broke out. We were born after."

"Right," Timothy said.

"So anybody who calls me a fluker," Fred said, "is going to get hit in the eye with my bull-roarer."

"And 'careboy,'" Timothy said, "that's a made-up word, too. It's from when stuff was dumped from jet planes and ships to people in a disaster area. They were called 'care parcels' because they came from people who cared."

"I know that," Fred said. "I didn't ask that."

"Well, I told you anyhow," Timothy said.

The two boys continued skinning the rabbit.

Jean Regan said to her husband, "Have you heard about the Connie Companion doll?" She glanced down the long rough-board table to make sure none of the other families was listening. "Sam," she said, "I heard it from Helen Morrison; she heard it from Tod and he heard it from Bill Ferner, I think. So it's probably true."

"What's true?" Sam said.

"That in the Oakland Fluke-pit they don't have Perky Pat; they have

Connie Companion . . . and it occurred to me that maybe some of this—you know, this sort of emptiness, this boredom we feel now and then—maybe if we saw the Connie Companion doll and how she lives, maybe we could add enough to our own layout to—" She paused, reflecting. "To make it more complete."

"I don't care for the name," Sam Regan said. "Connie Companion; it sounds cheap." He spooned up some of the plain, utilitarian grain-mash which the careboys had been dropping, of late. And, as he ate a mouthful, he thought, I'll bet Connie Companion doesn't eat slop like this; I'll bet she eats cheeseburgers with all the trimmings, at a high-type drive-in.

"Could we make a trek down there?" Jean asked.

"To Oakland Fluke-pit?" Sam stared at her. "It's *fifteen miles,* all the way on the other side of the Berkeley Fluke-pit!"

"But this is important," Jean said stubbornly. "And Bill says that a fluker from Oakland came all the way up here, in search of electronic parts or something . . . so if he can do it, we can. We've got the dust suits they dropped us. I know we could do it."

Little Timothy Schein, sitting with his family, had overheard her; now he spoke up. "Mrs. Regan, Fred Chamberlain and I, we could trek down that far, if you pay us. What do you say?" He nudged Fred, who sat beside him. "Couldn't we? For maybe five dollars."

Fred, his face serious, turned to Mrs. Regan and said, "We could get you a Connie Companion doll. For five dollars for *each* of us."

"Good grief," Jean Regan said, outraged. And dropped the subject.

But later, after dinner, she brought it up again when she and Sam were alone in their quarters.

"Sam, I've got to see it," she burst out. Sam, in a galvanized tub, was taking his weekly bath, so he had to listen to her. "Now that we know it exists we have to play against someone in the Oakland Fluke-pit; at least we can do that. Can't we? Please." She paced back and forth in the small room, her hands clasped tensely. "Connie Companion may have a Standard Station and an airport terminal with jet landing strip and color TV and a French restaurant where they serve escargot, like the one you and I went to when we were first married . . . I just have to see her layout."

"I don't know," Sam said hesitantly. "There's something about Connie Companion doll that—makes me uneasy."

"What could it possibly be?"

"I don't know."

Jean said bitterly, "It's because you know her layout is so much better than ours and she's so much more than Perky Pat."

"Maybe that's it," Sam murmured.

"If you don't go, if you don't try to make contact with them down at the Oakland Fluke-pit, someone else will—someone with more ambition will get ahead of you. Like Norman Schein. He's not afraid the way you are."

Sam said nothing; he continued with his bath. But his hands shook.

A careboy had recently dropped complicated pieces of machinery which were, evidently, a form of mechanical computer. For several weeks the computers—if that was what they were—had sat about the pit in their cartons, unused, but now Norman Schein was finding something to do with one. At the moment he was busy adapting some of its gears, the smallest ones, to form a garbage disposal unit for his Perky Pat's kitchen.

Using the tiny special tools—designed and built by inhabitants of the fluke-pit—which were necessary in fashioning environmental items for Perky Pat, he was busy at his hobby bench. Thoroughly engrossed in what he was doing, he all at once realized that Fran was standing directly behind him, watching.

"I get nervous when I'm watched," Norm said, holding a tiny gear with a pair of tweezers.

"Listen," Fran said, "I've thought of something. Does this suggest anything to you?" She placed before him one of the transistor radios which had been dropped the day before.

"It suggests that garage-door opener already thought of," Norm said irritably. He continued with his work, expertly fitting the miniature pieces together in the sink drain of Pat's kitchen; such delicate work demanded maximum concentration.

Fran said, "It suggests that there must be radio *transmitters* on Earth somewhere, or the careboys wouldn't have dropped these."

"So?" Norm said, uninterested.

"Maybe our Mayor has one," Fran said. "Maybe there's one right here in our own pit, and we could use it to call the Oakland Fluke-pit. Representatives from there could meet us halfway . . . say at the Berkeley Fluke-pit. And we could play there. So we wouldn't have that long fifteen-mile trip."

Norman hesitated in his work; he set the tweezers down and said slowly, "I think possibly you're right." But if their Mayor Hooker Glebe had a radio transmitter, would he let them use it? And if he did—

"We can try," Fran urged. "It wouldn't hurt to try."

"Okay," Norm said, rising from his hobby bench.

The short, sly-faced man in Army uniform, the Mayor of the Pinole Fluke-pit, listened in silence as Norm Schein spoke. Then he smiled a wise, cunning smile. "Sure, I have a radio transmitter. Had it all the time. Fifty-watt output. But why would you want to get in touch with the Oakland Fluke-pit?"

Guardedly, Norm said, "That's my business."

Hooker Glebe said thoughtfully, "I'll let you use it for fifteen dollars."

It was a nasty shock, and Norm recoiled. Good Lord; all the money he and his wife had—they needed every bill of it for use in playing Perky Pat. Money was the tender in the game; there was no other criterion by which one could tell if he had won or lost. "That's too much," he said aloud.

"Well, say ten," the Mayor said, shrugging.

In the end they settled for six dollars and a fifty-cent piece.

"I'll make the radio contact for you," Hooker Glebe said. "Because you don't know how. It will take time." He began turning a crank at the side of the generator of the transmitter. "I'll notify you when I've made contact with them. But give me the money now." He held out his hand for it, and, with great reluctance, Norm paid him.

It was not until late that evening that Hooker managed to establish contact with Oakland. Pleased with himself, beaming in self-satisfaction, he appeared at the Scheins' quarters, during their dinner hour. "All set," he announced. "Say, you know there are actually *nine* fluke-pits in Oakland? I didn't know that. Which you want? I've got one with the radio code of Red Vanilla." He chuckled. "They're tough and suspicious down there; it was hard to get any of them to answer."

Leaving his evening meal, Norman hurried to the Mayor's quarters, Hooker puffing along after him.

The transmitter, sure enough, was on, and static wheezed from the speaker of its monitoring unit. Awkwardly, Norm seated himself at the microphone. "Do I just talk?" he asked Hooker Glebe.

"Just say, This is Pinole Fluke-pit calling. Repeat that a couple of times and then when they acknowledge, you say what you want to say." The Mayor fiddled with controls of the transmitter, fussing in an important fashion.

"This is Pinole Fluke-pit," Norm said loudly into the microphone.

Almost at once a clear voice from the monitor said, "This is Red Vanilla Three answering." The voice was cold and harsh; it struck him forcefully as distinctly alien. Hooker was right.

"Do you have Connie Companion down there where you are?"

"Yes we do," the Oakland fluker answered.

"Well, I challenge you," Norman said, feeling the veins in his throat pulse with the tension of what he was saying. "We're Perky Pat in this area; we'll play Perky Pat against your Connie Companion. Where can we meet?"

"Perky Pat," the Oakland fluker echoed. "Yeah, I know about her. What would the stakes be, in your mind?"

"Up here we play for paper money mostly," Norman said, feeling that his response was somehow lame.

"We've got lots of paper money," the Oakland fluker said cuttingly. "That wouldn't interest any of us. What else?"

"I don't know." He felt hampered, talking to someone he could not see; he was not used to that. People should, he thought, be face-to-face, then you can see the other person's expression. This was not natural. "Let's meet halfway," he said, "and discuss it. Maybe we could meet at the Berkeley Fluke-pit; how about that?"

The Oakland fluker said, "That's too far. You mean lug our Connie Companion layout all that way? It's too heavy and something might happen to it."

"No, just to discuss rules and stakes," Norman said.

Dubiously, the Oakland fluker said, "Well, I guess we could do that. But you better understand—we take Connie Companion doll pretty damn seriously; you better be prepared to talk terms."

"We will," Norm assured him.

All this time Mayor Hooker Glebe had been cranking the handle of the generator; perspiring, his face bloated with exertion, he motioned angrily for Norm to conclude his palaver.

"At the Berkeley Fluke-pit," Norm finished. "In three days. And send your best player, the one who has the biggest and most authentic layout. Our Perky Pat layouts are works of art, you understand."

The Oakland fluker said, "We'll believe that when we see them. After all, we've got carpenters and electricians and plasterers here, building our layouts; I'll bet you're all unskilled."

"Not as much as you think," Norm said hotly, and laid down the microphone. To Hooker Glebe—who had immediately stopped cranking—he said, "We'll beat them. Wait'll they see the garbage disposal unit I'm making for my Perky Pat; did you know there were people back in the ol-days, I mean real alive human beings, who didn't have garbage disposal units?"

"I remember," Hooker said peevishly. "Say, you got a lot of cranking for your money; I think you gypped me, talking so long." He eyed Norm with such hostility that Norm began to feel uneasy. After all, the Mayor of the pit had the authority to evict any fluker he wished; that was their law.

"I'll give you the fire alarm box I just finished the other day," Norm said. "In my layout it goes at the corner of the block where Perky Pat's boyfriend Leonard lives."

"Good enough," Hooker agreed, and his hostility faded. It was replaced, at once, by desire. "Let's see it, Norm. I bet it'll go good in my layout; a fire alarm box is just what I need to complete my first block where I have the mailbox. Thank you."

"You're welcome," Norm sighed, philosophically.

When he returned from the two-day trek to the Berkeley Fluke-pit his face was so grim that his wife knew at once that the parley with the Oakland people had not gone well.

That morning a careboy had dropped cartons of a synthetic tea-like drink; she fixed a cup of it for Norman, waiting to hear what had taken place eight miles to the south.

"We haggled," Norm said, seated wearily on the bed which he and his wife and child all shared. "They don't want money; they don't want goods—naturally not goods, because the darn careboys are dropping regularly down there, too."

"What will they accept, then?"

Norm said, "Perky Pat herself." He was silent, then.

"Oh good Lord," she said, appalled.

"But if we win," Norm pointed out, "we win Connie Companion."

"And the layouts? What about them?"

"We keep our own. It's just Perky Pat herself, not Leonard, not anything else."

"But," she protested, "what'll we *do* if we lose Perky Pat?"

"I can make another one," Norm said. "Given time. There's still a big supply of thermoplastics and artificial hair, here in the pit. And I have plenty of different paints; it would take at least a month, but I could do it. I don't look forward to the job, I admit. But—" His eyes glinted. "Don't look on the dark side; *imagine what it would be like to win Connie Companion doll.* I think we may well win; their delegate seemed smart and, as Hooker said, tough . . . but the one I talked to didn't strike me as being very flukey. You know, on good terms with luck."

And, after all, the element of luck, of chance, entered into each stage of the game through the agency of the spinner.

"It seems wrong," Fran said, "to put up Perky Pat herself. But if you say so—" She managed to smile a little. "I'll go along with it. And if you won Connie Companion—who knows? You might be elected Mayor when Hooker dies. Imagine, to have won somebody else's *doll*—not just the game, the money, but the *doll itself.*"

"I can win," Norm said soberly. "Because I'm very flukey." He could feel it in him, the same flukeyness that had got him through the hydrogen war alive, that had kept him alive ever since. You either have it or you don't, he realized. And I do.

His wife said, "Shouldn't we ask Hooker to call a meeting of everyone in the pit, and send the best player out of our entire group. So as to be the surest of winning."

"Listen," Norm Schein said emphatically. "I'm the best player. I'm going. And so are you; we make a good team, and we don't want to break it up. Anyhow, we'll need at least two people to carry Perky Pat's layout." All in all, he judged, their layout weighed sixty pounds.

His plan seemed to him to be satisfactory. But when he mentioned it to the others living in the Pinole Fluke-pit he found himself facing sharp disagreement. The whole next day was filled with argument.

"You can't lug your layout all that way yourselves," Sam Regan said. "Either take more people with you or carry your layout in a vehicle of some sort. Such as a cart." He scowled at Norm.

"Where'd I get a cart?" Norm demanded.

"Maybe something could be adapted," Sam said. "I'll give you every bit of help I can. Personally, I'd go along but as I told my wife this whole idea worries me." He thumped Norm on the back. "I admire your courage, you and Fran, setting off this way. I wish I had what it takes." He looked unhappy.

In the end, Norm settled on a wheelbarrow. He and Fran would take turns pushing it. That way neither of them would have to carry any load above and beyond their food and water, and of course knives by which to protect them from the do-cats.

As they were carefully placing the elements of their layout in the wheelbarrow, Norm Schein's boy Timothy came sidling up to them. "Take me along, Dad," he pleaded. "For fifty cents I'll go as guide and scout, and also I'll help you catch food along the way."

"We'll manage fine," Norm said. "You stay here in the fluke-pit; you'll be safer here." It annoyed him, the idea of his son tagging along on an important venture such as this. It was almost—sacrilegious.

"Kiss us goodbye," Fran said to Timothy, smiling at him briefly; then her attention returned to the layout within the wheelbarrow. "I hope it doesn't tip over," she said fearfully to Norm.

"Not a chance," Norm said. "If we're careful." He felt confident.

A few moments later they began wheeling the wheelbarrow up the ramp to the lid at the top, to upstairs. Their journey to the Berkeley Fluke-pit had begun.

A mile outside the Berkeley Fluke-pit he and Fran began to stumble over empty drop-canisters and some only partly empty: remains of past care parcels such as littered the surface near their own pit. Norm Schein breathed a sigh of relief; the journey had not been so bad after all, except that his hands had become blistered from gripping the metal handles of the wheelbarrow, and Fran had turned her ankle so that now she walked with a painful limp. But it had taken them less time than he had anticipated, and his mood was one of buoyancy.

Ahead, a figure appeared, crouching low in the ash. A boy. Norm waved at him and called, "Hey, sonny—we're from the Pinole pit; we're supposed to meet a party from Oakland here . . . do you remember me?"

The boy, without answering, turned and scampered off.

"Nothing to be afraid of," Norm said to his wife. "He's going to tell their Mayor. A nice old fellow named Ben Fennimore."

Soon several adults appeared, approaching warily.

With relief, Norm set the legs of the wheelbarrow down into the ash, letting go and wiping his face with his handkerchief. "Has the Oakland team arrived yet?" he called.

"Not yet," a tall, elderly man with a white armband and ornate cap answered. "It's you Schein, isn't it?" he said, peering. This was Ben Fennimore. "Back already with your layout." Now the Berkeley flukers had begun crowding around the wheelbarrow, inspecting the Scheins' layout. Their faces showed admiration.

"They have Perky Pat here," Norm explained to his wife. "But—" He lowered his voice. "Their layouts are only basic. Just a house, wardrobe, and car . . . they've built almost nothing. No imagination."

One Berkeley fluker, a woman, said wonderingly to Fran, "And you made each of the pieces of furniture yourselves?" Marveling, she turned to the man beside her. "See what they've accomplished, Ed?"

"Yes," the man answered, nodding. "Say," he said to Fran and Norm, "can we see it all set up? You're going to set it up in our pit, aren't you?"

"We are indeed," Norm said.

The Berkeley flukers helped push the wheelbarrow the last mile. And before long they were descending the ramp, to the pit below the surface.

"It's a big pit," Norm said knowingly to Fran. "Must be two thousand people here. This is where the University of California was."

"I see," Fran said, a little timid at entering a strange pit; it was the first time in years—since the war, in fact—that she had seen any strangers. And so many at once. It was almost too much for her; Norm felt her shrink back, pressing against him in fright.

When they had reached the first level and were starting to unload the wheelbarrow, Ben Fennimore came up to them and said softly, "I think the Oakland people have been spotted; we just got a report of activity upstairs. So be prepared." He added, "We're rooting for you, of course, because you're Perky Pat, the same as us."

"Have you ever seen Connie Companion doll?" Fran asked him.

"No ma'am," Fennimore answered courteously. "But naturally we've heard about it, being neighbors to Oakland and all. I'll tell you one thing . . . we hear that Connie Companion doll is a bit older than Perky Pat. You know—more, um, *mature*." He explained, "I just wanted to prepare you."

Norm and Fran glanced at each other. "Thanks," Norm said slowly. "Yes, we should be as much prepared as possible. How about Paul?"

"Oh, he's not much," Fennimore said. "Connie runs things; I don't even think Paul has a real apartment of his own. But you better wait until the Oakland flukers get here; I don't want to mislead you—my knowledge is all hearsay, you understand."

Another Berkeley fluker, standing nearby, spoke up. "I saw Connie once, and she's much more grown up than Perky Pat."

"How old do you figure Perky Pat is?" Norm asked him.

"Oh, I'd say seventeen or eighteen," Norm was told.

"And Connie?" He waited tensely.

"Oh, she might be twenty-five, even."

From the ramp behind them they heard noises. More Berkeley flukers appeared, and, after them, two men carrying between them a platform on which, spread out, Norm saw a great, spectacular layout.

This was the Oakland team, and they weren't a couple, a man and wife; they were both men, and they were hard-faced with stern, remote eyes.

They jerked their heads briefly at him and Fran, acknowledging their presence. And then, with enormous care, they set down the platform on which their layout rested.

Behind them came a third Oakland fluker carrying a metal box, much like a lunch pail. Norm, watching, knew instinctively that in the box lay Connie Companion doll. The Oakland fluker produced a key and began unlocking the box.

"We're ready to begin playing any time," the taller of the Oakland men said. "As we agreed in our discussion, we'll use a numbered spinner instead of dice. Less chance of cheating that way."

"Agreed," Norm said. Hesitantly he held out his hand. "I'm Norman Schein and this is my wife and play-partner Fran."

The Oakland man, evidently the leader, said, "I'm Walter R. Wynn. This is my partner here, Charley Dowd, and the man with the box, that's Peter Foster. He isn't going to play; he just guards our layout." Wynn glanced about, at the Berkeley flukers, as if saying, I know you're all partial to Perky Pat, in here. But we don't care; we're not scared.

Fran said, "We're ready to play, Mr. Wynn." Her voice was low but controlled.

"What about money?" Fennimore asked.

"I think both teams have plenty of money," Wynn said. He laid out several thousand dollars in greenbacks, and now Norm did the same. "The money of course is not a factor in this, except as a means of conducting the game."

Norm nodded; he understood perfectly. Only the dolls themselves mattered. And now, for the first time, he saw Connie Companion doll.

She was being placed in her bedroom by Mr. Foster who evidently was in charge of her. And the sight of her took his breath away. Yes, she was older. A grown woman, not a girl at all . . . the difference between her and Perky Pat was acute. And so life-like. Carved, not poured; she obviously had been whittled out of wood and then painted—she was not a thermoplastic. And her hair. It appeared to be genuine hair.

He was deeply impressed.

"What do you think of her?" Walter Wynn asked, with a faint grin.

"Very—impressive," Norm conceded.

Now the Oaklanders were studying Perky Pat. "Poured thermoplastic," one of them said. "Artificial hair. Nice clothes, though; all stitched by hand, you can see that. Interesting; what we heard was correct. Perky Pat isn't a grown-up, she's just a teenager."

Now the male companion to Connie appeared; he was set down in the bedroom beside Connie.

"Wait a minute," Norm said. "You're putting Paul or whatever his name is, in her bedroom with her? Doesn't he have his own apartment?"

Wynn said, "They're married."

"*Married!*" Norman and Fran stared at him, dumbfounded.

"Why sure," Wynn said. "So naturally they live together. Your dolls, they're not, are they?"

"N-no," Fran said. "Leonard is Perky Pat's boyfriend . . ." Her voice trailed off. "Norm," she said, clutching his arm, "I don't believe him; I think he's just saying they're married to get the advantage. Because if they both start out from the same room—"

Norm said aloud, "You fellows, look here. It's not fair, calling them married."

Wynn said, "We're not 'calling' them married; they are married. Their names are Connie and Paul Lathrope, of 24 Arden Place, Piedmont. They've been married for a year, most players will tell you." He sounded calm.

Maybe, Norm thought, it's true. He was truly shaken.

"Look at them together," Fran said, kneeling down to examine the Oaklanders' layout. "In the same bedroom, in the same house. Why, Norm; do you see? There's just the one bed. A big double bed." Wild-eyed, she appealed to him. "How can Perky Pat and Leonard play against them?" Her voice shook. "It's not morally *right*."

"This is another type of layout entirely," Norm said to Walter Wynn. "This, that you have. Utterly different from what we're used to, as you can see." He pointed to his own layout. "I insist that in this game Connie and Paul *not* live together and *not* be considered married."

"But they are," Foster spoke up. "It's a fact. Look—their clothes are in the same closet." He showed them the closet. "And in the same bureau drawers." He showed them that, too. "And look in the bathroom. Two toothbrushes. His and hers, in the same rack. So you can see we're not making it up."

There was silence.

Then Fran said in a choked voice, "And if they're married—you mean they've been—intimate?"

Wynn raised an eyebrow, then nodded. "Sure, since they're married. Is there anything wrong with that?"

"Perky Pat and Leonard have never—" Fran began, and then ceased.

"Naturally not," Wynn agreed. "Because they're only going together. We understand that."

Fran said, "We just can't play. We can't." She caught hold of her husband's arm. "Let's go back to Pinole pit—please, Norman."

"Wait," Wynn said, at once. "If you don't play, you're conceding; you have to give up Perky Pat."

The three Oaklanders all nodded. And, Norm saw, many of the Berkeley flukers were nodding, too, including Ben Fennimore.

"They're right," Norm said heavily to his wife. "We'd have to give her up. We better play, dear."

"Yes," Fran said, in a dead, flat voice. "We'll play." She bent down and listlessly spun the needle of the spinner. It stopped at six.

Smiling, Walter Wynn knelt down and spun. He obtained a four.

The game had begun.

Crouching behind the strewn, decayed contents of a care parcel that had been dropped long ago, Timothy Schein saw coming across the surface of ash his mother and father, pushing the wheelbarrow ahead of them. They looked tired and worn.

"Hi," Timothy yelled, leaping out at them in joy at seeing them again; he had missed them very much.

"Hi, son," his father murmured, nodding. He let go of the handles of the wheelbarrow, then halted and wiped his face with his handkerchief.

Now Fred Chamberlain raced up, panting. "Hi, Mr. Schein; hi, Mrs.

Schein. Hey, did you win? Did you beat the Oakland flukers? I bet you did, didn't you?" He looked from one of them to the other and then back.

In a low voice Fran said, "Yes, Freddy. We won."

Norm said, "Look in the wheelbarrow."

The two boys looked. And, there among Perky Pat's furnishings, lay another doll. Larger, fuller-figured, much older than Pat . . . they stared at her and she stared up sightlessly at the gray sky overhead. So this is Connie Companion doll, Timothy said to himself. Gee.

"We were lucky," Norm said. Now several people had emerged from the pit and were gathering around them, listening. Jean and Sam Regan, Tod Morrison and his wife Helen, and now their Mayor, Hooker Glebe himself, waddling up excited and nervous, his face flushed, gasping for breath from the labor—unusual for him—of ascending the ramp.

Fran said, "We got a cancellation-of-debts card, just when we were most behind. We owed fifty thousand, and it made us even with the Oakland flukers. And then, after that, we got an advance-ten-squares card, and that put us right on the jackpot square, at least in our layout. We had a very bitter squabble, because the Oaklanders showed us that on their layout it was a tax lien slapped on real-estate-holdings square, but we had spun an odd number so that put us back on our own board." She sighed. "I'm glad to be back. It was hard, Hooker; it was a tough game."

Hooker Glebe wheezed, "Let's all get a look at the Connie Companion doll, folks." To Fran and Norm he said, "Can I lift her up and show them?"

"Sure," Norm said, nodding.

Hooker picked up Connie Companion doll. "She sure is realistic," he said, scrutinizing her. "Clothes aren't as nice as ours generally are; they look machine-made."

"They are," Norm agreed. "But she's carved, not poured."

"Yes, so I see." Hooker turned the doll about, inspecting her from all angles. "A nice job. She's—um, more filled out than Perky Pat. What's this outfit she has on? Tweed suit of some sort."

"A business suit," Fran said. "We won that with her; they had agreed on that in advance."

"You see, she has a job," Norm explained. "She's a psychology consultant for a business firm doing marketing research. In consumer preferences. A high-paying position . . . she earns twenty thousand a year, I believe Wynn said."

"Golly," Hooker said. "And Pat's just going to college; she's still in school." He looked troubled. "Well, I guess they were bound to be ahead of us in some ways. What matters is that you won." His jovial smile returned. "Perky Pat came out ahead." He held the Connie Companion doll up high, where everyone could see her. "Look what Norm and Fran came back with, folks!"

Norm said, "Be careful with her, Hooker." His voice was firm.

"Eh?" Hooker said, pausing. "Why, Norm?"

"Because," Norm said, "she's going to have a baby."

There was a sudden chill silence. The ash around them stirred faintly; that was the only sound.

"How do you know?" Hooker asked.

"They told us. The Oaklanders told us. And we won that, too—after a bitter argument that Fennimore had to settle." Reaching into the wheelbarrow he brought out a little leather pouch; from it he carefully took a carved pink newborn baby. "We won this too because Fennimore agreed that from a technical standpoint it's literally part of Connie Companion doll at this point."

Hooker stared a long, long time.

"She's married," Fran explained. "To Paul. They're not just going together. She's three months pregnant, Mr. Wynn said. He didn't tell us until after we won; he didn't want to, then, but they felt they had to. I think they were right; it wouldn't have done not to say."

Norm said, "And in addition there's actually an embryo outfit—"

"Yes," Fran said. "You have to open Connie up, of course, to see—"

"No," Jean Regan said. "Please, no."

Hooker said, "No, Mrs. Schein, don't." He backed away.

Fran said, "It shocked us of course at first, but—"

"You see," Norm put in, "it's logical; you have to follow the logic. Why, eventually Perky Pat—"

"No," Hooker said violently. He bent down, picked up a rock from the ash at his feet. "No," he said, and raised his arm. "You stop, you two. Don't say any more."

Now the Regans, too, had picked up rocks. No one spoke.

Fran said, at last, "Norm, we've got to get out of here."

"You're right," Tod Morrison told them. His wife nodded in grim agreement.

"You two go back down to Oakland," Hooker told Norman and Fran Schein. "You don't live here anymore. You're different than you were. You—changed."

"Yes," Sam Regan said slowly, half to himself. "I was right; there was something to fear." To Norm Schein he said, "How difficult a trip is it to Oakland?"

"We just went to Berkeley," Norm said. "To the Berkeley Fluke-pit." He seemed baffled and stunned by what was happening. "My God," he said, "we can't turn around and push this wheelbarrow back all the way to Berkeley again—we're worn out, we need rest!"

Sam Regan said, "What if somebody else pushed?" He walked up to the Scheins, then, and stood with them. "I'll push the darn thing. You lead the way, Schein." He looked toward his own wife, but Jean did not stir. And she did not put down her handful of rocks.

Timothy Schein plucked at his father's arm. "Can I come this time, Dad? Please let me come."

"Okay," Norm said, half to himself. Now he drew himself together. "So we're not wanted here." He turned to Fran. "Let's go. Sam's going to push the wheelbarrow; I think we can make it back there before nightfall. If not, we can sleep out in the open; Timothy'll help protect us against the do-cats."

Fran said, "I guess we have no choice." Her face was pale.

"And take this," Hooker said. He held out the tiny carved baby. Fran Schein accepted it and put it tenderly back in its leather pouch. Norm laid Connie Companion back down in the wheelbarrow, where she had been. They were ready to start back.

"It'll happen up here eventually," Norm said, to the group of people, to the Pinole flukers. "Oakland is just more advanced; that's all."

"Go on," Hooker Glebe said. "Get started."

Nodding, Norm started to pick up the handles of the wheelbarrow, but Sam Regan moved him aside and took them himself. "Let's go," he said.

The three adults, with Timothy Schein going ahead of them with his knife ready—in case a do-cat attacked—started into motion, in the direction of Oakland and the south. No one spoke. There was nothing to say.

"It's a shame this had to happen," Norm said at last, when they had gone almost a mile and there was no further sign of the Pinole flukers behind them.

"Maybe not," Sam Regan said. "Maybe it's for the good." He did not seem downcast. And after all, he had lost his wife; he had given up more than anyone else, and yet—he had survived.

"Glad you feel that way," Norm said somberly.

They continued on, each with his own thoughts.

After a while, Timothy said to his father, "All these big fluke-pits to the south . . . there's lots more things to do there, isn't there? I mean, you don't just sit around playing that game." He certainly hoped not.

His father said, "That's true, I guess."

Overhead, a care ship whistled at great velocity and then was gone again almost at once; Timothy watched it go but he was not really interested in it, because there was so much more to look forward to, on the ground and below the ground, ahead of them to the south.

His father murmured, "Those Oaklanders; their game, their particular doll, it taught them something. Connie had to grow and it forced them all to grow along with her. Our flukers never learned about that, not from Perky Pat. I wonder if they ever will. She'd have to grow up the way Connie did. Connie must have been like Perky Pat, once. A long time ago."

Not interested in what his father was saying—who really cared about dolls and games with dolls?—Timothy scampered ahead, peering to see what lay before them, the opportunities and possibilities, for him and for his mother and dad, for Mr. Regan also.

"I can't wait," he yelled back at his father, and Norm Schein managed a faint, fatigued smile in answer.

PRECIOUS ARTIFACT

Below the 'copter of Milt Biskle lay newly fertile lands. He had done well with his area of Mars, verdant from his reconstruction of the ancient water-network. Spring, two springs each year, had been brought to this autumn world of sand and hopping toads, a land once made of dried soil cracking with the dust of former times, of a dreary and unwatered waste. Victim of the recent Prox-Terra conflict.

Quite soon the first Terran emigrants would appear, stake their claims, and take over. He could retire. Perhaps he could return to Terra or bring his own family here, receive priority of land-acquisition—as a reconstruct engineer he deserved it. Area Yellow had progressed far faster than the other engineers' sections. And now his reward came.

Reaching forward, Milt Biskle touched the button of his long-range transmitter. "This is Reconstruct Engineer Yellow," he said. "I'd like a psychiatrist. Any one will do, so long as he's immediately available."

When Milt Biskle entered the office Dr. DeWinter rose and held out his hand. "I've heard," Dr. DeWinter said, "that you, of all the forty-odd reconstruct engineers, have been the most creative. It's no wonder you're tired. Even God had to rest after six days of such work, and you've been at it for years. As I was waiting for you to reach me I received a news memo from Terra that will interest you." He picked the memo up from his desk. "The initial transport of settlers is about to arrive here on Mars . . . and they'll go directly into your area. Congratulations, Mr. Biskle."

Rousing himself Milt Biskle said, "What if I returned to Earth?"

"But if you mean to stake a claim for your family, here—"

Milt Biskle said, "I want you to do something for me. I feel too tired, too—" He gestured. "Or depressed, maybe. Anyhow I'd like you to make arrangements for my gear, including my wug-plant, to be put aboard a transport returning to Terra."

"Six years of work," Dr. DeWinter said. "And now you're abandoning your recompense. Recently I visited Earth and it's just as you remember—"

"How do you know how I remember it?"

"Rather," DeWinter corrected himself smoothly, "I should say it's just as it was. Overcrowded, tiny conapts with seven families to a single cramped kitchen. Autobahns so crowded you can't make a move until eleven in the morning."

"For me," Milt Biskle said, "the overcrowding will be a relief after six years of robot autonomic equipment." He had made up his mind. In spite of what he had accomplished here, or perhaps because of it, he intended to go home. Despite the psychiatrist's arguments.

Dr. DeWinter purred, "What if your wife and children, Milt, are among the passengers of this first transport?" Once more he lifted a document from his neatly arranged desk. He studied the paper, then said, "Biskle, Fay, Mrs. Laura C. June C. Woman and two girl children. Your family?"

"Yes," Milt Biskle admitted woodenly; he stared straight ahead.

"So you see you can't head back to Earth. Put on your hair and prepare to meet them at Field Three. And exchange your teeth. You've got the stainless steel ones in, at the moment."

Chagrined, Biskle nodded. Like all Terrans he had lost his hair and teeth from the fallout during the war. For everyday service in his lonely job of re-reconstructing Yellow Area of Mars he made no use of the expensive wig which he had brought from Terra, and as to the teeth he personally found the steel ones far more comfortable than the natural-color plastic set. It indicated how far he had drifted from social interaction. He felt vaguely guilty; Dr. DeWinter was right.

But he had felt guilty ever since the defeat of the Proxmen. The war had embittered him; it didn't seem fair that one of the two competing cultures would have to suffer, since the needs of both were legitimate.

Mars itself had been the locus of contention. Both cultures needed it as a colony on which to deposit surplus populations. Thank God Terra had managed to gain tactical mastery during the last year of the war . . . hence it was Terrans such as himself, and not Proxmen, patching up Mars.

"By the way," Dr. DeWinter said. "I happen to know of your intentions regarding your fellow reconstruct engineers."

Milt Biskle glanced up swiftly.

"As a matter of fact," Dr. DeWinter said, "we know they're at this moment gathering in Red Area to hear your account." Opening his desk drawer he got out a yo-yo, stood up, and began to operate it expertly doing *walking the dog*. "Your panic-stricken speech to the effect that something is wrong, although you can't seem to say just what it might be."

Watching the yo-yo Biskle said, "That's a toy popular in the Prox system. At least so I read in a homeopape article, once."

"Hmm. I understood it originated in the Philippines." Engrossed, Dr. DeWinter now did *around the world*. He did it well. "I'm taking the liberty of sending a disposition to the reconstruct engineers' gathering, testifying to your mental condition. It will be read aloud—sorry to say."

"I still intend to address the gathering," Biskle said.

"Well, then there's a compromise that occurs to me. Greet your little family when it arrives here on Mars and then we'll arrange a trip to Terra for you. At our expense. And in exchange you'll agree not to address the gathering of reconstruct engineers or burden them in any way with your nebulous forebodings." DeWinter eyed him keenly. "After all, this is a critical moment. The first emigrants are arriving. We don't want trouble; we don't want to make anyone uneasy."

"Would you do me a favor?" Biskle asked. "Show me that you've got a wig on. And that your teeth are false. Just so I can be sure that you're a Terran."

Dr. DeWinter tilted his wig and plucked out his set of false teeth.

"I'll take the offer," Milt Biskle said. "If you'll agree to make certain that my wife obtains the parcel of land I set aside for her."

Nodding, DeWinter tossed him a small white envelope. "Here's your ticket. Round-trip, of course, since you'll be coming back."

I hope so, Biskle thought as he picked up the ticket. But it depends on what I see on Terra. Or rather on what they *let* me see.

He had a feeling they'd let him see very little. In fact as little as Proxmanly possible.

When his ship reached Terra a smartly uniformed guide waited for him. "Mr. Biskle?" Trim and attractive and exceedingly young, she stepped forward alertly. "I'm Mary Ableseth, your Tourplan companion. I'll show you around the planet during your brief stay here." She smiled brightly and very professionally. He was taken aback. "I'll be with you constantly, night and day."

"Night, too?" he managed to say.

"Yes, Mr. Biskle. That's my job. We expect you to be disoriented due to your years of labor on Mars . . . labor we of Terra applaud and honor, as is right." She fell in beside him, steering him toward a parked 'copter. "Where would you like to go first? New York City? Broadway? To the night clubs and theaters and restaurants . . ."

"No, to Central Park. To sit on a bench."

"But there is no more Central Park, Mr. Biskle. It was turned into a parking lot for government employees while you were on Mars."

"I see," Milt Biskle said. "Well, then Portsmouth Square in San Francisco will do." He opened the door of the 'copter.

"That, too, has become a parking lot," Miss Ableseth said, with a sad shake of her long, luminous red hair. "We're so darn overpopulated. Try again, Mr. Biskle; there are a few parks left, one in Kansas, I believe, and *two* in Utah in the south part near St. George."

"This is bad news," Milt said. "May I stop at that amphetamine dispenser and put in my dime? I need a stimulant to cheer me up."

"Certainly," Miss Ableseth said, nodding graciously.

Milt Biskle walked to the spaceport's nearby stimulant dispenser, reached into his pocket, found a dime, and dropped the dime in the slot.

The dime fell completely through the dispenser and bounced onto the pavement.

"Odd," Biskle said, puzzled.

"I think I can explain that," Miss Ableseth said. "That dime of yours is a Martian dime, made for a lighter gravity."

"Hmm," Milt Biskle said, as he retrieved the dime. As Miss Ableseth had predicted, he felt disoriented. He stood by as she put in a dime of her own and obtained the small tube of amphetamine stimulants for him. Certainly her explanation seemed adequate. But—

"It is now eight P.M. local time," Miss Ableseth said. "And I haven't had dinner, although of course you have, aboard your ship. Why not take me to dinner? We can talk over a bottle of Pinot Noir and you can tell me these vague forebodings which have brought you to Terra, that something dire is wrong and that all your marvelous reconstruct work is pointless. I'd adore to hear about it." She guided him back to the 'copter and the two of them entered, squeezing into the back seat together. Milt Biskle found her to be warm and yielding, decidedly Terran; he became embarrassed and felt his heart pounding in effort-syndrome. It had been some time since he had been this close to a woman.

"Listen," he said, as the automatic circuit of the 'copter caused it to rise from the spaceport parking lot, "I'm married. I've got two children and I came here on business. I'm on Terra to prove that the Proxmen really won and that we few remaining Terrans are slaves of the Prox authorities, laboring for—" He gave up; it was hopeless. Miss Ableseth remained pressed against him.

"You really think," Miss Ableseth said presently, as the 'copter passed above New York City, "that I'm a Prox agent?"

"N-no," Milt Biskle said. "I guess not." It did not seem likely, under the circumstances.

"While you're on Terra," Miss Ableseth said, "why stay in an overcrowded, noisy hotel? Why not stay with me at my conapt in New Jersey? There's plenty of room and you're more than welcome."

"Okay," Biskle agreed, feeling the futility of arguing.

"Good." Miss Ableseth gave an instruction to the 'copter; it turned north. "We'll have dinner there. It'll save money, and at all the decent restaurants there's a two-hour line this time of night, so it's almost impossible to get a table. You've probably forgotten. How wonderful it'll be when half our population can emigrate!"

"Yes," Biskle said tightly. "And they'll like Mars; we've done a good job." He felt a measure of enthusiasm returning to him, a sense of pride in the reconstruct work he and his compatriots had done. "Wait until you see it, Miss Ableseth."

"Call me Mary," Miss Ableseth said, as she arranged her heavy scarlet wig; it had become dislodged during the last few moments in the cramped quarters of the 'copter.

"Okay," Biskle said, and, except for a nagging awareness of disloyalty to Fay, he felt a sense of well-being.

"Things happen fast on Terra," Mary Ableseth said. "Due to the terrible pressure of overpopulation." She pressed her teeth in place; they, too, had become dislodged.

"So I see," Milt Biskle agreed, and straightened his own wig and teeth, too. *Could I have been mistaken?* he asked himself. After all he could see the lights of New York below; Terra was decidedly not a depopulated ruin and its civilization was intact.

Or was this all an illusion, imposed on his percept-system by Prox psychiatric techniques unfamiliar to him? It was a fact that his dime had fallen completely through the amphetamine dispenser. Didn't that indicate something was subtly, terribly wrong?

Perhaps the dispenser hadn't really been there.

The next day he and Mary Ableseth visited one of the few remaining parks. In the southern part of Utah, near the mountains, the park, although small, was bright green and attractive. Milt Biskle lolled on the grass watching a squirrel progressing toward a tree in wicket-like leaps, its tail flowing behind it in a gray stream.

"No squirrels on Mars," Milt Biskle said sleepily.

Wearing a slight sunsuit, Mary Ableseth stretched out on her back, eyes shut. "It's nice here, Milt. I imagine Mars is like this." Beyond the park heavy traffic moved along the freeway; the noise reminded Milt of the surf of the Pacific Ocean. It lulled him. All seemed well, and he tossed a peanut to the squirrel. The squirrel veered, wicket-hopped toward the peanut, its intelligent face twitching in response.

As it sat upright, holding the nut, Milt Biskle tossed a second nut off to the right. The squirrel heard it land among the maple leaves; its ears pricked up, and this reminded Milt of a game he once had played with a cat, an old sleepy tom which had belonged to him and his brother in the days before Terra had been so overpopulated, when pets were still legal. He had waited until Pumpkin—the tomcat—was almost asleep and then he had tossed a small object into the corner of the room. Pumpkin woke up. His eyes had flown open and his ears had pricked, turned, and he had sat for fifteen minutes listening and watching, brooding as to what had made the noise. It was a harmless way of teasing the old cat, and Milt felt sad, thinking how many years Pumpkin had been dead now, his last legal pet. On Mars, though, pets would be legal again. That cheered him.

In fact on Mars, during his years of reconstruct work, he had possessed a pet. A Martian plant. He had brought it with him to Terra and it now stood on the living-room coffee table in Mary Ableseth's conapt, its limbs draped rather unhappily. It had not prospered in the unfamiliar Terran climate.

"Strange," Milt murmured, "that my wug-plant isn't thriving. I'd have thought in such a moist atmosphere . . ."

"It's the gravity," Mary said, eyes still shut, her bosom rising and falling regularly. She was almost asleep. "Too much for it."

Milt regarded the supine form of the woman, remembering Pumpkin under similar circumstances. The hypnogogic moment, between waking and sleeping, when consciousness and unconsciousness became blended . . . reaching, he picked up a pebble.

He tossed the pebble into the leaves near Mary's head.

At once she sat up, eyes open startled, her sunsuit falling from her.

Both her ears pricked up.

"But we Terrans," Milt said, "have lost control of the musculature of our ears, Mary. On even a reflex basis."

"What?" she murmured, blinking in confusion as she retied her sunsuit.

"Our ability to prick up our ears has atrophied," Milt explained. "Unlike the dog and cat. Although to examine us morphologically you wouldn't know because the muscles are still there. So you made an error."

"I don't know what you're talking about," Mary said, with a trace of sullenness. She turned her attention entirely to arranging the bra of her sunsuit, ignoring him.

"Let's go back to the conapt," Milt said, rising to his feet. He no longer felt like lolling in the park, because he could no longer believe in the park. Unreal squirrel, unreal grass . . . was it actually? Would they ever show him the substance beneath the illusion? He doubted it.

The squirrel followed them a short way as they walked to their parked 'copter, then turned its attention to a family of Terrans which included two small boys; the children threw nuts to the squirrel and it scampered in vigorous activity.

"Convincing," Milt said. And it really was.

Mary said, "Too bad you couldn't have seen Dr. DeWinter more, Milt. He could have helped you." Her voice was oddly hard.

"I have no doubt of that," Milt Biskle agreed as they re-entered the parked 'copter.

When they arrived back at Mary's conapt he found his Martian wug-plant dead. It had evidently perished of dehydration.

"Don't try to explain this," he said to Mary as the two of them stood gazing down at the parched, dead stalks of the once active plant. "You know what it shows. Terra is supposedly more humid than Mars, even reconstructed Mars at its best. Yet this plant has completely dried out. There's no moisture left on Terra because I suppose the Prox blasts emptied the seas. Right?"

Mary said nothing.

"What I don't understand," Milt said, "is why it's worth it to you people to keep the illusion going. *I've finished my job.*"

After a pause Mary said, "Maybe there're more planets requiring re-construct work, Milt."

"Your population is that great?"

"I was thinking of Terra. Here," Mary said. "Reconstruct work on it will take generations; all the talent and ability you reconstruct engineers possess will be required." She added, "I'm just following your hypothetical logic, of course."

"So Terra's our next job. That's why you let me come here. In fact I'm going to *stay* here." He realized that, thoroughly and utterly, in a flash of insight. "I won't be going back to Mars and I won't see Fay again. You're replacing her." It all made sense.

"Well," Mary said, with a faint wry smile, "let's say I'm attempting to." She stroked his arm. Barefoot, still in her sunsuit, she moved slowly closer and closer to him.

Frightened, he backed away from her. Picking up the dead wug-plant, he numbly carried it to the apt's disposal chute and dropped the brittle, dry remains in. They vanished at once.

"And now," Mary said busily, "we're going to visit the Museum of Modern Art in New York and then, if we have time, the Smithsonian in Washington, D.C. They've asked me to keep you busy so you don't start brooding."

"But I am brooding," Milt said as he watched her change from her sunsuit to a gray wool knit dress. Nothing can stop that, he said to himself. And you know it now. And as each reconstruct engineer finishes his area it's going to happen again. I'm just the first.

At least I'm not alone, he realized. And felt somewhat better.

"How do I look?" Mary asked as she put on lipstick before the bedroom mirror.

"Fine," he said listlessly, and wondered if Mary would meet each reconstruct engineer in turn, become the mistress of each. Not only is she not what she seems, he thought, but I don't even get to keep her.

It seemed a gratuitous loss, easily avoided.

He was, he realized, beginning to like her. *Mary was alive;* that much was real. Terran or not. At least they had not lost the war to shadows; they had lost to authentic living organisms. He felt somewhat cheered.

"Ready for the Museum of Modern Art?" Mary said briskly, with a smile.

Later, at the Smithsonian, after he had viewed the Spirit of St. Louis and the Wright brothers' incredibly ancient plane—it appeared to be at least a million years old—he caught sight of an exhibit which he had been anticipating.

Saying nothing to Mary—she was absorbed in studying a case of semi-precious stones in their natural uncut state—he slipped off and, a moment later, stood before a glass-walled section entitled

PROX MILITARY OF 2014

Three Prox soldiers stood frozen, their dark muzzles stained and grimy, sidearms ready, in a makeshift shelter composed of the remains of one of their transports. A bloody Prox flag hung drably. This was a defeated enclave of the enemy; these three creatures were about to surrender or be killed.

A group of Terran visitors stood before the exhibit, gawking. Milt Biskle said to the man nearest him, "Convincing, isn't it?"

"Sure is," the man, middle-aged, with glasses and gray hair, agreed. "Were you in the war?" he asked Milt, glancing at him.

"I'm in reconstruct," Milt said. "Yellow Engineer."

"Oh." The man nodded, impressed. "Boy, these Proxmen look scary. You'd almost expect them to step out of that exhibit and fight us to the death." He grinned. "They put up a good fight before they gave in, those Proxmen; you have to give 'em credit for that."

Beside him the man's gray, taut wife said, "Those guns of theirs make me shiver. It's too realistic." Disapproving, she walked on.

"You're right," Milt Biskle said. "They do look frighteningly real, because of course they are." There was no point in creating an illusion of this sort because the genuine thing lay immediately at hand, readily available. Milt swung himself under the guardrail, reached the transparent glass of the exhibit, raised his foot, and smashed the glass; it burst and rained down with a furious racket of shivering fragments.

As Mary came running, Milt snatched a rifle from one of the frozen Proxmen in the exhibit and turned it toward her.

She halted, breathing rapidly, eyeing him but saying nothing.

"I am willing to work for you," Milt said to her, holding the rifle expertly. "After all, if my own race no longer exists I can hardly reconstruct a colony world for them; even I can see that. But I want to know the truth. Show it to me and I'll go on with my job."

Mary said, "No, Milt, if you knew the truth you wouldn't go on. You'd turn that gun on yourself." She sounded calm, even compassionate, but her eyes were bright and enlarged, wary.

"Then I'll kill you," he said. And, after that, himself.

"Wait." She pondered. "Milt—this is difficult. You know absolutely nothing and yet look how miserable you are. How do you expect to feel when you can see your planet as it is? It's almost too much for me and I'm—" She hesitated.

"Say it."

"I'm just a—" she choked out the word—"a visitor."

"But I am right," he said. "Say it. Admit it."

"You're right, Milt," she sighed.

Two uniformed museum guards appeared, holding pistols. "You okay, Miss Ableseth?"

"For the present," Mary said. She did not take her eyes off Milt and the rifle which he held. "Just wait," she instructed the guards.

"Yes ma'am." The guards waited. No one moved.

Milt said, "Did any Terran women survive?"

After a pause, Mary said, "No, Milt. But we Proxmen are within the same genus, as you well know. We can interbreed. Doesn't that make you feel better?"

"Sure," he said. "A lot better." And he did feel like turning the rifle on himself now, without waiting. It was all he could do to resist the impulse. So he had been right; that thing had not been Fay, there at Field Three on Mars. "Listen," he said to Mary Ableseth, "I want to go back to Mars again. I came here to learn something. I learned it, now I want to go back. Maybe I'll talk to Dr. DeWinter again, maybe he can help me. Any objection to that?"

"No." She seemed to understand how he felt. "After all, you did all your work there. You have a right to return. But eventually you have to begin here on Terra. We can wait a year or so, perhaps even two. But eventually Mars will be filled up and we'll need the room. And it's going to be so much harder here . . . as you'll discover." She tried to smile but failed; he saw the effort. "I'm sorry, Milt."

"So am I," Milt Biskle said. "Hell, I was sorry when that wug-plant died. I knew the truth then. It wasn't just a guess."

"You'll be interested to know that your fellow reconstruct engineer

Red, Cleveland Andre, addressed the meeting in your place. And passed your intimations on to them all, along with his own. They voted to send an official delegate here to Terra to investigate; he's on his way now."

"I'm interested," Milt said. "But it doesn't really matter. It hardly changes things." He put down the rifle. "Can I go back to Mars now?" He felt tired. "Tell Dr. DeWinter I'm coming." Tell him, he thought, to have every psychiatric technique in his repertory ready for me, because it will take a lot. "What about Earth's animals?" he asked. "Did any forms at all survive? How about the dog and the cat?"

Mary glanced at the museum guards; a flicker of communication passed silently between them and then Mary said, "Maybe it's all right after all."

"What's all right?" Milt Biskle said.

"For you to see. Just for a moment. You seem to be standing up to it better than we had expected. In our opinion you *are* entitled to that." She added, "Yes, Milt, the dog and cat survived; they live here among the ruins. Come along and look."

He followed after her, thinking to himself, Wasn't she right the first time? Do I really want to look? Can I stand up to what exists in actuality—what they've felt the need of keeping from me up until now?

At the exit ramp of the museum Mary halted and said, "Go on outside, Milt. I'll stay here. I'll be waiting for you when you come back in."

Haltingly, he descended the ramp.

And saw.

It was, of course, as she had said, ruins. The city had been decapitated, leveled three feet above ground level; the buildings had become hollow squares, without contents, like some infinite arrangements of useless, ancient courtyards. He could not believe that what he saw was *new*; it seemed to him as if these abandoned remnants had always been there, exactly as they were now. And—how long would they remain this way?

To the right an elaborate but small-scale mechanical system had plopped itself down on a debris-filled street. As he watched, it extended a host of pseudopodia which burrowed inquisitively into the nearby founda-tions. The foundations, steel and cement, were abruptly pulverized; the bare ground, exposed, lay naked and dark brown, seared over from the atomic heat generated by the repair autonomic rig—a construct, Milt Biskle thought, not much different from those I employ on Mars. At least to some meager extent the rig had the task of clearing away the old. He knew from his own reconstruct work on Mars that it would be followed, probably within minutes, by an equally elaborate mechanism which would lay the groundwork for the new structures to come.

And, standing off to one side in the otherwise deserted street, watching this limited clearing-work in progress, two gray, thin figures could be made out. Two hawk-nosed Proxmen with their pale, natural hair arranged in high coils, their earlobes elongated with heavy weights.

The victors, he thought to himself. Experiencing the satisfaction of this spectacle, witnessing the last artifacts of the defeated race being obliterated. Someday a purely Prox city will rise up here: Prox architecture, streets of the odd, wide Prox pattern, the uniform box-like buildings with their many subsurface levels. And citizens such as these will be treading the ramps, accepting the high-speed runnels in their daily routines. And what, he thought, about the Terran dogs and cats which now inhabit these ruins, as Mary said? Will even they disappear? Probably not entirely. There will be room for them, perhaps in museums and zoos, as oddities to be gaped at. Survivals of an ecology which no longer obtained. Or even mattered.

And yet—Mary was right. The Proxmen were within the same genus. Even if they did not interbreed with the remaining Terrans, the species as he had known it would go on. And they would interbreed, he thought. His own relationship with Mary was a harbinger. As individuals they were not so far apart. The results might even be good.

The results, he thought as he turned away and started back into the museum, may be a race not quite Prox and not quite Terran; something that is genuinely new may come from the melding. At least we can hope so.

Terra would be rebuilt. He had seen slight but real work in progress with his own eyes. Perhaps the Proxmen lacked the skill that he and his fellow reconstruct engineers possessed . . . but now that Mars was virtually done they could begin here. It was not absolutely hopeless. Not *quite*.

Walking up to Mary he said hoarsely, "Do me a favor. Get me a cat I can take back to Mars with me. I've always liked cats. Especially the orange ones with stripes."

One of the museum guards, after a glance at his companion, said, "We can arrange that, Mr. Biskle. We can get a—cub, is that the word?"

"Kitten, I think," Mary corrected.

On the trip back to Mars, Milt Biskle sat with the box containing the orange kitten on his lap, working out his plans. In fifteen minutes the ship would land on Mars and Dr. DeWinter—or the thing that posed as Dr. DeWinter anyhow—would be waiting to meet him. And it would be too late. From where he sat he could see the emergency escape hatch with its red warning light. His plans had become focused around the hatch. It was not ideal but it would serve.

In the box the orange kitten reached up a paw and batted at Milt's hand. He felt the sharp, tiny claws rake across his hand and he absently disengaged his flesh, retreating from the probing reach of the animal. You wouldn't have liked Mars anyhow, he thought, and rose to his feet.

Carrying the box, he strode swiftly toward the emergency hatch. Before the stewardess could reach him he had thrown open the hatch. He stepped forward and the hatch locked behind him. For an instant he was within the cramped unit, and then he began to twist open the heavy outer door.

"Mr. Biskle!" the stewardess's voice came, muffled by the door behind him. He heard her fumbling to reach him, opening the door and groping to catch hold of him.

As he twisted open the outer door the kitten within the box under his arm snarled.

You, too? Milt Biskle thought, and paused.

Death, the emptiness and utter lack of warmth of 'tween space, seeped around him, filtering past the partly opened outer door. He smelled it and something within him, as in the kitten, retreated by instinct. He paused, holding the box, not trying to push the outer door any farther open, and in that moment the stewardess grabbed him.

"Mr. Biskle," she said with a half-sob, "are you out of your mind? Good God, what are you doing?" She managed to tug the outer door shut, screw the emergency section back into shut position.

"You know exactly what I'm doing," Milt Biskle said as he allowed her to propel him back into the ship and to his seat. And don't think you stopped me, he said to himself. Because it wasn't you. I could have gone ahead and done it. But I decided not to.

He wondered why.

———

Later, at Field Three on Mars, Dr. DeWinter met him as he had expected.

The two of them walked to the parked 'copter and DeWinter in a worried tone of voice said, "I've just been informed that during the trip—"

"That's right. I attempted suicide. But I changed my mind. Maybe you know why. You're the psychologist, the authority as to what goes on inside us." He entered the 'copter, being careful not to bang the box containing the Terran kitten.

"You're going to go ahead and stake your landparcel with Fay?" Dr. DeWinter asked presently as the 'copter flew above green, wet fields of high protein wheat. "Even though—you know?"

"Yes." He nodded. After all, there was nothing else for him, as far as he could make out.

"You Terrans." DeWinter shook his head. "Admirable." Now he noticed the box on Milt Biskle's lap. "What's that you have there? A creature from Terra?" He eyed it suspiciously; obviously to him it was a manifestation of an alien form of life. "A rather peculiar-looking organism."

"It's going to keep me company," Milt Biskle said. "While I go on with my work, either building up my private parcel or—" Or helping you Proxmen with Terra, he thought.

"Is that what was called a 'rattlesnake'? I detect the sound of its rattles." Dr. DeWinter edged away.

"It's purring." Milt Biskle stroked the kitten as the autonomic circuit of the 'copter guided it across the dully red Martian sky. Contact with the one familiar life-form, he realized, will keep me sane. It will make it possible for me to go on. He felt grateful. My race may have been defeated and destroyed, but not all Terran creatures have perished. When we reconstruct Terra maybe we can induce the authorities to allow us to set up game preserves. We'll make that part of our task, he told himself, and again he patted the kitten. At least we can hope for that much.

Next to him, Dr. DeWinter was also deep in thought. He appreciated the intricate workmanship, by engineers stationed on the third planet, which had gone into the simulacrum resting in the box on Milt Biskle's lap. The technical achievement was impressive, even to him, and he saw clearly—as Milt Biskle of course did not. This artifact, accepted by the Terran as an authentic organism from his familiar past, would provide a pivot by which the man would hang onto his psychic balance.

But what about the other reconstruct engineers? What would carry each of them through and past the moment of discovery as each completed his work and had to—whether he liked it or not—awake?

It would vary from Terran to Terran. A dog for one, a more elaborate simulacrum, possibly that of a nubile human female, for another. In any case, each would be provided with an "exception" to the true state. One essential surviving entity, selected out of what had in fact totally vanished. Research into the past of each engineer would provide the clue, as it had in Biskle's instance; the cat-simulacrum had been finished weeks before his abrupt, panic-stricken trip home to Terra. For instance, in Andre's case a parrot-simulacrum was already under construction. It would be done by the time he made *his* trip home.

"I call him Thunder," Milt Biskle explained.

"Good name," Dr. DeWinter—as he titled himself these days—said. And thought, A shame we could not have shown him the real situation of Terra. Actually it's quite interesting that he accepted what he saw, because on some level he must realize that nothing survives a war of the kind we conducted. Obviously he desperately wanted to believe that a remnant, even though no more than rubble, endures. But it's typical of the Terran mind to fasten onto phantoms. That might help explain their defeat in the conflict; they were simply not realists.

"This cat," Milt Biskle said, "is going to be a mighty hunter of Martian sneak-mice."

"Right," Dr. DeWinter agreed, and thought, *As long as its batteries don't run down.* He, too, patted the kitten.

A switch closed and the kitten purred louder.

A GAME OF UNCHANCE

While rolling a fifty-gallon drum of water from the canal to his potato garden, Bob Turk heard the roar, glanced up into the haze of the midafternoon Martian sky, and saw the great blue interplan ship.

In the excitement he waved. And then he read the words painted on the side of the ship and his joy became alloyed with care. Because this great pitted hull, now lowering itself to a rear-end landing, was a carny ship, come to this region of the fourth planet to transact business.

The painting spelled out:

FALLING STAR ENTERTAINMENT ENTERPRISES
PRESENTS
FREAKS, MAGIC, TERRIFYING STUNTS, AND WOMEN!

The final word had been painted largest of all.

I better go tell the settlement council, Turk realized. He left his water drum and trotted toward the shop-area, panting as his lungs struggled to take in the thin, weak air of this unnatural, colonized world. Last time a carnival had come to their area they had been robbed of most of their crops—accepted by the pitchmen in barter—and had wound up with nothing more than an armload of useless plaster figurines. It would not happen again. And yet—

He felt the craving within him, the need to be entertained. And they all felt this way; the settlement yearned for the bizarre. Of course the pitchmen knew this, preyed off this. Turk thought, If only we could keep our heads. Barter excess food and cloth-fibers, not what we need . . . not become like a lot of kids. But life in the colony world was monotonous.

Carting water, fighting bugs, repairing fences, ceaselessly tinkering with the semi-autonomous robot farm machinery which sustained them . . . it wasn't enough; it had no—culture. No solemnity.

"Hey," Turk called as he reached Vince Guest's land; Vince sat aboard his one-cylinder plow, wrench in hand. "Hear the noise? Company! More sideshows, like last year—remember?"

"I remember," Vince said, not looking up. "They got all my squash. The hell with traveling shows." His face became dark.

"This is a different outfit," Turk explained, halting. "I never saw them before; they've got a *blue* ship and it looks like it's been everywhere. You know what we're going to do? Remember our plan?"

"Some plan," Vince said, closing the jaw of the wrench.

"Talent is talent," Turk babbled, trying to convince—not merely Vince—but himself as well; he talked against his own alarm. "All right, so Fred's sort of half-witted; his talent's genuine, I mean, we've tried it out a million times, and why we didn't use it against that carny last year I'll never know. But now we're organized. Prepared."

Raising his head Vince said, "You know what that dumb kid will do? He'll join the carny; he'll leave with it and he'll use his talent on their side—we can't trust him."

"I trust him," Turk said, and hurried on toward the buildings of the settlement, the dusty, eroded gray structures directly ahead. Already he could see their council chairman, Hoagland Rae, busy at his store; Hoagland rented tired pieces of equipment to settlement members and they all depended on him. Without Hoagland's contraptions no sheep would get sheared, no lambs would be distailed. It was no wonder that Hoagland had become their political—as well as economic—leader.

Stepping out onto the hard-packed sand, Hoagland shaded his eyes, wiped his wet forehead with a folded handkerchief, and greeted Bob Turk. "Different outfit this time?" His voice was low.

"Right," Turk said, his heart pounding. "And we can take them, Hoag! If we play it right; I mean, once Fred—"

"They'll be suspicious," Hoagland said thoughtfully. "No doubt other settlements have tried to use Psi to win. They may have one of those—what do you call them?—those anti-Psi folks with them. Fred's a p-k and if they have an anti-p-k—" He gestured, showing his resignation.

"I'll go tell Fred's parents to get him from school," Bob Turk panted. "It'd be natural for kids to show up right away; let's close the school for this afternoon so Fred's lost in the crowd, you know what I mean? He doesn't *look* funny, not to me, anyhow." He sniggered.

"True," Hoagland agreed, with dignity. "The Costner boy appears quite normal. Yes, we'll try; that's what we voted to do anyhow, we're committed. Go sound the surplus-gathering bell so these carny boys can see we've got good produce to offer—I want to see all those apples and walnuts and cabbages and squash and pumpkins piled up—" He pointed to the spot. "And an accurate inventory sheet, with three carbons, in my hands, within one hour." Hoagland got out a cigar, lit up with his lighter. "Get going."

Bob Turk went.

As they walked through their south pasture, among the black-face sheep who chewed the hard, dry grass, Tony Costner said to his son, "You think you can manage it, Fred? If not, say so. You don't have to."

Straining, Fred Costner thought he could dimly see the carnival, far off, arranged before the upended interplan ship. Booths, shimmering big banners and metal streamers that danced in the wind . . . and the recorded music, or was it an authentic calliope? "Sure," he muttered. "I can handle them; I've been practicing every day since Mr. Rae told me." To prove it he caused a rock lying ahead of them to skim up, pass in an arc, start toward them at high speed, and then drop abruptly back to the brown, dry grass. A sheep regarded it dully and Fred laughed.

A small crowd from the settlement, including children, had already manifested itself among the booths now being set up; he saw the cotton candy machine hard at work, smelled the frying popcorn, saw with delight a vast cluster of helium-filled balloons carried by a gaudily painted dwarf wearing a hobo costume.

His father said quietly, "What you must look for, Fred, is the game which offers the really valuable prizes."

"I know," he said, and began to scan the booths. We don't have a need for hula-hula dolls, he said to himself. Or boxes of saltwater taffy.

Somewhere in the carnival lay the real spoils. It might be in the money-pitching board or the spinning wheel or the bingo table; anyhow it was there. He scented it, sniffed it. And hurried.

In a weak, strained voice his father said, "Um, maybe I'll leave you, Freddy." Tony had seen one of the girl platforms and had turned toward it, unable to take his eyes from the scene. One of the girls was already—but then the rumble of a truck made Fred Costner turn, and he forgot about the high-breasted, unclad girl on the platform. The truck was bringing the produce of the settlement, to be bartered in exchange for tickets.

The boy started toward the truck, wondering how much Hoagland Rae had decided to put up this time after the awful licking they had taken before. It looked like a great deal and Fred felt pride; the settlement obviously had full confidence in his abilities.

He caught then the unmistakable stench of Psi.

It emanated from a booth to his right and he turned at once in that direction. This was what the carny people were protecting, this one game which they did not feel they could afford to lose. It was, he saw, a booth in which one of the freaks acted as the target; the freak was a no-head, the first Fred had ever seen, and he stopped, transfixed.

The no-head had no head at all and his sense organs, his eyes and nose and ears, had migrated to other parts of his body beginning in the period before birth. For instance, his mouth gaped from the center of his chest, and from each shoulder an eye gleamed; the no-head was deformed but not deprived, and Fred felt respect for him. The no-head could see, smell, and hear as good as anyone. But what exactly did he do in the game?

In the booth the no-head sat within a basket suspended above a tub of water. Behind the no-head Fred Costner saw a target and then he saw the heap of baseballs near at hand and he realized how the games worked; if the target were hit by a ball, the no-head would plunge into the tub of water. And it was to prevent this that the carny had directed its Psi powers; the stench here was overpowering. He could not, however, tell from whom the stench came, the no-head or the operator of the booth or from a third person as yet unseen.

The operator, a thin young woman wearing slacks and a sweater and tennis shoes, held a baseball toward Fred. "Ready to play, captain?" she demanded and smiled at him insinuatingly, as if it was utterly in the realm of the impossible that he might play and win.

"I'm thinking," Fred said. He was scrutinizing the prizes.

The no-head giggled and the mouth located in the chest said, "He's thinking—I doubt that!" It giggled again and Fred flushed.

His father came up beside him. "Is this what you want to play?" he said. Now Hoagland Rae appeared; the two men flanked the boy, all three of them studying the prizes. What were they? Dolls, Fred thought. At least that was their appearance; the vaguely male, small shapes lay in rows on the shelves to the left of the booth's operator. He could not for the life of him fathom the carny's reasons for protecting these; surely they were worthless. He moved closer, straining to see . . .

Leading him off to one side Hoagland Rae said worriedly, "But even if we win, Fred, what do we get? Nothing we can use, just those plastic figurines. We can't barter those with other settlements, even." He looked disappointed; the corners of his mouth turned down dismally.

"I don't think they're what they seem," Fred said. "But I don't actually know what they are. Anyhow, let me try, Mr. Rae; I know this is the one." And the carny people certainly believed so.

"I'll leave it up to you," Hoagland Rae said, with pessimism; he exchanged glances with Fred's father, then slapped the boy encouragingly on the back. "Let's go," he announced. "Do your best, kid." The group of them—joined now by Bob Turk—made their way back to the booth in which the no-head sat with shoulder eyes gleaming.

"Made up your mind, people?" the thin stony-faced girl who operated the booth asked, tossing a baseball and recatching it.

"Here." Hoagland handed Fred an envelope; it was the proceeds from the settlement's produce, in the form of carny tickets—this was what they had obtained in exchange. This was all there was, now.

"I'll try," Fred said to the thin girl, and handed her a ticket.

The thin girl smiled, showing sharp, small teeth.

"Put me in the drink!" the no-head babbled. "Dunk me and win a valuable prize!" It giggled again, in delight.

———

That night, in the workshop behind his store, Hoagland Rae sat with a jeweler's loupe in his right eye, examining one of the figurines which Tony Costner's boy had won at the Falling Star Entertainment Enterprises carnival earlier in the day.

Fifteen of the figurines lay in a row against the far wall of Hoagland's workshop.

With a tiny pair of pliers Hoagland pried open the back of the doll-like structure and saw, within, intricate wiring. "The boy was right," he said to Bob Turk, who stood behind him smoking a synthetic tobacco cigarette in jerky agitation. "It's not a doll; it's fully rigged. Might be UN property they stole; might even be a microrob. You know, one of those special automatic mechanisms the government uses for a million tasks from spying to reconstruct surgery for war vets." Now, gingerly, he opened the front of the figurine.

More wiring, and the miniature parts which even under the loupe were exceedingly difficult to make out. He gave up; after all, his ability was limited to repairing power harvesting equipment and the like. This was just too much. Again he wondered exactly how the settlement could make use of these microrobs. Sell them back to the UN? And meanwhile, the carnival had packed up and gone. No way to find out from them what these were.

"Maybe it walks and talks," Turk suggested.

Hoagland searched for a switch on the figurine, found none. Verbal order? he wondered. "Walk," he ordered it. The figurine remained inert. "I think we've got something here," he said to Turk. "But—" He gestured. "It'll take time; we've got to be patient." Maybe if they took one of the figurines to M City, where the truly professional engineers, electronics experts, and repairmen of all kinds could be found . . . but he wanted to do this himself; he distrusted the inhabitants of the one great urban area on the colony planet.

"Those carny people sure were upset when we won again and again," Bob Turk chuckled. "Fred, he said that they were exerting their own Psi all the time and it completely surprised them that—"

"Be quiet," Hoagland said. He had found the figurine's power supply; now he needed only to trace the circuit until he came to a break. By closing the break he could start the mechanism into activity; it was—or rather it seemed—as simple as that.

Shortly, he found the interruption in the circuit. A microscopic switch, disguised as the belt buckle, of the figurine . . . exulting, Hoagland closed the switch with his needle-nose pliers, set the figurine down on his workbench, and waited.

The figurine stirred. It reached into a pouch-like construct hanging at its side, a sort of purse; from the pouch it brought a tiny tube, which it pointed at Hoagland.

"Wait," Hoagland said feebly. Behind him Turk bleated and scuttled for cover. Something boomed in his face, a light that thrust him back; he shut his eyes and cried out in fright. *We're being attacked!* he shouted, but his voice did not sound; he heard nothing. He was crying uselessly in a darkness which had no end. Groping, he reached out imploringly . . .

The settlement's registered nurse was bending over him, holding a bottle of ammonia at his nostrils. Grunting, he managed to lift his head, open his eyes. He lay in his workshop; around him stood a ring of settlement adults, Bob Turk foremost, all with expressions of gray alarm.

"These dolls or whatever," Hoagland managed to whisper, "attacked us; be careful." He twisted, trying to see the line of dolls which he had so carefully placed against the far wall. "I set one off prematurely," he mumbled. "By completing the circuit; I tripped it so now we know." And then he blinked.

The dolls were gone.

"I went for Miss Beason," Bob Turk explained, "and when I got back they had disappeared. Sorry." He looked apologetic, as if it were his personal fault. "But you were hurt; I was worried you were maybe dead."

"Okay," Hoagland said, pulling himself up; his head ached and he felt nauseated. "You did right. Better get that Costner kid in here, get his opinion." He added, "Well, we've been taken. For the second year in a row. Only this time is worse." This time, he thought, we won. We were better off last year when we merely lost.

He had an intimation of true foreboding.

Four days later, as Tony Costner hoed weeds in his squash garden, a stirring of the ground made him pause; he reached silently for the pitchfork, thinking, It's an m-gopher, down under, eating the roots. I'll get it. He lifted the pitchfork, and, as the ground stirred once more, brought the tines of the fork savagely down to penetrate the loose, sandy soil.

Something beneath the surface squeaked in pain and fright. Tony Costner grabbed a shovel, dug the dirt away. A tunnel lay exposed and in it, dying in a heap of quivering, pulsating fur, lay—as he had from long experience anticipated—a Martian gopher, its eyes glazed in agony, elongated fangs exposed

He killed it, mercifully. And then bent down to examine it. Because something had caught his eye: a flash of metal.

The m-gopher wore a harness.

It was artificial, of course; the harness fitted snugly around the animal's thick neck. Almost invisible, hair-like wires passed from the harness and disappeared into the scalp of the gopher near the front of the skull.

"Lord," Tony Costner said, picking the gopher and its harness up and standing in futile anxiety, wondering what to do. Right away he connected this with the carnival dolls; they had gone off and done this, made this—the settlement, as Hoagland had said, was under attack.

He wondered what the gopher would have done had he not killed it.

The gopher had been up to something. Tunneling toward—his house!

Later, he sat beside Hoagland Rae in the workshop; Rae, with care, had opened the harness, inspected its interior.

"A transmitter," Hoagland said, and breathed out noisily, as if his childhood asthma had returned. "Short range, maybe half a mile. The gopher was directed by it, maybe gave back a signal that told where it was and what it was doing. The electrodes to the brain probably connect with pleasure and pain areas . . . that way the gopher could be controlled." He glanced at Tony Costner. "How'd you like to have a harness like that on you?"

"I wouldn't," Tony said, shivering. He wished, all at once, that he was back on Terra, overcrowded as it was; he longed for the press of the crowd, the smells and sounds of great throngs of men and women, moving along the hard sidewalks, among the lights. It occurred to him then, in a flash, that he had never really enjoyed it here on Mars. Far too lonely, he realized. I made a mistake. My wife; she made me come here.

It was a trifle late, however, to think that now.

"I guess," Hoagland said stonily, "that we'd better notify the UN military police." He went with dragging steps to the wallphone, cranked it, then dialed the emergency number. To Tony he said, half in apology, half in anger, "I can't take responsibility for handling this, Costner; it's too difficult."

"It's my fault too," Tony said. "When I saw that girl, she had taken off the upper part of her garment and—"

"UN regional security office," the phone declared, loudly enough for Tony Costner to hear it.

"We're in trouble," Hoagland said. And explained, then, about the Falling Star Entertainment Enterprises ship and what had happened. As he talked he wiped his streaming forehead with his handkerchief; he looked old and tired, and very much in need of a rest.

An hour later the military police landed in the middle of the settlement's sole street. A uniformed UN officer, middle-aged, with a briefcase, stepped out, glanced around in the yellow late-afternoon light, made out the sight of the crowd with Hoagland Rae placed officially in front. "You are General Mozart?" Hoagland said tentatively, holding his hand out.

"That's correct," the heavyset UN officer said, as they shook briefly. "May I see the construct, please?" He seemed a trifle disdainful of the somewhat grimy settlement people; Hoagland felt that acutely, and his sense of failure and depression burgeoned.

"Sure, General." Hoagland led the way to his store and the workshop in the rear.

After he had examined the dead m-gopher with its electrodes and harness, General Mozart said, "You may have won artifacts they did *not* want to give up, Mr. Rae. Their final—in other words actual—destination was probably not this settlement." Again his distaste showed, ill-disguised; who would want to bother this area? "But, and this is a guess, eventually Earth and the more populated regions. However, by your employment of a parapsychological bias on the ball-throwing game—" He broke off, glanced at his wristwatch. "We'll treat the fields in this vicinity with arsine gas, I think; you and your people will have to evacuate this whole region, as a matter of fact tonight; we'll provide a transport. May I use your phone? I'll order the transport—you assemble all your people." He smiled reflexively at Hoagland and then went to the telephone to place his call back to his office in M City.

"Livestock, too?" Rae said. "We can't sacrifice them." He wondered just

how he was supposed to get their sheep, dogs, and cattle into the UN transport in the middle of the night. What a mess, he thought dully.

"Of course livestock," General Mozart said unsympathetically, as if Rae
were some sort of idiot.

The third steer driven aboard the UN transport carried a harness at its
neck; the UN military policeman at the entrance hatch spotted it, shot the
steer at once, summoned Hoagland to dispose of the carcass.

Squatting by the dead steer, Hoagland Rae examined the harness and
its wiring. As with the m-gopher, the harness connected, by delicate leads,
the brain of the animal to the sentient organism—whatever it was—which
had installed the apparatus, located, he assumed, no farther than a mile
from the settlement. What was this animal supposed to do? he wondered as
he disconnected the harness. Gore one of us? Or—eavesdrop. More likely
that; the transmitter within the harness hummed audibly; it was perpetually on, picking up all sounds in the vicinity. So they know we've brought in
the military, Hoagland realized. And that we've detected two of these con-
structs, now.

He had a deep intuition that this meant the abolition of the settlement.
This area would soon be a battleground between the UN military and
the—whatever they were. Falling Star Entertainment Enterprises. He wondered where they were from. Outside the Sol System, evidently.

Kneeling momentarily beside him a blackjack—a black-clad UN secret
police officer—said, "Cheer up. This tipped their hand; we could never
prove those carnivals were hostile, before. Because of you they never made it
to Terra. You'll be reinforced; don't give up." He grinned at Hoagland, then
hurried off, disappearing into the darkness, where a UN tank sat parked.

Yes, Hoagland thought. We did the authorities a favor. And they'll
reward us by moving massively into this area.

He had a feeling that the settlement would never be quite the same
again, no matter what the authorities did. Because, if nothing else, the settlement had failed to solve its own problems; it had been forced to call for
outside help. For the big boys.

Tony Costner gave him a hand with the dead steer; together they dragged
it to one side, gasping for breath as they grappled with the still warm body.
"I feel responsible," Tony said, when they had set it down.

"Don't." Hoagland shook his head. "And tell your boy not to feel bad."

"I haven't seen Fred since this first came out," Tony said miserably. "He took off, terribly disturbed. I guess the UN MPs will find him; they're on the outskirts rounding everybody up." He sounded numb, as if he could not quite take in what was happening. "An MP told me that by morning we could come back. The arsine gas would have taken care of everything. You think they've run into this before? They're not saying but they seem so efficient. They seem so sure of what they're doing."

"Lord knows," Hoagland said. He lit a genuine Earth-made Optimo cigar and smoked in glum silence, watching a flock of black-face sheep being driven into the transport. Who would have thought the legendary, classic invasion of Earth would take this form? he asked himself. Starting here at our meager settlement, in terms of small wired figurines, a little over a dozen in all, which we labored to win from Falling Star Entertainment Enterprises; as General Mozart said, the invaders didn't even want to give them up. Ironic.

Bob Turk, coming up beside him, said quietly, "You realize we're going to be sacrificed. That's obvious. Arsine will kill all the gophers and rats but it won't kill the microrobs because they don't breathe. The UN will have to keep blackjack squads operating in this region for weeks, maybe months. This gas attack is just the beginning." He turned accusingly to Tony Costner. "If your kid—"

"All right," Hoagland said in a sharp voice. "That's enough. If I hadn't taken that one apart, closed the circuit—you can blame me, Turk; in fact I'll be glad to resign. You can run the settlement without me."

Through a battery-driven loudspeaker a vast UN voice boomed, "All persons within sound of my voice prepare to board! This area will be flooded with poisonous gas at 14:00. I repeat—" It repeated, as the loudspeakers turned in first one direction and then another; the noise echoed in the night darkness.

Stumbling, Fred Costner made his way over the unfamiliar, rough terrain, wheezing in sorrow and weariness; he paid no attention to his location, made no effort to see where he was going. All he wanted to do was get away. He had destroyed the settlement and everyone from Hoagland Rae on down knew it. Because of him—

Far away, behind him, an amplified voice boomed, "All persons within sound of my voice prepare to board! This area will be flooded with poisonous gas at 14:00. I repeat, all persons within sound of my voice—" It dinned on and on. Fred continued to stumble along, trying to shut out the racket of the voice, hurrying away from it.

The night smelled of spiders and dry weeds; he sensed the desolation of the landscape around him. Already he was beyond the final perimeter of cultivation; he had left the settlement's fields and now he stumbled over unplowed ground where no fences or even surveyor's stakes existed. But they would probably flood this area, too, however; the UN ships would coast back and forth, spraying the arsine gas, and then after that special forces troops would come in, wearing gas-masks, carrying flame throwers, with metal-sensitive detectors on their backs, to roust out the fifteen microrobs which had taken refuge underground in the burrows of rats and vermin. Where they belong, Fred Costner said to himself. And to think I wanted them for the settlement; I thought, because the carnival wanted to keep them, that they must be valuable.

He wondered, dimly, if there was any way he could undo what he had done. Find the fifteen microrobs, plus the activated one which had almost killed Hoagland Rae? And—he had to laugh; it was absurd. Even if he found their hideout—assuming that all of them had taken refuge together in one spot—how could he destroy them? And they were armed. Hoagland Rae had barely escaped, and that had been from one acting alone.

A light glowed ahead.

In the darkness he could not make out the shapes which moved at the edge of the light; he halted, waited, trying to orient himself. Persons came and went and he heard the voices, muted, both men's and women's. And the sound of machinery in motion. The UN would not be sending out women, he realized. This was not the authorities.

A portion of the sky, the stars and faint nocturnal swath of haze, had been blotted out, and he realized all at once that he was seeing the outline of a large stationary object.

It could be a ship, parked on its tail, awaiting take-off; the shape seemed roughly that.

———

He seated himself, shivering in the cold of the Martian night, scowling in an attempt to trace the passage of the indistinct forms busy with their activity. Had the carnival returned? Was this once more the Falling Star Entertainment Enterprises vehicle? Eerily, the thought came to him: the booths and banners and tents and platforms, the magic shows and girl platforms and freaks and games of chance were being erected here in the middle of the night, in this barren area lost in the emptiness between settlements. A hollow enactment of the festivity of the carny life, for no one to see or experience. Except—by chance—himself. And to him it was revolting; he had seen all he wanted of the carnival, its people and—things.

Something ran across his foot.

With his psycho-kinetic faculty he snared it, drew it back; reaching, he grabbed with both hands until all at once he had snatched out of the darkness a thrashing, hard shape. He held it, and saw with fright one of the microrobs; it struggled to escape and yet, reflexively, he held onto it. The microrob had been scurrying toward the parked ship, and he thought, the ship's picking them up. So they won't be found by the UN. They're getting away; then the carnival can go on with its plans.

A calm voice, a woman's, said from close by, "Put it down, please. It wants to go."

Jumping with shock he released the microrob and it scuttled off, rustling in the weeds, gone at once. Standing before Fred the thin girl, still wearing slacks and a sweater, faced him placidly, a flashlight in her hand; by its circle of illumination he made out her sharply traced features, her colorless jaw and intense, clear eyes. "Hi," Fred said stammeringly; he stood up, defensively, facing the girl. She was slightly taller than he and he felt afraid of her. But he did not catch the stench of Psi about her and he realized that it had definitely not been she there in the booth who had struggled against his own faculty during the game. So he had an advantage over her, and perhaps one she did not know about.

"You better get away from here," he said. "Did you hear the loudspeaker? They're going to gas this area."

"I heard." The girl surveyed him. "You're the big winner, aren't you, sonny? The master game-player; you dunked our anti-ceph sixteen times in a row." She laughed merrily. "Simon was furious; he caught cold from that and blames you. So I hope you don't run into him."

"Don't call me sonny," he said. His fear began to leave him.

"Douglas, our p-k, says you're strong. You wrestled him down every time; congratulations. Well, how pleased are you with your take?" Silently, she once more laughed; her small sharp teeth shone in the meager light. "You feel you got your produce's worth?"

"Your p-k isn't much good," Fred said. "I didn't have any trouble and I'm really not experienced. You could do a lot better."

"With you, possibly? Are you asking to join us? Is this a proposition from you to me, little boy?"

"No!" he said, startled and repelled.

"There was a rat," the girl said, "in the wall of your Mr. Rae's workshop; it had a transmitter on it and so we knew about your call to the UN as soon as you made it. So we've had plenty of time to regain our—" She paused a moment. "Our merchandise. If we cared to. Nobody meant to hurt you; it isn't our fault that busybody Rae stuck the tip of his screwdriver into the control-circuit of that one microrob. Is it?"

"He started the cycle prematurely. It would have done that eventually anyhow." He refused to believe otherwise; he knew the settlement was in the right. "And it's not going to do you any good to collect all those micro-robs because the UN knows and—"

"'Collect'?" The girl rocked with amusement. "We're not collecting the sixteen microrobs you poor little people won. We're going ahead—you forced us to. The ship is unloading the rest of them." She pointed with the flashlight and he saw in that brief instant the horde of microrobs disgorged, spreading out, seeking shelter like so many photophobic insects.

He shut his eyes and moaned.

"Are you still sure," the girl said purringly, "that you don't want to come with us? It'll ensure your future, sonny. And otherwise—" She gestured. "Who knows? Who really can guess what'll become of your tiny settlement and you poor tiny people?"

"No," he said. "I'm still not coming."

When he opened his eyes again the girl had gone off. She stood with the no-head, Simon, examining a clipboard which the no-head held.

Turning, Fred Costner ran back the way he had come, toward the UN military police.

The lean, tall, black-uniformed UN secret police general said, "I have replaced General Mozart who is unfortunately ill-equipped to deal with domestic subversion; he is a military man exclusively." He did not extend his hand to Hoagland Rae. Instead he began to pace about the workshop, frowning. "I wish I had been called in last night. For example I could have told you one thing immediately . . . which General Mozart did not understand." He halted, glanced searchingly at Hoagland. "You realize, of course, that you did not beat the carnival people. They wanted to lose those sixteen microrobs."

Hoagland Rae nodded silently; there was nothing to say. It now did appear obvious, as the blackjack general had pointed out.

"Prior appearances of the carnival," General Wolff said, "in former years, was to set you up, to set each settlement up in turn. They knew you'd have to plan to win this time. So this time they brought their microrobs. And had their weak Psi ready to engage in an ersatz 'battle' for supremacy."

"All I want to know," Hoagland said, "is whether we're going to get protection." The hills and plains surrounding the settlement, as Fred had told them, were now swarming with the microrobs; it was unsafe to leave the downtown buildings.

"We'll do what we can." General Wolff resumed pacing. "But obviously we're not primarily concerned with you, or with any other particular settlement or locale that's been infested. It's the overall situation that we have to deal with. That ship has been forty places in the last twenty-four hours; how they've moved so swiftly—" He broke off. "They had every step prepared. And you thought you conned them." He glowered at Hoagland Rae. "Every settlement along the line thought that as they won their boxload of microrobs."

"I guess," Hoagland said presently, "that's what we get for cheating." He did not meet the blackjack general's gaze.

"That's what you get for pitting your wits against an adversary from another system," General Wolff said bitingly. "Better look at it that way. And the next time a vehicle *not* from Terra shows up—don't try to mastermind a strategy to defeat them: *call us.*"

Hoagland Rae nodded. "Okay. I understand." He felt only dull pain, not indignation; he deserved—they all deserved—this chewing out. If they were lucky their reprimand would end at this. It was hardly the settlement's greatest problem. "What do they want?" he asked General Wolff. "Are they after this area for colonization? Or is this an economic—"

"Don't try," General Wolff said.

"P-pardon?"

"It's not something you can understand, now or at any other time. We know what they're after—and *they* know what they're after. Is it important that you know, too? Your job is to try to resume your farming as before. Or if you can't do that, pull back and return to Earth."

"I see," Hoagland said, feeling trivial.

"Your kids can read about it in the history books," General Wolff said. "That ought to be good enough for you."

"It's just fine," Hoagland Rae said, miserably. He seated himself half-heartedly at his workbench, picked up a screwdriver, and began to tinker with a malfunctioning autonomic tractor guidance-turret.

"Look," General Wolff said, and pointed.

In a corner of the workshop, almost invisible against the dusty wall, a microrob crouched watching them.

"Jeez!" Hoagland wailed, groping around on his workbench for the old .32 revolver which he had gotten out and loaded.

Long before his fingers found the revolver the microrob had vanished. General Wolff had not even moved; he seemed, in fact, somewhat amused: he stood with his arms folded, watching Hoagland fumbling with the antiquated sidearm.

"We're working on a central device," General Wolff said, "which would cripple all of them simultaneously. By interrupting the flow of current from their portable power-packs. Obviously to destroy them one by one is absurd; we never even considered it. However—" He paused thoughtfully, his forehead wrinkling. "There's reason to believe they—the outspacers—have anticipated us and have diversified the power-sources in such a way that—" He shrugged philosophically. "Well, perhaps something else will come to mind. In time."

"I hope so," Hoagland said. And tried to resume his repair of the defective tractor turret.

"We've pretty much given up the hope of holding Mars," General Wolff said, half to himself.

Hoagland slowly set down his screwdriver, stared at the secret policeman.

"What we're going to concentrate on is Terra," General Wolff said, and scratched his nose reflectively.

"Then," Hoagland said after a pause, "there's really no hope for us here; that's what you're saying."

The blackjack general did not answer. He did not need to.

As he bent over the faintly greenish, scummy surface of the canal where botflies and shiny black beetles buzzed, Bob Turk saw, from the corner of his vision, a small shape scuttle. Swiftly he spun, reached for his laser cane; he brought it up, fired it, and destroyed—oh happy day!—a heap of rusted, discarded fuel drums, nothing more. The microrob had already departed.

Shakily he returned the laser cane to his belt and again bent over the bug-infested water. As usual the 'robs had been active here during the night; his wife had seen them, heard their rat-like scratchings. What the hell had they done? Bob Turk wondered dismally, and sniffed long and hard at the water.

It seemed to him that the customary odor of the stagnant water was somehow subtly changed.

"Damn," he said, and stood up, feeling futile. The 'robs had put some contaminator in the water; that was obvious. Now it would have to be given a thorough chemical analysis and that would take days. Meanwhile, what would keep his potato crop alive? Good question.

Raging in baffled helplessness, he pawed the laser cane, wishing for a target—and knowing he could never, not in a million years, have one. As always the 'robs did their work at night; steadily, surely, they pushed the settlement back.

Already ten families had packed up and taken passage for Terra. To resume—if they could—the old lives which they had abandoned.

And, soon, it would be his turn.

If only there was something they could do. Some way they could fight back. He thought, I'd do anything, give anything, for a chance to get those 'robs. I swear it. I'd go into debt or bondage or servitude or anything, just for a *chance* of freeing the area of them.

He was shuffling morosely away from the canal, hands thrust deep in the pockets of his jacket, when he heard the booming roar of the inter-system ship overhead.

Calcified, he stood peering up, his heart collapsing inside him. Them back? he asked himself. The Falling Star Entertainment Enterprises ship . . . are they going to hit us all over again, finish us off finally? Shielding his eyes he peered frantically, not able even to run, his body not knowing its way even to instinctive, animal panic.

The ship, like a gigantic orange, lowered. Shaped like an orange, colored like an orange . . . it was not the blue tubular ship of the Falling Star people; he could see that. But also it was not from Terra; it was not UN. He had never seen a ship exactly like it before and he knew that he was definitely seeing another vehicle from beyond the Sol System, much more blatantly so than the blue ship of the Falling Star creatures. Not even a cursory attempt had been made to make it appear Terran.

And yet, on its sides, it had huge letters, which spelled out words in English.

His lips moving, he read the words as the ship settled to a landing northeast of the spot at which he stood.

SIX SYSTEM EDUCATIONAL PLAYTIME ASSOCIATES IN A RIOT OF FUN AND FROLIC FOR ALL!

It was—God in heaven—another itinerant carnival company.

He wanted to look away, to turn and hurry off. And yet he could not; the old familiar drive within him, the craving, the fixated curiosity, was too strong. So he continued to watch; he could see several hatches open and autonomic mechanisms beginning to nose, like flattened doughnuts, out onto the sand.

They were pitching camp.

Coming up beside him his neighbor Vince Guest said hoarsely, "Now what?"

"You can see." Turk gestured frantically. "Use your eyes." Already the auto-mechs were erecting a central tent; colored streamers hurled themselves upward into the air and then rained down on the still two-dimensional booths. And the first humans—or humanoids—were emerging. Vince and Bob saw men wearing bright clothing and then women in tights. Or rather something considerably less than tights.

"Wow," Vince managed to say, swallowing. "You see those ladies? You ever seen women with such—"

"I see them," Turk said. "But I'm never going back to one of these non-Terran carnivals from beyond the system and neither is Hoagland; I know that as well as I know my own name."

How rapidly they were going to work. No time wasted; already faint, tinny music, of a carousel nature, filtered to Bob Turk. And the smells. Cotton candy, roasting peanuts, and with those the subtle smell of adventure and exciting sights, of the illicit. One woman with long braided red hair had hopped lithely up onto a platform; she wore a meager bra and wisp of silk at her waist and as he watched fixedly she began to practice her dance. Faster and faster she spun until at last, carried away by the rhythm, she discarded entirely what little she wore. And the funny thing about it all was that it seemed to him real art; it was not the usual carny shimmying at the midsection. There was something beautiful and alive about her movements; he found himself spellbound.

"I—better go get Hoagland," Vince managed to say, finally. Already a few settlers, including a number of children, were moving as if hypnotized toward the lines of booths and the gaudy streamers that fluttered and shone in the otherwise drab Martian air.

"I'll go over and get a closer look," Bob Turk said, "while you're locating him." He started toward the carnival on a gradually accelerated run, scuffling sand as he hurried.

To Hoagland, Tony Costner said, "At least let's *see* what they have to offer. You know they're not the same people; it wasn't them who dumped those horrible damn microrobs off here—you can see that."

"Maybe it's something worse," Hoagland said, but he turned to the boy, Fred. "What do you say?" he demanded.

"I want to look," Fred Costner said. He had made up his mind.

"Okay," Hoagland said, nodding. "That's good enough for me. It won't hurt us to look. As long as we remember what that UN secret police general told us. Let's not kid ourselves into imagining we can outsmart them." He put down his wrench, rose from his workbench, and walked to the closet to get his fur-lined outdoor coat.

When they reached the carnival they found that the games of chance had been placed—conveniently—ahead of even the girly shows and the freaks. Fred Costner rushed forward, leaving the group of adults behind; he sniffed the air, took in the scents, heard the music, saw past the games of chance the first freak platform: it was his favorite abomination, one he remembered from previous carnivals, only this one was superior. It was a no-body. In the midday Martian sunlight it reposed quietly: a bodiless head complete with hair, ears, intelligent eyes; heaven only knew what kept it alive . . . in any case he knew intuitively that it was genuine.

"Come and see Orpheus, the head without a visible body!" the pitch-man called through his megaphone, and a group, mostly children, had gathered in awe to gape. "How does it stay alive? How does it propel itself? Show them, Orpheus." The pitchman tossed a handful of food pellets—Fred Costner could not see precisely what—at the head; it opened its mouth to enormous, frightening proportions, managed to snare most of what landed near it. The pitchman laughed and continued with his spiel. The no-body was now rolling industriously after the bits of food which it had missed. Gee, Fred thought.

"Well?" Hoagland said, coming up beside him. "Do you see any games we might profit from?" His tone was drenched with bitterness. "Care to throw a baseball at anything?" He started away, then, not waiting, a tired little fat man who had been defeated too much, who had already lost too many times. "Let's go," he said to the other adults of the settlement. "Let's get out of here before we get into another—"

"Wait," Fred said. He had caught it, the familiar, pleasing stench. It came from a booth on his right and he turned at once in that direction.

A plump, gray-colored middle-aged woman stood in a ringtoss booth, her hands full of the light wicker rings.

Behind Fred his father said to Hoagland Rae, "You get the rings over the merchandise; you win whatever you manage to toss the ring onto so that it stays." With Fred he walked slowly in that direction. "It would be a natural," he murmured, "for a psychokinetic. I would think."

"I suggest," Hoagland said, speaking to Fred, "that you look more closely this time at the prizes. At the merchandise." However, he came along, too.

At first Fred could not make out what the neat stacks were, each of them exactly alike, intricate and metallic; he came up to the edge of the booth and the middle-aged woman began her chant-like litany, offering him a handful of rings. For a dollar, or whatever of equal value the settlement had to offer.

"What are they?" Hoagland said, peering. "I—think they're some kind of machines."

Fred said, "I know what they are." And we've got to play, he realized. We must round up every item in the settlement that we can possibly trade these people, every cabbage and rooster and sheep and wool blanket.

Because, he realized, this is our chance. Whether General Wolff knows about it or likes it.

"My God," Hoagland said quietly. "Those are traps."

"That's right, mister," the middle-aged woman chanted. "Homeostatic traps; they do all the work, think for themselves, you just let them go and they travel and travel and they never give up until they catch—" She winked. "*You know what.* Yes, you know what they catch, mister, those little pesky things you can't ever possibly catch by yourselves, that are poisoning your water and killing your steers and ruining your settlement—win a trap, a valuable, useful trap, and you'll see, you'll see!" She tossed a wicker ring and it nearly settled over one of the complex, sleek-metal traps; it might very well have, if she had thrown it just a little more carefully. At least that was the impression given. They all felt this.

Hoagland said to Tony Costner and Bob Turk, "We'll need a couple hundred of them at least."

"And for that," Tony said, "we'll have to hock everything we own. But it's worth it; at least we won't be completely wiped out." His eyes gleamed. "Let's get started." To Fred he said, "Can you play this game? Can you win?"

"I—think so," Fred said. Although somewhere nearby, someone in the carnival was ready with a contrary power of psychokinesis. But not enough, he decided. *Not quite enough.*

It was almost as if they worked it that way on purpose.

WE CAN REMEMBER IT FOR YOU WHOLESALE

He awoke—and wanted Mars. The valleys, he thought. What would it be like to trudge among them? Great and greater yet: the dream grew as he became fully conscious, the dream and the yearning. He could almost feel the enveloping presence of the other world, which only Government agents and high officials had seen. A clerk like himself? Not likely.

"Are you getting up or not?" his wife, Kirsten, asked drowsily, with her usual hint of fierce crossness. "If you are, push the hot coffee button on the darn stove."

"Okay," Douglas Quail said, and made his way barefoot from the bedroom of their conapt to the kitchen. There, having dutifully pressed the hot coffee button, he seated himself at the kitchen table, brought out a yellow, small tin of fine Dean Swift snuff. He inhaled briskly, and the Beau Nash mixture stung his nose, burned the roof of his mouth. But still he inhaled; it woke him up and allowed his dreams, his nocturnal desires and random wishes, to condense into a semblance of rationality.

I will go, he said to himself. *Before I die I'll see Mars.*

It was, of course, impossible, and he knew this even as he dreamed. But the daylight, the mundane noise of his wife now brushing her hair before the bedroom mirror—everything conspired to remind him of what he was. *A miserable little salaried employee,* he said to himself with bitterness. Kirsten reminded him of this at least once a day and he did not blame her; it was a wife's job to bring her husband down to Earth. *Down to Earth,* he thought, and laughed. The figure of speech in this was literally apt.

"What are you sniggering about?" his wife asked as she swept into the kitchen, her long busy-pink robe wagging after her. "A dream, I bet. You're always full of them."

"Yes," he said, and gazed out the kitchen window at the hover-cars and traffic runnels, and all the little energetic people hurrying to work. In a little while he would be among them. As always.

"I'll bet it had to do with some woman," Kirsten said witheringly.

"No," he said. "A god. The god of war. He has wonderful craters with every kind of plant-life growing deep down in them."

"Listen." Kirsten crouched down beside him and spoke earnestly, the harsh quality momentarily gone from her voice. "The bottom of the ocean— *our* ocean is much more, an infinity of times more beautiful. You know that; everyone knows that. Rent an artificial gill-outfit for both of us, take a week off from work, and we can descend and live down there at one of those year-round aquatic resorts. And in addition—" She broke off. "You're not listening. You should be. Here is something a lot better than that compulsion, that obsession you have about Mars, and you don't even listen!" Her voice rose piercingly. "God in heaven, you're doomed, Doug! What's going to become of you?"

"I'm going to work," he said, rising to his feet, his breakfast forgotten. "That's what's going to become of me."

She eyed him. "You're getting worse. More fanatical every day. Where's it going to lead?"

"To Mars," he said, and opened the door to the closet to get down a fresh shirt to wear to work.

Having descended from the taxi Douglas Quail slowly walked across three densely populated foot runnels and to the modern, attractively inviting doorway. There he halted, impeding mid-morning traffic, and with caution read the shifting-color neon sign. He had, in the past, scrutinized this sign before . . . but never had he come so close. This was very different; what he did now was something else. Something which sooner or later had to happen.

REKAL, INCORPORATED

Was this the answer? After all, an illusion, no matter how convincing, remained nothing more than an illusion. At least objectively. But subjectively—quite the opposite entirely.

And anyhow he had an appointment. Within the next five minutes.

Taking a deep breath of mildly smog-infested Chicago air, he walked through the dazzling polychromatic shimmer of the doorway and up to the receptionist's counter.

The nicely articulated blonde at the counter, bare-bosomed and tidy, said pleasantly, "Good morning, Mr. Quail."

"Yes," he said. "I'm here to see about a Rekal course. As I guess you know."

"Not 'rekal' but *recall*," the receptionist corrected him. She picked up the receiver of the vidphone by her smooth elbow and said into it, "Mr. Douglas Quail is here, Mr. McClane. May he come inside, now? Or is it too soon?"

"Giz wetwa wum-wum wamp," the phone mumbled.

"Yes, Mr. Quail," she said. "You may go in; Mr. McClane is expecting you." As he started off uncertainly she called after him, "Room D, Mr. Quail. To your right."

After a frustrating but brief moment of being lost he found the proper room. The door hung open and inside, at a big genuine walnut desk, sat a genial-looking man, middle-aged, wearing the latest Martian frog-pelt gray suit; his attire alone would have told Quail that he had come to the right person.

"Sit down, Douglas," McClane said, waving his plump hand toward a chair which faced the desk. "So you want to have gone to Mars. Very good."

Quail seated himself, feeling tense. "I'm not so sure this is worth the fee," he said. "It costs a lot and as far as I can see I really get nothing." *Costs almost as much as going,* he thought.

"You get tangible proof of your trip," McClane disagreed emphatically. "All the proof you'll need. Here; I'll show you." He dug within a drawer of his impressive desk. "Ticket stub." Reaching into a manila folder, he produced a small square of embossed cardboard. "It proves you went—and returned. Postcards." He laid out four franked picture 3-D full-color postcards in a neatly arranged row on the desk for Quail to see. "Film. Shots you took of local sights on Mars with a rented moving camera." To Quail he displayed those, too. "Plus the names of people you met, two hundred poscreds' worth of souvenirs, which will arrive—from Mars—within the following month. And passport, certificates listing the shots you received.

And more." He glanced up keenly at Quail. "You'll know you went, all right," he said. "You won't remember us, won't remember me or ever having been here. It'll be a real trip in your mind; we guarantee that. A full two weeks of recall; every last piddling detail. Remember this: if at any time you doubt that you really took an extensive trip to Mars you can return here and get a full refund. You see?"

"But I didn't go," Quail said. "I won't have gone, no matter what proofs you provide me with." He took a deep, unsteady breath. "And I never was a secret agent with Interplan." It seemed impossible to him that Rekal, Incorporated's extra-factual memory implant would do its job—despite what he had heard people say.

"Mr. Quail," McClane said patiently. "As you explained in your letter to us, you have no chance, no possibility in the slightest, of ever actually getting to Mars; you can't afford it, and what is much more important, you could never qualify as an undercover agent for Interplan or anybody else. This is the only way you can achieve your, ahem, lifelong dream; am I not correct, sir? You can't be this; you can't actually do this." He chuckled. "But you can *have been* and *have done.* We see to that. And our fee is reasonable; no hidden charges." He smiled encouragingly.

"Is an extra-factual memory that convincing?" Quail asked.

"More than the real thing, sir. Had you really gone to Mars as an Interplan agent, you would by now have forgotten a great deal; our analysis of true-mem systems—authentic recollections of major events in a person's life—shows that a variety of details are very quickly lost to the person. Forever. Part of the package we offer you is such deep implantation of recall that nothing is forgotten. The packet which is fed to you while you're comatose is the creation of trained experts, men who have spent years on Mars; in every case we verify details down to the last iota. And you've picked a rather easy extra-factual system; had you picked Pluto or wanted to be Emperor of the Inner Planet Alliance we'd have much more difficulty . . . and the charges would be considerably greater."

Reaching into his coat for his wallet, Quail said, "Okay. It's been my lifelong ambition and so I see I'll never really do it. So I guess I'll have to settle for this."

"Don't think of it that way," McClane said severely. "You're not accepting second best. The actual memory, with all its vagueness, omissions, and ellipses, not to say distortions—that's second best." He accepted the money and pressed a button on his desk. "All right, Mr. Quail," he said, as the door of his office opened and two burly men swiftly entered. "You're on your way to Mars as a secret agent." He rose, came over to shake Quail's nervous, moist hand. "Or rather, you have been on your way. This afternoon at four-thirty you will, um, arrive back here on Terra; a cab will leave you off at your conapt and, as I say, you will never remember seeing me or coming here; you won't, in fact, even remember having heard of our existence."

His mouth dry with nervousness, Quail followed the two technicians from the office; what happened next depended on them.

Will I actually believe I've been on Mars? he wondered. *That I managed to fulfill my lifetime ambition?* He had a strange, lingering intuition that something would go wrong. But just what—he did not know.

He would have to wait and find out.

The intercom on McClane's desk, which connected him with the work area of the firm, buzzed and a voice said, "Mr. Quail is under sedation now, sir. Do you want to supervise this one, or shall we go ahead?"

"It's routine," McClane observed. "You may go ahead, Lowe; I don't think you'll run into any trouble." Programming an artificial memory of a trip to another planet—with or without the added fillip of being a secret agent—showed up on the firm's work schedule with monotonous regularity. *In one month,* he calculated wryly, *we must do twenty of these . . . ersatz interplanetary travel has become our bread and butter.*

"Whatever you say, Mr. McClane," Lowe's voice came, and thereupon the intercom shut off.

Going to the vault section in the chamber behind his office, McClane searched about for a Three packet—trip to Mars—and a Sixty-two packet: secret Interplan spy. Finding the two packets, he returned with them to his desk, seated himself comfortably, poured out the contents—merchandise which would be planted in Quail's conapt while the lab technicians busied themselves installing false memory.

A one-poscred sneaky-pete side arm, McClane reflected; *that's the largest item. Sets us back financially the most.* Then a pellet-sized transmitter, which could be swallowed if the agent were caught. Code book that astonishingly resembled the real thing . . . the firm's models were highly accurate: based, whenever possible, on actual U.S. military issue. Odd bits which made no intrinsic sense but which would be woven into the warp and woof of Quail's imaginary trip, would coincide with his memory: half an ancient silver fifty-cent piece, several quotations from John Donne's sermons written incorrectly, each on a separate piece of transparent tissue-thin paper, several match folders from bars on Mars, a stainless steel spoon engraved PROPERTY OF DOME-MARS NATIONAL KIBBUZIM, a wiretapping coil which—

The intercom buzzed. "Mr. McClane, I'm sorry to bother you but something rather ominous has come up. Maybe it would be better if you were in here after all. Quail is already under sedation; he reacted well to the narkidrine; he's completely unconscious and receptive. But—"

"I'll be in." Sensing trouble, McClane left his office; a moment later he emerged in the work area.

On a hygienic bed lay Douglas Quail, breathing slowly and regularly, his eyes virtually shut; he seemed dimly—but only dimly—aware of the two technicians and now McClane himself.

"There's no space to insert false memory-patterns?" McClane felt irritation. "Merely drop out two work weeks; he's employed as a clerk at the West Coast Emigration Bureau, which is a government agency, so he undoubtedly has or had two weeks' vacation within the last year. That ought to do it." Petty details annoyed him. And always would.

"Our problem," Lowe said sharply, "is something quite different." He bent over the bed, said to Quail, "Tell Mr. McClane what you told us." To McClane he said, "Listen closely."

The gray-green eyes of the man lying supine in the bed focussed on McClane's face. The eyes, he observed uneasily, had become hard; they had a polished, inorganic quality, like semi-precious tumbled stones. He was not sure that he liked what he saw; the brilliance was too cold. "What do you want now?" Quail said harshly. "You've broken my cover. Get out of here before I take you all apart." He studied McClane. "Especially you," he continued. "You're in charge of this counter-operation."

Lowe said, "How long were you on Mars?"

"One month," Quail said gratingly.

"And your purpose there?" Lowe demanded.

The meager lips twisted; Quail eyed him and did not speak. At last, drawling the words out so that they dripped with hostility, he said, "Agent for Interplan. As I already told you. Don't you record everything that's said? Play your vid-aud tape back for your boss and leave me alone." He shut his eyes, then; the hard brilliance ceased. McClane felt, instantly, a rushing splurge of relief.

Lowe said quietly, "This is a tough man, Mr. McClane."

"He won't be," McClane said, "after we arrange for him to lose his memory-chain again. He'll be as meek as before." To Quail he said, "So *this* is why you wanted to go to Mars so terribly bad."

Without opening his eyes Quail said, "I never wanted to go to Mars. I was assigned it—they handed it to me and there I was: stuck. Oh yeah, I admit I was curious about it; who wouldn't be?" Again he opened his eyes and surveyed the three of them, McClane in particular. "Quite a truth drug you've got here; it brought up things I had absolutely no memory of." He pondered. "I wonder about Kirsten," he said, half to himself. "Could she be in on it? An Interplan contact keeping an eye on me . . . to be certain I didn't regain my memory? No wonder she's been so derisive about my wanting to go there." Faintly, he smiled; the smile—one of understanding—disappeared almost at once.

McClane said, "Please believe me, Mr. Quail; we stumbled onto this entirely by accident. In the work we do—"

"I believe you," Quail said. He seemed tired, now; the drug was continuing to pull him under, deeper and deeper. "Where did I say I'd been?" he murmured. "Mars? Hard to remember—I know I'd like to see it; so would everybody else. But me—" His voice trailed off. "Just a clerk, a nothing clerk."

Straightening up, Lowe said to his superior, "He wants a false memory implanted that corresponds to a trip he actually took. And a false reason which is the real reason. He's telling the truth; he's a long way down in the narkidrine. The trip is very vivid in his mind—at least under sedation. But apparently he doesn't recall it otherwise. Someone, probably at a government military-sciences lab, erased his conscious memories; all he knew was that going to Mars meant something special to him, and so did being a secret agent. They couldn't erase that; it's not a memory but a desire, undoubtedly the same one that motivated him to volunteer for the assignment in the first place."

The other technician, Keeler, said to McClane, "What do we do? Graft a false memory-pattern over the real memory? There's no telling what the results would be; he might remember some of the genuine trip, and the confusion might bring on a psychotic interlude. He'd have to hold two opposite premises in his mind simultaneously: that he went to Mars and that he didn't. That he's a genuine agent for Interplan and he's not, that it's spurious. I think we ought to revive him without any false memory implantation and send him out of here; this is hot."

"Agreed," McClane said. A thought came to him. "Can you predict what he'll remember when he comes out of sedation?"

"Impossible to tell," Lowe said. "He probably will have some dim, diffuse memory of his actual trip, now. And he'd probably be in grave doubt as to its validity; he'd probably decide our programming slipped a gear-tooth. And he'd remember coming here; that wouldn't be erased—unless you want it erased."

"The less we mess with this man," McClane said, "the better I like it. This is nothing for us to fool around with; we've been foolish enough to— or unlucky enough to—uncover a genuine Interplan spy who has a cover so perfect that up to now even he didn't know what he was—or rather is." The sooner they washed their hands of the man calling himself Douglas Quail the better.

"Are you going to plant packets Three and Sixty-two in his conapt?" Lowe said.

"No," McClane said. "And we're going to return half his fee."

"'Half'! Why half?"

McClane said lamely, "It seems to be a good compromise."

As the cab carried him back to his conapt at the residential end of Chicago, Douglas Quail said to himself, *It's sure good to be back on Terra.*

Already the month-long period on Mars had begun to waver in his memory; he had only an image of profound gaping craters, an ever-present ancient erosion of hills, of vitality, of motion itself. A world of dust where little happened, where a good part of the day was spent checking and rechecking one's portable oxygen source. And then the life-forms, the unassuming and modest gray-brown cacti and maw-worms.

As a matter of fact he had brought back several moribund examples of Martian fauna; he had smuggled them through customs. After all, they posed no menace; they couldn't survive in Earth's heavy atmosphere.

Reaching into his coat pocket, he rummaged for the container of Martian maw-worms—

And found an envelope instead.

Lifting it out, he discovered, to his perplexity, that it contained five hundred and seventy poscreds, in cred bills of low denomination.

Where'd I get this? he asked himself. *Didn't I spend every 'cred I had on my trip?*

With the money came a slip of paper marked: *One-half fee ret'd. By McClane.* And then the date. Today's date.

"Recall," he said aloud.

"Recall what, sir or madam?" the robot driver of the cab inquired respectfully.

"Do you have a phone book?" Quail demanded.

"Certainly, sir or madam." A slot opened; from it slid a microtape phone book for Cook County.

"It's spelled oddly," Quail said as he leafed through the pages of the yellow section. He felt fear, then; abiding fear. "Here it is," he said. "Take me there, to Rekal, Incorporated. I've changed my mind; I don't want to go home."

"Yes, sir or madam, as the case may be," the driver said. A moment later the cab was zipping back in the opposite direction.

"May I make use of your phone?" he asked.

"Be my guest," the robot driver said. And presented a shiny new emperor 3-D color phone to him.

He dialed his own conapt. And after a pause found himself confronted by a miniature but chillingly realistic image of Kirsten on the small screen. "I've been to Mars," he said to her.

"You're drunk." Her lips writhed scornfully. "Or worse."

" 's God's truth."

"When?" she demanded.

"I don't know." He felt confused. "A simulated trip, I think. By means of one of those artificial or extra-factual or whatever it is memory places. It didn't take."

Kirsten said witheringly, "You *are* drunk." And broke the connection at her end. He hung up, then, feeling his face flush. *Always the same tone,* he said hotly to himself. *Always the retort, as if she knows everything and I know nothing. What a marriage. Keerist,* he thought dismally.

A moment later the cab stopped at the curb before a modern, very attractive little pink building, over which a shifting polychromatic neon sign read: REKAL, INCORPORATED.

The receptionist, chic and bare from the waist up, started in surprise, then gained masterful control of herself. "Oh, hello, Mr. Quail," she said nervously. "H-how are you? Did you forget something?"

"The rest of my fee back," he said.

More composed now, the receptionist said, "Fee? I think you are mistaken, Mr. Quail. You were here discussing the feasibility of an extra-factual trip for you, but—" She shrugged her smooth pale shoulders. "As I understand it, no trip was taken."

Quail said, "I remember everything, miss. My letter to Rekal, Incorporated, which started this whole business off. I remember my arrival here, my visit with Mr. McClane. Then the two lab technicians taking me in tow and administering a drug to put me out." No wonder the firm had returned half his fee. The false memory of his "trip to Mars" hadn't taken—at least not entirely, not as he had been assured.

"Mr. Quail," the girl said, "although you are a minor clerk you are a good-looking man and it spoils your features to become angry. If it would make you feel any better, I might, ahem, let you take me out . . ."

He felt furious, then. "I remember you," he said savagely. "For instance the fact that your breasts are sprayed blue; that stuck in my mind. And I remember Mr. McClane's promise that if I remembered my visit to Rekal, Incorporated I'd receive my money back in full. Where is Mr. McClane?"

After a delay—probably as long as they could manage—he found himself once more seated facing the imposing walnut desk, exactly as he had been an hour or so earlier in the day.

"Some technique you have," Quail said sardonically. His disappointment—and resentment—was enormous, by now. "My so-called 'memory' of a trip to Mars as an undercover agent for Interplan is hazy and vague and shot full of contradictions. And I clearly remember my dealings here with you people. I ought to take this to the Better Business Bureau." He was burning angry, at this point; his sense of being cheated had overwhelmed him, had destroyed his customary aversion to participating in a public squabble.

Looking morose, as well as cautious, McClane said, "We capitulate, Quail. We'll refund the balance of your fee. I fully concede the fact that we did absolutely nothing for you." His tone was resigned.

Quail said accusingly, "You didn't even provide me with the various artifacts that you claimed would 'prove' to me I had been on Mars. All that song-and-dance you went into—it hasn't materialized into a damn thing. Not even a ticket stub. Nor postcards. Nor passport. Nor proof of immunization shots. Nor—"

"Listen, Quail," McClane said. "Suppose I told you—" He broke off. "Let it go." He pressed a button on his intercom. "Shirley, will you disburse five hundred and seventy more 'creds in the form of a cashier's check made out to Douglas Quail? Thank you." He released the button, then glared at Quail.

Presently the check appeared; the receptionist placed it before McClane and once more vanished out of sight, leaving the two men alone, still facing each other across the surface of the massive walnut desk.

"Let me give you a word of advice," McClane said as he signed the check and passed it over. "Don't discuss your, ahem, recent trip to Mars with anyone."

"What trip?"

"Well, that's the thing." Doggedly, McClane said, "The trip you partially remember. Act as if you don't remember; pretend it never took place. Don't ask me why; just take my advice: it'll be better for all of us." He had begun to perspire. Freely. "Now, Mr. Quail, I have other business, other clients to see." He rose, showed Quail to the door.

Quail said, as he opened the door, "A firm that turns out such bad work shouldn't have any clients at all." He shut the door behind him.

On the way home in the cab Quail pondered the wording of his letter of complaint to the Better Business Bureau, Terra Division. As soon as he could get to his typewriter he'd get started; it was clearly his duty to warn other people away from Rekal, Incorporated.

When he got back to his conapt he seated himself before his Hermes

Rocket portable, opened the drawers, and rummaged for carbon paper—and noticed a small, familiar box. A box which he had carefully filled on Mars with Martian fauna and later smuggled through customs.

Opening the box he saw, to his disbelief, six dead maw-worms and several varieties of the unicellular life on which the Martian worms fed. The protozoa were dried up, dusty, but he recognized them; it had taken him an entire day picking among the vast dark alien boulders to find them. A wonderful, illuminated journey of discovery.

But I didn't go to Mars, he realized.

Yet on the other hand—

Kirsten appeared at the doorway to the room, an armload of pale brown groceries gripped. "Why are you home in the middle of the day?" Her voice, in an eternity of sameness, was accusing.

"Did I go to Mars?" he asked her. "You would know."

"No, of course you didn't go to Mars; *you* would know that, I would think. Aren't you always bleating about going?"

He said, "By God, I think I went." After a pause he added, "And simultaneously I think I didn't go."

"Make up your mind."

"How can I?" He gestured. "I have both memory-tracks grafted inside my head; one is real and one isn't but I can't tell which is which. Why can't I rely on you? They haven't tinkered with you." She could do this much for him at least—even if she never did anything else.

Kirsten said in a level, controlled voice, "Doug, if you don't pull yourself together, we're through. I'm going to leave you."

"I'm in trouble." His voice came out husky and coarse. And shaking. "Probably I'm heading into a psychotic episode; I hope not, but—maybe that's it. It would explain everything, anyhow."

Setting down the bag of groceries, Kirsten stalked to the closet. "I was not kidding," she said to him quietly. She brought out a coat, got it on, walked back to the door of the conapt. "I'll phone you one of these days soon," she said tonelessly. "This is goodbye, Doug. I hope you pull out of this eventually; I really pray you do. For your sake."

"Wait," he said desperately. "Just tell me and make it absolute; I did go or I didn't—tell me which one." *But they may have altered your memory-track also,* he realized.

The door closed. His wife had left. Finally!

A voice behind him said, "Well, that's that. Now put up your hands, Quail. And also please turn around and face this way."

He turned, instinctively, without raising his hands.

The man who faced him wore the plum uniform of the Interplan Police Agency, and his gun appeared to be UN issue. And, for some odd reason, he seemed familiar to Quail; familiar in a blurred, distorted fashion which he could not pin down. So, jerkily, he raised his hands.

"You remember," the policeman said, "your trip to Mars. We know all your actions today and all your thoughts—in particular your very important thoughts on the trip home from Rekal, Incorporated." He explained, "We have a tele-transmitter wired within your skull; it keeps us constantly informed."

A telepathic transmitter; use of a living plasma that had been discovered on Luna. He shuddered with self-aversion. The thing lived inside him, within his own brain, feeding, listening, feeding. But the Interplan police used them; that had come out even in the homeopapes. So this was probably true, dismal as it was.

"Why me?" Quail said huskily. What had he done—or thought? And what did this have to do with Rekal, Incorporated?

"Fundamentally," the Interplan cop said, "this has nothing to do with Rekal; it's between you and us." He tapped his right ear. "I'm still picking up your mentational processes by way of your cephalic transmitter." In the man's ear Quail saw a small white-plastic plug. "So I have to warn you: anything you think may be held against you." He smiled. "Not that it matters now; you've already thought and spoken yourself into oblivion. What's annoying is the fact that under narkidrine at Rekal, Incorporated you told them, their technicians and the owner, Mr. McClane, about your trip—where you went, for whom, some of what you did. They're very frightened. They wish they had never laid eyes on you." He added reflectively, "They're right."

Quail said, "I never made any trip. It's a false memory-chain improperly planted in me by McClane's technicians." But then he thought of the box, in his desk drawer, containing the Martian life-forms. And the trouble and hardship he had had gathering them. The memory seemed real. And the box of life-forms; that certainly was real. Unless McClane had planted it. Perhaps this was one of the "proofs" which McClane had talked glibly about.

The memory of my trip to Mars, he thought, *doesn't convince me—but unfortunately it has convinced the Interplan Police Agency. They think I really went to Mars and they think I at least partially realize it.*

"We not only know you went to Mars," the Interplan cop agreed, in answer to his thoughts, "but we know that you now remember enough to be difficult for us. And there's no use expunging your conscious memory of all this, because if we do you'll simply show up at Rekal, Incorporated again and start over. And we can't do anything about McClane and his operation because we have no jurisdiction over anyone except our own people. Anyhow, McClane hasn't committed any crime." He eyed Quail. "Nor, technically, have you. You didn't go to Rekal, Incorporated with the idea of regaining your memory; you went, as we realize, for the usual reason people go there—a love by plain, dull people for adventure." He added, "Unfortunately you're not plain, not dull, and you've already had too much excitement; the last thing in the universe you needed was a course from Rekal, Incorporated. Nothing could have been more lethal for you or for us. And, for that matter, for McClane."

Quail said, "Why is it 'difficult' for you if I remember my trip—my alleged trip—and what I did there?"

"Because," the Interplan harness bull said, "what you did is not in accord with our great white all-protecting father public image. You did, for us, what we never do. As you'll presently remember—thanks to narkidrine. That box of dead worms and algae has been sitting in your desk drawer for six months, ever since you got back. And at no time have you shown the slightest curiosity about it. We didn't even know you had it until you remembered it on your way home from Rekal; then we came here on the double to look for it." He added, unnecessarily, "Without any luck; there wasn't enough time."

A second Interplan cop joined the first one; the two briefly conferred. Meanwhile, Quail thought rapidly. He did remember more, now; the cop had been right about the narkidrine. They—Interplan—probably used it themselves. Probably? He knew darn well they did; he had seen them putting a prisoner on it. Where would *that* be? Somewhere on Terra? More

likely on Luna, he decided, viewing the image rising from his highly defective—but rapidly less so—memory.

And he remembered something else. Their reason for sending him to
Mars; the job he had done.

No wonder they had expunged his memory.

"Oh, God," the first of the two Interplan cops said, breaking off his
conversation with his companion. Obviously, he had picked up Quail's
thoughts. "Well, this is a far worse problem, now; as bad as it can get." He
walked toward Quail, again covering him with his gun. "We've got to kill
you," he said. "And right away."

Nervously, his fellow officer said, "Why right away? Can't we simply
cart him off to Interplan New York and let them—"

"*He* knows why it has to be right away," the first cop said; he too looked
nervous, now, but Quail realized that it was for an entirely different reason.
His memory had been brought back almost entirely, now. And he fully
understood the officer's tension.

"On Mars," Quail said hoarsely, "I killed a man. After getting past fifteen bodyguards. Some armed with sneaky-pete guns, the way you are." He
had been trained, by Interplan, over a five-year period to be an assassin. A
professional killer. He knew ways to take out armed adversaries . . . such as
these two officers; and the one with the ear-receiver knew it, too.

If he moved swiftly enough—

The gun fired. But he had already moved to one side, and at the same
time he chopped down the gun-carrying officer. In an instant he had possession of the gun and was covering the other, confused, officer.

"Picked my thoughts up," Quail said, panting for breath. "He knew
what I was going to do, but I did it anyhow."

Half sitting up, the injured officer grated, "He won't use that gun on
you, Sam; I pick that up, too. He knows he's finished, and he knows we
know it, too. Come on, Quail." Laboriously, grunting with pain, he got
shakily to his feet. He held out his hand. "The gun," he said to Quail.
"You can't use it, and if you turn it over to me I'll guarantee not to kill
you; you'll be given a hearing, and someone higher up in Interplan will
decide, not me. Maybe they can erase your memory once more, I don't
know. But you know the thing I was going to kill you for; I couldn't keep

you from remembering it. So my reason for wanting to kill you is in a sense past."

Quail, clutching the gun, bolted from the conapt, sprinted for the elevator. *If you follow me,* he thought, *I'll kill you. So don't.* He jabbed at the elevator button and, a moment later, the doors slid back.

The police hadn't followed him. Obviously they had picked up his terse, tense thoughts and had decided not to take the chance.

With him inside the elevator descended. He had gotten away—for a time. But what next? Where could he go?

The elevator reached the ground floor; a moment later Quail had joined the mob of peds hurrying along the runnels. His head ached and he felt sick. But at least he had evaded death; they had come very close to shooting him on the spot, back in his own conapt.

And they probably will again, he decided. *When they find me. And with this transmitter inside me, that won't take too long.*

Ironically, he had gotten exactly what he had asked Rekal, Incorporated for. Adventure, peril, Interplan police at work, a secret and dangerous trip to Mars in which his life was at stake—everything he had wanted as a false memory.

The advantages of it being a memory—and nothing more—could now be appreciated.

On a park bench, alone, he sat dully watching a flock of perts: a semi-bird imported from Mars's two moons, capable of soaring flight, even against Earth's huge gravity.

Maybe I can find my way back to Mars, he pondered. But then what? It would be worse on Mars; the political organization whose leader he had assassinated would spot him the moment he stepped from the ship; he would have Interplan and *them* after him, there.

Can you hear me thinking? he wondered. Easy avenue to paranoia; sitting here alone he felt them tuning in on him, monitoring, recording, discussing . . . He shivered, rose to his feet, walked aimlessly, his hands deep in his pockets. *No matter where I go,* he realized, *you'll always be with me. As long as I have this device inside my head.*

I'll make a deal with you, he thought to himself—and to them. *Can you imprint a false-memory template on me again, as you did before, that I lived an average, routine life, never went to Mars? Never saw an Interplan uniform up close and never handled a gun?*

A voice inside his brain answered, "As has been carefully explained to you: that would not be enough."

Astonished, he halted.

"We formerly communicated with you in this manner," the voice continued. "When you were operating in the field, on Mars. It's been months since we've done it; we assumed, in fact, that we'd never have to do so again. Where are you?"

"Walking," Quail said, "to my death." *By your officers' guns,* he added as an afterthought. "How can you be sure it wouldn't be enough?" he demanded. "Don't the Rekal techniques work?"

"As we said. If you're given a set of standard, average memories you get—restless. You'd inevitably seek out Rekal or one of its competitors again. We can't go through this a second time."

"Suppose," Quail said, "once my authentic memories have been canceled, something more vital than standard memories are implanted. Something which would act to satisfy my craving," he said. "That's been proved; that's probably why you initially hired me. But you ought to be able to come up with something else—something equal. I was the richest man on Terra but I finally gave all my money to educational foundations. Or I was a famous deep-space explorer. Anything of that sort; wouldn't one of those do?"

Silence.

"Try it," he said desperately. "Get some of your top-notch military psychiatrists; explore my mind. Find out what my most expansive daydream is." He tried to think. "Women," he said. "Thousands of them, like Don Juan had. An interplanetary playboy—a mistress in every city on Earth, Luna, and Mars. Only I gave that up, out of exhaustion. Please," he begged. "Try it."

"You'd voluntarily surrender, then?" the voice inside his head asked. "If we agreed to arrange such a solution? *If* it's possible?"

After an interval of hesitation he said, "Yes." *I'll take the risk,* he said to himself, *that you don't simply kill me.*

"You make the first move," the voice said presently. "Turn yourself over to us. And we'll investigate that line of possibility. If we can't do it, however, if your authentic memories begin to crop up again as they've done at this time, then—" There was silence and then the voice finished, "We'll have to destroy you. As you must understand. Well, Quail, you still want to try?"

"Yes," he said. Because the alternative was death now—and for certain. At least this way he had a chance, slim as it was.

"You present yourself at our main barracks in New York," the voice of the Interplan cop resumed. "At 580 Fifth Avenue, floor twelve. Once you've surrendered yourself, we'll have our psychiatrists begin on you; we'll have personality-profile tests made. We'll attempt to determine your absolute, ultimate fantasy wish—then we'll bring you back to Rekal, Incorporated, here; get them in on it, fulfilling that wish in vicarious surrogate retrospection. And—good luck. We do owe you something; you acted as a capable instrument for us." The voice lacked malice; if anything, they—the organization—felt sympathy toward him.

"Thanks," Quail said. And began searching for a robot cab.

"Mr. Quail," the stern-faced, elderly Interplan psychiatrist said, "you possess a most interesting wish-fulfillment dream fantasy. Probably nothing such as you consciously entertain or suppose. This is commonly the way; I hope it won't upset you too much to hear about it."

The senior-ranking Interplan officer present said briskly, "He better not be too much upset to hear about it, not if he expects not to get shot."

"Unlike the fantasy of wanting to be an Interplan undercover agent," the psychiatrist continued, "which, being relatively speaking a product of maturity, had a certain plausibility to it, this production is a grotesque dream of your childhood; it is no wonder you fail to recall it. Your fantasy is this: you are nine years old, walking alone down a rustic lane. An unfamiliar variety of space vessel from another star system lands directly in front of you. No one on Earth but you, Mr. Quail, sees it. The creatures within are very small and helpless, somewhat on the order of field mice, although they are attempting to invade Earth; tens of thousands of other ships will soon be on their way, when this advance party gives the go-ahead signal."

"And I suppose I stop them," Quail said, experiencing a mixture of amusement and disgust. "Single-handed I wipe them out. Probably by stepping on them with my foot."

"No," the psychiatrist said patiently. "You halt the invasion, but not by destroying them. Instead, you show them kindness and mercy, even though by telepathy—their mode of communication—you know why they have come. They have never seen such humane traits exhibited by any sentient organism, and to show their appreciation they made a covenant with you."

Quail said, "They won't invade Earth as long as I'm alive."

"Exactly." To the Interplan officer the psychiatrist said, "You can see it does fit his personality, despite his feigned scorn."

"So by merely existing," Quail said, feeling a growing pleasure, "by simply being alive, I keep Earth safe from alien rule. I'm in effect, then, the most important person on Terra. Without lifting a finger."

"Yes, indeed, sir," the psychiatrist said. "And this is bedrock in your psyche; this is a lifelong childhood fantasy. Which, without depth and drug therapy, you never would have recalled. But it has always existed in you; it went underneath, but never ceased."

To McClane, who sat intently listening, the senior police official said, "Can you implant an extra-factual memory pattern that extreme in him?"

"We get handed every possible type of wish-fantasy there is," McClane said. "Frankly, I've heard a lot worse than this. Certainly we can handle it. Twenty-four hours from now he won't just *wish* he'd saved Earth; he'll devoutly believe it really happened."

The senior police official said, "You can start the job, then. In preparation we've already once again erased the memory in him of his trip to Mars."

Quail said, "What trip to Mars?"

No one answered him, so reluctantly he shelved the question. And anyhow a police vehicle had now put in its appearance; he, McClane, and the senior police officer crowded into it, and presently they were on their way to Chicago and Rekal, Incorporated.

"You had better make no errors this time," the police officer said to heavyset, nervous-looking McClane.

"I can't see what could go wrong," McClane mumbled, perspiring. "This has nothing to do with Mars or Interplan. Single-handedly stopping an invasion of Earth from another star-system." He shook his head at that.

"Wow, what a kid dreams up. And by pious virtue, too; not by force. It's sort of quaint." He dabbed at his forehead with a large linen pocket handkerchief.

Nobody said anything.

"In fact," McClane said, "it's touching."

"But arrogant," the police official said starkly. "Inasmuch as when he dies the invasion will resume. No wonder he doesn't recall it; it's the most grandiose fantasy I ever ran across." He eyed Quail with disapproval. "And to think we put this man on our payroll."

When they reached Rekal, Incorporated the receptionist, Shirley, met them breathlessly in the outer office. "Welcome back, Mr. Quail," she fluttered, her melon-shaped breasts—today painted an incandescent orange—bobbing with agitation. "I'm sorry everything worked out so badly before; I'm sure this time it'll go better."

Still repeatedly dabbing at his shiny forehead with his neatly folded Irish linen handkerchief, McClane said, "It better." Moving with rapidity he rounded up Lowe and Keeler, escorted them and Douglas Quail to the work area, and then, with Shirley and the senior police officer, returned to his familiar office. To wait.

"Do we have a packet made up for this, Mr. McClane?" Shirley asked, bumping against him in her agitation, then coloring modestly.

"I think we do." He tried to recall, then gave up and consulted the formal chart. "A combination," he decided aloud, "of packets Eighty-one, Twenty, and Six." From the vault section of the chamber behind his desk he fished out the appropriate packets, carried them to his desk for inspection. "From Eighty-one," he explained, "a magic healing rod given him—the client in question, this time Mr. Quail—by the race of beings from another system. A token of their gratitude."

"Does it work?" the police officer asked curiously.

"It did once," McClane explained. "But he, ahem, you see, used it up years ago, healing right and left. Now it's only a memento. But he remembers it working spectacularly." He chuckled, then opened packet Twenty. "Document from the UN Secretary General thanking him for saving Earth; this isn't precisely appropriate, because part of Quail's fantasy is that no one knows of the invasion except himself, but for the sake of verisimilitude we'll throw it in." He inspected packet Six, then. What came from this?

He couldn't recall; frowning, he dug into the plastic bag as Shirley and the Interplan police officer watched intently.

"Writing," Shirley said. "In a funny language."

"This tells who they were," McClane said, "and where they came from. Including a detailed star map logging their flight here and the system of origin. Of course it's in *their* script, so he can't read it. But he remembers them reading it to him in his own tongue." He placed the three artifacts in the center of the desk. "These should be taken to Quail's conapt," he said to the police officer. "So that when he gets home he'll find them. And it'll confirm his fantasy. SOP—standard operating procedure." He chuckled apprehensively, wondering how matters were going with Lowe and Keeler.

The intercom buzzed. "Mr. McClane, I'm sorry to bother you." It was Lowe's voice; he froze as he recognized it, froze and became mute. "But something's come up. Maybe it would be better if you came in here and supervised. Like before, Quail reacted well to the narkidrine; he's unconscious, relaxed and receptive. But—"

McClane sprinted for the work area.

On a hygienic bed Douglas Quail lay breathing slowly and regularly, eyes half-shut, dimly conscious of those around him.

"We started interrogating him," Lowe said, white-faced. "To find out exactly when to place the fantasy-memory of him single-handedly having saved Earth. And strangely enough—"

"They told me not to tell," Douglas Quail mumbled in a dull drug-saturated voice. "That was the agreement. I wasn't even supposed to remember. But how could I forget an event like that?"

I guess it would be hard, McClane reflected. *But you did—until now.*

"They even gave me a scroll," Quail mumbled, "of gratitude. I have it hidden in my conapt; I'll show it to you."

To the Interplan officer who had followed after him, McClane said, "Well, I offer the suggestion that you better not kill him. If you do they'll return."

"They also gave me a magic invisible destroying rod," Quail mumbled, eyes totally shut now. "That's how I killed that man on Mars you sent me to take out. It's in my drawer along with the box of Martian maw-worms and dried-up plant life."

Wordlessly, the Interplan officer turned and stalked from the work area.

I might as well put those packets of proof-artifacts away, McClane said to himself resignedly. He walked, step by step, back to his office. *Including the citation from the UN Secretary General. After all—*

The real one probably would not be long in coming.

FAITH OF OUR FATHERS

On the streets of Hanoi he found himself facing a legless peddler who rode a little wooden cart and called shrilly to every passerby. Chien slowed, listened, but did not stop; business at the Ministry of Cultural Artifacts cropped into his mind and deflected his attention: it was as if he were alone, and none of those on bicycles and scooters and jet-powered motorcycles remained. And likewise it was as if the legless peddler did not exist.

"Comrade," the peddler called, however, and pursued him on his cart; a helium battery operated the drive and sent the cart scuttling expertly after Chien. "I possess a wide spectrum of time-tested herbal remedies complete with testimonials from thousands of loyal users; advise me of your malady and I can assist."

Chien, pausing, said, "Yes, but I have no malady." Except, he thought, for the chronic one of those employed by the Central Committee, that of career opportunism testing constantly the gates of each official position. Including mine.

"I can cure for example radiation sickness," the peddler chanted, still pursuing him. "Or expand, if necessary, the element of sexual prowess. I can reverse carcinomatous progressions, even the dreaded melanomae, what you would call black cancers." Lifting a tray of bottles, small aluminum cans, and assorted powders in plastic jars, the peddler sang, "If a rival persists in trying to usurp your gainful bureaucratic position, I can purvey an ointment which, appearing as a dermal balm, is in actuality a desperately effective toxin. And my prices, comrade, are low. And as a special favor to one so distinguished in bearing as yourself I will accept the postwar inflationary paper dollars reputedly of international exchange but in reality damn near no better than bathroom tissue."

"Go to hell," Chien said, and signaled a passing hover-car taxi; he was already three and one half minutes late for his first appointment of the day, and his various fat-assed superiors at the Ministry would be making quick mental notations—as would, to an even greater degree, his subordinates.

The peddler said quietly, "But, comrade; you *must* buy from me."

"Why?" Chien demanded. Indignation.

"Because, comrade, I am a war veteran. I fought in the Colossal Final War of National Liberation with the People's Democratic United Front against the Imperialists; I lost my pedal extremities at the battle of San Francisco." His tone was triumphant now, and sly. "*It is the law.* If you refuse to buy wares offered by a veteran you risk a fine and possible jail sentence—and in addition disgrace."

Wearily, Chien nodded the hovercab on. "Admittedly," he said. "Okay, I must buy from you." He glanced summarily over the meager display of herbal remedies, seeking one at random. "That," he decided, pointing to a paper-wrapped parcel in the rear row.

The peddler laughed. "That, comrade, is a spermatocide, bought by women who for political reasons cannot qualify for The Pill. It would be of shallow use to you, in fact none at all, since you are a gentleman."

"The law," Chien said bitingly, "does not require me to purchase anything useful from you; only that I purchase something. I'll take that." He reached into his padded coat for his billfold, huge with the postwar inflationary bills in which, four times a week, he as a government servant was paid.

"Tell me your problems," the peddler said.

Chien stared at him, appalled by the invasion of privacy—and done by someone outside the government.

"All right, comrade," the peddler said, seeing his expression. "I will not probe; excuse me. But as a doctor—an herbal healer—it is fitting that I know as much as possible." He pondered, his gaunt features somber. "Do you watch television unusually much?" he asked abruptly.

Taken by surprise, Chien said, "Every evening. Except on Friday, when I go to my club to practice the esoteric imported art from the defeated West of steer-roping." It was his only indulgence; other than that he had totally devoted himself to Party activities.

The peddler reached, selected a gray paper packet. "Sixty trade dollars," he stated. "With a full guarantee; if it does not do as promised, return the unused portion for a full and cheery refund."

"And what," Chien said cuttingly, "is it guaranteed to do?"

"It will rest eyes fatigued by the countenance of meaningless official monologues," the peddler said. "A soothing preparation; take it as soon as you find yourself exposed to the usual dry and lengthy sermons which—"

Chien paid the money, accepted the packet, and strode off. Balls, he said to himself. It's a racket, he decided, the ordinance setting up war vets as a privileged class. They prey off us—we, the younger ones—like raptors.

Forgotten, the gray packet remained deposited in his coat pocket as he entered the imposing Postwar Ministry of Cultural Artifacts building, and his own considerable stately office, to begin his workday.

A portly, middle-aged Caucasian male, wearing a brown Hong Kong silk suit, double-breasted with vest, waited in his office. With the unfamiliar Caucasian stood his own immediate superior, Ssu-Ma Tso-pin. Tso-pin introduced the two of them in Cantonese, a dialect which he used badly.

"Mr. Tung Chien, this is Mr. Darius Pethel. Mr. Pethel will be headmaster at the new ideological and cultural establishment of didactic character soon to open at San Fernando, California." He added, "Mr. Pethel has had a rich and full lifetime supporting the people's struggle to unseat imperialist-bloc countries via pedagogic media; therefore this high post."

They shook hands.

"Tea?" Chien asked the two of them; he pressed the switch of his infrared hibachi and in an instant the water in the highly ornamented ceramic pot—of Japanese origin—began to burble. As he seated himself at his desk he saw that trustworthy Miss Hsi had laid out the information poop-sheet (confidential) on Comrade Pethel; he glanced over it, meanwhile pretending to be doing nothing in particular.

"The Absolute Benefactor of the People," Tso-pin said, "has personally met Mr. Pethel and trusts him. This is rare. The school in San Fernando will appear to teach run-of-the-mill Taoist philosophies but will, of course, in actuality maintain for us a channel of communication to the liberal and intellectual youth segment of western U.S. There are many of them still alive, from San Diego to Sacramento; we estimate at least ten thousand. The school will accept two thousand. Enrollment will be mandatory for those we select. Your relationship to Mr. Pethel's programming is grave. Ahem; your tea water is boiling."

"Thank you," Chien murmured, dropping in the bag of Lipton's tea.

Tso-pin continued, "Although Mr. Pethel will supervise the setting up of the courses of instruction presented by the school to its student body, all examination papers will, oddly enough, be relayed here to your office for your own expert, careful, ideological study. In other words, Mr. Chien, you will determine who among the two thousand students is reliable, who is truly responding to the programming and who is not."

"I will now pour my tea," Chien said, doing so ceremoniously.

"What we have to realize," Pethel rumbled in Cantonese even worse than that of Tso-pin, "is that, once having lost the global war to us, the American youth has developed a talent for dissembling." He spoke the last word in English; not understanding it, Chien turned inquiringly to his superior.

"Lying," Tso-pin explained.

Pethel said, "Mouthing the proper slogans for surface appearance, but on the inside believing them false. Test papers by this group will closely resemble those of genuine—"

"You mean that the test papers of *two thousand* students will be passing through my office?" Chien demanded. He could not believe it. "That's a full-time job in itself; I don't have time for anything remotely resembling that." He was appalled. "To give critical, official approval or denial of the astute variety which you're envisioning—" He gestured. "Screw that," he said, in English.

Blinking at the strong, Western vulgarity, Tso-pin said, "You have a staff. Plus you can requisition several more from the pool; the Ministry's budget, augmented this year, will permit it. And remember: the Absolute Benefactor of the People has handpicked Mr. Pethel." His tone now had become ominous, but only subtly so. Just enough to penetrate Chien's hysteria, and to wither it into submission. At least temporarily. To underline his point, Tso-pin walked to the far end of the office; he stood before the full-length 3-D portrait of the Absolute Benefactor, and after an interval his proximity triggered the tape-transport mounted behind the portrait; the face of the Benefactor moved, and from it came a familiar homily, in more than familiar accents. "Fight for peace, my sons," it intoned gently, firmly.

"Ha," Chien said, still perturbed, but concealing it. Possibly one of the Ministry's computers could sort the examination papers; a yes-no-maybe structure could be employed, in conjunction with a pre-analysis of the pattern of ideological correctness—and incorrectness. The matter could be made routine. Probably.

Darius Pethel said, "I have with me certain material which I would like you to scrutinize, Mr. Chien." He unzipped an unsightly, old-fashioned, plastic briefcase. "Two examination essays," he said as he passed the documents to Chien. "This will tell us if you're qualified." He then glanced at Tso-pin; their gazes met. "I understand," Pethel said, "that if you are successful in this venture you will be made vice-councilor of the Ministry, and His Greatness the Absolute Benefactor of the People will personally confer Kisterigian's medal on you." Both he and Tso-pin smiled in wary unison.

"The Kisterigian medal," Chien echoed; he accepted the examination papers, glanced over them in a show of leisurely indifference. But within him his heart vibrated in ill-concealed tension. "Why these two? By that I mean, what am I looking for, sir?"

"One of them," Pethel said, "is the work of a dedicated progressive, a loyal Party member of thoroughly researched conviction. The other is by a young *stilyagi* whom we suspect of holding petit-bourgeois imperialist degenerate crypto-ideas. It is up to you, sir, to determine which is which."

Thanks a lot, Chien thought. But, nodding, he read the title of the top paper.

DOCTRINES OF THE ABSOLUTE BENEFACTOR ANTICIPATED IN THE POETRY OF BAHA AD-DIN ZUHAYR OF THIRTEENTH-CENTURY ARABIA

Glancing down the initial pages of the essay, Chien saw a quatrain familiar to him; it was called "Death," and he had known it most of his adult, educated life.

Once he will miss, twice he will miss,
He only chooses one of many hours;
For him nor deep nor hill there is,
But all's one level plain he hunts for flowers.

"Powerful," Chien said. "This poem."

"He makes use of the poem," Pethel said, observing Chien's lips moving as he reread the quatrain, "to indicate the age-old wisdom, displayed by the Absolute Benefactor in our current lives, that no individual is safe; everyone is mortal, and only the supra-personal, historically essential cause survives. As it should be. Would you agree with him? With this student, I mean? Or—" Pethel paused. "Is he in fact perhaps satirizing the Absolute Benefactor's promulgations?"

Cagily, Chien said, "Give me a chance to inspect the other paper."

"You need no further information; decide."

Haltingly, Chien said, "I—I had never thought of this poem that way." He felt irritable. "Anyhow, it isn't by Baha ad-Din Zuhayr; it's part of the *Thousand and One Nights* anthology. It is, however, thirteenth century; I admit that." He quickly read over the text of the paper accompanying the poem. It appeared to be a routine, uninspired rehash of Party clichés, all of them familiar to him from birth. The blind, imperialist monster who moved down and snuffed out (mixed metaphor) human aspiration, the calculations of the still extant anti-Party group in eastern United States . . . He felt dully bored, and as uninspired as the student's paper. We must persevere, the paper declared. Wipe out the Pentagon remnants in the Catskills, subdue Tennessee and most especially the pocket of die-hard reaction in the red hills of Oklahoma. He sighed.

"I think," Tso-pin said, "we should allow Mr. Chien the opportunity of observing this difficult matter at his leisure." To Chien he said, "You have permission to take them home to your condominium, this evening, and adjudge them on your own time." He bowed, half mockingly, half solicitously. In any case, insult or not, he had gotten Chien off the hook, and for that Chien was grateful.

"You are most kind," he murmured, "to allow me to perform this new and highly stimulating labor on my own time. Mikoyan, were he alive today, would approve." You bastard, he said to himself. Meaning both his superior and the Caucasian Pethel. Handing me a hot potato like this, and on my own time. Obviously the CP U.S.A. is in trouble; its indoctrination academies aren't managing to do their job with the notoriously mulish, eccentric Yank youths. And you've passed that hot potato on and on until it reaches me.

Thanks for nothing, he thought acidly.

That evening in his small but well-appointed condominium apartment he read over the other of the two examination papers, this one by a Marion Culper, and discovered that it, too, dealt with poetry. Obviously this was speciously a poetry class, and he felt ill. It had always run against his grain, the use of poetry—of any art—for social purposes. Anyhow, comfortable in his special spine-straightening, simulated-leather easy chair, he lit a Cuesta Rey Number One English Market immense corona cigar and began to read.

The writer of the paper, Miss Culper, had selected as her text a portion of a poem of John Dryden, the seventeenth-century English poet, final lines from the well-known "A Song for St. Cecilia's Day."

> . . . So when the last and dreadful hour
> rumbling pageant shall devour,
> The trumpet shall be heard on high,
> The dead shall live, the living die,
> And Music shall untune the sky.

Well, that's a hell of a thing, Chien thought to himself bitingly. Dryden, we're supposed to believe, anticipated the fall of capitalism? That's what he meant by the "crumbling pageant"? Christ. He leaned over to take hold of his cigar and found that it had gone out. Groping in his pockets for his Japanese-made lighter, he half rose to his feet.

Tweeeeeee! the TV set at the far end of the living room said.

Aha, Chien thought. We're about to be addressed by the Leader. By the Absolute Benefactor of the People, up there in Peking, where he's lived for ninety years now; or is it one hundred? Or, as we sometimes like to think of him, the Ass—

"May the ten thousand blossoms of abject self-assumed poverty flower in your spiritual courtyard," the TV announcer said. With a groan, Chien rose to his feet, bowed the mandatory bow of response; each TV set came equipped with monitoring devices to narrate to the Secpol, the Security Police, whether its owner was bowing and/or watching.

On the screen a clearly defined visage manifested itself, the wide, unlined, healthy features of the one-hundred-and-twenty-year-old leader of CP East, ruler of many—far too many, Chien reflected. Blah to you, he thought, and reseated himself in his simulated-leather easy chair, now facing the TV screen.

"My thoughts," the Absolute Benefactor said in his rich and slow tones, "are on you, my children. And especially on Mr. Tung Chien of Hanoi, who faces a difficult task ahead, a task to enrich the people of Democratic East, plus the American West Coast. We must think in unison about this noble, dedicated man and the chore which he faces, and I have chosen to take several moments of my time to honor him and encourage him. Are you listening, Mr. Chien?"

"Yes, Your Greatness," Chien said, and pondered to himself the odds against the Party Leader singling *him* out this particular evening. The odds caused him to feel uncomradely cynicism; it was unconvincing. Probably this transmission was being beamed into his apartment building alone— or at least to this city. It might also be a lip-synch job, done at Hanoi TV, Incorporated. In any case he was required to listen and watch—and absorb. He did so, from a lifetime of practice. Outwardly he appeared to be rigidly attentive. Inwardly he was still mulling over the two test papers, wondering which was which; where did devout Party enthusiasm end and sardonic lampoonery begin? Hard to say . . . which of course explained why they had dumped the task in his lap.

Again he groped in his pockets for his lighter—and found the small gray envelope which the war-veteran peddler had sold him. Gawd, he thought, remembering what it had cost. Money down the drain and what did this herbal remedy do? Nothing. He turned the packet over and saw, on the back, small printed words. Well, he thought, and began to unfold the packet with care. The words had snared him—as of course they were meant to do.

Failing as a Party member and human?
Afraid of becoming obsolete and discarded
    on the ash heap of history by . . .

He read rapidly through the text, ignoring its claims, seeking to find out what he had purchased.

Meanwhile, the Absolute Benefactor droned on.

Snuff. The package contained snuff. Countless tiny black grains, like gunpowder, which sent up an interesting aromatic to tickle his nose. The title of the particular blend was Princes Special, he discovered. And very pleasing, he decided. At one time he had taken snuff—smoking tobacco for a time having been illegal for reasons of health—back during his student days at Peking U; it had been the fad, especially the amatory mixes prepared in Chungking, made from God knew what. Was this that? Almost any aromatic could be added to snuff, from essence of organe to pulverized baby-crab . . . or so some seemed, especially an English mixture called High Dry Toast, which had in itself more or less put an end to his yearning for nasal, inhaled tobacco.

On the TV screen the Absolute Benefactor rumbled monotonously on as Chien sniffed cautiously at the powder, read the claims—it cured everything from being late to work to falling in love with a woman of dubious political background. Interesting. But typical of claims—

His doorbell rang.

Rising, he walked to the door, opened it with full knowledge of what he would find. There, sure enough, stood Mou Kuei, the Building Warden, small and hard-eyed and alert to his task; he had his arm band and metal helmet on, showing that he meant business. "Mr. Chien, comrade Party worker. I received a call from the television authority. You are failing to watch your television screen and are instead fiddling with a packet of doubtful content." He produced a clipboard and ballpoint pen. "Two red marks, and hithertonow you are summarily ordered to repose yourself in a comfortable, stress-free posture before your screen and give the Leader your unexcelled attention. His words, this evening, are directed particularly to you, sir; to you."

"I doubt that," Chien heard himself say.

Blinking, Kuei said, "What do you mean?"

"The Leader rules eight billion comrades. He isn't going to single me out." He felt wrathful; the punctuality of the warden's reprimand irked him.

Kuei said, "But I distinctly heard with my own ears. You were mentioned."

Going over to the TV set, Chien turned the volume up. "But now he's talking about failures in People's India; that's of no relevance to me."

"Whatever the Leader expostulates is relevant." Mou Kuei scratched a mark on his clipboard sheet, bowed formally, turned away. "My call to come up here to confront you with your slackness originated at Central. Obviously they regard your attention as important; I must order you to set in motion your automatic transmission recording circuit and replay the earlier portions of the Leader's speech."

Chien farted. And shut the door.

Back to the TV set, he said to himself. Where our leisure hours are spent. And there lay the two student examination papers; he had that weighing him down, too. And all on my own time, he thought savagely. The hell with them. Up theirs. He strode to the TV set, started to shut it off; at once a red warning light winked on, informing that he did not have permission to shut off the set—could not in fact end its tirade and image even if he unplugged it. Mandatory speeches, he thought, will kill us all, bury us; if I could be free of the noise of speeches, free of the din of the Party baying as it hounds mankind . . .

There was no known ordinance, however, preventing him from taking snuff while he watched the Leader. So, opening the small gray packet, he shook out a mound of the black granules onto the back of his left hand. He then, professionally, raised his hand to his nostrils and deeply inhaled, drawing the snuff well up into his sinus cavities. Imagine the old superstition, he thought to himself. That the sinus cavities are connected to the brain, and hence an inhalation of snuff directly affects the cerebral cortex. He smiled, seated himself once more, fixed his gaze on the TV screen and the gesticulating individual known so utterly to them all.

The face dwindled away, disappeared. The sound ceased. He faced an emptiness, a vacuum. The screen, white and blank, confronted him and from the speaker a faint hiss sounded.

The frigging snuff, he said to himself. And inhaled greedily at the remainder of the powder on his hand, drawing it up avidly into his nose, his sinuses, and, or so it felt, into his brain; he plunged into the snuff, absorbing it elatedly.

The screen remained blank and then, by degrees, an image once more formed and established itself. It was not the Leader. Not the Absolute Benefactor of the People, in point of fact not a human figure at all.

He faced a dead mechanical construct, made of solid-state circuits, of swiveling pseudopodia, lenses, and a squawk-box. And the box began, in a droning din, to harangue him.

Staring fixedly, he thought, *What is this?* Reality? Hallucination, he thought. The peddler came across some of the psychedelic drugs used during the War of Liberation—he's selling the stuff and I've taken some, taken a whole lot!

Making his way unsteadily to the vidphone, he dialed the Secpol station nearest his building. "I wish to report a pusher of hallucinogenic drugs," he said into the receiver.

"Your name, sir, and conapt location?" Efficient, brisk, and impersonal bureaucrat of the police.

He gave them the information, then haltingly made it back to his simulated-leather easy chair, once again to witness the apparition on the TV screen. This is lethal, he said to himself. It must be some preparation developed in Washington, D.C., or London—stronger and stranger than the LSD-25 which they dumped so effectively into our reservoirs. And I thought it was going to relieve me of the burden of the Leader's speeches . . . this is far worse, this electronic, sputtering, swiveling, metal and plastic monstrosity yammering away—this is terrifying.

To have to face *this* the remainder of my life—

It took ten minutes for the Secpol two-man team to come rapping at his door. And by then, in a deteriorating set of stages, the familiar image of the Leader had seeped back into focus on the screen, had supplanted the horrible artificial construct which waved its podia and squalled on and on. He let the two cops in shakily, led them to the table on which he had left the remains of the snuff in its packet.

"Psychedelic toxin," he said thickly. "Of short duration. Absorbed into the bloodstream directly, through nasal capillaries. I'll give you details as to where I got it, from whom, all that." He took a deep shaky breath; the presence of the police was comforting.

Ballpoint pens ready, the two officers waited. And all the time, in the background, the Leader rattled out his endless speech. As he had done a thousand evenings before in the life of Tung Chien. But, he thought, it'll never be the same again, at least not for me. Not after inhaling that near-toxic snuff.

He wondered, Is that what they intended?

It seemed odd to him, thinking of a *they*. Peculiar—but somehow correct. For an instant he hesitated, to giving out the details, not telling the police enough to find the man. A peddler, he started to say. I don't know where; can't remember. But he did; he remembered the exact street intersection. So, with unexplainable reluctance, he told them.

"Thank you, comrade Chien." The boss of the team of police carefully gathered up the remaining snuff—most of it remained—and placed it in his uniform—smart, sharp uniform—pocket. "We'll have it analyzed at the first available moment," the cop said, "and inform you immediately in case counter-medical measures are indicated for you. Some of the old wartime psychedelics were eventually fatal, as you have no doubt read."

"I've read," he agreed. That had been specifically what he had been thinking.

"Good luck and thanks for notifying us," both cops said, and departed. The affair, for all their efficiency, did not seem to shake them; obviously such a complaint was routine.

The lab report came swiftly—surprisingly so, in view of the vast state bureaucracy. It reached him by vidphone before the Leader had finished his TV speech.

"It's not a hallucinogen," the Secpol lab technician informed him.

"No?" he said, puzzled and, strangely, not relieved. Not at all.

"On the contrary. It's a phenothiazine, which as you doubtless know is anti-hallucinogenic. A strong dose per gram of admixture, but harmless. Might lower your blood pressure or make you sleepy. Probably stolen from a wartime cache of medical supplies. Left by the retreating barbarians. I wouldn't worry."

Pondering, Chien hung up the vidphone in slow motion. And then walked to the window of his conapt—the window with the fine view of other Hanoi high-rise conapts—to think.

The doorbell rang. Feeling as if he were in a trance, he crossed the carpeted living room to answer it.

The girl standing there, in a tan raincoat with a babushka over her dark, shiny, and very long hair, said in a timid little voice, "Um, Comrade Chien? Tung Chien? Of the Ministry of—"

He let her in, reflexively, and shut the door after her. "You've been monitoring my vidphone," he told her; it was a shot in darkness, but something in him, an unvoiced certitude, told him that she had.

"Did—they take the rest of the snuff?" She glanced about. "Oh, I hope not; it's so hard to get these days."

"Snuff," he said, "is easy to get. Phenothiazine isn't. Is that what you mean?"

The girl raised her head, studied him with large, moon-darkened eyes. "Yes. Mr. Chien—" She hesitated, obviously as uncertain as the Secpol cops had been assured. "Tell me what you saw; it's of great importance for us to be certain."

"I had a choice?" he said acutely.

"Y-yes, very much so. That's what confuses us; that's what is not as we planned. We don't understand it; it fits nobody's theory." Her eyes even darker and deeper, she said, "Was it the aquatic horror shape? The thing with slime and teeth, the extraterrestrial life-form? Please tell me; we have to know." She breathed irregularly, with effort, the tan raincoat rising and falling; he found himself watching its rhythm.

"A machine," he said.

"Oh!" She ducked her head, nodding vigorously. "Yes, I understand; a mechanical organism in no way resembling a human. Not a simulacrum, or something constructed to resemble a man."

He said, "This did not look like a man." He added to himself, And it failed—did not try—to talk like a man.

"You understand that it was not a hallucination."

"I've been officially told that what I took was a phenothiazine. That's all I know." He said as little as possible; he did not want to talk but to hear. Hear what the girl had to say.

"Well, Mr. Chien—" She took a deep, unstable breath. "If it was not a hallucination, then what was it? What does that leave? What is called 'extra-consciousness'—could that be it?"

He did not answer; turning his back, he leisurely picked up the two student test papers, glanced over them, ignoring her. Waiting for her next attempt.

At his shoulder, she appeared, smelling of spring rain, smelling of sweetness and agitation, beautiful in the way she smelled, and looked, and, he thought, speaks. So different from the harsh plateau speech patterns we hear on the TV—have heard since I was a baby.

"Some of them," she said huskily, "who take the stelazine—it was stelazine you got, Mr. Chien—see one apparition, some another. But distinct categories have emerged; there is not an infinite variety. Some see what you saw; we call it the Clanker. Some the aquatic horror; that's the Gulper. And then there's the Bird, and the Climbing Tube, and—" She broke off. "But other reactions tell you very little. Tell *us* very little." She hesitated, then plunged on. "Now that this has happened to you, Mr. Chien, we would like you to join our gathering. Join your particular group, those who see what you see. Group Red. We want to know what it *really* is, and—" She gestured with tapered, wax smooth fingers. "It can't be *all* those manifestations." Her tone was poignant, naively so. He felt his caution relax—a trifle.

He said, "What do you see? You in particular?"

"I'm a part of Group Yellow. I see—a storm. A whining, vicious whirlwind. That roots everything up, crushes condominium apartments built to last a century." She smiled wanly. "The Crusher. Twelve groups in all, Mr. Chien. Twelve absolutely different experiments, all from the same phenothiazines, all of the Leader as he speaks over TV. As *it* speaks, rather." She smiled up at him, lashes long—probably protracted artificially—and gaze engaging, even trusting. As if she thought he knew something or could do something.

"I should make a citizen's arrest of you," he said presently.

"There is no law, not about this. We studied Soviet judicial writings before we—found people to distribute the stelazine. We don't have much of it; we have to be very careful whom we give it to. It seemed to us that you constituted a likely choice . . . a well-known, postwar, dedicated young career man on his way up." From his fingers she took the examination papers. "They're having you pol-read?" she asked.

" 'Pol-read'?" He did not know the term.

"Study something said or written to see if it fits the Party's current worldview. You in the hierarchy merely call it 'read,' don't you?" Again she smiled. "When you rise one step higher, up with Mr. Tso-pin, you will know that expression." She added somberly, "And with Mr. Pethel. He's very far up. Mr. Chien, there is no ideological school in San Fernando; these are forged exam papers, designed to read back to them a thorough analysis of *your* political ideology. And have you been able to distinguish which paper is orthodox and which is heretical?" Her voice was pixielike, taunting with amused malice. "Choose the wrong one and your budding career stops dead, cold, in its tracks. Choose the proper one—"

"Do you know which is which?" he demanded.

"Yes." She nodded soberly. "We have listening devices in Mr. Tso-pin's inner offices; we monitored his conversation with Mr. Pethel—who is not Mr. Pethel but the Higher Secpol Inspector Judd Craine. You have probably heard mention of him; he acted as chief assistant to Judge Vorlawsky at the '98 war-crimes trial in Zurich."

With difficulty he said, "I—see." Well, that explained that.

The girl said, "My name is Tanya Lee."

He said nothing; he merely nodded, too stunned for any cerebration.

"Technically, I am a minor clerk," Miss Lee said, "at your Ministry. You have never run into me, however, that I can at least recall. We try to hold posts wherever we can. As far up as possible. My own boss—"

"Should you be telling me this?" he gestured at the TV set, which remained on. "Aren't they picking this up?"

Tanya Lee said, "We introduced a noise factor in the reception of both vid and aud material from this apartment building; it will take them almost an hour to locate the sheathing. So we have"—she examined the tiny wristwatch on her slender wrist—"fifteen more minutes. And still be safe."

"Tell me," he said, "which paper is orthodox."

"Is that what you care about? Really?"

"What," he said, "should I care about?"

"Don't you see, Mr. Chien? You've learned something. The Leader is not the Leader; he is something else, but we can't tell what. Not yet. Mr. Chien, with all due respect, have you ever had your drinking water analyzed? I know it sounds paranoiac, but have you?"

"No," he said. "Of course not." Knowing what she was going to say.

Miss Lee said briskly, "Our tests show that it's saturated with hallucinogens. It is, has been, will continue to be. Not the ones used during the war; not the disorientating ones, but a synthetic quasi-ergot derivative called Datrox-3. You drink it here in the building from the time you get up; you drink it in restaurants and other apartments that you visit. You drink it at the Ministry; it's all piped from a central, common source." Her tone was bleak and ferocious. "We solved that problem; we knew, as soon as we discovered it, that any good phenothiazine would counter it. What we did not know, of course, was this—a *variety* of authentic experiences; that makes no sense, rationally. It's the hallucination which should differ from person to person, and the reality experience which should be ubiquitous—it's all turned around. We can't even construct an ad hoc theory which accounts for that, and God knows we've tried. Twelve mutually exclusive hallucinations—that would be easily understood. But not one hallucination and twelve realities." She ceased talking then, and studied the two test papers, her forehead wrinkling. "The one with the Arabic poem is orthodox," she stated. "If you tell them that they'll trust you and give you a higher post. You'll be another notch up in the hierarchy of Party officialdom." Smiling—her teeth were perfect and lovely—she finished, "Look what you received back for your investment this morning. Your career is underwritten for a time. And by us."

He said, "I don't believe you." Instinctively, his caution operated within him, always, the caution of a lifetime lived among the hatchet men of the Hanoi branch of the CP East. They knew an infinitude of ways by which to ax a rival out of contention—some of which he himself had employed; some of which he had seen done to himself and to others. This could be a novel way, one unfamiliar to him. It could always be.

"Tonight," Miss Lee said, "in the speech the Leader singled you out. Didn't this strike you as strange? You, of all people? A minor officeholder in a meager ministry—"

"Admitted," he said. "It struck me that way; yes."

"That was legitimate. His Greatness is grooming an elite cadre of younger men, postwar men, he hopes will infuse new life into the hidebound, moribund hierarchy of old fogies and Party hacks. His Greatness singled you out for the same reason that we singled you out; if pursued properly, your career could lead you all the way to the top. At least for a time . . . as we know. That's how it goes."

He thought: So virtually everyone has faith in me. Except myself; and certainly not after this, the experience with the anti-hallucinatory snuff. It had shaken years of confidence, and no doubt rightly so. However, he was beginning to regain his poise; he felt it seeping back, a little at first, then with a rush.

Going to the vidphone, he lifted the receiver and began, for the second time that night, to dial the number of the Hanoi Security Police.

"Turning me in," Miss Lee said, "would be the second most regressive decision you could make. I'll tell them that you brought me here to bribe me; you thought, because of my job at the Ministry, I would know which examination paper to select."

He said, "And what would be my first most regressive decision?"

"Not taking a further dose of phenothiazine," Miss Lee said evenly.

Hanging up the phone, Tung Chien thought to himself, I don't understand what's happening to me. Two forces, the Party and His Greatness on one hand—this girl with her alleged group on the other. One wants me to rise as far as possible in the Party hierarchy; the other—*What did Tanya Lee want?* Underneath the words, inside the membrane of an almost trivial contempt for the Party, the Leader, the ethical standards of the People's Democratic United Front—what was she after in regard to him?

He said curiously, "Are you anti-Party?"

"No."

"But—" He gestured. "That's all there is: Party and anti-Party. You must be Party, then." Bewildered, he stared at her; with composure she returned the stare. "You have an organization," he said, "and you meet. What do you intend to destroy? The regular function of government? Are you like the treasonable college students of the United States during the Vietnam War who stopped troop trains, demonstrated—"

Wearily Miss Lee said, "It wasn't like that. But forget it; that's not the issue. What we want to know is this: who or what is leading us? We must penetrate far enough to enlist someone, some rising young Party theoretician, who could conceivably be invited to a tête-à-tête with the Leader—you see?" Her voice lifted; she consulted her watch, obviously anxious to get away: the fifteen minutes were almost up. "Very few persons actually see the Leader, as you know. I mean really see him."

"Seclusion," he said. "Due to his advanced age."

"We have hope," Miss Lee said, "that if you pass the phony test which they have arranged for you—and with my help you have—you will be invited to one of the stag parties which the Leader has from time to time, which of course the papers don't report. Now do you see?" Her voice rose shrilly, in a frenzy of despair. "Then we would know; if you could go in there under the influence of the anti-hallucinogenic drug, could see him face-to-face as he actually is—"

Thinking aloud, he said, "And end my career of public service. If not my life."

"You owe us something," Tanya Lee snapped, her cheeks white. "If I hadn't told you which exam paper to choose you would have picked the wrong one and your dedicated public-service career would be over anyhow; you would have failed—failed at a test you didn't even realize you were taking!"

He said mildly, "I had a fifty-fifty chance."

"No." She shook her head fiercely. "The heretical one is faked up with a lot of Party jargon; they deliberately constructed the two texts to trap you. They *wanted* you to fail!"

Once more he examined the two papers, feeling confused. Was she right? Possibly. Probably. It rang true, knowing the Party functionaries as he did, and Tso-pin, his superior, in particular. He felt weary then. Defeated. After a time he said to the girl, "What you're trying to get out of me is a quid pro quo. You did something for me—you got, or claim you got, the answer to this Party inquiry. But you've already done your part. What's to keep me from tossing you out of here on your head? I don't have to do a goddamn thing." He heard his voice, toneless, sounding the poverty of empathic emotionality so usual in Party circles.

Miss Lee said, "There will be other tests, as you continue to ascend. And we will monitor for you with them too." She was calm, at ease; obviously she had foreseen his reaction.

"How long do I have to think it over?" he said.

"I'm leaving now. We're in no rush; you're not about to receive an invitation to the Leader's Yangtze River villa in the next week or even month." Going to the door, opening it, she paused. "As you're given covert rating tests we'll be in contact, supplying the answers—so you'll see one or more of us on those occasions. Probably it won't be me; it'll be that disabled war veteran who'll sell you the correct response sheets as you leave the Ministry building." She smiled a brief, snuffed-out-candle smile. "But one of these days, no doubt unexpectedly, you'll get an ornate, official, very formal invitation to the villa, and when you go you'll be heavily sedated with stelazine . . . possibly our last dose of our dwindling supply. Good night." The door shut after her; she had gone.

My God, he thought. They can blackmail me. For what I've done. And she didn't even bother to mention it; in view of what they're involved with it was not worth mentioning.

But blackmail for what? He had already told the Secpol squad that he had been given a drug which had proved to be a phenothiazine. *Then they know,* he realized. They'll watch me; they're alert. Technically, I haven't broken a law, but—they'll be watching, all right.

However, they always watched anyhow. He relaxed slightly, thinking that. He had, over the years, become virtually accustomed to it, as had everyone.

I will see the Absolute Benefactor of the People as he is, he said to himself. Which possibly no one else had done. What will it be? Which of the subclasses of non-hallucination? Classes which I do not even know about . . . a view which may totally overthrow me. How am I going to be able to get through the evening, to keep my poise, if it's like the shape I saw on the TV screen? The Crusher, the Clanker, the Bird, the Climbing Tube, the Gulper—or worse.

He wondered what some of the other views consisted of . . . and then gave up that line of speculation; it was unprofitable. And too anxiety-inducing.

The next morning Mr. Tso-pin and Mr. Darius Pethel met him in his office, both of them calm but expectant. Wordlessly, he handed them one of the two "exam papers." The orthodox one, with its short and heart-smothering Arabian poem.

"This one," Chien said tightly, "is the product of a dedicated Party member or candidate for membership. The other—" He slapped the remaining sheets. "Reactionary garbage." He felt anger. "In spite of a superficial—"

"All right, Mr. Chien," Pethel said, nodding. "We don't have to explore each and every ramification; your analysis is correct. You heard the mention regarding you in the Leader's speech last night on TV?"

"I certainly did," Chien said.

"So you have undoubtedly inferred," Pethel said, "that there is a good deal involved in what we are attempting, here. The leader has his eye on you; that's clear. As a matter of fact, he has communicated to myself regarding you." He opened his bulging briefcase and rummaged. "Lost the goddamn thing. Anyhow—" He glanced at Tso-pin, who nodded slightly. "His Greatness would like to have you appear for dinner at the Yangtze River Ranch next Thursday night. Mrs. Fletcher in particular appreciates—"

Chien said, "'Mrs. Fletcher'? Who is 'Mrs. Fletcher'?"

After a pause Tso-pin said dryly, "The Absolute Benefactor's wife. His name—which you of course had never heard—is Thomas Fletcher."

"He's a Caucasian," Pethel explained. "Originally from the New Zealand Communist Party; he participated in the difficult takeover there. This news is not in the strict sense secret, but on the other hand it hasn't been noised about." He hesitated, toying with his watch chain. "Probably it would be better if you forgot about that. Of course, as soon as you meet him, see him face-to-face, you'll realize that, realize that he's a Cauc. As I am. As many of us are."

"Race," Tso-pin pointed out, "has nothing to do with loyalty to the leader and the Party. As witness Mr. Pethel, here."

But His Greatness, Chien thought, jolted. He did not appear, on the TV screen, to be Occidental. "On TV—" he began.

"The image," Tso-pin interrupted, "is subjected to a variegated assortment of skillful refinements. For ideological purposes. Most persons holding higher offices are aware of this." He eyed Chien with hard criticism.

So everyone agrees, Chien thought. What we see every night is not real. The question is, How unreal? Partially? Or—completely?

"I will be prepared," he said tautly. And he thought, There has been a slip-up. They weren't prepared for me—the people that Tanya Lee represents—to gain entry so soon. Where's the anti-hallucinogen? Can they get it to me or not? Probably not on such short notice.

He felt, strangely, relief. He would be going into the presence of His Greatness in a position to see him as a human being, see him as he—and everybody else—saw him on TV. It would be a most stimulating and cheerful dinner party, with some of the most influential Party members in Asia. I think we can do without the phenothiazine, he said to himself. And his sense of relief grew.

"Here it is, finally," Pethel said suddenly, producing a white envelope from his briefcase. "Your card of admission. You will be flown by Sinorocket to the Leader's villa Thursday morning; there the protocol officer will brief you on your expected behavior. It will be formal dress, white tie and tails, but the atmosphere will be cordial. There are always a great number of toasts." He added, "I have attended two such stag get-togethers. Mr. Tso-pin"—he smiled creakily—"has not been honored in such a fashion. But, as they say, all things come to him who waits. Ben Franklin said that."

Tso-pin said, "It has come for Mr. Chien rather prematurely, I would say." He shrugged philosophically. "But my opinion has never at any time been asked."

"One thing," Pethel said to Chien. "It is possible that when you see His Greatness in person you will be in some regards disappointed. Be alert that you do not let this make itself apparent, if you should so feel. We have, always, tended—been trained—to regard him as more than a man. But at table he is"—he gestured—"a forked radish. In certain respects like ourselves. He may for instance indulge in moderately human oral-aggressive and -passive activity; he possibly may tell an off-color joke or drink too much . . . To be candid, no one ever knows in advance how these things will work out, but they do generally hold forth until late the following morning. So it would be wise to accept the dosage of amphetamines which the protocol officer will offer you."

"Oh?" Chien said. This was news to him, and interesting.

"For stamina. And to balance the liquor. His Greatness has amazing staying power; he often is still on his feet and raring to go after everyone else has collapsed."

"A remarkable man," Tso-pin chimed in. "I think his—indulgences only show that he is a fine fellow. And fully in the round; he is like the ideal Renaissance man; as, for example, Lorenzo de'Medici."

"That does come to mind," Pethel said; he studied Chien with such intensity that some of last night's chill returned. Am I being led into one trap after another? Chien wondered. That girl—was she in fact an agent of the Secpol probing me, trying to ferret out a disloyal, anti-Party streak in me?

I think, he decided, I will make sure that the legless peddler of herbal remedies does not snare me when I leave work; I'll take a totally different route back to my conapt.

He was successful. That day he avoided the peddler, and the same the next, and so on until Thursday.

On Thursday morning the peddler scooted from beneath a parked truck and blocked his way, confronting him.

"My medication?" the peddler demanded. "It helped? I know it did; the formula goes back to the Sung Dynasty—I can tell it did. Right?"

Chien said, "Let me go."

"Would you be kind enough to answer?" The tone was not the expected, customary whining of a street peddler operating in a marginal fashion, and that tone came across to Chien; he heard loud and clear . . . as the Imperialist puppet troops of long ago phrased.

"I know what you gave me," Chien said. "And I don't want any more. If I change my mind I can pick it up at a pharmacy. Thanks." He started on, but the cart, with the legless occupant, pursued him.

"Miss Lee was talking to me," the peddler said loudly.

"Hmmm," Chien said, and automatically increased his pace; he spotted a hovercab and began signaling for it.

"It's tonight you're going to the stag dinner at the Yangtze River villa," the peddler said, panting for breath in his effort to keep up. "Take the medication—now!" He held out a flat packet, imploringly. "Please, Party Member Chien; for your own sake, for all of us. So we can tell what it is we're up against. Good Lord, it may be non-Terran; that's our most basic fear. Don't you understand, Chien? What's your goddamn career compared with that? If we can't find out—"

The cab bumped to a halt on the pavement; its doors slid open. Chien started to board it.

The packet sailed past him, landed on the entrance sill of the cab, then slid onto the floor, damp from earlier rain.

"Please," the peddler said. "And it won't cost you anything; today it's free. Just take it, use it before the stag dinner. And don't use the amphetamines; they're a thalamic stimulant, contraindicated whenever an adrenal suppressant such as a phenothiazine is—"

The door of the cab closed after Chien. He seated himself.

"Where to, comrade?" the robot drive-mechanism inquired.

He gave the ident tag number of his conapt.

"That halfwit of a peddler managed to infiltrate his seedy wares into my clean interior," the cab said. "Notice; it reposes by your foot."

He saw the packet—no more than an ordinary-looking envelope. I guess, he thought, this is how drugs come to you; all of a sudden they're there. For a moment he sat, and then he picked it up.

As before, there was a written enclosure above and beyond the medication, but this time, he saw, it was handwritten. A feminine script—from Miss Lee:

We were surprised at the suddenness. But thank heaven we were ready. Where were you Tuesday and Wednesday? Anyhow, here it is, and good luck. I will approach you later in the week; I don't want you to try to find me.

He ignited the note, burned it up in the cab's disposal ashtray.

And kept the dark granules.

All this time, he thought. Hallucinogens in our water supply. Year after year. Decades. And not in wartime but in peacetime. And not to the enemy camp but here in our own. The evil bastards, he said to himself. Maybe I ought to take this; maybe I ought to find out what he or it is and let Tanya's group know.

I will, he decided. And—he was curious.

A bad emotion, he knew. Curiosity was, especially in Party activities, often a terminal state careerwise.

A state which, at the moment, gripped him thoroughly. He wondered if it would last through the evening, if, when it came right down to it, he would actually take the inhalant.

Time would tell. Tell that and everything else. We are blooming flowers, he thought, on the plain, which he picks. As the Arabic poem had put it. He tried to remember the rest of the poem but could not.

That probably was just as well.

The villa protocol officer, a Japanese named Kimo Okubara, tall and husky, obviously a quondam wrestler, surveyed him with innate hostility, even after he presented his engraved invitation and had successfully managed to prove his identity.

"Surprise you bother to come," Okubara muttered. "Why not stay home and watch on TV? Nobody miss you. We got along fine without you up to right now."

Chien said tightly, "I've already watched on TV." And anyhow the stag dinners were rarely televised; they were too bawdy.

Okubara's crew double-checked him for weapons, including the possibility of an anal suppository, and then gave him his clothes back. They did not find the phenothiazine, however. Because he had already taken it. The effects of such a drug, he knew, lasted approximately four hours; that would be more than enough. And, as Tanya had said, it was a major dose; he felt sluggish and inept and dizzy, and his tongue moved in spasms of pseudo-Parkinsonism—an unpleasant side effect which he had failed to anticipate.

A girl, nude from the waist up, with long coppery hair down her shoulders and back, walked by. Interesting.

Coming the other way, a girl nude from the bottom up made her appearance. Interesting, too. Both girls looked vacant and bored, and totally self-possessed.

"You go in like that too," Okubara informed Chien.

Startled, Chien said, "I understood white tie and tails."

"Joke," Okubara said. "At your expense. Only girls wear nude; you even get so you enjoy, unless you homosexual."

Well, Chien thought, I guess I had better like it. He wandered on with the other guests—they, like him, wore white tie and tails, or, if women, floor-length gowns—and felt ill at ease, despite the tranquilizing effect of the stelazine. Why am I here? he asked himself. The ambiguity of his situation did not escape him. He was here to advance his career in the Party apparatus, to obtain the intimate and personal nod of approval from His Greatness . . . and in addition he was here to decipher His Greatness as a fraud; he did not know what variety of fraud, but there it was: fraud against the Party, against all the peace-loving democratic peoples of Terra. Ironic, he thought. And continued to mingle.

A girl with small, bright, illuminated breasts approached him for a match; he absentmindedly got out his lighter. "What makes your breasts glow?" he asked her. "Radioactive injections?"

She shrugged, said nothing, passed on, leaving him alone. Evidently he had responded in the incorrect way.

Maybe it's a wartime mutation, he pondered.

"Drink, sir." A servant graciously held out a tray; he accepted a martini—which was the current fad among the higher Party classes in People's China—and sipped the ice-cold dry flavor. Good English gin, he said to himself. Or possibly the original Holland compound; juniper or whatever they added. Not bad. He strolled on, feeling better; in actuality he found the atmosphere here a pleasant one. The people here were self-assured; they had been successful and now they could relax. It evidently was a myth that proximity to His Greatness produced neurotic anxiety: he saw no evidence here, at least, and felt little himself.

A heavyset elderly man, bald, halted him by the simple means of holding his drink glass against Chien's chest. "That frably little one who asked you for a match," the elderly man said, and sniggered. "The quig with the Christmas-tree breasts—that was a boy, in drag." He giggled. "You have to be cautious around here."

"Where, if anywhere," Chien said, "do I find authentic women? In white ties and tails?"

"Darn near," the elderly man said, and departed with a throng of hyperactive guests, leaving Chien alone with his martini.

A handsome, tall woman, well dressed, standing near Chien, suddenly put her hand on his arm; he felt her fingers tense and she said, "Here he comes. His Greatness. This is the first time for me; I'm a little scared. Does my hair look all right?"

"Fine," Chien said reflexively, and followed her gaze, seeking a glimpse—his first—of the Absolute Benefactor.

What crossed the room toward the table in the center was not a man.

And it was not, Chien realized, a mechanical construct either; it was not what he had seen on TV. That evidently was simply a device for speech-making, as Mussolini had once used an artificial arm to salute long and tedious processions.

God, he thought, and felt ill. Was this what Tanya Lee had called the "aquatic horror" shape? It had no shape. Nor pseudopodia, either flesh or metal. It was, in a sense, not there at all; when he managed to look directly at it, the shape vanished; he saw through it, saw the people on the far side—

but not it. Yet if he turned his head, caught it out of a sidelong glance, he could determine its boundaries.

It was terrible; it blasted him with its awareness. As it moved it drained the life from each person in turn; it ate the people who had assembled, passed on, ate again, ate more with an endless appetite. It hated; he felt its hate. It loathed; he felt its loathing for everyone present—in fact he shared its loathing. All at once he and everyone else in the big villa were each a twisted slug, and over the fallen slug carcasses the creature savored, lingered, but all the time coming directly toward him—or was that an illusion? If this is a hallucination, Chien thought, it is the worst I have ever had; if it is not, then it is evil reality; it's an evil thing that kills and injures. He saw the trail of stepped-on, mashed men and women remnants behind it; he saw them trying to reassemble, to operate their crippled bodies; he heard them attempting speech.

I know who you are, Tung Chien thought to himself. You, the supreme head of the worldwide Party structure. You, who destroy whatever living object you touch; I see that Arabic poem, the searching for the flowers of life to eat them—I see you astride the plain which to you is Earth, plain without hills, without valleys. You go anywhere, appear anytime, devour anything; you engineer life and then guzzle it, and you enjoy that.

He thought, You are God.

"Mr. Chien," the voice said, but it came from inside his head, not from the mouthless spirit that fashioned itself directly before him. "It is good to meet you again. You know nothing. Go away. I have no interest in you. Why should I care about slime? Slime; I am mired in it, I must excrete it, and I choose to. I could break you; I can break even myself. Sharp stones are under me; I spread sharp pointed things upon the mire. I make the hiding places, the deep places, boil like a pot; to me the sea is like a lot of ointment. The flakes of my flesh are joined to everything. You are me. I am you. It makes no difference, just as it makes no difference whether the creature with ignited breasts is a girl or boy; you could learn to enjoy either." It laughed.

He could not believe it was speaking to him; he could not imagine—it was too terrible—that it had picked him out.

"I have picked everybody out," it said. "No one is too small, each falls and dies and I am there to watch. I don't need to do anything but watch; it is automatic; it was arranged that way." And then it ceased talking to him; it disjoined itself. But he still saw it; he felt its manifold presence. It was a globe which hung in the room, with fifty thousand eyes, a million eyes—billions: an eye for each living thing as it waited for each thing to fall, and then stepped on the living thing as it lay in a broken state. Because of this it had created the things, and he knew; he understood. What had seemed in the Arabic poem to be death was not death but God; or rather God was death, it was one force, one hunter, one cannibal thing, and it missed again and again but, having all eternity, it could afford to miss. Both poems, he realized; the Dryden one too. The crumbling; that is our world and you are doing it. Warping it to come out that way; bending us.

But at least, he thought, I still have my dignity. With dignity he set down his drink glass, turned, walked toward the doors of the room. He passed through the doors. He walked down a long carpeted hall. A villa servant dressed in purple opened a door for him; he found himself standing out in the night darkness, on a veranda, alone.

Not alone.

It had followed after him. Or it had already been here before him; yes, it had been expecting. It was not really through with him.

"Here I go," he said, and made a dive for the railing; it was six stories down, and there below gleamed the river and death, not what the Arabic poem had seen.

As he tumbled over, it put an extension of itself on his shoulder.

"Why?" he said. But, in fact, he paused. Wondering. Not understanding, not at all.

"Don't fall on my account," it said. He could not see it because it had moved behind him. But the piece of it on his shoulder—it had begun to look like a human hand.

And then it laughed.

"What's funny?" he demanded, as he teetered on the railing, held back by its pseudo-hand.

"You're doing my task for me," it said. "You aren't waiting; don't have time to wait? I'll select you out from among the others; you don't need to speed the process up."

"What if I do?" he said. "Out of revulsion for you?"

It laughed. And didn't answer.

"You won't even say," he said.

Again no answer. He started to slide back, onto the veranda. And at once the pressure of its pseudo-hand lifted.

"You founded the Party?" he asked.

"I founded everything. I founded the anti-Party and the Party that isn't a Party, and those who are for it and those who are against, those that you call Yankee Imperialists, those in the camp of reaction, and so on endlessly. I founded it all. As if they were blades of grass."

"And you're here to enjoy it?" he said.

"What I want," it said, "is for you to see me, as I am, as you have seen me, and then trust me."

"What?" he said, quavering. "Trust you to what?"

It said, "Do you believe in me?"

"Yes," he said. "I can see you."

"Then go back to your job at the Ministry. Tell Tanya Lee that you saw an overworked, overweight, elderly man who drinks too much and likes to pinch girls' rear ends."

"Oh, Christ," he said.

"As you live on, unable to stop, I will torment you," it said. "I will deprive you, item by item, of everything you possess or want. And then when you are crushed to death I will unfold a mystery."

"What's the mystery?"

"The dead shall live, the living die. I kill what lives; I save what has died. And I will tell you this: *there are things worse than I.* But you won't meet them because by then I will have killed you. Now walk back into the dining room and prepare for dinner. Don't question what I'm doing; I did it long before there was a Tung Chien and I will do it long after."

He hit it as hard as he could.

And experienced violent pain in his head.

And darkness, with the sense of falling.

After that, darkness again. He thought, I will get you. I will see that you die too. That you suffer; you're going to suffer, just like us, exactly in every way we do. I'll nail you; I swear to God I'll nail you up somewhere. And it will hurt. As much as I hurt now.

He shut his eyes.

Roughly, he was shaken. And heard Mr. Kimo Okubara's voice. "Get to your feet, common drunk. Come on!"

Without opening his eyes he said, "Get me a cab."

"Cab already waiting. You go home. Disgrace. Make a violent scene out of yourself."

Getting shakily to his feet, he opened his eyes and examined himself. Our leader whom we follow, he thought, is the One True God. And the enemy whom we fight and have fought is God too. They are right, he is everywhere. But I didn't understand what that meant. Staring at the protocol officer, he thought, You are God too. So there is no getting away, probably not even by jumping. As I started, instinctively, to do. He shuddered.

"Mix drinks with drugs," Okubara said witheringly. "Ruin career. I see it happen many times. Get lost."

Unsteadily, he walked toward the great central door of the Yangtze River villa; two servants, dressed like medieval knights, with crested plumes, ceremoniously opened the door for him and one of them said, "Good night, sir."

"Up yours," Chien said, and passed out into the night.

At a quarter to three in the morning, as he sat sleepless in the living room of his conapt, smoking one Cuesta Rey Astoria after another, a knock sounded at the door.

When he opened it he found himself facing Tanya Lee in her trenchcoat, her face pinched with cold. Her eyes blazed, questioningly.

"Don't look at me like that," he said roughly. His cigar had gone out; he relit it. "I've been looked at enough," he said.

"You saw it," she said.

He nodded.

She seated herself on the arm of the couch and after a time she said, "Want to tell me about it?"

"Go as far from here as possible," he said. "Go a long way." And then he remembered: no way was long enough. He remembered reading that too. "Forget it," he said; rising to his feet, he walked clumsily into the kitchen to start up the coffee.

Following after him, Tanya said, "Was—it that bad?"

"We can't win," he said. "You can't win; I don't mean me. I'm not in this; I just wanted to do my job at the Ministry and forget it. Forget the whole damned thing."

"Is it nonterrestrial?"

"Yes." He nodded.

"Is it hostile to us?"

"Yes," he said. "No. Both. Mostly hostile."

"Then we have to—"

"Go home," he said, "and go to bed." He looked her over carefully; he had sat a long time and he had done a great deal of thinking. About a lot of things. "Are you married?" he said.

"No. Not now. I used to be."

He said, "Stay with me tonight. The rest of tonight, anyhow. Until the sun comes up." He added, "The night part is awful."

"I'll stay," Tanya said, unbuckling the belt of her raincoat, "but I have to have some answers."

"What did Dryden mean," Chien said, "about music untuning the sky? I don't get that. What does music do to the sky?"

"All the celestial order of the universe ends," she said as she hung her raincoat up in the closet of the bedroom; under it she wore an orange striped sweater and stretchpants.

He said, "And that's bad?"

Pausing, she reflected. "I don't know. I guess so."

"It's a lot of power," he said, "to assign to music."

"Well, you know that old Pythagorean business about the 'music of the spheres.'" Matter-of-factly she seated herself on the bed and removed her slipper-like shoes.

"Do you believe in that?" he said. "Or do you believe in God?"

"'God'!" She laughed. "That went out with the donkey steam engine. What are you talking about? God, or god?" She came over close beside him, peering into his face.

"Don't look at me so closely," he said sharply, drawing back. "I don't ever want to be looked at again." He moved away, irritably.

"I think," Tanya said, "that if there is a God He has very little interest in human affairs. That's my theory, anyhow. I mean, He doesn't seem to care if evil triumphs or people or animals get hurt and die. I frankly don't see Him anywhere around. And the Party has always denied any form of—"

"Did you ever see Him?" he asked. "When you were a child?"

"Oh, sure, as a child. But I also believed—"

"Did it ever occur to you," Chien said, "that good and evil are names for the same thing? That God could be both good and evil at the same time?"

"I'll fix you a drink," Tanya said, and padded barefoot into the kitchen.

Chien said, "The Crusher. The Clanker. The Gulper and the Bird and the Climbing Tube—plus other names, forms, I don't know. I had a hallucination. At the stag dinner. A big one. A terrible one."

"But the stelazine—"

"It brought on a worse one," he said.

"Is there any way," Tanya said somberly, "that we can fight this thing you saw? This apparition you call a hallucination but which very obviously was not?"

He said, "Believe in it."

"What will that do?"

"Nothing," he said wearily. "Nothing at all. I'm tired; I don't want a drink—let's just go to bed."

"Okay." She padded back into the bedroom, began pulling her striped sweater over her head. "We'll discuss it more thoroughly later."

"A hallucination," Chien said, "is merciful. I wish I had it; I want mine back. I want to be before your peddler got me with that phenothiazine."

"Just come to bed. It'll be toasty. All warm and nice."

He removed his tie, his shirt—and saw, on his right shoulder, the mark, the stigma, which it had left when it stopped him from jumping. Livid marks which looked as if they would never go away. He put his pajama top on then; it hid the marks.

"Anyhow," Tanya said as he got into the bed beside her, "your career is immeasurably advanced. Aren't you glad about that?"

"Sure," he said, nodding sightlessly in the darkness. "Very glad."

"Come over against me," Tanya said, putting her arms around him. "And forget everything else. At least for now."

He tugged her against him then, doing what she asked and what he wanted to do. She was neat; she was swiftly active; she was successful and she did her part. They did not bother to speak until at last she said, "Oh!" And then she relaxed.

"I wish," he said, "that we could go on forever."

"We did," Tanya said. "It's outside of time; it's boundless, like an ocean. It's the way we were in Cambrian times, before we migrated up onto the land; it's the ancient primary waters. This is the only time we get to go back, when this is done. That's why it means so much. And in those days we weren't separate; it was like a big jelly, like those blobs that float up on the beach."

"Float up," he said, "and are left there to die."

"Could you get me a towel?" Tanya asked. "Or a washcloth? I need it."

He padded into the bathroom for a towel. There—he was naked now—he once more saw his shoulder, saw where it had seized hold of him and held on, dragging him back, possibly to toy with him a little more.

The marks, unaccountably, were bleeding.

He sponged the blood away. More oozed forth at once and, seeing that, he wondered how much time he had left. Probably only hours.

Returning to bed, he said, "Could you continue?"

"Sure. If you have any energy left; it's up to you." She lay gazing up at him unwinkingly, barely visible in the dim nocturnal light.

"I have," he said. And hugged her to him.

THE ELECTRIC ANT

At four-fifteen in the afternoon, T.S.T., Garson Poole woke up in his hospital bed, knew that he lay in a hospital bed in a three-bed ward, and realized in addition two things: that he no longer had a right hand and that he felt no pain.

They had given me a strong analgesic, he said to himself as he stared at the far wall with its window showing downtown New York. Webs in which vehicles and peds darted and wheeled glimmered in the late afternoon sun, and the brilliance of the aging light pleased him. It's not yet out, he thought. And neither am I.

A fone lay on the table beside his bed; he hesitated, then picked it up and dialed for an outside line. A moment later he was faced by Louis Danceman, in charge of Tri-Plan's activities while he, Garson Poole, was elsewhere.

"Thank God you're alive," Danceman said, seeing him; his big, fleshy face with its moon's surface of pock marks flattened with relief. "I've been calling all—"

"I just don't have a right hand," Poole said.

"But you'll be okay. I mean, they can graft another one on."

"How long have I been here?" Poole said. He wondered where the nurses and doctors had gone to; why weren't they clucking and fussing about him making a call?

"Four days," Danceman said. "Everything here at the plant is going splunkishly. In fact we've splunked orders from three separate police systems, all here on Terra. Two in Ohio, one in Wyoming. Good solid orders, with one third in advance and the usual three-year lease-option."

"Come get me out of here," Poole said.

"I can't get you out until the new hand—"

"I'll have it done later." He wanted desperately to get back to familiar surroundings; memory of the mercantile squib looming grotesquely on the pilot screen careened at the back of his mind; if he shut his eyes he felt himself back in his damaged craft as it plunged from one vehicle to another, piling up enormous damage as it went. The kinetic sensations . . . he winced, recalling them. I guess I'm lucky, he said to himself.

"Is Sarah Benton there with you?" Danceman asked.

"No." Of course; his personal secretary—if only for job considerations—would be hovering close by, mothering him in her jejune, infantile way. All heavyset women like to mother people, he thought. And they're dangerous; if they fall on you they can kill you. "Maybe that's what happened to me," he said aloud. "Maybe Sarah fell on my squib."

"No, no; a tie rod in the steering fin of your squib split apart during the heavy rush-hour traffic and you—"

"I remember." He turned in his bed as the door of the ward opened; a white-clad doctor and two blue-clad nurses appeared, making their way toward his bed. "I'll talk to you later," Poole said and hung up the fone. He took a deep, expectant breath.

"You shouldn't be foning quite so soon," the doctor said as he studied his chart. "Mr. Garson Poole, owner of Tri-Plan Electronics. Maker of random ident darts that track their prey for a circle-radius of a thousand miles, responding to unique enceph wave patterns. You're a successful man, Mr. Poole. But, Mr. Poole, you're not a man. You're an electric ant."

"Christ," Poole said, stunned.

"So we can't really treat you here, now that we've found out. We knew, of course, as soon as we examined your injured right hand; we saw the electronic components and then we made torso X-rays and of course they bore out our hypothesis."

"What," Poole said, "is an 'electric ant'?" But he knew; he could decipher the term.

A nurse said, "An organic robot."

"I see," Poole said. Frigid perspiration rose to the surface of his skin, across all his body.

"You didn't know," the doctor said.

"No." Poole shook his head.

The doctor said, "We get an electric ant every week or so. Either brought in here from a squib accident—like yourself—or one seeking voluntary admission . . . one who, like yourself, has never been told, who has functioned alongside humans, believing himself—itself—human. As to your hand—" He paused.

"Forget my hand," Poole said savagely.

"Be calm." The doctor leaned over him, peered acutely down into Poole's face. "We'll have a hospital boat convey you over to a service facility where repairs, or replacement, on your hand can be made at a reasonable expense, either to yourself, if you're self-owned, or to your owners, if such there are. In any case you'll be back at your desk at Tri-Plan functioning just as before."

"Except," Poole said, "now I know." He wondered if Danceman or Sarah or any of the others at the office knew. Had they—or one of them—purchased him? Designed him? A figurehead, he said to himself; that's all I've been. I must never really have run the company; it was a delusion implanted in me when I was made . . . along with the delusion that I am human and alive.

"Before you leave for the repair facility," the doctor said, "could you kindly settle your bill at the front desk?"

Poole said acidly, "How can there be a bill if you don't treat ants here?"

"For our services," the nurse said. "Up until the point we knew."

"Bill me," Poole said, with furious, impotent anger. "Bill my firm." With massive effort he managed to sit up; his head swimming, he stepped haltingly from the bed and onto the floor. "I'll be glad to leave here," he said as he rose to a standing position. "And thank you for your humane attention."

"Thank you, too, Mr. Poole," the doctor said. "Or rather I should say just Poole."

At the repair facility he had his missing hand replaced.

It proved fascinating, the hand; he examined it for a long time before he let the technicians install it. On the surface it appeared organic—in fact on the surface, it was. Natural skin covered natural flesh, and true blood filled the veins and capillaries. But, beneath that, wires and circuits, miniaturized components, gleamed . . . looking deep into the wrist he saw surge gates, motors, multi-stage valves, all very small. Intricate. And—the hand cost forty frogs. A week's salary, insofar as he drew it from the company payroll.

"Is this guaranteed?" he asked the technicians as they fused the "bone" section of the hand to the balance of his body.

"Ninety days, parts and labor," one of the technicians said. "Unless subjected to unusual or intentional abuse."

"That sounds vaguely suggestive," Poole said.

The technician, a man—all of them were men—said, regarding him keenly, "You've been posing?"

"Unintentionally," Poole said.

"And now it's intentional?"

Poole said, "Exactly."

"Do you know why you never guessed? There must have been signs . . . clickings and whirrings from inside you, now and then. You never guessed because you were programmed not to notice. You'll now have the same difficulty finding out why you were built and for whom you've been operating."

"A slave," Poole said. "A mechanical slave."

"You've had fun."

"I've lived a good life," Poole said. "I've worked hard."

He paid the facility its forty frogs, flexed his new fingers, tested them out by picking up various objects such as coins, then departed. Ten minutes later he was aboard a public carrier, on his way home. It had been quite a day.

At home, in his one-room apartment, he poured himself a shot of Jack Daniel's Purple Label—sixty years old—and sat sipping it, meanwhile gazing through his sole window at the building on the opposite side of the street. Shall I go to the office? he asked himself. If so, why? If not, why? Choose one. Christ, he thought, it undermines you, knowing this. I'm a freak, he realized. An inanimate object mimicking an animate one. But— he felt alive. Yet . . . he felt differently, now. About himself. Hence about everyone, especially Danceman and Sarah, everyone at Tri-Plan.

I think I'll kill myself, he said to himself. But I'm probably programmed not to do that; it would be a costly waste which my owner would have to absorb. And he wouldn't want to.

386 SELECTED STORIES OF PHILIP K. DICK

Programmed. In me somewhere, he thought, there is a matrix fitted in place, a grid screen that cuts me off from certain thoughts, certain actions. And forces me into others. I am not free. I never was, but now I know it; that makes it different.

Turning his window to opaque, he snapped on the overhead light, carefully set about removing his clothing, piece by piece. He had watched carefully as the technicians at the repair facility had attached his new hand: he had a rather clear idea, now, of how his body had been assembled. Two major panels, one in each thigh; the technicians had removed the panels to check the circuit complexes beneath. If I'm programmed, he decided, the matrix probably can be found there.

The maze of circuitry baffled him. I need help, he said to himself. Let's see . . . what's the fone code for the class BBB computer we hire at the office?

He picked up the fone, dialed the computer at its permanent location in Boise, Idaho.

"Use of this computer is prorated at a five-frogs-per-minute basis," a mechanical voice from the fone said. "Please hold your mastercredit-chargeplate before the screen."

He did so.

"At the sound of the buzzer you will be connected with the computer," the voice continued. "Please query it as rapidly as possible, taking into account the fact that its answer will be given in terms of a microsecond, while your query will—" He turned the sound down, then. But quickly turned it up as the blank audio input of the computer appeared on the screen. At this moment the computer had become a giant ear, listening to him—as well as fifty thousand other queriers throughout Terra.

"Scan me visually," he instructed the computer. "And tell me where I will find the programming mechanism which controls my thoughts and behavior." He waited. On the fone's screen a great active eye, multi-lensed, peered at him; he displayed himself for it, there in his one-room apartment.

The computer said, "Remove your chest panel. Apply pressure at your breastbone and then ease outward."

He did so. A section of his chest came off; dizzily, he set it down on the floor.

"I can distinguish control modules," the computer said, "but I can't tell which—" It paused as its eye roved about on the fone screen. "I distinguish a roll of punched tape mounted above your heart mechanism. Do you see it?" Poole craned his neck, peered. He saw it, too. "I will have to sign off," the computer said. "After I have examined the data available to me I will contact you and give you an answer. Good day." The screen died out.

I'll yank the tape out of me, Poole said to himself. Tiny . . . no larger than two spools of thread, with a scanner mounted between the delivery drum and the take-up drum. He could not see any sign of motion; the spools seemed inert. They must cut in as override, he reflected, when specific situations occur. Override to my encephalic processes. And they've been doing it all my life.

He reached down, touched the delivery drum. All I have to do is tear this out, he thought, and—

The fone screen relit. "Mastercreditchargeplate number 3-BNX-882-HQR446-T," the computer's voice came. "This is BBB-307DR recontacting you in response to your query of sixteen seconds lapse, November 4, 1992. The punched tape roll above your heart mechanism is not a programming turret but is in fact a reality-supply construct. All sense stimuli received by your central neurological system emanate from that unit and tampering with it would be risky if not terminal." It added, "You appear to have no programming circuit. Query answered. Good day." It flicked off.

Poole, standing naked before the fone screen, touched the tape drum once again, with calculated, enormous caution. I see, he thought wildly. Or do I see? This unit—

If I cut the tape, he realized, my world will disappear. Reality will continue for others, but not for me. Because my reality, my universe, is coming to me from this minuscule unit. Fed into the scanner and then into my central nervous system as it snailishly unwinds.

It has been unwinding for years, he decided.

Getting his clothes, he redressed, seated himself in his big armchair—a luxury imported into his apartment from Tri-Plan's main offices—and lit a tobacco cigarette. His hands shook as he laid down his initialed lighter; leaning back, he blew smoke before himself, creating a nimbus of gray.

I have to go slowly, he said to himself. What am I trying to do? Bypass my programming? But the computer found no programming circuit. Do I want to interfere with the reality tape? And if so, *why*?

Because, he thought, if I control that, I control reality. At least so far as

I'm concerned. My subjective reality . . . but that's all there is. Objective reality is a synthetic construct, dealing with a hypothetical universalization of a multitude of subjective realities.

My universe is lying within my fingers, he realized. If I can just figure out how the damn thing works. All I set out to do originally was to search for and locate my programming circuits so I could gain true homeostatic functioning: control of myself. But with this—

With this he did not merely gain control of himself; he gained control over everything.

And this sets me apart from every human who ever lived and died, he thought somberly.

Going over to the fone, he dialed his office. When he had Danceman on the screen he said briskly, "I want you to send a complete set of microtools and enlarging screen over to my apartment. I have some microcircuitry to work on." Then he broke the connection, not wanting to discuss it.

A half hour later a knock sounded on his door. When he opened up he found himself facing one of the shop foremen, loaded down with microtools of every sort. "You didn't say exactly what you wanted," the foreman said, entering the apartment. "So Mr. Danceman had me bring everything."

"And the enlarging-lens system?"

"In the truck, up on the roof."

Maybe what I want to do, Poole thought, is die. He lit a cigarette, stood smoking and waiting as the shop foreman lugged the heavy enlarging screen, with its power-supply and control panel, into the apartment. This is suicide, what I'm doing here. He shuddered.

"Anything wrong, Mr. Poole?" the shop foreman said as he rose to his feet, relieved of the burden of the enlarging-lens system. "You must still be rickety on your pins from your accident."

"Yes," Poole said quietly. He stood tautly waiting until the foreman left.

Under the enlarging-lens system the plastic tape assumed a new shape: a wide track along which hundreds of thousands of punch-holes worked their way. I thought so, Poole thought. Not recorded as charges on a ferrous oxide layer but actually punched-free slots.

Under the lens the strip of tape visibly oozed forward. Very slowly, but it did, at uniform velocity, move in the direction of the scanner.

The way I figure it, he thought, is that the punched holes are *on* gates. It functions like a player piano; solid is no, punch-hole is yes. How can I test this?

Obviously by filling in a number of holes.

He measured the amount of tape left on the delivery spool, calculated—at great effort—the velocity of the tape's movement, and then came up with a figure. If he altered the tape visible at the in-going edge of the scanner, five to seven hours would pass before that particular time period arrived. He would in effect be painting out stimuli due a few hours from now.

With a microbrush he swabbed a large—relatively large—section of tape with opaque varnish . . . obtained from the supply kit accompanying the microtools. I have smeared out stimuli for about half an hour, he pondered. Have covered at least a thousand punches.

It would be interesting to see what change, if any, overcame his environment, six hours from now.

Five and a half hours later he sat at Krackter's, a superb bar in Manhattan, having a drink with Danceman.

"You look bad," Danceman said.

"I am bad," Poole said. He finished his drink, a Scotch sour, and ordered another.

"From the accident?"

"In a sense, yes."

Danceman said, "Is it—something you found out about yourself?"

Raising his head, Poole eyed him in the murky light of the bar. "Then you know."

"I know," Danceman said, "that I should call you 'Poole' instead of 'Mr. Poole.' But I prefer the latter, and will continue to do so."

"How long have you known?" Poole said.

"Since you took over the firm. I was told that the actual owners of Tri-Plan, who are located in the Prox System, wanted Tri-Plan run by an electric ant whom they could control. They wanted a brilliant and forceful—"

"The real owners?" This was the first he had heard about that. "We have two thousand stockholders. Scattered everywhere."

"Marvis Bey and her husband, Ernan, on Prox 4, control fifty-one per-cent of the voting stock. This has been true from the start."

"Why didn't I know?"

"I was told not to tell you. You were to think that you yourself made all company policy. With my help. But actually I was feeding you what the Beys fed to me."

"I'm a figurehead," Poole said.

"In a sense, yes." Danceman nodded. "But you'll always be 'Mr. Poole' to me."

A section of the far wall vanished. And with it, several people at tables nearby. And—

Through the big glass side of the bar, the skyline of New York City flickered out of existence.

Seeing his face, Danceman said, "What is it?"

Poole said hoarsely, "Look around. Do you see any changes?"

After looking around the room, Danceman said, "No. What like?"

"You still see the skyline?"

"Sure. Smoggy as it is. The lights wink—"

"Now I know," Poole said. He had been right; every punch-hole cov-ered up meant the disappearance of some object in his reality world. Standing, he said, "I'll see you later, Danceman. I have to get back to my apartment; there's some work I'm doing. Goodnight." He strode from the bar and out onto the street, searching for a cab.

No cabs.

Those, too, he thought. I wonder what else I painted over. Prostitutes? Flowers? Prisons?

There, in the bar's parking lot, Danceman's squib. I'll take that, he decided. There are still cabs in Danceman's world; he can get one later. Anyhow it's a company car, and I hold a copy of the key.

Presently he was in the air, turning toward his apartment.

New York City had not returned. To the left and right vehicles and buildings, streets, ped-runners, signs . . . and in the center nothing. How can I fly into that? he asked himself. I'd disappear.

Or would I? He flew toward the nothingness.

Smoking one cigarette after another he flew in a circle for fifteen minutes . . . and then, soundlessly, New York reappeared. He could finish his trip. He stubbed out his cigarette (a waste of something so valuable) and shot off in the direction of his apartment.

If I insert a narrow opaque strip, he pondered as he unlocked his apartment door, I can—

His thoughts ceased. Someone sat in his living room chair, watching a captain kirk on the TV. "Sarah," he said, nettled.

She rose, well-padded but graceful. "You weren't at the hospital, so I came here. I still have that key you gave me back in March after we had that awful argument. Oh . . . you look so depressed." She came up to him, peeped into his face anxiously. "Does your injury hurt that badly?"

"It's not that." He removed his coat, tie, shirt, and then his chest panel; kneeling down he began inserting his hands into the microtool gloves. Pausing, he looked up at her and said, "I found out I'm an electric ant. Which from one standpoint opens up certain possibilities, which I am exploring now." He flexed his fingers and, at the far end of the left waldo, a micro screwdriver moved, magnified into visibility by the enlarging-lens system. "You can watch," he informed her. "If you so desire."

She had begun to cry.

"What's the matter?" he demanded savagely, without looking up from his work.

"I—it's just so sad. You've been such a good employer to all of us at Tri-Plan. We respect you so. And now it's all changed."

The plastic tape had an unpunched margin at top and bottom; he cut a horizontal strip, very narrow, then, after a moment of great concentration, cut the tape itself four hours away from the scanning head. He then rotated the cut strip into a right-angle piece in relation to the scanner, fused it in place with a micro heat element, then reattached the tape reel to its left and right sides. He had, in effect, inserted a dead twenty minutes into the unfolding flow of his reality. It would take effect—according to his calculations—a few minutes after midnight.

"Are you fixing yourself?" Sarah asked timidly.

Poole said, "I'm freeing myself." Beyond this he had several alterations in mind. But first he had to test his theory; blank, unpunched tape meant no stimuli, in which case the *lack* of tape . . .

"That look on your face," Sarah said. She began gathering up her purse, coat, rolled-up aud-vid magazine. "I'll go; I can see how you feel about finding me here."

"Stay," he said. "I'll watch the captain kirk with you." He got into his shirt. "Remember years ago when there were—what was it?—twenty or twenty-two TV channels? Before the government shut down the independents?"

She nodded.

"What would it have looked like," he said, "if this TV set projected all channels onto the cathode ray screen *at the same time*? Could we have distinguished anything, in the mixture?"

"I don't think so."

"Maybe we could learn to. Learn to be selective; do our own job of perceiving what we wanted to and what we didn't. Think of the possibilities, if our brains could handle twenty images at once; think of the amount of knowledge which could be stored during a given period. I wonder if the brain, the human brain—" He broke off. "The human brain couldn't do it," he said, presently, reflecting to himself. "But in theory a quasi-organic brain might."

"Is that what you have?" Sarah asked.

"Yes," Poole said.

They watched the captain kirk to its end, and then they went to bed. But Poole sat up against his pillows, smoking and brooding. Beside him, Sarah stirred restlessly, wondering why he did not turn off the light.

Eleven-fifty. It would happen anytime, now.

"Sarah," he said. "I want your help. In a very few minutes something strange will happen to me. It won't last long, but I want you to watch me carefully. See if I—" He gestured. "Show any changes. If I seem to go to sleep, or if I talk nonsense, or—" He wanted to say, if I disappear. But he did not. "I won't do you any harm, but I think it might be a good idea if you armed yourself. Do you have your anti-mugging gun with you?"

"In my purse." She had become fully awake now; sitting up in bed, she gazed at him with wild fright, her ample shoulders tanned and freckled in the light of the room.

He got her gun for her.

The room stiffened into paralyzed immobility. Then the colors began to drain away. Objects diminished until, smoke-like, they flitted away into shadows. Darkness filmed everything as the objects in the room became weaker and weaker.

The last stimuli are dying out, Poole realized. He squinted, trying to see. He made out Sarah Benton, sitting in the bed: a two-dimensional figure that doll-like had been propped up, there to fade and dwindle. Random gusts of dematerialized substance eddied about in unstable clouds; the elements collected, fell apart, then collected once again. And then the last heat, energy, and light dissipated; the room closed over and fell into itself, as if sealed off from reality. And at that point absolute blackness replaced everything, space without depth, not nocturnal but rather stiff and unyielding. And in addition he heard nothing.

Reaching, he tried to touch something. But he had nothing to reach with. Awareness of his own body had departed along with everything else in the universe. He had no hands, and even if he had, there would be nothing for them to feel.

I am still right about the way the damn tape works, he said to himself, using a nonexistent mouth to communicate an invisible message.

Will this pass in ten minutes? he asked himself. Am I right about that, too? He waited . . . but knew intuitively that his time sense had departed with everything else. I can only wait, he realized. And hope it won't be long.

To pace himself, he thought, I'll make up an encyclopedia; I'll try to list everything that begins with an "a." Let's see. He pondered. Apple, automobile, acksetron, atmosphere, Atlantic, tomato aspic, advertising—he thought on and on, categories slithering through his fright-haunted mind.

All at once light flickered on.

He lay on the couch in the living room, and mild sunlight spilled in through the single window. Two men bent over him, their hands full of tools. Maintenance men, he realized. They've been working on me.

"He's conscious," one of the technicians said. He rose, stood back; Sarah Benton, dithering with anxiety, replaced him.

"Thank God!" she said, breathing wetly in Poole's ear. "I was so afraid; I called Mr. Danceman finally about—"

"What happened?" Poole broke in harshly. "Start from the beginning and for God's sake speak slowly. So I can assimilate it all."

Sarah composed herself, paused to rub her nose, and then plunged on nervously, "You passed out. You just lay there, as if you were dead. I waited until two-thirty and you did nothing. I called Mr. Danceman, waking him up unfortunately, and he called the electric-ant maintenance—I mean, the organic-roby maintenance people, and these two men came about four-forty-five, and they've been working on you ever since. It's now six-fifteen in the morning. And I'm very cold and I want to go to bed; I can't make it in to the office today; I really can't." She turned away, sniffling. The sound annoyed him.

One of the uniformed maintenance men said, "You've been playing around with your reality tape."

"Yes," Poole said. Why deny it? Obviously they had found the inserted solid strip. "I shouldn't have been out that long," he said. "I inserted a ten-minute strip only."

"It shut off the tape transport," the technician explained. "The tape stopped moving forward; your insertion jammed it, and it automatically shut down to avoid tearing the tape. Why would you want to fiddle around with that? Don't you know what you could do?"

"I'm not sure," Poole said.

"But you have a good idea."

Poole said acridly, "That's why I'm doing it."

"Your bill," the maintenance man said, "is going to be ninety-five frogs. Payable in installments, if you so desire."

"Okay," he said; he sat up groggily, rubbed his eyes, and grimaced. His head ached and his stomach felt totally empty.

"Shave the tape next time," the primary technician told him. "That way it won't jam. Didn't it occur to you that it had a safety factor built into it? So it would stop rather than—"

"What happens," Poole interrupted, his voice low and intently careful, "if no tape passed under the scanner? No tape—nothing at all. The photo-cell shining upward without impedance?"

The technicians glanced at each other. One said, "All the neuro circuits jump their gaps and short out."

"Meaning what?" Poole said.

"Meaning it's the end of the mechanism."

Poole said, "I've examined the circuit. It doesn't carry enough voltage to do that. Metal won't fuse under such slight loads of current, even if the terminals are touching. We're talking about a millionth of a watt along a cesium channel perhaps a sixteenth of an inch in length. Let's assume there are a billion possible combinations at one instant arising from the punch-outs on the tape. The total output isn't cumulative; the amount of current depends on what the battery details for that module, and it's not much. With all gates open and going."

"Would we lie?" one of the technicians asked wearily.

"Why not?" Poole said. "Here I have an opportunity to experience everything. Simultaneously. To know the universe and its entirety, to be momentarily in contact with all reality. Something that no human can do. A symphonic score entering my brain outside of time, all notes, all instruments sounding at once. And all symphonies. Do you see?"

"It'll burn you out," both technicians said, together.

"I don't think so," Poole said.

Sarah said, "Would you like a cup of coffee, Mr. Poole?"

"Yes," he said; he lowered his legs, pressed his cold feet against the floor, shuddered. He then stood up. His body ached. They had me lying all night on the couch, he realized. All things considered, they could have done better than that.

At the kitchen table in the far corner of the room, Garson Poole sat sipping coffee across from Sarah. The technicians had long since gone.

"You're not going to try any more experiments on yourself, are you?" Sarah asked wistfully.

Poole grated, "I would like to control time. To reverse it." I will cut a segment of tape out, he thought, and fuse it in upside down. The causal sequences will then flow the other way. Thereupon I will walk backward down the steps from the roof field, back up to my door, push a locked door open, walk backward to the sink, where I will get out a stack of dirty dishes. I will seat myself at this table before the stack, fill each dish with food produced from my stomach . . . I will then transfer the food to the refrigerator. The next day I will take the food out of the refrigerator, pack it in bags, carry the bags to a supermarket, distribute the food here and there in the store. And at last, at the front counter, they will pay me money for this, from their cash register. The food will be packed with other food in big plastic boxes, shipped out of the city into the hydroponic plants on the Atlantic, there to be joined back to trees and bushes or the bodies of dead animals or pushed deep into the ground. But what would all that prove? A video tape running backward . . . I would know no more than I know now, which is not enough.

What I want, he realized, is ultimate and absolute reality, for one micro-second. After that it doesn't matter, because all will be known; nothing will be left to understand or see.

I might try one other change, he said to himself. Before I try cutting the tape. I will prick new punch-holes in the tape and see what presently emerges. It will be interesting because I will not know what the holes I make mean.

Using the tip of a microtool, he punched several holes, at random, on the tape. As close to the scanner as he could manage . . . he did not want to wait.

"I wonder if you'll see it," he said to Sarah. Apparently not, insofar as he could extrapolate. "Something may show up," he said to her. "I just want to warn you; I don't want you to be afraid."

"Oh dear," Sarah said tinnily.

He examined his wristwatch. One minute passed, then a second, a third. And then—

In the center of the room appeared a flock of green-and-black ducks. They quacked excitedly, rose from the floor, fluttered against the ceiling in a dithering mass of feathers and wings and frantic in their vast urge, their instinct, to get away.

"Ducks," Poole said, marveling. "I punched a hole for a flight of wild ducks."

Now something else appeared. A park bench with an elderly, tattered man seated on it, reading a torn, bent newspaper. He looked up, dimly made out Poole, smiled briefly at him with badly made dentures, and then returned to his folded-back newspaper. He read on.

"Do you see him?" Poole asked Sarah. "And the ducks." At that moment the ducks and the park bum disappeared. Nothing remained of them. The interval of their punch-holes had quickly passed.

"They weren't real," Sarah said. "Were they? So how—"

"You're not real," he told Sarah. "You're a stimulus-factor on my reality tape. A punch-hole that can be glazed over. Do you also have an existence in another reality tape, or one in an objective reality?" He did not know; he couldn't tell. Perhaps Sarah did not know, either. Perhaps she existed in a thousand reality tapes; perhaps on every reality tape ever manufactured. "If I cut the tape," he said, "you will be everywhere and nowhere. Like everything else in the universe. At least as far as I am aware of it."

Sarah faltered, "I am real."

"I want to know you completely," Poole said. "To do that I must cut the tape. If I don't do it now, I'll do it some other time; it's inevitable that eventually I'll do it." So why wait? he asked himself. And there is always the possibility that Danceman has reported back to my maker, that they will be making moves to head me off. Because, perhaps, I'm endangering their property—myself.

"You make me wish I had gone to the office after all," Sarah said, her mouth turned down with dimpled gloom.

"Go," Poole said.

"I don't want to leave you alone."

"I'll be fine," Poole said.

"No, you're not going to be fine. You're going to unplug yourself or something, kill yourself because you've found out you're just an electric ant and not a human being."

He said, presently, "Maybe so." Maybe it boiled down to that.

"And I can't stop you," she said.

"No." He nodded in agreement.

"But I'm going to stay," Sarah said. "Even if I can't stop you. Because if I do leave and you do kill yourself, I'll always ask myself for the rest of my life what would have happened if I had stayed. You see?"

Again he nodded.

"Go ahead," Sarah said.

He rose to his feet. "It's not pain I'm going to feel," he told her. "Although it may look like that to you. Keep in mind the fact that organic robots have minimal pain-circuits in them. I will be experiencing the most intense—"

"Don't tell me any more," she broke in. "Just do it if you're going to, or don't do it if you're not."

Clumsily—because he was frightened—he wriggled his hands into the microglove assembly, reached to pick up a tiny tool: a sharp cutting blade. "I am going to cut a tape mounted inside my chest panel," he said, as he gazed through the enlarging-lens system. "That's all." His hand shook as it lifted the cutting blade. In a second it can be done, he realized. All over. And—I will have time to fuse the cut ends of the tape back together, he realized. A half hour at least. If I change my mind.

He cut the tape.

Staring at him, cowering, Sarah whispered, "Nothing happened."

"I have thirty or forty minutes." He reseated himself at the table, having drawn his hands from the gloves. His voice, he noticed, shook; undoubtedly Sarah was aware of it, and he felt anger at himself, knowing that he had alarmed her. "I'm sorry," he said, irrationally; he wanted to apologize to her. "Maybe you ought to leave," he said in panic; again he stood up. So did she, reflexively, as if imitating him; bloated and nervous, she stood there palpitating. "Go away," he said thickly. "Back to the office where you ought to be. Where we both ought to be." I'm going to fuse the tape-ends together, he told himself; the tension is too great for me to stand.

Reaching his hands toward the gloves he groped to pull them over his straining fingers. Peering into the enlarging screen, he saw the beam from the photoelectric gleam upward, pointed directly into the scanner; at the same time he saw the end of the tape disappearing under the scanner . . . he saw this, understood it; I'm too late, he realized. It has passed through. God, he thought, help me. It has begun winding at a rate greater than I calculated. So it's *now* that—

He saw apples, and cobblestones and zebras. He felt warmth, the silky texture of cloth; he felt the ocean lapping at him and a great wind, from the north, plucking at him as if to lead him somewhere. Sarah was all around him, so was Danceman. New York glowed in the night, and the squibs about him scuttled and bounced through night skies and daytime and flooding and drought. Butter relaxed into liquid on his tongue, and at the same time hideous odors and tastes assailed him: the bitter presence of poisons and lemons and blades of summer grass. He drowned; he fell; he lay in the arms of a woman in a vast white bed which at the same time dinned shrilly in his ear: the warning noise of a defective elevator in one of the ancient, ruined downtown hotels. I am living, I have lived, I will never live, he said to himself, and with his thoughts came every word, every sound; insects squeaked and raced, and he half sank into a complex body of homeostatic machinery located somewhere in Tri-Plan's labs.

He wanted to say something to Sarah. Opening his mouth he tried to bring forth words—a specific string of them out of the enormous mass of them brilliantly lighting his mind, scorching him with their utter meaning.

His mouth burned. He wondered why.

Frozen against the wall, Sarah Benton opened her eyes and saw the curl of smoke ascending from Poole's half-opened mouth. Then the roby sank down, knelt on elbows and knees, then slowly spread out in a broken, crumpled heap. She knew without examining it that it had "died."

Poole did it to itself, she realized. And it couldn't feel pain; it said so itself. Or at least not very much pain; maybe a little. Anyhow, now it is over.

I had better call Mr. Danceman and tell him what's happened, she decided. Still shaky, she made her way across the room to the fone; picking it up, she dialed from memory.

It thought I was a stimulus-factor on its reality tape, she said to herself. So it thought I would die when it "died." How strange, she thought. Why did it imagine that? It had never been plugged into the real world; it had "lived" in an electronic world of its own. How bizarre.

"Mr. Danceman," she said when the circuit to his office had been put through. "Poole is gone. It destroyed itself right in front of my eyes. You'd better come over."

"So we're finally free of it."

"Yes, won't it be nice?"

Danceman said, "I'll send a couple of men over from the shop." He saw past her, made out the sight of Poole lying by the kitchen table. "You go home and rest," he instructed Sarah. "You must be worn out by all this."

"Yes," she said. "Thank you, Mr. Danceman." She hung up and stood, aimlessly.

And then she noticed something.

My hands, she thought. She held them up. Why is it I can see through them?

The walls of the room, too, had become ill-defined.

Trembling, she walked back to the inert roby, stood by it, not knowing what to do. Through her legs the carpet showed, and then the carpet
became dim, and she saw, through it, farther layers of disintegrating matter
beyond.

Maybe if I can fuse the tape-ends back together, she thought. But she
did not know how. And already Poole had become vague.

The wind of early morning blew about her. She did not feel it; she had
begun, now, to cease to feel.

The winds blew on.

A LITTLE SOMETHING FOR US TEMPUNAUTS

Wearily, Addison Doug plodded up the long path of synthetic redwood rounds, step by step, his head down a little, moving as if he were in actual physical pain. The girl watched him, wanting to help him, hurt within her to see how worn and unhappy he was, but at the same time she rejoiced that he was there at all. On and on, toward her, without glancing up, going by feel . . . like he's done this many times, she thought suddenly. Knows the way too well. Why?

"Addi," she called, and ran toward him. "They said on the TV you were dead. All of you were killed!"

He paused, wiping back his dark hair, which was no longer long; just before the launch they had cropped it. But he had evidently forgotten. "You believe everything you see on TV?" he said, and came on again, haltingly, but smiling now. And reaching up for her.

God, it felt good to hold him, and to have him clutch at her again, with more strength than she had expected. "I was going to find somebody else," she gasped. "To replace you."

"I'll knock your head off if you do," he said. "Anyhow, that isn't possible; nobody could replace me."

"But what about the implosion?" she said. "On reentry; they said—"

"I forget," Addison said, in the tone he used when he meant, I'm not going to discuss it. The tone had always angered her before, but not now. This time she sensed how awful the memory was. "I'm going to stay at your place a couple of days," he said, as together they moved up the path toward the open front door of the tilted A-frame house. "If that's okay. And Benz and Crayne will be joining me, later on; maybe even as soon as tonight. We've got a lot to talk over and figure out."

"Then all three of you survived." She gazed up into his careworn face. "Everything they said on TV . . ." She understood, then. Or believed she did. "It was a cover story. For—political purposes, to fool the Russians. Right? I mean, the Soviet Union'll think the launch was a failure because on reentry—"

"No," he said. "A chrononaut will be joining us, most likely. To help figure out what happened. General Toad said one of them is already on his way here; they got clearance already. Because of the gravity of the situation."

"Jesus," the girl said, stricken. "Then who's the cover story for?"

"Let's have something to drink," Addison said. "And then I'll outline it all for you."

"Only thing I've got at the moment is California brandy."

Addison Doug said, "I'd drink anything right now, the way I feel." He dropped to the couch, leaned back, and sighed a ragged, distressed sigh, as the girl hurriedly began fixing both of them a drink.

The FM radio in the car yammered, ". . . grieves at the stricken turn of events precipitating out of an unheralded . . ."

"Official nonsense babble," Crayne said, shutting off the radio. He and Benz were having trouble finding the house, having been there only once before. It struck Crayne that this was a somewhat informal way of convening a conference of this importance, meeting at Addison's chick's pad out here in the boondocks of Ojai. On the other hand, they wouldn't be pestered by the curious. And they probably didn't have much time. But that was hard to say; about that no one knew for sure.

The hills on both sides of the road had once been forests, Crayne observed. Now housing tracts and their melted, irregular, plastic roads marred every rise in sight. "I'll bet this was nice once," he said to Benz, who was driving.

"The Los Padres National Forest is near here," Benz said. "I got lost in there when I was eight. For hours I was sure a rattler would get me. Every stick was a snake."

"The rattler's got you now," Crayne said.

"All of us," Benz said.

"You know," Crayne said, "it's a hell of an experience to be dead."

"Speak for yourself."

"But technically—"

"If you listen to the radio and TV." Benz turned toward him, his big gnome face bleak with admonishing sternness. "We're no more dead than anyone else on the planet. The difference for us is that our death date is in the past, whereas everyone else's is set somewhere at an uncertain time in the future. Actually, some people have it pretty damn well set, like people in cancer wards; they're as certain as we are. More so. For example, how long can we stay here before we go back? We have a margin, a latitude that a terminal cancer victim doesn't have."

Crayne said cheerfully, "The next thing you'll be telling us to cheer us up is that we're in no pain."

"Addi is. I watched him lurch off earlier today. He's got it psychosomatically—made it into a physical complaint. Like God's kneeling on his neck; you know, carrying a much-too-great burden that's unfair, only he won't complain out loud . . . just points now and then at the nail hole in his hand." He grinned.

"Addi has got more to live for than we do."

"Everyman has more to live for than any other man. I don't have a cute chick to sleep with, but I'd like to see the semis rolling along Riverside Freeway at sunset a few more times. It's not what you have to live for; it's that you want to live to see it, to be there—that's what is so damn sad."

They rode on in silence.

In the quiet living room of the girl's house the three tempunauts sat around smoking, taking it easy; Addison Doug thought to himself that the girl looked unusually foxy and desirable in her stretched-tight white sweater and micro-skirt and he wished, wistfully, that she looked a little less interesting. He could not really afford to get embroiled in such stuff, at this point. He was too tired.

"Does she know," Benz said, indicating the girl, "what this is all about? I mean, can we talk openly? It won't wipe her out?"

"I haven't explained it to her yet," Addison said.

"You goddam well better," Crayne said.

"What is it?" the girl said, stricken, sitting upright with one hand directly between her breasts. As if clutching at a religious artifact that isn't there, Addison thought.

"We got snuffed on reentry," Benz said. He was, really, the cruelest of the three. Or at least the most blunt. "You see, Miss . . ."

"Hawkins," the girl whispered.

"Glad to meet you, Miss Hawkins." Benz surveyed her in his cold, lazy fashion. "You have a first name?"

"Merry Lou."

"Okay, Merry Lou," Benz said. To the other two men he observed, "Sounds like the name a waitress has stitched on her blouse. Merry Lou's my name and I'll be serving you dinner and breakfast and lunch and dinner and breakfast for the next few days or however long it is before you all give up and go back to your own time; that'll be fifty-three dollars and eight cents, please, not including tip. And I hope y'all never come back, y'hear?" His voice had begun to shake; his cigarette, too. "Sorry, Miss Hawkins," he said then. "We're all screwed up by the implosion at reentry. As soon as we got here in ETA we learned about it. We've known longer than anyone else; we knew as soon as we hit Emergence Time."

"But there's nothing we could do," Crayne said.

"There's nothing anyone can do," Addison said to her, and put his arm around her. It felt like a déjà vu thing but then it hit him. We're in a closed time loop, he thought, we keep going through this again and again, trying to solve the reentry problem, each time imagining it's the first time, the only time . . . and never succeeding. Which attempt is this? Maybe the millionth; we have sat here a million times, raking the same facts over and over again and getting nowhere. He felt bone-weary, thinking that. And he felt a sort of vast philosophical hate toward all other men, who did not have this enigma to deal with. We all go to one place, he thought, as the Bible says. But . . . for the three of us, we have been there already. Are lying there now. So it's wrong to ask us to stand around on the surface of Earth afterward and argue and worry about it and try to figure out what malfunctioned. That should be, rightly, for our heirs to do. We've had enough already.

He did not say this aloud, though—for their sake.

"Maybe you bumped into something," the girl said.

Glancing at the others, Benz said sardonically, "Maybe we 'bumped into something.'"

"The TV commentators kept saying that," Merry Lou said, "about the hazard in reentry of being out of phase spatially and colliding right down to the molecular level with tangent objects, any one of which—" She gestured. "You know. 'No two objects can occupy the same space at the same time.' So everything blew up, for that reason." She glanced around questioningly.

"That is the major risk factor," Crayne acknowledged. "At least theoretically, as Dr. Fein at Planning calculated when they got into the hazard question. But we had a variety of safety locking devices provided that functioned automatically. Reentry couldn't occur unless these assists had stabilized us spatially so we would not overlap. Of course, all those devices, in sequence, might have failed. One after the other. I was watching my feedback metric scopes on launch, and they agreed, every one of them, that we were phased properly at that time. And I heard no warning tones. Saw none, neither." He grimaced. "At least it didn't happen then."

Suddenly Benz said, "Do you realize that our next of kin are now rich? All our Federal and commercial life-insurance payoff. Our 'next of kin'— God forbid, that's us, I guess. We can apply for tens of thousands of dollars, cash on the line. Walk into our brokers' offices and say, 'I'm dead; lay the heavy bread on me.'"

Addison Doug was thinking, The public memorial services. That they have planned, after the autopsies. That long line of black-draped Cads going down Pennsylvania Avenue, with all the government dignitaries and double-domed scientist types—*and we'll be there*. Not once but twice. Once in the oak hand-rubbed brass-fitted flag-draped caskets, but also . . . maybe riding in open limos, waving at the crowds of mourners.

"The ceremonies," he said aloud.

The others stared at him, angrily, not comprehending. And then, one by one, they understood; he saw it on their faces.

"No," Benz grated. "That's—impossible."

Crayne shook his head emphatically. "They'll order us to be there, and we will be. Obeying orders."

"Will we have to *smile*?" Addison said. "To fucking *smile*?"

"No," General Toad said slowly, his great wattled head shivering about on his broomstick neck, the color of his skin dirty and mottled, as if the mass of decorations on his stiff-board collar had started part of him decaying away. "You are not to smile, but on the contrary are to adopt a properly grief-stricken manner. In keeping with the national mood of sorrow at this time."

"That'll be hard to do," Crayne said.

The Russian chrononaut showed no response; his thin beaked face, narrow within his translating earphones, remained strained with concern.

"The nation," General Toad said, "will become aware of your presence among us once more for this brief interval; cameras of all major TV networks will pan up to you without warning, and at the same time, the various commentators have been instructed to tell their audiences something like the following." He got out a piece of typed material, put on his glasses, cleared his throat, and said, "'We seem to be focusing on three figures riding together. Can't quite make them out. Can you?'" General Toad lowered the paper. "At this point they'll interrogate their colleagues extempore. Finally they'll exclaim, 'Why, Roger,' or Walter or Ned, as the case may be, according to the individual network—"

"Or Bill," Crayne said. "In case it's the Bufonidae network, down there in the swamp."

General Toad ignored him. "They will severally exclaim, 'Why Roger I believe we're seeing the three tempunauts themselves! Does this indeed mean that somehow the difficulty—?' And then the colleague commentator says in his somewhat more somber voice, 'What we're seeing at this time, I think, David,' or Henry or Pete or Ralph, whichever it is, 'consists of mankind's first verified glimpse of what the technical people refer to as Emergence Time Activity or ETA. Contrary to what might seem to be the case at first sight, these are *not*—repeat, not—our three valiant tempunauts as such, as we would ordinarily experience them, but more likely picked up by our cameras as the three of them are temporarily suspended in their voyage to the future, which we initially had reason to hope would take place in a time continuum roughly a hundred years from now . . . but it would seem that they somehow undershot and are here now, at this moment, which of course is, as we know, our present.'"

Addison Doug closed his eyes and thought, Crayne will ask him if he can be panned up on by the TV cameras holding a balloon and eating cotton candy. I think we're all going nuts from this, all of us. And then he wondered, How many times have we gone through this idiotic exchange?

I can't prove it, he thought wearily. But I know it's true. We've sat here, done this minuscule scrabbling, listened to and said all this crap, many times. He shuddered. Each rinky-dink word . . .

"What's the matter?" Benz said acutely.

The Soviet chrononaut spoke up for the first time. "What is the maximum interval of ETA possible to your three-man team? And how large a per cent has been exhausted by now?"

After a pause Crayne said, "They briefed us on that before we came in here today. We've consumed approximately one-half of our maximum total ETA interval."

"However," General Toad rumbled, "we have scheduled the Day of National Mourning to fall within the expected period remaining to them of ETA time. This required us to speed up the autopsy and other forensic findings, but in view of public sentiment, it was felt . . ."

The autopsy, Addison Doug thought, and again he shuddered; this time he could not keep his thoughts within himself and he said, "Why don't we adjourn this nonsense meeting and drop down to pathology and view a few tissue sections enlarged and in color, and maybe we'll brainstorm a couple of vital concepts that'll aid medical science in its quest for explanations? Explanations—that's what we need. Explanations for problems that don't exist yet; we can develop the problems later." He paused. "Who agrees?"

"I'm not looking at my spleen up there on the screen," Benz said. "I'll ride in the parade but I won't participate in my own autopsy."

"You could distribute microscopic purple-stained slices of your own gut to the mourners along the way," Crayne said. "They could provide each of us with a doggy bag; right, General? We can strew tissue sections like confetti. I still think we should smile."

"I have researched all the memoranda about smiling," General Toad said, riffling the pages stacked before him, "and the consensus at policy is that smiling is not in accord with national sentiment. So that issue must be ruled closed. As far as your participating in the autopsical procedures which are now in progress—"

"We're missing out as we sit here," Crayne said to Addison Doug. "I always miss out."

Ignoring him, Addison addressed the Soviet chrononaut. "Officer N. Gauki," he said into his microphone, dangling on his chest, "what in your mind is the greatest terror facing a time traveler? That there will be an implosion due to coincidence on reentry, such as has occurred in our launch? Or did other traumatic obsessions bother you and your comrade during your own brief but highly successful time flight?"

N. Gauki, after a pause, answered, "R. Plenya and I exchanged views at several informal times. I believe I can speak for us both when I respond to your question by emphasizing our perpetual fear that we had inadvertently entered a closed time loop and would never break out."

"You'd repeat it forever?" Addison Doug asked.

"Yes, Mr. A. Doug," the chrononaut said, nodding somberly.

A fear that he had never experienced before overcame Addison Doug. He turned helplessly to Benz and muttered, "Shit." They gazed at each other.

"I really don't believe this is what happened," Benz said to him in a low voice, putting his hand on Doug's shoulder; he gripped hard, the grip of friendship. "We just imploded on reentry, that's all. Take it easy."

"Could we adjourn soon?" Addison Doug said in a hoarse, strangling voice, half rising from his chair. He felt the room and the people in it rushing in at him, suffocating him. Claustrophobia, he realized. Like when I was in grade school, when they flashed a surprise test on our teaching machines, and I saw I couldn't pass it. "Please," he said simply, standing. They were all looking at him, with different expressions. The Russian's face was especially sympathetic, and deeply lined with care. Addison wished—

"I want to go home," he said to them all, and felt stupid.

He was drunk. It was late at night, at a bar on Hollywood Boulevard; fortunately, Merry Lou was with him, and he was having a good time.

Everyone was telling him so, anyhow. He clung to Merry Lou and said, "The great unity in life, the supreme unity and meaning, is man and woman. Their absolute unity; right?"

"I know," Merry Lou said. "We studied that in class." Tonight, at his request, Merry Lou was a small blonde girl, wearing purple bellbottoms and high heels and an open midriff blouse. Earlier she had had a lapis lazuli in her navel, but during dinner at Ting Ho's it had popped out and been lost. The owner of the restaurant had promised to keep on searching for it, but Merry Lou had been gloomy ever since. It was, she said, symbolic. But of what she did not say. Or anyhow he could not remember; maybe that was it. She had told him what it meant, and he had forgotten.

An elegant young black at a nearby table, with an Afro and striped vest and overstuffed red tie, had been staring at Addison for some time. He obviously wanted to come over to their table but was afraid to; meanwhile, he kept on staring.

"Did you ever get the sensation," Addison said to Merry Lou, "that you knew exactly what was about to happen? What someone was going to say? Word for word? Down to the slightest detail. As if you had already lived through it once before?"

"Everybody gets into that space," Merry Lou said. She sipped a Bloody Mary.

The black rose and walked toward them. He stood by Addison. "I'm sorry to bother you, sir."

Addison said to Merry Lou, "He's going to say, 'Don't I know you from somewhere? Didn't I see you on TV?'"

"That was precisely what I intended to say," the black said.

Addison said, "You undoubtedly saw my picture on page forty-six of the current issue of *Time,* the section on new medical discoveries. I'm the G.P. from a small town in Iowa catapulted to fame by my invention of a widespread, easily available cure for eternal life. Several of the big pharmaceutical houses are already bidding on my vaccine."

"That might have been where I saw your picture," the black said, but he did not appear convinced. Nor did he appear drunk; he eyed Addison Doug intensely. "May I seat myself with you and the lady?"

"Sure," Addison Doug said. He now saw, in the man's hand, the ID of the U.S. security agency that had ridden herd on the project from the start.

"Mr. Doug," the security agent said as he seated himself beside Addison, "you really shouldn't be here shooting off your mouth like this. If I recognized you some other dude might and break out. It's all classified until the Day of Mourning. Technically, you're in violation of a Federal Statute by being here; did you realize that? I should haul you in. But this is a difficult situation; we don't want to do something uncool and make a scene. Where are your two colleagues?"

"At my place," Merry Lou said. She had obviously not seen the ID. "Listen," she said sharply to the agent, "why don't you get lost? My husband here has been through a grueling ordeal, and this is his only chance to unwind."

Addison looked at the man. "I knew what you were going to say before you came over here." Word for word, he thought. I am right, and Benz is wrong, and this will keep happening, this replay.

"Maybe," the security agent said, "I can induce you to go back to Miss Hawkins's place voluntarily. Some info arrived"—he tapped the tiny earphone in his right ear—"just a few minutes ago, to all of us, to deliver to you, marked urgent, if we located you. At the launchsite ruins . . . they've been combing through the rubble, you know?"

"I know," Addison said.

"They think they have their first clue. Something was brought back by one of you. From ETA, over and above what you took, in violation of all your prelaunch training."

"Let me ask you this," Addison Doug said. "Suppose somebody does see me? Suppose somebody does recognize me? So what?"

"The public believes that even though reentry failed, the flight into time, the first American time-travel launch, was successful. Three U.S. tempunauts were thrust a hundred years into the future—roughly twice as far as the Soviet launch of last year. That you only went a *week* will be less of a shock if it's believed that you three chose deliberately to remanifest at this continuum because you wished to attend, in fact felt compelled to attend—"

"We wanted to be in the parade," Addison interrupted. "Twice."

"You were drawn to the dramatic and somber spectacle of your own funeral procession, and will be glimpsed there by the alert camera crews of all major networks. Mr. Doug, really, an awful lot of high-level planning and expense have gone into this to help correct a dreadful situation; trust us, believe me. It'll be easier on the public, and that's vital, if there's ever to be another U.S. time shot. And that is, after all, what we all want."

Addison Doug stared at him. "We want what?"

Uneasily, the security agent said, "To take further trips into time. As you have done. Unfortunately, you yourself cannot ever do so again, because of the tragic implosion and death of the three of you. But other tempunauts—"

"We want what? Is that what we want?" Addison's voice rose; people at nearby tables were watching now. Nervously.

"Certainly," the agent said. "And keep your voice down."

"I don't want that," Addison said. "I want to stop. To stop forever. To just lie in the ground, in the dust, with everyone else. To see no more summers—the *same* summer."

"Seen one, you've seen them all," Merry Lou said hysterically. "I think he's right, Addi; we should get out of here. You've had too many drinks, and it's late, and this news about the—"

Addison broke in, "What was brought back? How much extra mass?"

The security agent said, "Preliminary analysis shows that machinery weighing about one hundred pounds was lugged back into the time-field of the module and picked up along with you. This much mass—" The agent gestured. "That blew up the pad right on the spot. It couldn't begin to compensate for that much more than had occupied its open area at launch time."

"Wow!" Merry Lou said, eyes wide. "Maybe somebody sold one of you a quadraphonic phono for a dollar ninety-eight including fifteen-inch air-suspension speakers and a lifetime supply of Neil Diamond records." She tried to laugh, but failed; her eyes dimmed over. "Addi," she whispered, "I'm sorry. But it's sort of—weird. I mean, it's absurd; you all were briefed, weren't you, about your return weight? You weren't even to add so much as a piece of paper to what you took. I even saw Dr. Fein demonstrating the reasons on TV. And one of you hoisted a hundred pounds of machinery into that field? You must have been trying to self-destruct, to do that!" Tears slid from her eyes; one tear rolled out onto her nose and hung there. He reached reflexively to wipe it away, as if helping a little girl rather than a grown one.

"I'll fly you to the analysis site," the security agent said, standing up. He and Addison helped Merry Lou to her feet; she trembled as she stood a moment, finishing her Bloody Mary. Addison felt acute sorrow for her, but then, almost at once, it passed. He wondered why. One can weary even of that, he conjectured. Of caring for someone. If it goes on too long—on and on. Forever. And, at last, even after that, into something no one before, not God Himself, maybe, had ever had to suffer and in the end, for all His great heart, succumb to.

As they walked through the crowded bar toward the street, Addison Doug said to the security agent, "Which one of us—"

"They know which one," the agent said as he held the door to the street open for Merry Lou. The agent stood, now, behind Addison, signaling for a gray Federal car to land at the red parking area. Two other security agents, in uniform, hurried toward them.

"Was it me?" Addison Doug asked.

"You better believe it," the security agent said.

The funeral procession moved with aching solemnity down Pennsylvania Avenue, three flag-draped caskets and dozens of black limousines passing between rows of heavily coated, shivering mourners. A low haze hung over the day, gray outlines of buildings faded into the rain-drenched murk of the Washington March day.

Scrutinizing the lead Cadillac through prismatic binoculars, TV's top news and public-events commentator, Henry Cassidy, droned on at his vast unseen audience, ". . . sad recollections of that earlier train among the wheatfields carrying the coffin of Abraham Lincoln back to burial and the nation's capital. And what a sad day this is, and what appropriate weather, with its dour overcast and sprinkles!" In his monitor he saw the zoomar lens pan up on the fourth Cadillac, as it followed those with the caskets of the dead tempunauts.

His engineer tapped him on the arm.

"We appear to be focusing on three unfamiliar figures so far not identified, riding together," Henry Cassidy said into his neck mike, nodding agreement. "So far I'm unable to quite make them out. Are your location and vision any better from where you're placed, Everett?" he inquired of his colleague and pressed the button that notified Everett Branton to replace him on the air.

"Why, Henry," Branton said in a voice of growing excitement, "I believe we're actually eyewitness to the three American tempunauts as they remanifest themselves on their historic journey into the future!"

"Does this signify," Cassidy said, "that somehow they have managed to solve and overcome the—"

"Afraid not, Henry," Branton said in his slow, regretful voice. "What we're eyewitnessing to our complete surprise consists of the Western world's first verified glimpse of what the technical people refer to as Emergence Time Activity."

"Ah, yes, ETA," Cassidy said brightly, reading it off the official script the Federal authorities had handed to him before air time.

"Right, Henry. Contrary to what *might* seem to be the case at first sight, these are not—repeat *not*—our three brave tempunauts as such, as we would ordinarily experience them—"

"I grasp it now, Everett," Cassidy broke in excitedly, since his authorized script read CASS BREAKS IN EXCITEDLY. "Our three tempunauts have momentarily been suspended in their historic voyage to the future, which we believe will span across a time-continuum roughly a century from now . . . It would seem that the overwhelming grief and drama of this unanticipated day of mourning has caused them to—"

"Sorry to interrupt, Henry," Everett Branton said, "but I think, since the procession has momentarily halted on its slow march forward, that we might be able to—"

"No!" Cassidy said, as a note was handed him in a swift scribble, reading: *Do not interview nauts. Urgent. Dis. previous inst.* "I don't think we're going to be able to . . ." he continued, ". . . to speak briefly with tempunauts Benz, Crayne, and Doug, as you had hoped, Everett. As we had all briefly hoped to." He wildly waved the boom-mike back; it had already begun to swing out expectantly toward the stopped Cadillac. Cassidy shook his head violently at the mike technician and his engineer.

Perceiving the boom-mike swinging at them Addison Doug stood up in the back of the open Cadillac. Cassidy groaned. He wants to speak, he realized. Didn't they reinstruct *him*? Why am I the only one they get across to? Other boom-mikes representing other networks plus radio station interviewers on foot now were rushing out to thrust up their microphones into the faces of the three tempunauts, especially Addison Doug's. Doug was already beginning to speak, in response to a question shouted up to him by a reporter. With his boom-mike off, Cassidy couldn't hear the question, nor Doug's answer. With reluctance, he signaled for his own boom-mike to trigger on.

". . . before," Doug was saying loudly.

"In what manner, 'All this has happened before'?" the radio reporter, standing close to the car, was saying.

"I mean," U.S. tempunaut Addison Doug declared, his face red and strained, "that I have stood here in this spot and said again and again, and all of you have viewed this parade and our deaths at reentry endless times, a closed cycle of trapped time which must be broken."

"Are you seeking," another reporter jabbered up at Addison Doug, "for a solution to the reentry implosion disaster which can be applied in retrospect so that when you do return to the past you will be able to correct the malfunction and avoid the tragedy which cost—or for you three, will cost—your lives?"

Tempunaut Benz said, "We are doing that, yes."

"Trying to ascertain the cause of the violent implosion and eliminate the cause before we return," tempunaut Crayne added, nodding. "We have learned already that, for reasons unknown, a mass of nearly one hundred pounds of miscellaneous Volkswagen motor parts, including cylinders, the head . . ."

This is awful, Cassidy thought. "This is amazing!" he said aloud, into his neck mike. "The already tragically deceased U.S. tempunauts, with a determination that could emerge only from the rigorous training and discipline to which they were subjected—and we wondered why at the time but can clearly see why now—have already analyzed the mechanical slip-up responsible, evidently, for their own deaths, and have begun the laborious process of sifting through and eliminating causes of that slip-up so that they can return to their original launch site and reenter without mishap."

"One wonders," Branton mumbled onto the air and into his feedback earphone, "what the consequences of this alteration of the near past will be. If in reentry they do *not* implode and are *not* killed, then they will not—

well, it's too complex for me, Henry, these time paradoxes that Dr. Fein at the Time Extrusion Labs in Pasadena has so frequently and eloquently brought to our attention."

Into all the microphones available, of all sorts, tempunaut Addison Doug was saying, more quietly now, "We must not eliminate the cause of reentry implosion. The only way out of this trap is for us to die. Death is the only solution for this. For the three of us." He was interrupted as the procession of Cadillacs began to move forward.

Shutting off his mike momentarily, Henry Cassidy said to his engineer, "Is he nuts?"

"Only time will tell," his engineer said in a hard-to-hear voice.

"An extraordinary moment in the history of the United States's involvement in time travel," Cassidy said, then, into his now live mike. "Only time will tell—if you will pardon the inadvertent pun—whether tempunaut Doug's cryptic remarks, uttered impromptu at this moment of supreme suffering for him, as in a sense to a lesser degree it is for all of us, are the words of a man deranged by grief or an accurate insight into the macabre dilemma that in theoretical terms we knew all along might eventually confront—confront and strike down with its lethal blow—a time-travel launch, either ours or the Russians'."

He segued, then, to a commercial.

"You know," Branton's voice muttered in his ear, not on the air but just to the control room and to him, "if he's right they ought to let the poor bastards die."

"They ought to release them," Cassidy agreed. "My God, the way Doug looked and talked, you'd imagine he'd gone through this for a thousand years and then some! I wouldn't be in his shoes for anything."

"I'll bet you fifty bucks," Branton said, "they have gone through this before. Many times."

"Then we have, too," Cassidy said.

Rain fell now, making all the lined-up mourners shiny. Their faces, their eyes, even their clothes—everything glistened in wet reflections of broken, fractured light, bent and sparkling, as, from gathering gray formless layers above them, the day darkened.

"Are we on the air?" Branton asked.

Who knows? Cassidy thought. He wished the day would end.

The Soviet chrononaut N. Gauki lifted both hands impassionedly and spoke to the Americans across the table from him in a voice of extreme urgency. "It is the opinion of myself and my colleague R. Plenya, who for his pioneering achievements in time travel has been certified a Hero of the Soviet People, and rightly so, that based on our own experience and on theoretical material developed both in your own academic circles and in the Soviet Academy of Sciences of the USSR, we believe that tempunaut A. Doug's fears may be justified. And his deliberate destruction of himself and his teammates at reentry, by hauling a huge mass of auto back with him from ETA, in violation of his orders, should be regarded as the act of a desperate man with no other means of escape. Of course, the decision is up to you. We have only advisory position in this matter."

Addison Doug played with his cigarette lighter on the table and did not look up. His ears hummed, and he wondered what that meant. It had an electronic quality. Maybe we're within the module again, he thought. But he didn't perceive it; he felt the reality of the people around him, the table, the blue plastic lighter between his fingers. No smoking in the module during reentry, he thought. He put the lighter carefully away in his pocket.

"We've developed no concrete evidence whatsoever," General Toad said, "that a closed time loop has been set up. There's only the subjective feelings of fatigue on the part of Mr. Doug. Just his belief that he's done all this repeatedly. As he says, it is very probably psychological in nature." He rooted, piglike, among the papers before him. "I have a report, not disclosed to the media, from four psychiatrists at Yale on his psychological makeup. Although unusually stable, there is a tendency toward cyclothymia on his part, culminating in acute depression. This naturally was taken into account long before the launch, but it was calculated that the joyful qualities of the two others in the team would offset this functionally. Anyhow, that depressive tendency in him is exceptionally high, now." He held the paper out, but no one at the table accepted it. "Isn't it true, Dr. Fein," he said, "that an acutely depressed person experiences time in a peculiar way, that is, circular time, time repeating itself, getting nowhere, around and around? The person gets so psychotic that he refuses to let go of the past. Reruns it in his head constantly."

"But you see," Dr. Fein said, "this subjective sensation of being trapped is perhaps all we would have." This was the research physicist whose basic work had laid the theoretical foundation for the project. "If a closed loop did unfortunately lock into being."

"The general," Addison Doug said, "is using words he doesn't understand."

"I researched the one I was unfamiliar with," General Toad said. "The technical psychiatric terms . . . I know what they mean."

To Addison Doug, Benz said, "Where'd you get all those VW parts, Addi?"

"I don't have them yet," Addison Doug said.

"Probably picked up the first junk he could lay his hands on," Crayne said. "Whatever was available, just before we started back."

"Will start back," Addison Doug corrected.

"Here are my instructions to the three of you," General Toad said. "You are not in any way to attempt to cause damage or implosion or malfunction during reentry, either by lugging back extra mass or by any other method that enters your mind. You are to return as scheduled and in replica of the prior simulations. This especially applies to you, Mr. Doug." The phone by his right arm buzzed. He frowned, picked up the receiver. An interval passed, and then he scowled deeply and set the receiver back down, loudly.

"You've been overruled," Dr. Fein said.

"Yes, I have," General Toad said. "And I must say at this time that I am personally glad because my decision was an unpleasant one."

"Then we can arrange for implosion at reentry," Benz said after a pause.

"The three of you are to make the decision," General Toad said. "Since it involves your lives. It's been entirely left up to you. Whichever way you want it. If you're convinced you're in a closed time loop, and you believe a massive implosion at reentry will abolish it—" He ceased talking, as tempunaut Doug rose to his feet. "Are you going to make another speech, Doug?" he said.

"I just want to thank everyone involved," Addison Doug said. "For letting us decide." He gazed haggard-faced and wearily around at all the individuals seated at the table. "I really appreciate it."

"You know," Benz said slowly, "blowing us up at reentry could add nothing to the chances of abolishing a closed loop. In fact that could do it, Doug."

"Not if it kills us all," Crayne said.

"You agree with Addi?" Benz said.

"Dead is dead," Crayne said. "I've been pondering it. What other way is more likely to get us out of this? Than if we're dead? What possible other way?"

"You may be in no loop," Dr. Fein pointed out.

"But we may be," Crayne said.

Doug, still on his feet, said to Crayne and Benz, "Could we include Merry Lou in our decision-making?"

"Why?" Benz said.

"I can't think too clearly anymore," Doug said. "Merry Lou can help me; I depend on her."

"Sure," Crayne said. Benz, too, nodded.

General Toad examined his wristwatch stoically and said, "Gentlemen, this concludes our discussion."

Soviet chrononaut Gauki removed his headphones and neck mike and hurried toward the three U.S. tempunauts, his hand extended; he was apparently saying something in Russian, but none of them could understand it. They moved away somberly, clustering close.

"In my opinion you're nuts, Addi," Benz said. "But it would appear that I'm the minority now."

"If he *is* right," Crayne said, "if—one chance in a billion—if we are going back again and again forever, that would justify it."

"Could we go see Merry Lou?" Addison Doug said. "Drive over to her place now?"

"She's waiting outside," Crayne said.

Striding up to stand beside the three tempunauts, General Toad said, "You know, what made the determination go the way it did was the public reaction to how you, Doug, looked and behaved during the funeral procession. The NSC advisors came to the conclusion that the public would, like you, rather be certain it's over for all of you. That it's more of a relief to them to know you're free of your mission than to save the project and obtain a perfect reentry. I guess you really made a lasting impression on them, Doug. That whining you did." He walked away, then, leaving the three of them standing there alone.

"Forget him," Crayne said to Addison Doug. "Forget everyone like him. We've got to do what we have to."

"Merry Lou will explain it to me," Doug said. She would know what to do, what would be right.

"I'll go get her," Crayne said, "and after that the four of us can drive somewhere, maybe to her place, and decide what to do. Okay?"

"Thank you," Addison Doug said, nodding; he glanced around for her hopefully, wondering where she was. In the next room, perhaps, somewhere close. "I appreciate that," he said.

Benz and Crayne eyed each other. He saw that, but did not know what it meant. He knew only that he needed someone, Merry Lou most of all, to help him understand what the situation was. And what to finalize on to get them out of it.

Merry Lou drove them north from Los Angeles in the superfast lane of the freeway toward Ventura, and after that inland to Ojai. The four of them said very little. Merry Lou drove well, as always; leaning against her, Addison Doug felt himself relax into a temporary sort of peace.

"There's nothing like having a chick drive you," Crayne said, after many miles had passed in silence.

"It's an aristocratic sensation," Benz murmured. "To have a woman do the driving. Like you're nobility being chauffeured."

Merry Lou said, "Until she runs into something. Some big slow object."

Addison Doug said, "When you saw me trudging up to your place . . . up the redwood round path the other day. What did you think? Tell me honestly."

"You looked," the girl said, "as if you'd done it many times. You looked worn and tired and—ready to die. At the end." She hesitated. "I'm sorry, but that's how you looked, Addi. I thought to myself, he knows the way too well."

"Like I'd done it too many times."

"Yes," she said.

"Then you vote for implosion," Addison Doug said.

"Well—"

"Be honest with me," he said.

Merry Lou said, "Look in the back seat. The box on the floor."

With a flashlight from the glove compartment the three men examined the box. Addison Doug, with fear, saw its contents. VW motor parts, rusty and worn. Still oily.

"I got them from behind a foreign-car garage near my place," Merry Lou said. "On the way to Pasadena. The first junk I saw that seemed as if it'd be heavy enough. I had heard them say on TV at launch time that anything over fifty pounds up to—"

"It'll do it," Addison Doug said. "It did do it."

"So there's no point in going to your place," Crayne said. "It's decided. We might as well head south toward the module. And initiate the procedure for getting out of ETA. And back to reentry." His voice was heavy but evenly pitched. "Thanks for your vote, Miss Hawkins."

She said, "You are all so tired."

"I'm not," Benz said. "I'm mad. Mad as hell."

"At me?" Addison Doug said.

"I don't know," Benz said. "It's just—Hell." He lapsed into brooding silence then. Hunched over, baffled and inert. Withdrawn as far as possible from the others in the car.

At the next freeway junction she turned the car south. A sense of freedom seemed now to fill her, and Addison Doug felt some of the weight, the fatigue, ebbing already.

On the wrist of each of the three men the emergency alert receiver buzzed its warning tone; they all started.

"What's that mean?" Merry Lou said, slowing the car.

"We're to contact General Toad by phone as soon as possible," Crayne said. He pointed. "There's a Standard Station over there; take the next exit, Miss Hawkins. We can phone in from there."

A few minutes later Merry Lou brought her car to a halt beside the outdoor phone booth. "I hope it's not bad news," she said.

"I'll talk first," Doug said, getting out. Bad news, he thought with labored amusement. Like what? He crunched stiffly across to the phone booth, entered, shut the door behind him, dropped in a dime, and dialed the toll-free number.

"Well, do I have news!" General Toad said when the operator had put him on the line. "It's a good thing we got hold of you. Just a minute—I'm going to let Dr. Fein tell you this himself. You're more apt to believe him than me." Several clicks, and then Dr. Fein's reedy, precise, scholarly voice, but intensified by urgency.

"What's the bad news?" Addison Doug said.

"Not bad, necessarily," Dr. Fein said. "I've had computations run since our discussion, and it would appear—by that I mean it is statistically probable but still unverified for a certainty—that you are right, Addison. You are in a closed time loop."

Addison Doug exhaled raggedly. You nowhere autocratic mother, he thought. You probably knew all along.

"However," Dr. Fein said excitedly, stammering a little, "I also calculate—we jointly do, largely through Cal Tech—that the greatest likelihood of maintaining the loop is to implode on reentry. Do you understand, Addison? If you lug all those rusty VW parts back and implode, then your statistical chances of closing the loop forever is greater than if you simply reenter and all goes well."

Addison Doug said nothing.

"In fact, Addi—and this is the severe part that I have to stress—implosion at reentry, especially a massive, calculated one of the sort we seem to see shaping up—do you grasp all this, Addi? Am I getting through to you? For Chrissake, Addi? Virtually *guarantees* the locking in of an absolutely unyielding loop such as you've got in mind. Such as we've all been worried about from the start." A pause. "Addi? Are you there?"

Addison Doug said, "I want to die."

"That's your exhaustion from the loop. God knows how many repetitions there've been already of the three of you—"

"No," he said and started to hang up.

"Let me speak with Benz and Crayne," Dr. Fein said rapidly. "Please, before you go ahead with reentry. Especially Benz; I'd like to speak with him in particular. Please, Addison. For their sake; your almost total exhaustion has—"

He hung up. Left the phone booth, step by step.

As he climbed back into the car, he heard their two alert receivers still buzzing. "General Toad said the automatic call for us would keep your two receivers doing that for a while," he said. And shut the car door after him. "Let's take off."

"Doesn't he want to talk to us?" Benz said.

Addison Doug said, "General Toad wanted to inform us that they have a little something for us. We've been voted a special Congressional Citation for valor or some damn thing like that. A special medal they never voted anyone before. To be awarded posthumously."

"Well, hell—that's about the only way it can be awarded," Crayne said.

Merry Lou, as she started up the engine, began to cry.

"It'll be a relief," Crayne said presently, as they returned bumpily to the freeway, "when it's over."

It won't be long now, Addison Doug's mind declared.

On their wrists the emergency alert receivers continued to put out their combined buzzing.

"They will nibble you to death," Addison Doug said. "The endless wearing down by various bureaucratic voices."

The others in the car turned to gaze at him inquiringly, with uneasiness mixed with perplexity.

"Yeah," Crayne said. "These automatic alerts are really a nuisance." He sounded tired. As tired as I am, Addison Doug thought. And, realizing this, he felt better. It showed how right he was.

Great drops of water struck the windshield; it had now begun to rain. That pleased him too. It reminded him of that most exalted of all experiences within the shortness of his life: the funeral procession moving slowly down Pennsylvania Avenue, the flag-draped caskets. Closing his eyes he leaned back and felt good at last. And heard, all around him once again, the sorrow-bent people. And, in his head, dreamed of the special Congressional Medal. For weariness, he thought. A medal for being tired.

He saw, in his head, himself in other parades too, and in the deaths of many. But really it was one death and one parade. Slow cars moving along the street in Dallas and with Dr. King as well . . . He saw himself return again and again, in his closed cycle of life, to the national mourning that he could not and they could not forget. He would be there; they would always be there; it would always be, and every one of them would return together again and again forever. To the place, the moment, they wanted to be. The event which meant the most to all of them.

This was his gift to them, the people, his country. He had bestowed upon the world a wonderful burden. The dreadful and weary miracle of eternal life.

THE EXIT DOOR LEADS IN

Bob Bibleman had the impression that robots wouldn't look you in the eye. And when one had been in the vicinity small valuable objects disappeared. A robot's idea of order was to stack everything into one pile. Nonetheless, Bibleman had to order lunch from robots, since vending ranked too low on the wage scale to attract humans.

"A hamburger, fries, strawberry shake, and—" Bibleman paused, reading the printout. "Make that a supreme double cheeseburger, fries, a chocolate malt—"

"Wait a minute," the robot said. "I'm already working on the burger. You want to buy into this week's contest while you're waiting?"

"I don't get the royal cheeseburger," Bibleman said.

"That's right."

It was hell living in the twenty-first century. Information transfer had reached the velocity of light. Bibleman's older brother had once fed a ten-word plot outline into a robot fiction machine, changed his mind as to the outcome, and found that the novel was already in print. He had had to program a sequel in order to make his correction.

"What's the prize structure in the contest?" Bibleman asked.

At once the printout posted all the odds, from first prize down to last. Naturally, the robot blanked out the display before Bibleman could read it.

"What is first prize?" Bibleman said.

"I can't tell you that," the robot said. From its slot came a hamburger, french fries, and a strawberry shake. "That'll be one thousand dollars in cash."

"Give me a hint," Bibleman said as he paid.

"It's everywhere and nowhere. It's existed since the seventeenth century. Originally it was invisible. Then it became royal. You can't get it unless you're smart, although cheating helps and so does being rich. What does the word 'heavy' suggest to you?"

"Profound."

"No, the literal meaning."

"Mass." Bibleman pondered. "What is this, a contest to see who can figure out what the prize is? I give up."

"Pay the six dollars," the robot said, "to cover our costs, and you'll receive an—"

"Gravity," Bibleman broke in. "Sir Isaac Newton. The Royal College of England. Am I right?"

"Right," the robot said. "Six dollars entitles you to a chance to go to college—a statistical chance, at the posted odds. What's six dollars? Pratfare."

Bibleman handed over a six-dollar coin.

"You win," the robot said. "You get to go to college. You beat the odds, which were two trillion to one against. Let me be the first to congratulate you. If I had a hand, I'd shake hands with you. This will change your life. This has been your lucky day."

"It's a setup," Bibleman said, feeling a rush of anxiety.

"You're right," the robot said, and it looked Bibleman right in the eye. "It's also mandatory that you accept your prize. The college is a military college located in Buttfuck, Egypt, so to speak. But that's no problem; you'll be taken there. Go home and start packing."

"Can't I eat my hamburger and drink—"

"I'd suggest you start packing right away."

Behind Bibleman a man and woman had lined up; reflexively he got out of their way, trying to hold on to his tray of food, feeling dizzy.

"A charbroiled steak sandwich," the man said, "onion rings, root beer, and that's it."

The robot said, "Care to buy into the contest? Terrific prizes." It flashed the odds on its display panel.

When Bob Bibleman unlocked the door of his one-room apartment, his telephone was on. It was looking for him.

"There you are," the telephone said.

"I'm not going to do it," Bibleman said.

"Sure you are," the phone said. "Do you know who this is? Read over your certificate, your first-prize legal form. You hold the rank of shavetail. I'm Major Casals. You're under my jurisdiction. If I tell you to piss purple, you'll piss purple. How soon can you be on a transplan rocket? Do you have friends you want to say goodbye to? A sweetheart, perhaps? Your mother?"

"Am I coming back?" Bibleman said with anger. "I mean, who are we fighting, this college? For that matter, what college is it? Who is on the faculty? Is it a liberal arts college or does it specialize in the hard sciences? Is it government-sponsored? Does it offer—"

"Just calm down," Major Casals said quietly.

Bibleman seated himself. He discovered that his hands were shaking. To himself he thought, I was born in the wrong century. A hundred years ago this wouldn't have happened and a hundred years from now it will be illegal. What I need is a lawyer.

His life had been a quiet one. He had, over the years, advanced to the modest position of floating-home salesman. For a man twenty-two years old, that wasn't bad. He almost owned his one-room apartment; that is, he rented with an option to buy. It was a small life, as lives went; he did not ask too much and he did not complain—normally—at what he received. Although he did not understand the tax structure that cut through his income, he accepted it; he accepted a modified state of penury the same way he accepted it when a girl would not go to bed with him. In a sense this defined him; this was his measure. He submitted to what he did not like, and he regarded this attitude as a virtue. Most people in authority over him considered him a good person. As to those over whom *he* had authority, that was a class with zero members. His boss at Cloud Nine Homes told him what to do and his customers, really, told him what to do. The government told everyone what to do, or so he assumed. He had very few dealings with the government. That was neither a virtue nor a vice; it was simply good luck.

Once he had experienced vague dreams. They had to do with giving to the poor. In high school he had read Charles Dickens and a vivid idea of the oppressed had fixed itself in his mind to the point where he could see them: all those who did not have a one-room apartment and a job and a high school education. Certain vague place names had floated through his head, gleaned from TV, places like India, where heavy-duty machinery swept up the dying. Once a teaching machine had told him, *You have a good heart.* That amazed him—not that a machine would say so, but that it would say it to him. A girl had told him the same thing. He marveled at this. Vast forces colluding to tell him that he was not a bad person! It was a mystery and a delight.

But those days had passed. He no longer read novels, and the girl had been transferred to Frankfurt. Now he had been set up by a robot, a cheap machine, to shovel shit in the boonies, dragooned by a mechanical scam that was probably pulling citizens off the streets in record numbers. This was not a college he was going to; he had won nothing. He had won a stint at some kind of forced-labor camp, most likely. The exit door leads in, he thought to himself. Which is to say, when they want you they already have you; all they need is the paperwork. And a computer can process the forms at the touch of a key. The H key for hell and the S key for slave, he thought. And the Y key for you.

Don't forget your toothbrush, he thought. You may need it.

On the phone screen Major Casals regarded him, as if silently estimating the chances that Bob Bibleman might bolt. Two trillion to one I will, Bibleman thought. But the one will win, as in the contest; I'll do what I'm told.

"Please," Bibleman said, "let me ask you one thing, and give me an honest answer."

"Of course," Major Casals said.

"If I hadn't gone up to that Earl's Senior robot and—"

"We'd have gotten you anyhow," Major Casals said.

"Okay," Bibleman said, nodding. "Thanks. It makes me feel better. I don't have to tell myself stupid stuff like, If only I hadn't felt like a hamburger and fries. If only—" He broke off. "I'd better pack."

Major Casals said, "We've been running an evaluation on you for several months. You're overly endowed for the kind of work you do. And undereducated. You need more education. You're *entitled* to more education."

Astonished, Bibleman said, "You're talking about it as if it's a genuine college!"

"It is. It's the finest in the system. It isn't advertised; something like this can't be. No one selects it; the college selects you. Those were not joke odds that you saw posted. You can't really imagine being admitted to the finest college in the system by this method, can you, Mr. Bibleman? You have a lot to learn."

"How long will I be at the college?" Bibleman said.

Major Casals said, "Until you have learned."

They gave him a physical, a haircut, a uniform, and a place to bunk down, and many psychological tests. Bibleman suspected that the true purpose of the tests was to determine if he were a latent homosexual, and then he suspected that his suspicions indicated that he *was* a latent homosexual, so he abandoned the suspicions and supposed instead that they were sly intelligence and aptitude tests, and he informed himself that he was showing both: intelligence and aptitude. He also informed himself that he looked great in his uniform, even though it was the same uniform that everyone else wore. That is why they call it a uniform, he reminded himself as he sat on the edge of his bunk reading his orientation pamphlets.

The first pamphlet pointed out that it was a great honor to be admitted to the College. That was its name—the one word. How strange, he thought, puzzled. It's like naming your cat Cat and your dog Dog. This is my mother, Mrs. Mother, and my father, Mr. Father. Are these people working right? he wondered. It had been a phobia of his for years that someday he would fall into the hands of madmen—in particular, madmen who seemed sane up until the last moment. To Bibleman this was the essence of horror.

As he sat scrutinizing the pamphlets, a red-haired girl, wearing the College uniform, came over and seated herself beside him. She seemed perplexed.

"Maybe you can help me," she said. "What is a syllabus? It says here that we'll be given a syllabus. This place is screwing up my head."

Bibleman said, "We've been dragooned off the streets to shovel shit."

"You think so?"

"I know so."

"Can't we just leave?"

"You leave first," Bibleman said. "And I'll wait and see what happens to you."

The girl laughed. "I guess you don't know what a syllabus is."

"Sure I do. It's an abstract of courses or topics."

"Yes, and pigs can whistle."

He regarded her. The girl regarded him.

"We're going to be here forever," the girl said.

Her name, she told him, was Mary Lorne. She was, he decided, pretty, wistful, afraid, and putting up a good front. Together they joined the other new students for a showing of a recent Herbie the Hyena cartoon which Bibleman had seen; it was the episode in which Herbie attempted to assassinate the Russian monk Rasputin. In his usual fashion, Herbie the Hyena poisoned his victim, shot him, blew him up six times, stabbed him, tied him up with chains and sank him in the Volga, tore him apart with wild horses, and finally shot him to the moon strapped to a rocket. The cartoon bored Bibleman. He did not give a damn about Herbie the Hyena or Russian history and he wondered if this was a sample of the College's level of pedagogy. He could imagine Herbie the Hyena illustrating Heisenberg's indeterminacy principle. Herbie—in Bibleman's mind—chased after by a subatomic particle fruitlessly, the particle bobbing up at random here and there . . . Herbie making wild swings at it with a hammer; then a whole flock of subatomic particles jeering at Herbie, who was doomed as always to fuck up.

"What are you thinking about?" Mary whispered to him.

The cartoon ended; the hall lights came on. There stood Major Casals on the stage, larger than on the phone. The fun is over, Bibleman said to himself. He could not imagine Major Casals chasing subatomic particles fruitlessly with wild swings of a sledgehammer. He felt himself grow cold and grim and a little afraid.

The lecture had to do with classified information. Behind Major Casals a giant hologram lit up with a schematic diagram of a homeostatic drilling rig. Within the hologram the rig rotated so that they could see it from all angles. Different stages of the rig's interior glowed in various colors.

"I asked what you were thinking," Mary whispered.

"We have to listen," Bibleman said quietly.

Mary said, equally quietly, "It finds titanium ore on its own. Big deal. Titanium is the ninth most abundant element in the crust of the planet. I'd be impressed if it could seek out and mine pure wurtzite, which is found only at Potosi, Bolivia; Butte, Montana; and Goldfield, Nevada."

"Why is that?" Bibleman said.

"Because," Mary said, "wurtzite is unstable at temperatures below one thousand degrees centigrade. And further—" She broke off. Major Casals had ceased talking and was looking at her.

"Would you repeat that for all of us, young woman?" Major Casals said.

Standing, Mary said, "Wurtzite is unstable at temperatures below one thousand degrees centigrade." Her voice was steady.

Immediately the hologram behind Major Casals switched to a readout of data on zinc-sulfide minerals.

"I don't see 'wurtzite' listed," Major Casals said.

"It's given on the chart in its inverted form," Mary said, her arms folded. "Which is sphalerite. Correctly, it is ZnS, of the sulfide group of the AX type. It's related to greenockite."

"Sit down," Major Casals said. The readout within the hologram now showed the characteristics of greenockite.

As she seated herself, Mary said, "I'm right. They don't have a homeostatic drilling rig for wurtzite because there is no—"

"Your name is?" Major Casals said, pen and pad poised.

"Mary Wurtz." Her voice was totally without emotion. "My father was Charles-Adolphe Wurtz."

"The discoverer of wurtzite?" Major Casals said uncertainly; his pen wavered.

"That's right," Mary said. Turning toward Bibleman, she winked.

"Thank you for the information," Major Casals said. He made a motion and the hologram now showed a flying buttress and, in comparison to it, a normal buttress.

"My point," Major Casals said, "is simply that certain information such as architectural principles of long-standing—"

"Most architectural principles are long-standing," Mary said.

Major Casals paused.

"Otherwise they'd serve no purpose," Mary said.

"Why not?" Major Casals said, and then he colored.

Several uniformed students laughed.

"Information of that type," Major Casals continued, "is not classified.

But a good deal of what you will be learning is classified. This is why the college is under military charter. To reveal or transmit or make public classified information given you during your schooling here falls under the jurisdiction of the military. For a breach of these statutes you would be tried by a military tribunal."

The students murmured. To himself Bibleman thought, Banged, ganged, and then some. No one spoke. Even the girl beside him was silent. A complicated expression had crossed her face, however; a deeply introverted look, somber and—he thought—unusually mature. It made her seem older, no longer a girl. It made him wonder just how old she really was. It was as if in her features a thousand years had surfaced before him as he scrutinized her and pondered the officer on the stage and the great information hologram behind him. What is she thinking? he wondered. Is she going to say something more? How can she not be afraid to speak up? We've been told we are under military law.

Major Casals said, "I am going to give you an instance of a strictly classified cluster of data. It deals with the Panther Engine." Behind him the hologram, surprisingly, became blank.

"Sir," one of the students said, "the hologram isn't showing anything."

"This is not an area that will be dealt with in your studies here," Major Casals said. "The Panther Engine is a two-rotor system, opposed rotors serving a common main shaft. Its main advantage is a total lack of centrifugal torque in the housing. A cam chain is thrown between the opposed rotors, which permits the main shaft to reverse itself without hysteresis."

Behind him the big hologram remained blank. Strange, Bibleman thought. An eerie sensation: information without information, as if the computer had gone blind.

Major Casals said, "The College is forbidden to release any information about the Panther Engine. It cannot be programmed to do otherwise. In fact, it knows nothing about the Panther Engine; it is programmed to destroy any information it receives in that sector."

Raising his hand, a student said, "So even if someone fed information into the College about the Panther—"

"It would eject the data," Major Casals said.

"Is this a unique situation?" another student asked.

"No," Major Casals said.

"Then there're a number of areas we can't get printouts for," a student murmured.

"Nothing of importance," Major Casals said. "At least as far as your studies are concerned."

The students were silent.

"The subjects which you will study," Major Casals said, "will be assigned to you, based on your aptitude and personality profiles. I'll call off your names and you will come forward for your allocation of topic assignment. The College itself has made the final decision for each of you, so you can be sure no error has been made."

What if I get proctology? Bibleman asked himself. In panic he thought, Or podiatry. Or herpetology. Or suppose the College in its infinite computeroid wisdom decides to ram into me all the information in the universe pertaining to or resembling herpes labialis . . . or things even worse. If there is anything worse.

"What you want," Mary said, as the names were read alphabetically, "is a program that'll earn you a living. You have to be practical. I know what I'll get; I know where my strong point lies. It'll be chemistry."

His name was called; rising, he walked up the aisle to Major Casals. They looked at each other, and then Casals handed him an unsealed envelope.

Stiffly, Bibleman returned to his seat.

"You want me to open it?" Mary said.

Wordlessly, Bibleman passed the envelope to her. She opened it and studied the printout.

"Can I earn a living with it?" he said.

She smiled. "Yes, it's a high-paying field. Almost as good as—well, let's just say that the colony planets are really in need of this. You could go to work anywhere."

Looking over her shoulder, he saw the words on the page.

COSMOLOGY COSMOGONY PRE-SOCRATICS

"Pre-Socratic philosophy," Mary said. "Almost as good as structural engineering." She passed him the paper. "I shouldn't kid you. No, it's not really something you can making a living at, unless you teach . . . but maybe it interests you. Does it interest you?"

"No," he said shortly.

"I wonder why the college picked it, then," Mary said.

"What the hell," he said, "is cosmogony?"

"How the universe came into being. Aren't you interested in how the universe—" She paused, eyeing him. "You certainly won't be asking for printouts of any classified material," she said meditatively. "Maybe that's it," she murmured, to herself. "They won't have to watchdog you."

"I can be trusted with classified material," he said.

"Can you? Do you know yourself? But you'll be getting into that when the College bombards you with early Greek thought. 'Know thyself.' Apollo's motto at Delphi. It sums up half of Greek philosophy."

Bibleman said, "I'm not going up before a military tribunal for making public classified military material." He thought, then, about the Panther Engine and he realized, fully realized, that a really grim message had been spelled out in that little lecture by Major Casals. "I wonder what Herbie the Hyena's motto is," he said.

" 'I am determined to prove a villain,' " Mary said. " 'And hate the idle pleasures of these days. Plots have I laid.' " She reached out to touch him on the arm. "Remember? The Herbie the Hyena cartoon version of *Richard the Third*."

"Mary Lorne," Major Casals said, reading off the list.

"Excuse me." She went up, returned with her envelope, smiling. "Leprology," she said to Bibleman. "The study and treatment of leprosy. I'm kidding; it's chemistry."

"You'll be studying classified material," Bibleman said.

"Yes," she said. "I know."

On the first day of his study program, Bob Bibleman set his College input-output terminal on AUDIO and punched the proper key for his coded course.

"Thales of Miletus," the terminal said. "The founder of the Ionian school of natural philosophy."

"What did he teach?" Bibleman said.

"That the world floated on water, was sustained by water, and originated in water."

"That's really stupid," Bibleman said.

The College terminal said, "Thales based this on the discovery of fossil fish far inland, even at high altitudes. So it is not as stupid as it sounds." It showed on its holoscreen a great deal of written information, no part of which struck Bibleman as very interesting. Anyhow, he had requested AUDIO. "It is generally considered that Thales was the first rational man in history," the terminal said.

"What about Ikhnaton?" Bibleman said.

"He was strange."

"Moses?"

"Likewise strange."

"Hammurabi?"

"How do you spell that?"

"I'm not sure. I've just heard the name."

"Then we will discuss Anaximander," the College terminal said. "And, in a cursory initial survey, Anaximenes, Xenophanes, Paramenides, Melissus—wait a minute; I forgot Heraclitus and Cratylus. And we will study Empedocles, Anaxagoras, Zeno—"

"Christ," Bibleman said.

"That's another program," the College terminal said.

"Just continue," Bibleman said.

"Are you taking notes?"

"That's none of your business."

"You seem to be in a state of conflict."

Bibleman said, "What happens to me if I flunk out of the College?"

"You go to jail."

"I'll take notes."

"Since you are so driven—"

"What?"

"Since you are so full of conflict, you should find Empedocles interesting. He was the first dialectical philosopher. Empedocles believed that the basis of reality was an antithetical conflict between the forces of Love and Strife. Under Love the whole cosmos is a duly proportioned mixture, called a *krasis*. This *krasis* is a spherical deity, a single perfect mind which spends all its time—"

"Is there any practical application to any of this?" Bibleman interrupted.

"The two antithetical forces of Love and Strife resemble the Taoist elements of Yang and Yin with their perpetual interaction from which all change takes place."

"Practical application."

"Twin mutually opposed constituents." On the holoscreen a schematic diagram, very complex, formed. "The two-rotor Panther Engine."

"What?" Bibleman said, sitting upright in his seat. He made out the large words PANTHER HYDRODRIVE SYSTEM TOP SECRET above the schematic comprising the readout. Instantly he pressed the PRINT key; the machinery of the terminal whirred and three sheets of paper slid down into the RETRIEVE slot.

They overlooked it, Bibleman realized, this entry in the College's memory banks relating to the Panther Engine. Somehow the cross-referencing got lost. No one thought of pre-Socratic philosophy—who would expect an entry on an engine, a modern-day top-secret engine, under the category PHILOSOPHY, PRE-SOCRATIC, subheading EMPEDOCLES?

I've got it in my hands, he said to himself as he swiftly lifted out the three sheets of paper. He folded them up and stuck them into the notebook the College had provided.

I've hit it, he thought. Right off the bat. Where the hell am I going to put these schematics? Can't hide them in my locker. And then he thought, Have I committed a crime already, by asking for a written printout?

"Empedocles," the terminal was saying, "believed in four elements as being perpetually rearranged: earth, water, air, and fire. These elements eternally—"

Click. Bibleman had shut the terminal down. The holoscreen faded to opaque gray.

Too much learning doth make a man slow, he thought as he got to his feet and started from the cubicle. Fast of wit but slow of foot. Where the hell am I going to hide the schematics? he asked himself again as he walked rapidly down the hall toward the ascent tube. Well, he realized, they don't know I have them; I can take my time. The thing to do is hide them at a random place, he decided, as the tube carried him to the surface. And even if they find them they won't be able to trace them back to me, not unless they go to the trouble of dusting for fingerprints.

This could be worth billions of dollars, he said to himself. A great joy filled him and then came the fear. He discovered that he was trembling. Will they ever be pissed, he said to himself. When they find out, *I* won't be pissing purple, *they'll* be pissing purple. The College itself will, when it discovers its error.

And the error, he thought, is on its part, not mine. The College fucked up and that's too bad.

In the dorm where his bunk was located, he found a laundry room maintained by a silent robot staff, and when no robot was watching he hid the three pages of schematics near the bottom of a huge pile of bedsheets. As high as the ceiling, this pile. They won't get down to the schematics this year. I have plenty of time to decide what to do.

Looking at his watch, he saw that the afternoon had almost come to an end. At five o'clock he would be seated in the cafeteria, eating dinner with Mary.

She met him a little after five o'clock; her face showed signs of fatigue.

"How'd it go?" she asked him as they stood in line with their trays.

"Fine," Bibleman said.

"Did you get to Zeno? I always like Zeno; he proved that motion is impossible. So I guess I'm still in my mother's womb. You look strange." She eyed him.

"Just sick of listening to how the earth rests on the back of a giant turtle."

"Or is suspended on a long string," Mary said. Together they made their way among the other students to an empty table. "You're not eating much."

"Feeling like eating," Bibleman said as he drank his cup of coffee, "is what got me here in the first place."

"You could flunk out."

"And go to jail."

Mary said, "The College is programmed to say that. Much of it is probably just threats. Talk loudly and carry a small stick, so to speak."

"I have it," Bibleman said.

"You have what?" She ceased eating and regarded him.

He said, "The Panther Engine."

Gazing at him, the girl was silent.

"The schematics," he said.

"Lower your goddam voice."

"They missed a citation in the memory storage. Now that I have them I don't know what to do. Just start walking, probably. And hope no one stops me."

"They don't know? The College didn't self-monitor?"

"I have no reason to think it's aware of what it did."

"Jesus Christ," Mary said softly. "On your first day. You had better do a lot of slow, careful thinking."

"I can destroy them," he said.

"Or sell them."

He said, "I looked them over. There's an analysis on the final page. The Panther—"

"Just say *it*," Mary said.

"It can be used as a hydroelectric turbine and cut costs in half. I couldn't understand the technical language, but I did figure out that. Cheap power source. Very cheap."

"So everyone would benefit."

He nodded.

"They really screwed up," Mary said. "What was it Casals told us? 'Even if someone fed data into the College about the—about it, the College would eject the data.'" She began eating slowly, meditatively. "And they're withholding it from the public. It must be industry pressure. Nice."

"What should I do?" Bibleman said.

"I can't tell you that."

"What I was thinking is that I could take the schematics to one of the colony planets where the authorities have less control. I could find an independent firm and make a deal with them. The government wouldn't know how—"

"They'd figure out where the schematics came from," Mary said. "They'd trace it back to you."

"Then I better burn them."

Mary said, "You have a very difficult decision to make. On the one hand, you have classified information in your possession which you obtained illegally. On the other—"

"I didn't obtain it illegally. The College screwed up."

Calmly, she continued, "You broke the law, military law, when you asked for a written transcript. You should have reported the breach of security as soon as you discovered it. They would have rewarded you. Major Casals would have said nice things to you."

"I'm scared," Bibleman said, and he felt the fear moving around inside him, shifting about and growing; as he held his plastic coffee cup it shook, and some of the coffee spilled onto his uniform.

Mary, with a paper napkin, dabbed at the coffee stain.

"It won't come off," she said.

"Symbolism," Bibleman said. "Lady Macbeth. I always wanted to have a dog named Spot so I could say, 'Out, out, damned Spot.'"

"I am not going to tell you what to do," Mary said. "This is a decision that you will make alone. It isn't ethical for you even to discuss it with me; that could be considered conspiracy and put us both in prison."

"Prison," he echoed.

"You have it within your—Christ, I was going to say, 'You have it within your power to provide a cheap power source to human civilization.'" She laughed and shook her head. "I guess this scares me, too. Do what you think is right. If you think it's right to publish the schematics—"

"I never thought of that. Just publish them. Some magazine or newspaper. A slave printing construct could print it and distribute it all over the solar system in fifteen minutes." All I have to do, he realized, is pay the fee and then feed in the three pages of schematics. As simple as that. And then spend the rest of my life in jail or anyhow in court. Maybe the adjudication would go in my favor. There are precedents in history where vital classified material—military classified material—was stolen and published, and not only was the person found innocent but we now realize that he was a hero; he served the welfare of the human race itself, and risked his life.

Approaching their table, two armed military security guards closed in on Bob Bibleman; he stared at them, not believing what he saw but think-ing, *Believe it.*

"Student Bibleman?" one of them said.

"It's on my uniform," Bibleman said.

"Hold out your hands, Student Bibleman." The larger of the two secu-rity guards snapped handcuffs on him.

Mary said nothing; she continued slowly eating.

In Major Casals's office Bibleman waited, grasping the fact that he was being—as the technical term had it—"detained." He felt glum. He won-dered what they would do. He wondered if he had been set up. He won-dered what he would do if he were charged. He wondered why it was taking so long. And then he wondered what it was all about really and he won-dered whether he would understand the grand issues if he continued with his courses in COSMOLOGY COSMOGONY PRE-SOCRATICS.

Entering the office, Major Casals said briskly, "Sorry to keep you waiting."

"Can these handcuffs be removed?" Bibleman said. They hurt his wrists; they had been clapped on to him as tightly as possible. His bone structure ached.

"We couldn't find the schematics," Casals said, seating himself behind his desk.

"What schematics?"

"For the Panther Engine."

"There aren't supposed to be any schematics for the Panther Engine. You told us that in orientation."

"Did you program your terminal for that deliberately? Or did it just happen to come up?"

"My terminal programmed itself to talk about water," Bibleman said. "The universe is composed of water."

"It automatically notified security when you asked for a written tran-script. All written transcripts are monitored."

"Fuck you," Bibleman said.

Major Casals said, "I tell you what. We're only interested in getting the schematics back; we're not interested in putting you in the slam. Return them and you won't be tried."

"Return what?" Bibleman said, but he knew it was a waste of time. "Can I think it over?"

"Yes."

"Can I go? I feel like going to sleep. I'm tired. I feel like having these cuffs off."

Removing the cuffs, Major Casals said, "We made an agreement, with all of you, an agreement between the College and the students, about classified material. You entered into that agreement."

"Freely?" Bibleman said.

"Well, no. But the agreement was known to you. When you discovered the schematics for the Panther Engine encoded in the College's memory and available to anyone who happened for any reason, any reason whatsoever, to ask for a practical application of pre-Socratic—"

"I was as surprised as hell," Bibleman said. "I still am."

"Loyalty is an ethical principle. I'll tell you what; I'll waive the punishment factor and put it on the basis of loyalty to the College. A responsible person obeys laws and agreements entered into. Return the schematics and you can continue your courses here at the College. In fact, we'll give you permission to select what subjects you want; they won't be assigned to you. I think you're good college material. Think it over and report back to me tomorrow morning, between eight and nine, here in my office. Don't talk to anyone; don't try to discuss it. You'll be watched. Don't try to leave the grounds. Okay?"

"Okay," Bibleman said woodenly.

He dreamed that night that he had died. In his dream vast spaces stretched out, and his father was coming toward him, very slowly, out of a dark glade and into the sunlight. His father seemed glad to see him, and Bibleman felt his father's love.

When he awoke, the feeling of being loved by his father remained. As he put on his uniform, he thought about his father and how rarely, in actual life, he had gotten that love. It made him feel lonely, now, his father being dead and his mother as well. Killed in a nuclear-power accident, along with a whole lot of other people.

They say someone important to you waits for you on the other side, he thought. Maybe by the time I die Major Casals will be dead and he will be waiting for me, to greet me gladly. Major Casals and my father combined as one.

What am I going to do? he asked himself. They have waived the punitive aspects; it's reduced to essentials, a matter of loyalty. Am I a loyal person? Do I qualify?

The hell with it, he said to himself. He looked at his watch. Eight-thirty. My father would be proud of me, he thought. For what I am going to do.

Going into the laundry room, he scoped out the situation. No robots in sight. He dug down in the pile of bedsheets, found the pages of schematics, took them out, looked them over, and headed for the tube that would take him to Major Casals's office.

"You have them," Casals said as Bibleman entered. Bibleman handed the three sheets of paper over to him.

"And you made no other copies?" Casals asked.

"No."

"You give me your word of honor?"

"Yes," Bibleman said.

"You are herewith expelled from the College," Major Casals said.

"What?" Bibleman said.

Casals pressed a button on his desk. "Come in."

The door opened and Mary Lorne stood there.

"I do not represent the College," Major Casals said to Bibleman. "You were set up."

"I am the College," Mary said.

Major Casals said, "Sit down, Bibleman. She will explain it to you before you leave."

"I failed?" Bibleman said.

"You failed me," Mary said. "The purpose of the test was to teach you to stand on your own feet, even if it meant challenging authority. The covert message of institutions is: 'Submit to that which you psychologically construe as an authority.' A good school trains the whole person; it isn't a matter of data and information; I was trying to make you morally and psychologically complete. But a person can't be commanded to disobey. You can't order someone to rebel. All I could do was give you a model, an example."

Bibleman thought, When she talked back to Casals at the initial orientation. He felt numb.

"The Panther Engine is worthless," Mary said, "as a technological artifact. This is a standard test we use on each student, no matter what study course he is assigned."

"They *all* got a readout on the Panther Engine?" Bibleman said with disbelief. He stared at the girl.

"They will, one by one. Yours came very quickly. First you are told that it is classified; you are told the penalty for releasing classified information; then you are leaked the information. It is hoped that you will make it public or at least try to make it public."

Major Casals said, "You saw on the third page of the printout that the engine supplied an economical source of hydroelectric power. That was important. You knew that the public would benefit if the engine design was released."

"And legal penalties were waived," Mary said. "So what you did was not done out of fear."

"Loyalty," Bibleman said. "I did it out of loyalty."

"To what?" Mary said.

He was silent; he could not think.

"To a holoscreen?" Major Casals said.

"To you," Bibleman said.

Major Casals said, "I am someone who insulted you and derided you. Someone who treated you like dirt. I told you that if I ordered you to piss purple, you—"

"Okay," Bibleman said. "Enough."

"Goodbye," Mary said.

"What?" Bibleman said, startled.

"You're leaving. You're going back to your life and job, what you had before we picked you."

Bibleman said, "I'd like another chance."

"But," Mary said, "you know how the test works now. So it can never be given to you again. You know what is really wanted from you by the College. I'm sorry."

"I'm sorry, too," Major Casals said.

Bibleman said nothing.

Holding out her hand, Mary said, "Shake?"

Blindly, Bibleman shook hands with her. Major Casals only stared at him blankly; he did not offer his hand. He seemed to be engrossed in some other topic, perhaps some other person. Another student was on his mind, perhaps. Bibleman could not tell.

Three nights later, as he wandered aimlessly through the mixture of lights and darkness of the city, Bob Bibleman saw ahead of him a robot food vendor at its eternal post. A teenage boy was in the process of buying a taco and an apple turnover. Bob Bibleman lined up behind the boy and stood waiting, his hands in his pockets, no thoughts coming to him, only a dull feeling, a sense of emptiness. As if the inattention which he had seen on Casals's face had taken him over, he thought to himself. He felt like an object, an object among objects, like the robot vendor. Something which, as he well knew, did not look you directly in the eye.

"What'll it be, sir?" the robot asked.

Bibleman said, "Fries, a cheeseburger, and a strawberry shake. Are there any contests?"

After a pause the robot said, "Not for you, Mr. Bibleman."

"Okay," he said, and stood waiting.

The food came, on its little throwaway plastic tray, in its little throwaway cartons.

"I'm not paying," Bibleman said, and walked away.

The robot called after him, "Eleven hundred dollars. Mr. Bibleman. You're breaking the law!"

He turned, got out his wallet.

"Thank you, Mr. Bibleman," the robot said. "I am very proud of you."

RAUTAVAARA'S CASE

The three technicians of the floating globe monitored fluctuations in interstellar magnetic fields, and they did a good job up until the moment they died.

Basalt fragments, traveling at enormous velocity in relation to their globe, ruptured their barrier and abolished their air supply. The two males were slow to react and did nothing. The young female technician from Finland, Agneta Rautavaara, managed to get her emergency helmet on in time, but the hoses tangled; she aspirated and died: a melancholy death, strangling on her own vomit. Herewith ended the survey task of EX208, their floating globe. In another month, the technicians would have been relieved and returned to Earth.

We could not get there in time to save the three Earth persons, but we did dispatch a robot to see if any of them could be regenerated from death. Earth persons do not like us, but in this case their survey globe was operating in our vicinity. There are rules governing such emergencies that are binding on all races in the galaxy. We had no desire to help Earth persons, but we obey the rules.

The rules called for an attempt on our part to restore life to the three dead technicians, but we allowed a robot to take on the responsibility, and perhaps there we erred. Also, the rules required us to notify the closest Earthship of the calamity and we chose not to. I will not defend this omission nor analyze our reasoning at the time.

The robot signaled that it had found no brain function in the two males and that their neural tissue had degenerated. Regarding Agneta Rautavaara, a slight brain wave could be detected. So in Rautavaara's case the robot would begin a restoration attempt. However, since it could not make a judgment decision on its own, it contacted us. We told it to make the attempt. The fault—the guilt, so to speak—therefore lies with us. Had we been on the scene, we would have known better. We accept the blame.

An hour later the robot signaled that it had restored significant brain function in Rautavaara by supplying her brain with oxygen-rich blood from her dead body. The oxygen, but not the nutriments, came from the robot. We instructed it to begin synthesis of nutriments by processing Rautavaara's body, by using it as raw material. This is the point at which the Earth authorities later made their most profound objection. But we did not have any other source of nutriments. Since we ourselves are a plasma we could not offer our own bodies.

The objection that we could have used the bodies of Rautavaara's dead companions was not phrased properly when we introduced it as evidence. Briefly, we felt that, based on the robot's reports, the other bodies were too contaminated by radioactivity and hence were toxic to Rautavaara; nutriments derived from that source would soon poison her brain. If you do not accept our logic, it does not matter to us; this was the situation as we construed it from our remote point. This is why I say our real error lay in sending a robot in rather than going ourselves. If you wish to indict us, indict us for that.

We asked the robot to patch into Rautavaara's brain and transmit her thoughts to us, so that we could assess the physical condition of her neural cells.

The impression that we received was sanguine. It was at this point that we notified the Earth authorities. We informed them of the accident that had destroyed EX208; we informed them that two of the technicians, the males, were irretrievably dead; we informed them that through swift efforts on our part we had the one female showing stable cephalic activity, which is to say, we had her brain alive.

"Her *what*?" the Earth person radio operator said, in response to our call.

"We are supplying her nutriments derived from her body—"

"Oh Christ," the Earth person radio operator said. "You can't feed her brain that way. What good is a brain qua brain?"

"It can think," we said.

"All right; we'll take over now," the Earth person radio operator said. "But there will be an inquiry."

"Was it not right to save her brain?" we asked. "After all, the psyche is located in the brain, the personality. The physical body is a device by which the brain relates to—"

"Give me the location of EX208," the Earth person radio operator said. "We'll send a ship there at once. You should have notified us at once before trying your own rescue efforts. You Approximations simply do not understand somatic life-forms."

It is offensive to us to hear the term "Approximations." It is an Earth slur regarding our origin in the Proxima Centaurus System. What it implies is that we are not authentic, that we merely simulate life.

This was our reward in the Rautavaara Case. To be derided. And, indeed, there was an inquiry.

Within the depths of her damaged brain, Agneta Rautavaara tasted acid vomit and recoiled in fear and aversion. All around her, EX208 lay in splinters. She could see Travis and Elms; they had been torn to bloody bits and the blood had frozen. Ice covered the interior of the globe. Air gone, temperature gone . . . what's keeping me alive? she wondered. She put her hands up and touched her face—or rather tried to touch her face. My helmet, she thought. I got it on in time.

The ice, which covered everything, began to melt. The severed arms and legs of her two companions rejoined their bodies. Basalt fragments, embedded in the hull of the globe, withdrew and flew away.

Time, Agneta realized, is running backward. How strange!

Air returned; she heard the dull tone of the indicator horn. And then, slowly, temperature. Travis and Elms, groggily, got to their feet. They stared around them, bewildered. She felt like laughing, but it was too grim for that. Apparently the force of the impact had caused a local time perturbation.

"Both of you sit down," she said.

Travis said thickly, "I—okay; you're right." He seated himself at his console and pressed the button that strapped him securely in place. Elms, however, just stood.

"We were hit by rather large particles," Agneta said.

"Yes," Elms said.

"Large enough and with enough impact to perturb time," Agneta said. "So we've gone back to before the event."

"Well, the magnetic fields are partly responsible," Travis said. He rubbed his eyes; his hands shook. "Get your helmet off, Agneta. You don't need it."

"But the impact is coming," she said.

Both men glanced at her.

"We'll repeat the accident," she said.

"Shit," Travis said, "I'll take the EX out of here." He pushed many keys on his console. "It'll miss us."

Agneta removed her helmet. She stepped out of her boots, picked them up . . . and then saw the Figure.

The Figure stood behind the three of them. It was Christ.

"Look," she said to Travis and Elms.

Both men looked.

The Figure wore a traditional white robe, sandals; his hair was long and pale with what looked like moonlight. Bearded, his face was gentle and wise. Just like in the holo-ads the churches back home put out, Agneta thought. Robed, bearded, wise and gentle and his arms slightly raised. Even the nimbus is there. How odd that our preconceptions were so accurate.

"Oh my God," Travis said. Both men stared and she stared, too. "He's come for us."

"Well, it's fine with me," Elms said.

"Sure, it would be fine with you," Travis said bitterly. "You have no wife and children. And what about Agneta? She's only three hundred years old; she's a baby."

Christ said, "I am the vine, you are the branches. Whoever remains in me, with me in him, bears fruit in plenty; for cut off from me, you can do nothing."

"I'm getting the EX out of this vector," Travis said.

"My little children," Christ said, "I shall not be with you much longer."

"Good," Travis said. The EX was now moving at peak velocity in the direction of the Sirius axis; their star chart showed massive flux.

"Damn you, Travis," Elms said savagely. "This is a great opportunity. I mean, how many people have seen Christ? I mean, it *is* Christ. You are Christ, aren't you?" he asked the Figure.

Christ said, "I am the Way, the Truth, and the Life. No one can come to the Father except through me. If you know me, you know my Father too. From this moment, you know him and have seen him."

"There," Elms said, his face showing happiness. "See? I want it known that I am very glad of this occasion, Mr.—" He broke off. "I was going to say, 'Mr. Christ.' That's stupid; that is really stupid. Christ, Mr. Christ, will you sit down? You can sit at my console or at Ms. Rautavaara's. Isn't that right, Agneta? This here is Walter Travis; he's not a Christian, but I am; I've been a Christian all my life. Well, most of my life. I'm not sure about Ms. Rautavaara. What do you say, Agneta?"

"Stop the babbling, Elms," Travis said.

To him, Elms said, "He's going to judge us."

Christ said, "If anyone hears my words and does not keep them faithfully, it is not I who shall condemn him, since I have come not to condemn the world but to save the world; he who rejects me and refuses my words has his judge already."

"There," Elms said, nodding.

Frightened, Agneta said to the Figure, "Go easy on us. The three of us have been through a major trauma." She wondered, suddenly, if Travis and Elms remembered that they had been killed, that their bodies had been destroyed.

The Figure smiled at her, as if to reassure her.

"Travis," Agneta said, bending down over him as he sat at his console, "I want you to listen to me. Neither you nor Elms survived the accident, survived the basalt particles. That's why he's here. I'm the only one who wasn't—" She hesitated.

"Killed," Elms said. "We're dead and he has come for us." To the Figure, he said, "I'm ready, Lord. Take me."

"Take both of them," Travis said. "I'm sending out a radio H.E.L.P. call. And I'm telling them what's taking place here. I'm going to report it before he takes me or tries to take me."

"You're *dead*," Elms told him.

"I can still file a radio report," Travis said, but his face showed his dismay. And his resignation.

To the Figure, Agneta said, "Give Travis a little time. He doesn't fully understand. But I guess you know that; you know everything."

The Figure nodded.

We and the Earth Board of Inquiry listened to and watched this activity in Rautavaara's brain, and we realized jointly what had happened. But we did not agree on our evaluation of it. Whereas the six Earth persons saw it as pernicious, we saw it as grand—both for Agneta Rautavaara and for us. By means of her damaged brain, restored by an ill-advised robot, we were in touch with the next world and the powers that ruled it.

The Earth persons' view distressed us.

"She's hallucinating," the spokesperson of the Earth people said. "Since she has no sensory data coming. Since her body is dead. Look what you've done to her."

We made the point that Agneta Rautavaara was happy.

"What we must do," the human spokesperson said, "is shut down her brain."

"And cut us off from the next world?" we objected. "This is a splendid opportunity to view the afterlife. Agneta Rautavaara's brain is our lens. This is a matter of gravity. The scientific merit outweighs the humanitarian."

This was the position we took at the inquiry. It was a position of sincerity, not of expedience.

The Earth persons decided to keep Rautavaara's brain at full function, with both video and audio transduction, which of course was recorded; meanwhile the matter of censuring us was put in suspension.

I personally found myself fascinated by the Earth idea of the Savior. It was, for us, an antique and quaint conception; not because it was anthropomorphic but because it involved a schoolroom adjudication of the departed soul. Some kind of tote board was involved listing good and bad acts: a transcendent report card, such as one finds employed in the teaching and grading of children.

This, to us, was a primitive conception of the Savior, and as I watched and listened—as we watched and listened as a polyencephalic entity—I wondered what Agneta Rautavaara's reaction would have been to a Savior, a Guide of the Soul, based on *our* expectations. Her brain, after all, was maintained by our equipment, by the original mechanism that our rescue robot had brought to the scene of the accident. It would have been too risky to disconnect it; too much brain damage had occurred already. The total apparatus, involving her brain, had been transferred to the site of the judicial inquiry, a neutral ark located between the Proxima System and the Sol System.

Later, in discreet discussion with my companions, I suggested that we attempt to infuse our own conception of the Afterlife Guide of the Soul into Rautavaara's artificially sustained brain. My point: It would be interesting to see how she reacted.

At once my companions pointed out to me the contradiction in my logic. I had argued at the inquiry that Rautavaara's brain was a window on the next world and hence justified—which exculpated us. Now I argued that what she experienced was a projection of her own mental presuppositions, nothing more.

"Both propositions are true," I said. "It is a genuine window on the next world and it is a presentation of Rautavaara's own cultural racial propensities."

What we had, in essence, was a model into which we could introduce carefully selected variables. We could introduce into Rautavaara's brain our own conception of the Guide of the Soul, and thereby see how our rendition differed practically from the puerile one of the Earth persons'.

This was a novel opportunity to test our own theology. In our opinion, the Earth persons' had been tested sufficiently and been found wanting.

We decided to perform the act, since we maintained the gear supporting Rautavaara's brain. To us, this was a much more interesting issue than the outcome of the inquiry. Blame is a mere cultural matter; it does not travel across species boundaries.

I suppose the Earth persons could regard our intentions as malign. I deny that; *we* deny that. Call it, instead, a game. It would provide us aesthetic enjoyment to witness Rautavaara confronted by *our* Savior, rather than hers.

———

To Travis, Elms, and Agneta, the Figure, raising its arms, said, "I am the Resurrection. If anyone believes in me, even though he dies he will live, and whoever lives and believes in me will never die. Do you believe this?"

"I sure do," Elms said heartily.

Travis said, "It's bilge."

To herself, Agneta Rautavaara thought, I'm not sure. I just don't know.

"We're supposed to decide," Elms said. "We have to decide if we're going to go with him. Travis, you're done for; you're out. Sit there and rot—that's your fate." To Agneta, he said, "I hope you find for Christ, Agneta. I want you to have eternal life like I'm going to have. Isn't that right, Lord?" he asked the Figure.

The Figure nodded.

Agneta said, "Travis, I think—well, I feel you should go along with this. I—" She did not want to press the point that Travis was dead. But he had to understand the situation; otherwise, as Elms said, he was doomed. "Go with us," she said.

"You're going, then?" Travis said, bitterly.

"Yes," she said.

Elms, gazing at the Figure, said in a low voice, "Quite possibly I'm mistaken, but it seems to be changing."

She looked, but saw no change. Yet Elms seemed frightened.

The Figure, in its white robe, walked slowly toward the seated Travis. The Figure halted close by Travis, stood for a time, and then, bending, bit Travis's face.

Agneta screamed. Elms stared, and Travis, locked into his seat, thrashed. The Figure, calmly, ate him.

"Now you see," the spokesperson for the Board of Inquiry said, "this brain must be shut down. The deterioration is severe; the experience is terrible for her; it must end now."

I said, "No. We from the Proxima System find this turn of events highly interesting."

"But the Savior is eating Travis!" another of the Earth persons exclaimed.

"In your religion," I said, "is it not the case that you eat the flesh of your God and drink his blood? All that has happened here is a mirror image of that Eucharist."

"I order her brain shut down!" the spokesperson for the Board said. His face was pale; drops of sweat stood out on his forehead.

"We should see more before we shut down," I said. I found it highly exciting, this enactment of our own sacrament, our highest sacrament, in which our Savior consumes us, his worshippers.

"Agneta," Elms whispered, "did you see that? Christ ate Travis. There's nothing left but his gloves and boots."

Oh God, Agneta Rautavaara thought. What is happening?

She moved away from the Figure, over to Elms. Instinctively.

"He is my blood," the Figure said as it licked its lips. "I drink of this blood, the blood of eternal life. When I have drunk it, I will live forever. He is my body. I have no body of my own; I am only a plasma. By eating his body, I obtain everlasting life. This is the new truth that I proclaim, that I am eternal."

"He's going to eat us, too," Elms said.

Yes, Agneta Rautavaara thought. He is. She could see now that the Figure was an Approximation. It is a Proxima life-form, she realized. He's right; he has no body of his own. The only way he can get a body is—

"I'm going to kill him," Elms said. He popped the emergency laser rifle from its rack and pointed it at the figure.

The Figure said, "Father, the hour has come."

"Stay away from me," Elms said.

"In a short time, you will no longer see me," the Figure said, "unless I drink of your blood and eat of your body. Glorify yourself that I may live." The Figure moved toward Elms.

Elms fired the laser rifle. The Figure staggered and bled. It was Travis's blood, Agneta realized. In him. Not his own blood. This is terrible; she put her hands to her face, terrified.

"Quick," she said to Elms. "Say 'I am innocent of this man's blood.' Say it before it's too late."

"'I am innocent of this man's blood,'" Elms said.

The Figure fell. Bleeding, it lay dying. It was no longer a bearded man. It was something else, but Agneta Rautavaara could not tell what it was. It said, "*Eli, Eli, lama sabachthani?*"

As she and Elms gazed down at it, the Figure died.

"I killed it," Elms said. "I killed Christ." He held the laser rifle pointed at himself, groping for the trigger.

"That wasn't Christ," Agneta said. "It was something else. The opposite of Christ." She took the gun from Elms.

Elms was weeping.

The Earth persons on the Board of Inquiry possessed the majority vote and they voted to abolish all activity in Rautavaara's artificially sustained brain. This disappointed us, but there was no remedy for us.

We had seen the beginning of an absolutely stunning scientific experiment: the theology of one race grafted onto that of another. Shutting down the Earth person's brain was a scientific tragedy. For example, in terms of the basic relationship to God, the Earth race held a diametrically opposite view from us. This of course must be attributed to the fact that they are a somatic race and we are a plasma. They drink the blood of their God; they eat his flesh; that way they become immortal. To them, there is no scandal in this. They find it perfectly natural. Yet, to us it is dreadful. That the worshipper should eat and drink its God? Awful to us; awful indeed. A disgrace and a shame—an abomination. The higher should always prey on the lower; the God should consume the worshipper.

We watched as the Rautavaara Case was closed—closed by the shutting down of her brain so that all EEG activity ceased and the monitors indicated nothing. We felt disappointment, and in addition the Earth persons voted out a verdict of censure of us for our handling of the rescue mission in the first place.

It is striking, the gulf which separates races developing in different star systems. We have tried to understand the Earth persons and we have failed. We are aware, too, that they do not understand us and are appalled in turn by some of our customs. This was demonstrated in the Rautavaara Case. But were we not serving the purposes of detached scientific study? I myself was amazed at Rautavaara's reaction when the Savior ate Mr. Travis. I would have wished to see this most holy of the sacraments fulfilled with the others, with Rautavaara and Elms as well.

But we were deprived of this. And the experiment, from our standpoint, failed.

And we live now, too, under the ban of unnecessary moral blame.

I HOPE I SHALL ARRIVE SOON

After takeoff the ship routinely monitored the condition of the sixty people sleeping in its cryonic tanks. One malfunction showed, that of person nine. His EEG revealed brain activity.

Shit, the ship said to itself.

Complex homeostatic devices locked into circuit feed, and the ship contacted person nine.

"You are slightly awake," the ship said, utilizing the psychotronic route; there was no point in rousing person nine to full consciousness—after all, the flight would last a decade.

Virtually unconscious, but unfortunately still able to think, person nine thought, Someone is addressing me. He said, "Where am I located? I don't see anything."

"You're in faulty cryonic suspension."

He said, "Then I shouldn't be able to hear you."

"'Faulty,' I said. That's the point; you can hear me. Do you know your name?"

"Victor Kemmings. Bring me out of this."

"We are in flight."

"Then put me under."

"Just a moment." The ship examined the cryonic mechanisms; it scanned and surveyed and then it said, "I will try."

Time passed. Victor Kemmings, unable to see anything, unaware of his body, found himself still conscious. "Lower my temperature," he said. He could not hear his voice; perhaps he only imagined he spoke. Colors floated toward him and then rushed at him. He liked the colors; they reminded him of a child's paint box, the semianimated kind, an artificial life-form. He had used them in school, two hundred years ago.

"I can't put you under," the voice of the ship sounded inside Kemmings's head. "The malfunction is too elaborate; I can't correct it and I can't repair it. You will be conscious for ten years."

The semianimated colors rushed toward him, but now they possessed a sinister quality, supplied to them by his own fear. "Oh my God," he said. Ten years! The colors darkened.

As Victor Kemmings lay paralyzed, surrounded by dismal flickerings of light, the ship explained to him its strategy. This strategy did not represent a decision on its part; the ship had been programmed to seek this solution in case of a malfunction of this sort.

"What I will do," the voice of the ship came to him, "is feed you sensory stimulation. The peril to you is sensory deprivation. If you are conscious for ten years without sensory data, your mind will deteriorate. When we reach the LR4 System, you will be a vegetable."

"Well, what do you intend to feed me?" Kemmings said in panic. "What do you have in your information storage banks? All the video soap operas of the last century? Wake me up and I'll walk around."

"There is no air in me," the ship said. "Nothing for you to eat. No one to talk to, since everyone else is under."

Kemmings said, "I can talk to you. We can play chess."

"Not for ten years. Listen to me; I say, I have no food and no air. You must remain as you are . . . a bad compromise, but one forced on us. You are talking to me now. I have no particular information stored. Here is policy in these situations: I will feed you your own buried memories, emphasizing the pleasant ones. You possess two hundred and six years of memories and most of them have sunk down into your unconscious. This is a splendid source of sensory data for you to receive. Be of good cheer. This situation, which you are in, is not unique. It has never happened within my domain before, but I am programmed to deal with it. Relax and trust me. I will see that you are provided with a world."

"They should have warned me," Kemmings said, "before I agreed to emigrate."

"Relax," the ship said.

He relaxed, but he was terribly frightened. Theoretically, he should have gone under, into the successful cryonic suspension, then awakened a moment later at his star of destination; or rather the planet, the colony planet, of that star. Everyone else aboard the ship lay in an unknowing state—he was the exception, as if bad karma had attacked him for obscure reasons. Worst of all, he had to depend totally on the goodwill of the ship. Suppose it elected to feed him monsters? The ship could terrorize him for ten years—ten objective years and undoubtedly more from a subjective standpoint. He was, in effect, totally in the ship's power. Did interstellar ships enjoy such a situation? He knew little about interstellar ships; his field was microbiology. Let me think, he said to himself. My first wife, Martine; the lovely little French girl who wore jeans and a red shirt open at the waist and cooked delicious crepes.

"I hear," the ship said. "So be it."

The rushing colors resolved themselves into coherent, stable shapes. A building: a little old yellow wooden house that he had owned when he was nineteen years old, in Wyoming. "Wait," he said in panic. "The foundation was bad; it was on a mud sill. And the roof leaked." But he saw the kitchen, with the table that he had built himself. And he felt glad.

"You will not know, after a little while," the ship said, "that I am feeding you your own buried memories."

"I haven't thought of that house in a century," he said wonderingly; entranced, he made out his old electric drip coffeepot with the box of paper filters beside it. This is the house where Martine and I lived, he realized. "Martine!" he said aloud.

"I'm on the phone," Martine said from the living room.

The ship said, "I will cut in only when there is an emergency. I will be monitoring you, however, to be sure you are in a satisfactory state. Don't be afraid."

"Turn down the rear right burner on the stove," Martine called. He could hear her and yet not see her. He made his way from the kitchen through the dining room and into the living room. At the VF, Martine stood in rapt conversation with her brother; she wore shorts and she was barefoot. Through the front windows of the living room he could see the street; a commercial vehicle was trying to park, without success.

It's a warm day, he thought. I should turn on the air conditioner.

———

He seated himself on the old sofa as Martine continued her VF conversation, and he found himself gazing at his most cherished possession, a framed poster on the wall above Martine: Gilbert Shelton's "Fat Freddy Says" drawing in which Freddy Freak sits with his cat on his lap, and Fat Freddy is trying to say "Speed kills," but he is so wired on speed—he holds in his hand every kind of amphetamine tablet, pill, spansule, and capsule that exists—that he can't say it, and the cat is gritting his teeth and wincing in a mixture of dismay and disgust. The poster is signed by Gilbert Shelton himself; Kemmings's best friend Ray Torrance gave it to him and Martine as a wedding present. It is worth thousands. It was signed by the artist back in the 1980s. Long before either Victor Kemmings or Martine lived.

If we ever run out of money, Kemmings thought to himself, we could sell the poster. It was not *a* poster; it was *the* poster. Martine adored it. The Fabulous Furry Freak Brothers—from the golden age of a long-ago society. No wonder he loved Martine so; she herself loved back, loved the beauties of the world, and treasured and cherished them as she treasured and cherished him; it was a protective love that nourished but did not stifle. It had been her idea to frame the poster; he would have tacked it up on the wall, so stupid was he.

"Hi," Martine said, off the VF now. "What are you thinking?"

"Just that you keep alive what you love," he said.

"I think that's what you're supposed to do," Martine said. "Are you ready for dinner? Open some red wine, a cabernet."

"Will an '07 do?" he said, standing up; he felt, then, like taking hold of his wife and hugging her.

"Either an '07 or a '12." She trotted past him, through the dining room and into the kitchen.

Going down into the cellar, he began to search among the bottles, which, of course, lay flat. Musty air and dampness; he liked the smell of the cellar, but then he noticed the redwood planks lying half-buried in the dirt and he thought, I know I've got to get a concrete slab poured. He forgot about the wine and went over to the far corner, where the dirt was piled highest; bending down, he poked at a board . . . he poked with a trowel and then he thought, Where did I get this trowel? I didn't have it a minute ago. The board crumbled against the trowel. This whole house is collapsing, he realized. Christ sake. I better tell Martine.

Going back upstairs, the wine forgotten, he started to say to her that the foundations of the house were dangerously decayed, but Martine was nowhere in sight. And nothing cooked on the stove—no pots, no pans. Amazed, he put his hands on the stove and found it cold. Wasn't she just cooking? he asked himself.

"Martine!" he said loudly.

No response. Except for himself, the house was empty. Empty, he thought, and collapsing. Oh my God. He seated himself at the kitchen table and felt the chair give slightly under him; it did not give much, but he felt it; he felt the sagging.

I'm afraid, he thought. Where did she go?

He returned to the living room. Maybe she went next door to borrow some spices or butter or something, he reasoned. Nonetheless, panic now filled him.

He looked at the poster. It was unframed. And the edges had been torn.

I know she framed it, he thought; he ran across the room to it, to examine it closely. Faded . . . the artist's signature had faded; he could scarcely make it out. She insisted on framing it and under glare-free, reflection-free glass. But it isn't framed and it's torn! The most precious thing we own!

Suddenly he found himself crying. It amazed him, his tears. Martine is gone; the poster is deteriorated; the house is crumbling away; nothing is cooking on the stove. This is terrible, he thought. And I don't understand it.

The ship understood it. The ship had been carefully monitoring Victor Kemmings's brain wave patterns, and the ship knew that something had gone wrong. The wave-forms showed agitation and pain. I must get him out of this feed-circuit or I will kill him, the ship decided. Where does the flaw lie? it asked itself. Worry dormant in the man; underlying anxieties. Perhaps if I intensify the signal. I will use the same source, but amp up the charge. What has happened is that massive subliminal insecurities have taken possession of him; the fault is not mine, but lies, instead, in his psychological makeup.

I will try an earlier period in his life, the ship decided. Before the neurotic anxieties got laid down.

In the backyard, Victor scrutinized a bee that had gotten itself trapped in a spider's web. The spider wound up the bee with great care. That's wrong, Victor thought. I'll let the bee loose. Reaching up, he took hold of the encapsulated bee, drew it from the web, and, scrutinizing it carefully, began to unwrap it.

The bee stung him; it felt like a little patch of flame.

Why did it sting me? he wondered. I was letting it go.

He went indoors to his mother and told her, but she did not listen; she was watching television. His finger hurt where the bee had stung it, but, more important, he did not understand why the bee would attack its rescuer. I won't do that again, he said to himself.

"Put some Bactine on it," his mother said at last, roused from watching the TV.

He had begun to cry. It was unfair. It made no sense. He was perplexed and dismayed and he felt a hatred toward small living things, because they were dumb. They didn't have any sense.

He left the house, played for a time on his swings, his slide, in his sandbox, and then he went into the garage because he heard a strange flapping, whirring sound, like a kind of fan. Inside the gloomy garage, he found that a bird was fluttering against the cobwebbed rear window, trying to get out. Below it, the cat, Dorky, leaped and leaped, trying to reach the bird.

He picked up the cat; the cat extended its body and its front legs; it extended its jaws and bit into the bird. At once the cat scrambled down and ran off with the still-fluttering bird.

Victor ran into the house. "Dorky caught a bird!" he told his mother.

"That goddam cat." His mother took the broom from the closet in the kitchen and ran outside, trying to find Dorky. The cat had concealed itself under the bramble bushes; she could not reach it with the broom. "I'm going to get rid of that cat," his mother said.

Victor did not tell her that he had arranged for the cat to catch the bird;

he watched in silence as his mother tried and tried to pry Dorky out from her hiding place; Dorky was crunching up the bird; he could hear the sound of breaking bones, small bones. He felt a strange feeling, as if he should tell his mother what he had done, and yet if he told her she would punish him. I won't do that again, he said to himself. His face, he realized, had turned red. What if his mother figured it out? What if she had some secret way of knowing? Dorky couldn't tell her and the bird was dead. No one would ever know. He was safe.

But he felt bad. That night he could not eat his dinner. Both his parents noticed. They thought he was sick; they took his temperature. He said nothing about what he had done. His mother told his father about Dorky and they decided to get rid of Dorky. Seated at the table, listening, Victor began to cry.

"All right," his father said gently. "We won't get rid of her. It's natural for a cat to catch a bird."

The next day he sat playing in his sandbox. Some plants grew up through the sand. He broke them off. Later his mother told him that had been a wrong thing to do.

Alone in the backyard, in his sandbox, he sat with a pail of water, forming a small mound of wet sand. The sky, which had been blue and clear, became by degrees overcast. A shadow passed over him and he looked up. He sensed a presence around him, something vast that could think.

You are responsible for the death of the bird, the presence thought; he could understand its thoughts.

"I know," he said. He wished, then, that he could die. That he could replace the bird and die for it, leaving it as it had been, fluttering against the cobwebbed window of the garage.

The bird wanted to fly and eat and live, the presence thought.

"Yes," he said miserably.

"You must never do that again," the presence told him.

"I'm sorry," he said, and wept.

This is a very neurotic person, the ship realized. I am having an awful lot of trouble finding happy memories. There is too much fear in him and too much guilt. He has buried it all, and yet it is still there, worrying him like a dog worrying a rag. Where can I go in his memories to find him solace? I must come up with ten years of memories, or his mind will be lost.

Perhaps, the ship thought, the error that I am making is in the area of choice on my part; I should allow him to select his own memories. However, the ship realized, this will allow an element of fantasy to enter. And that is not usually good. Still—

I will try the segment dealing with his first marriage once again, the ship decided. He really loved Martine. Perhaps this time if I keep the intensity of the memories at a greater level the entropic factor can be abolished. What happened was a subtle vitiation of the remembered world, a decay of structure. I will try to compensate for that. So be it.

"Do you suppose Gilbert Shelton really signed this?" Martine said pensively; she stood before the poster, her arms folded; she rocked back and forth slightly, as if seeking a better perspective on the brightly colored drawing hanging on their living room wall. "I mean, it could have been forged. By a dealer somewhere along the line. During Shelton's lifetime or after."

"The letter of authentication," Victor Kemmings reminded her.

"Oh, that's right!" She smiled her warm smile. "Ray gave us the letter that goes with it. But suppose the letter is a forgery? What we need is another letter certifying that the first letter is authentic." Laughing, she walked away from the poster.

"Ultimately," Kemmings said, "we would have to have Gilbert Shelton here to personally testify that he signed it."

"Maybe he wouldn't know. There's that story about the man bringing the Picasso picture to Picasso and asking him if it was authentic, and Picasso immediately signed it and said, 'Now it's authentic.'" She put her arm around Kemmings and, standing on tiptoe, kissed him on the cheek. "It's genuine. Ray wouldn't have given us a forgery. He's the leading expert on counterculture art of the twentieth century. Do you know that he owns an actual lid of dope? It's preserved under—"

"Ray is dead," Victor said.

"What?" She gazed at him in astonishment. "Do you mean something happened to him since we last—"

"He's been dead two years," Kemmings said. "I was responsible. I was driving the buzzcar. I wasn't cited by the police, but it was my fault."

"Ray is living on Mars!" She stared at him.

"I know I was responsible. I never told you. I never told anyone. I'm sorry. I didn't mean to do it. I saw it flapping against the window, and Dorky was trying to reach it, and I lifted Dorky up, and I don't know why but Dorky grabbed it—"

"Sit down, Victor." Martine led him to the overstuffed chair and made him seat himself. "Something's wrong," she said.

"I know," he said. "Something terrible is wrong. I'm responsible for the taking of a life, a precious life that can never be replaced. I'm sorry. I wish I could make it okay, but I can't."

After a pause, Martine said, "Call Ray."

"The cat—" he said.

"What cat?"

"There." He pointed. "In the poster. On Fat Freddy's lap. That's Dorky. Dorky killed Ray."

Silence.

"The presence told me," Kemmings said. "It was God. I didn't realize it at the time, but God saw me commit the crime. The murder. And he will never forgive me."

His wife stared at him numbly.

"God sees everything you do," Kemmings said. "He sees even the falling sparrow. Only in this case it didn't fall; it was grabbed. Grabbed out of the air and torn down. God is tearing this house down which is my body, to pay me back for what I've done. We should have had a building contractor look this house over before we bought it. It's just falling goddam to pieces. In a year there won't be anything left of it. Don't you believe me?"

Martine faltered, "I—"

"Watch." Kemmings reached up his arms toward the ceiling; he stood; he reached; he could not touch the ceiling. He walked to the wall and then, after a pause, put his hand through the wall.

Martine screamed.

The ship aborted the memory retrieval instantly. But the harm had been done.

He has integrated his early fears and guilts into one interwoven grid, the ship said to itself. There is no way I can serve up a pleasant memory to him because he instantly contaminates it. However pleasant the original experience in itself was. This is a serious situation, the ship decided. The man is already showing signs of psychosis. And we are hardly into the trip; years lie ahead of him.

After allowing itself time to think the situation through, the ship decided to contact Victor Kemmings once more.

"Mr. Kemmings," the ship said.

"I'm sorry," Kemmings said. "I didn't mean to foul up those retrievals. You did a good job, but I—"

"Just a moment," the ship said. "I'm not equipped to do psychiatric reconstruction of you; I am a simple mechanism, that's all. What is it you want? Where do you want to be and what do you want to be doing?"

"I want to arrive at our destination," Kemmings said. "I want this trip to be over."

Ah, the ship thought. That is the solution.

One by one the cryonic systems shut down. One by one the people returned to life, among them Victor Kemmings. What amazed him was the lack of a sense of the passage of time. He had entered the chamber, lain down, had felt the membrane cover him and the temperature begin to drop—

And now he stood on the ship's external platform, the unloading platform, gazing down at a verdant planetary landscape. This, he realized, is LR4–6, the colony world to which I have come in order to begin a new life.

"Looks good," a heavyset woman beside him said.

"Yes," he said, and felt the newness of the landscape rush up at him, its promise of a beginning. Something better than he had known the past two hundred years. I am a fresh person in a fresh world, he thought. And he felt glad.

Colors raced at him, like those of a child's semianimate kit. Saint Elmo's fire, he realized. That's right; there is a great deal of ionization in this planet's atmosphere. A free light show, such as they had back in the twentieth century.

"Mr. Kemmings," a voice said. An elderly man had come up beside him, to speak to him. "Did you dream?"

"During the suspension?" Kemmings said. "No, not that I can remember."

"I think I dreamed," the elderly man said. "Would you take my arm on the descent ramp? I feel unsteady. The air seems thin. Do you find it thin?"

"Don't be afraid," Kemmings said to him. He took the elderly man's arm. "I'll help you down the ramp. Look; there's a guide coming this way. He'll arrange our processing for us; it's part of the package. We'll be taken to a resort hotel and given first-class accommodations. Read your brochure." He smiled at the uneasy older man to reassure him.

"You'd think our muscles would be nothing but flab after ten years in suspension," the elderly man said.

"It's just like freezing peas," Kemmings said. Holding on to the timid older man, he descended the ramp to the ground. "You can store them forever if you get them cold enough."

"My name's Shelton," the elderly man said.

"What?" Kemmings said, halting. A strange feeling moved through him.

"Don Shelton." The elderly man extended his hand; reflexively, Kemmings accepted it and they shook. "What's the matter, Mr. Kemmings? Are you all right?"

"Sure," he said. "I'm fine. But hungry. I'd like to get something to eat. I'd like to get to our hotel, where I can take a shower and change my clothes." He wondered where their baggage could be found. Probably it would take the ship an hour to unload it. The ship was not particularly intelligent.

In an intimate, confidential tone, elderly Mr. Shelton said, "You know what I brought with me? A bottle of Wild Turkey bourbon. The finest bourbon on Earth. I'll bring it over to our hotel room and we'll share it." He nudged Kemmings.

"I don't drink," Kemmings said. "Only wine." He wondered if there were any good wines here on this distant colony world. Not distant now, he reflected. It is Earth that's distant. I should have done like Mr. Shelton and brought a few bottles with me.

Shelton. What did the name remind him of? Something in his far past, in his early years. Something precious, along with good wine and a pretty, gentle young woman making crepes in an old-fashioned kitchen. Aching memories; memories that hurt.

Presently he stood by the bed in his hotel room, his suitcase open; he had begun to hang up his clothes. In the corner of the room, a TV hologram showed a newscaster; he ignored it, but, liking the sound of a human voice, he kept it on.

Did I have any dreams? he asked himself. During these past ten years?

His hand hurt. Gazing down, he saw a red welt, as if he had been stung. A bee stung me, he realized. But when? How? While I lay in cryonic suspension? Impossible. Yet he could see the welt and he could feel the pain. I better get something to put on it, he realized. There's undoubtedly a robot doctor in the hotel; it's a first-rate hotel.

When the robot doctor had arrived and was treating the bee sting, Kemmings said, "I got this as punishment for killing the bird."

"Really?" the robot doctor said.

"Everything that ever meant anything to me has been taken away from me," Kemmings said. "Martine, the poster—my little old house with the wine cellar. We had everything and now it's gone. Martine left me because of the bird."

"The bird you killed," the robot doctor said.

"God punished me. He took away all that was precious to me because of my sin. It wasn't Dorky's sin; it was my sin."

"But you were just a little boy," the robot doctor said.

"How did you know that?" Kemmings said. He pulled his hand away from the robot doctor's grasp. "Something's wrong. You shouldn't have known that."

"Your mother told me," the robot doctor said.

"My mother didn't know!"

The robot doctor said, "She figured it out. There was no way the cat could have reached the bird without your help."

"So all the time that I was growing up she knew. But she never said anything."

"You can forget about it," the robot doctor said.

Kemmings said, "I don't think you exist. There is no possible way that you could know these things. I'm still in cryonic suspension and the ship is still feeding me my own buried memories. So I won't become psychotic from sensory deprivation."

"You could hardly have a memory of completing the trip."

"Wish fulfillment, then. It's the same thing. I'll prove it to you. Do you have a screwdriver?"

"Why?"

Kemmings said, "I'll remove the back of the TV set and you'll see; there's nothing inside it; no components, no parts, no chassis—nothing."

"I don't have a screwdriver."

"A small knife, then. I can see one in your surgical supply bag." Bending, Kemmings lifted up a small scalpel. "This will do. If I show you, will you believe me?"

"If there's nothing inside the TV cabinet—"

Squatting down, Kemmings removed the screws holding the back panel of the TV set in place. The panel came loose and he set it down on the floor.

There was nothing inside the TV cabinet. And yet the color hologram continued to fill a quarter of the hotel room, and the voice of the newscaster issued forth from his three-dimensional image.

"Admit you're the ship," Kemmings said to the robot doctor.

"Oh dear," the robot doctor said.

Oh dear, the ship said to itself. And I've got almost ten years of this lying ahead of me. He is hopelessly contaminating his experiences with childhood guilt; he imagines that his wife left him because, when he was four years old, he helped a cat catch a bird. The only solution would be for Martine to return to him, but how am I going to arrange that? She may not still be alive. On the other hand, the ship reflected, maybe she is alive. Maybe she could be induced to do something to save her former husband's sanity. People by and large have very positive traits. And ten years from now it will take a lot to save—or rather restore—his sanity; it will take something drastic, something I myself cannot do alone.

Meanwhile, there was nothing to be done but recycle the wish fulfillment arrival of the ship at its destination. I will run him through the arrival, the ship decided, then wipe his conscious memory clean and run him through it again. The only positive aspect of this, it reflected, is that it will give me something to do, which may help preserve *my* sanity.

Lying in cryonic suspension—faulty cryonic suspension—Victor Kemmings imagined, once again, that the ship was touching down and he was being brought back to consciousness.

"Did you dream?" a heavyset woman asked him as the group of passengers gathered on the outer platform. "I have the impression that I dreamed. Early scenes from my life . . . over a century ago."

"None that I can remember," Kemmings said. He was eager to reach his hotel; a shower and a change of clothes would do wonders for his morale. He felt slightly depressed and wondered why.

"There's our guide," an elderly lady said. "They're going to escort us to our accommodations."

"It's in the package," Kemmings said. His depression remained. The others seemed so spirited, so full of life, but over him only a weariness lay, a weighing-down sensation, as if the gravity of this colony planet were too much for him. Maybe that's it, he said to himself. But, according to the brochure, the gravity here matched Earth's; that was one of the attractions.

Puzzled, he made his way slowly down the ramp, step by step, holding on to the rail. I don't really deserve a new chance at life anyhow, he realized. I'm just going through the motions . . . I am not like these other people. There is something wrong with me; I cannot remember what it is, but nonetheless it is there. In me. A bitter sense of pain. Of lack of worth.

An insect landed on the back of Kemmings's right hand, an old insect, weary with flight. He halted, watched it crawl across his knuckles. I could crush it, he thought. It's so obviously infirm; it won't live much longer anyhow.

He crushed it—and felt great inner horror. What have I done? he asked himself. My first moment here and I have wiped out a little life. Is this my new beginning?

Turning, he gazed back up at the ship. Maybe I ought to go back, he thought. Have them freeze me forever. I am a man of guilt, a man who destroys. Tears filled his eyes.

And, within its sentient works, the interstellar ship moaned.

During the ten long years remaining in the trip to the LR4 System, the ship had plenty of time to track down Martine Kemmings. It explained the situation to her. She had emigrated to a vast orbiting dome in the Sirius System, found her situation unsatisfactory, and was en route back to Earth. Roused from her own cryonic suspension, she listened intently and then agreed to be at the colony world LR4–6 when her ex-husband arrived—if it was at all possible.

Fortunately, it was possible.

"I don't think he'll recognize me," Martine said to the ship. "I've allowed myself to age. I don't really approve of entirely halting the aging process."

He'll be lucky if he recognizes anything, the ship thought.

At the intersystem spaceport on the colony world of LR4–6, Martine stood waiting for the people aboard the ship to appear on the outer platform. She wondered if she would recognize her former husband. She was a little afraid, but she was glad that she had gotten to LR4–6 in time. It had been close. Another week and his ship would have arrived before hers. Luck is on my side, she said to herself, and scrutinized the newly landed interstellar ship.

People appeared on the platform. She saw him. Victor had changed very little.

As he came down the ramp, holding on to the railing as if weary and hesitant, she came up to him, her hands thrust deep in the pockets of her coat; she felt shy and when she spoke she could hardly hear her own voice.

"Hi, Victor," she managed to say.

He halted, gazed at her. "I know you," he said.

"It's Martine," she said.

Holding out his hand, he said, smiling, "You heard about the trouble on the ship?"

"The ship contacted me." She took his hand and held it. "What an ordeal."

"Yeah," he said. "Recirculating memories forever. Did I ever tell you about a bee that I was trying to extricate from a spider's web when I was four years old? The idiotic bee stung me." He bent down and kissed her. "It's good to see you," he said.

"Did the ship—"

"It said it would try to have you here. But it wasn't sure if you could make it."

As they walked toward the terminal building, Martine said, "I was lucky; I managed to get a transfer to a military vehicle, a high-velocity-drive ship that just shot along like a mad thing. A new propulsion system entirely."

Victor Kemmings said, "I have spent more time in my own unconscious mind than any other human in history. Worse than early-twentieth-century psychoanalysis. And the same material over and over again. Did you know I was scared of my mother?"

"*I* was scared of your mother," Martine said. They stood at the baggage depot, waiting for his luggage to appear. "This looks like a really nice little planet. Much better than where I was . . . I haven't been happy at all."

"So maybe there's a cosmic plan," he said grinning. "You look great."

"I'm old."

"Medical science—"

"It was my decision. I like older people." She surveyed him. He has been hurt a lot by the cryonic malfunction, she said to herself. I can see it in his eyes. They look broken. Broken eyes. Torn down into pieces by fatigue and—defeat. As if his buried early memories swam up and destroyed him. But it's over, she thought. And I did get here in time.

At the bar in the terminal building, they sat having a drink.

"This old man got me to try Wild Turkey bourbon," Victor said. "It's amazing bourbon. He says it's the best on Earth. He brought a bottle with him from . . ." His voice died into silence.

"One of your fellow passengers," Martine finished.

"I guess so," he said.

"Well, you can stop thinking of the birds and the bees," Martine said.

"Sex?" he said, and laughed.

"Being stung by a bee, helping a cat catch a bird. That's all past."

"That cat," Victor said, "has been dead one hundred and eighty-two years. I figured it out while they were bringing us out of suspension. Probably just as well. Dorky. Dorky, the killer cat. Nothing like Fat Freddy's cat."

"I had to sell the poster," Martine said. "Finally."

He frowned.

"Remember?" she said. "You let me have it when we split up. Which I always thought was really good of you."

"How much did you get for it?"

"A lot. I should pay you something like—" She calculated. "Taking inflation into account, I should pay you about two million dollars."

"Would you consider," he said, "instead, in place of the money, my share of the sale of the poster, spending some time with me? Until I get used to this planet?"

"Yes," she said. And she meant it. Very much.

They finished their drinks and then, with his luggage transported by robot spacecap, made their way to his hotel room.

"This is a nice room," Martine said, perched on the edge of the bed. "And it has a hologram TV. Turn it on."

"There's no use turning it on," Victor Kemmings said. He stood by the open closet, hanging up his shirts.

"Why not?"

Kemmings said, "There's nothing on it."

Going over to the TV set, Martine turned it on. A hockey game materialized, projected out into the room, in full color, and the sound of the game assailed her ears.

"It works fine," she said.

"I know," he said. "I can prove it to you. If you have a nail file or something, I'll unscrew the back plate and show you."

"But I can—"

"Look at this." He paused in his work of hanging up his clothes. "Watch me put my hand through the wall." He placed the palm of his right hand against the wall. "See?"

His hand did not go through the wall because hands do not go through walls; his hand remained pressed against the wall, unmoving.

"And the foundation," he said, "is rotting away."

"Come and sit down by me," Martine said.

"I've lived this often enough now," he said. "I've lived this over and over again. I come out of suspension; I walk down the ramp; I get my luggage; sometimes I have a drink at the bar and sometimes I come directly to my room. Usually I turn on the TV and then—" He came over and held his hand toward her. "See where the bee stung me?"

She saw no mark on his hand; she took his hand and held it.

"There is no bee sting," she said.

"And when the robot doctor comes, I borrow a tool from him and take off the back plate of the TV set. To prove to him that it has no chassis, no components in it. And then the ship starts me over again."

"Victor," she said. "Look at your hand."

"This is the first time you've been here, though," he said.

"Sit down," she said.

"Okay." He seated himself on the bed, beside her, but not too close to her.

"Won't you sit closer to me?" she said.

"It makes me too sad," he said. "Remembering you. I really loved you. I wish this was real."

Martine said, "I will sit with you until it is real for you."

"I'm going to try reliving the part with the cat," he said, "and this time *not* pick up the cat and *not* let it get the bird. If I do that, maybe my life will change so that it turns into something happy. Something that is real. My real mistake was separating from you. Here; I'll put my hand through you." He placed his hand against her arm. The pressure of his muscles was vigorous; she felt the weight, the physical presence of him, against her. "See?" he said. "It goes right through you."

"And all this," she said, "because you killed a bird when you were a little boy."

"No," he said. "All this because of a failure in the temperature-regulating assembly aboard the ship. I'm not down to the proper temperature. There's just enough warmth left in my brain cells to permit cerebral activity." He stood up then, stretched, smiled at her. "Shall we go get some dinner?" he asked.

She said, "I'm sorry. I'm not hungry."

"I am. I'm going to have some of the local seafood. The brochure says it's terrific. Come along anyhow; maybe when you see the food and smell it you'll change your mind."

Gathering up her coat and purse, she came with him.

"This is a beautiful little planet," he said. "I've explored it dozens of times. I know it thoroughly. We should stop downstairs at the pharmacy for some Bactine, though. For my hand. It's beginning to swell and it hurts like hell." He showed her his hand. "It hurts more this time than ever before."

"Do you want me to come back to you?" Martine said.

"Are you serious?"

"Yes," she said. "I'll stay with you as long as you want. I agree; we should never have been separated."

Victor Kemmings said, "The poster is torn."

"What?" she said.

"We should have framed it," he said. "We didn't have sense enough to take care of it. Now it's torn. And the artist is dead."

PUBLISHER'S ACKNOWLEDGMENTS

The publisher wishes to acknowledge Lawrence Sutin, Jonathan Lethem, and Russell Galen for their assistance in putting together this collection.

All of the stories in this collection have been previously published.

Some stories first appeared in the following publications: *Amazing, Astounding, Beyond Fantasy Fiction, Fantastic Universe, Fantasy & Science Fiction, Galaxy, Imagination, Omni, Orbit Science Fiction, Planet Stories, Playboy, Rolling Stone College Papers, Space Science Fiction.*

"Faith of Our Fathers" in *Dangerous Visions*, edited by Harlan Ellison (Doubleday, 1967); "A Little Something for Us Tempunauts" in *Final Stage*, edited by Edward L. Ferman and Barry N. Malzburg (Charterhouse, 1974); "Foster, You're Dead" in *Star Science Fiction Stories No. 3*, edited by Frederick Pohl (Ballantine Books, 1955).

"The Electric Ant," "The Exit Door Leads In," "Faith of Our Fathers," "A Game of Unchance," "I Hope I Shall Arrive Soon," "A Little Something for Us Tempunauts," "Precious Artifact," and "Rautavaara's Case" from *The Eye of the Sibyl & Other Classic Stories by Philip K. Dick.* Copyright © 1987 by the Estate of Philip K. Dick (Kensington Publishing Corp., 1992).

These stories subsequently appeared in the following works published as Citadel Press Books by Carol Publishing Group:
"Beyond Lies the Wub," "The King of the Elves," "Paycheck," and "Roog" from *The Collected Stories of Philip K. Dick: The Short Happy Life of the Brown Oxford, vol. 1;* "Foster, You're Dead," "Second Variety," and "Upon the Dull Earth" from *The Collected Stories of Philip K. Dick, vol 3;*

"Autofac," "The Days of Perky Pat," and "The Minority Report" from *The Collected Stories of Philip K. Dick: The Minority Report;* "Adjustment Team," "Imposter," and "We Can Remember It for You Wholesale" from *We Can Remember It for You Wholesale.* All works copyright © 1987 by the Estate of Philip K. Dick.

ABOUT THE AUTHOR

Philip K. Dick was born in Chicago in 1928 and lived most of his life in California. He briefly attended the University of California but dropped out before completing any classes. He began writing professionally in 1952 and published many novels and short-story collections. He won the Hugo Award for best novel in 1963 for *The Man in the High Castle* and the John W. Campbell Memorial Award for best novel in 1975 for *Flow My Tears, the Policeman Said*. Philip K. Dick died on March 2, 1982, in Santa Ana, California, of heart failure following a stroke.